FATE NOT CHOSEN

BOOK ONE

TARA LYTLE

SCRIBBLED READS

Copyright © 2020 by Tara Lytle

Published by Scribbled Reads

E-Book ISBN: 978-1-7363067-8-9

Paperback ISBN: 978-1-960319-15-9

Hardcover ISBN: 978-1-7363067-5-8

Acknowledgements

I started writing this novel fifteen years ago. This story has carried me through most of the major events of my life. It has been the last thing I thought of before I went to sleep and the first thing I thought of when I woke up. To say that I am thrilled to finally release this book would be an understatement. I would like to give my heartfelt thanks to my mother, Sandy Shelburne, for helping me with my children so I could have time to write. You have been a blessing to me. To my father, David Shelburne, for reading through the numerous drafts and always showing me encouragement. To my dear husband, Seth Lytle. I think he's poured as much of his heart and soul into this book as I have to get it ready to publish. I love you all dearly. To our friends who have shown their support; thank you from the bottom of my heart. I would also like to express my love to the readers who pick this book up and give me a chance to prove how amazing the world of Aberron is.

ABERRON
PORTS END
JAYDORIA
DRAMERA
FRESTAN
HAYLORE
STRELL
BERUND
ORINDALER
N
W
E
S

KORRUN
CARASMILLE
LAND
THIMBLETON
LOCHENLOCK
TRIVAIL FOREST
ABERRON CLIFFS
PRASTIS
KISTER
SAREN
MANARIA
CAILEN
PENDRA
CALLAN OUTPOST
NEDRA
Isabelle's Journey

PROLOGUE

I HELD ON TO MY brother's hand as we walked in the redwood forest near our home. The moss-covered trees seemed to touch the sky. Large ferns tickled my legs with every step forward, but I didn't mind. The wind blew softly, giving us relief from the hot summer air. I liked the fresh, earthy smell and breathed deeply.

I tugged on my brother's hand, digging my boots into the dirt. "Joshua, it's not ready!"

"Sure it is, Isabelle." He smiled and pulled me along. "Da just hasn't added all your toys."

We stopped in front of the redwood tree Da had been making into a playhouse. It looked like a plain tree on the outside, matching all the others. The magical illusion hid the door and window.

I touched the bark. "Is this the right one?"

"Say the password and find out." Joshua shrugged.

I giggled. "Bubbles."

Above my head a circle window appeared, and in front of me, a small red door. I grinned and bounced on my feet. "It worked!"

Joshua turned the handle. "Go inside. I have a present for you."

I looked up at my big brother. "You only give me presents when you don't want Mama to know you snuck off."

"Come on, Isabelle, I've been chasing you around the forest for an hour," he begged, hands out in front of him. "I won't be long, promise."

I frowned. "Mama says I'm not old enough to be on my own."

"Mama said that when you were four. You've been five for a week." Joshua leaned against the doorway. "Just stay in there till I come back. You promise?"

"All right." I hoped Mama wouldn't get mad if she caught me. I'd tell on Joshua if she did.

He smiled wide. "You're the best, little sister."

I stepped inside. As the door shut, I heard him say, "Pop." I knew that meant the magical illusion was back in place. I hurried up the stairs and found a soft pink bear with a white bow on the floor of the empty room.

I hugged it to my chest and went to the window to watch Joshua leave, but he had already run out of sight. I skipped around the room and pointed things out to my new bear. "The table will go here in the middle. My toy chest will go there, and by the window—" I rushed to it, imagination flying, and looked out.

I froze.

Many grungy men, each holding a weapon, surrounded Mama and Da below. Their clothes were ripped, filthy, and bloody. Sweat dripped off their dirty faces. I shook with fear.

Da's dark brown hair was messy, and a cut above his eye bled down his bruised cheek, falling into the whiskers on his chin. His hands were tied behind him with thick rope, and his knees sank into the soft dirt.

Mama knelt next to him. Her black hair flowed down her back, covering the rope that bound her hands. No bruises or cuts showed on her face, but I saw the anger in her green eyes and shivered. She wiggled closer until her shoulders touched Da, trying but failing to reach his hands.

"Da! Mama!" I pounded on the glass with my fist, my bear safely under my arm. Tears fell down my cheeks as I yelled out their names, but no one heard me.

Da opened his mouth. I stopped to listen. "Your plan failed. The King still lives."

A man stepped forward and spoke with authority—like Mama did when I got in trouble. "That may be so." He played with a knife between his dirty hands. "But this is not the end of us. We will rise again and in greater numbers and power."

Mama laughed harshly. "Rise again, and the good people of Aberron will send you running like cowering dogs with your tails tucked between your legs."

"No!" the man screamed, throwing the knife. It raced by Mama and stuck into a tree. "Braidus will obtain what is rightfully his, only this time, you won't be in his way." He raised his hand. "Goodbye."

The men rushed forward. Multiple swords stabbed Mama and Da. Blood spilled onto their clothes as they fell to the ground, dead.

My bear dropped to the floor.

CHAPTER ONE

You're not blocking fast enough!" Nathan paced, his boots crushing the dry grass. He pointed his sword at my chest. "If this were a real fight, you'd be dead quicker than a jackrabbit can jump for cover. Come on, Isabelle! Put those skinny arms to good use, and block!" He swung the blade toward me, his muscles bulging through the thin cotton shirt.

"Give me a break," I said as I fended off his attack. "We put the final touches on my sword yesterday. I'm not used to it yet." I stepped backward, light on my feet, and rubbed my forehead. The morning had just begun, and I could already tell that today was going to be a scorcher.

"Oh, poor Isabelle ..." Nathan mocked, putting a hand over his heart. "Does the delicate little thing want me to go easier?" He spoke as if I were a baby, not seventeen years old.

Grinning through his red beard, he pushed a few strands of hair away from his blue eyes. Sweat dripped off his brow, sliding down his round face and falling into his beard, but it didn't deter him. Nothing ever did. Nathan was as hard as granite, and I envied his ability to stay strong through all kinds of circumstances.

I laughed, wrapping my fingers tighter against the leather handle. "Go easier? Never." Squinting my eyes against the sun, I shifted and danced on the balls of my feet.

"That's my girl!" Nathan's blue eyes lit up as he surged forward, his blade coming down on me.

This time, I felt ready and blocked with fierce determination.

"That's better." He nodded approvingly, stepping back.

"Hey, Iz!"

I turned around and grinned. "Stefan!" I sheathed my weapon and ran through the garden, carefully navigating through the row of carrots to the dirt road. Stefan opened his arms wide, enveloping me in a warm hug as I reached him. We broke apart and held each other at arm's length, wearing matching sloppy grins.

"Fencing on Gods Day? You never cease to surprise me," Stefan said.

"You always work on Gods Day; what's the difference?" I asked.

"Mail waits for no one." He shrugged nonchalantly.

We measured our days in increments of seven. On First Day through Fifth Day, we worked, followed by Kings Day and Gods Day. On Kings Day people petitioned their leaders about problems they faced. On Gods Day, everyone visited family, feasted, or prayed to the Gods in the temples. Many considered Gods Day a day of rest and relaxation.

"What are you doing here?" I asked. "Why aren't you at work with Mr. Travers?"

Stefan pushed his dirty blonde hair back from his pale blue eyes and grinned. "Mr. Travers sent me on a special assignment. I've got a delivery just for you."

"Special assignment?" I raised my eyebrows. "More like you begged."

He laughed and kicked at the tall grass growing on the edge of the dirt road. "All right, you caught me."

"I'm glad you did. It's so nice to see you," I answered delightedly, letting my hands fall down to my sides. "I didn't think I'd get to see you until Mava's celebration tonight." Stefan was like a ray of sunshine, and I couldn't help but feel happy around him.

He grinned and opened the flap of his leather bag, pulling out a medium-size parcel wrapped with twine and stamped with a red seal. He handed it to me.

"What is it?" I tilted my head with confusion as I accepted the package.

Stefan shrugged. "I don't know. Mr. Travers said a new post rider came thundering in this morning making all kinds of racket down Shop Street.

He threw the letters and your package at him before taking off again faster than a fox after a chicken." He shook his head and rolled his eyes. "You should have seen Mr. Travers when I came in this morning.

"In a foul mood, muttering curses and banging everything with his cane, going on and on about the new rider who woke him up at the crack of dawn. I think he was happy to send me off and get the parcel out of the post room. He kept staring at it like it was going to open up on its own and eat him." He stuck his thumbs in his front pockets, shifting his feet side to side.

"Oh Travers, what does he know?" I rolled my eyes and put a hand on my hip. "Hardly anybody sends anything magical through the post and especially not to Saren. He should know farmers and magic don't mix."

"Yeah, well, he still can't seem to forget that time Benner ordered that 'Grow plants in a day' potion or whatnot and it spilled onto Silla's seed packets. In a matter of minutes, the whole post room erupted in plants. It took us weeks to clear out the mess." Stefan shuddered.

"Yes, but that was a year and a half ago, and I'm pretty sure Benner learned his lesson," I said.

"Oh yeah, he won't be doing that again." He nodded.

"I bet it's that pocket-size book I ordered for Nathan. His birthday is coming up soon," I whispered, holding the package to my side. "At any rate, I don't think Travers should be too worried—"

"Hey! I thought we were supposed to be fencing," Nathan interrupted, calling from the dry patch of grass we called the practice area behind the garden. "Stefan can chase after you at the celebration tonight."

I glanced at my adoptive father over my shoulder; he had both hands on his hips, and his foot tapped in the grass. Little puffs of dirt rose from the ground around his leather boots. Those that did not know him would have found him intimidating, with his stern glare and large, muscular form. But I knew better. Underneath that hard exterior was a man as soft as butter.

"All right, I'm coming!" I faced Stefan.

"You and that sword," he laughed. "You're the only girl in Saren brave enough to pick one up."

"If the men in Aberron stopped acting like it's a crime, then I'm sure we'd see more women with swords tied to their belts. We have just as much a right to defend ourselves as men do," I said indignantly.

"And you're going to be the one to change that?" Stefan smirked.

I nodded. "That's right, I am."

"You know what?" he said suddenly. "I believe you will."

I grinned. "Thanks for delivering the package to me. See you at the party tonight."

Stefan leaned in and kissed me on the cheek. "See you."

I blushed, stumbling backward as I waved farewell.

"Hey, none of that!" Nathan protested. "You're too young to be thinking romance."

I walked to Nathan until I stood an arm's length away, package in hand. "And yet we are going to Mava's wedding celebration tonight. You know she's only a few months older than I am."

"Yeah, well ... I don't have a say in Mava's life like I do yours." Nathan glanced at the parcel. "So, what's in the box?"

"Oh, nothing important." I shrugged. "I'm pretty sure it's something I ordered from Carasmille."

He snorted. "Don't tell me it's another book. We can barely hold the ones we have. The study is crammed full."

I leaned forward and lightly slapped his arm. "You're the one who encouraged me to read in the first place, and it's not my fault we live in the smallest farming community in Aberron. The only information we ever get in Saren is through books."

"All right, you win that battle," he conceded, folding his arms.

I grinned. "Thought so." I trotted back to the garden, setting the package down at the base of the apple tree.

I faced Nathan again and unsheathed my blade. "You ready to practice?"

He drew his sword and smiled so wide it reached his eyes. "I'm always ready. Let's do this."

"Isabelle, Nathan." Adel called to us from the back door.

"Oh, what now?" Nathan groaned, his shoulders slumping.

I laughed. "Might as well give up. We can practice again tomorrow."

"Fine, but no interruptions, not even if the King himself shows up." He pointed his saber at my chest.

"Agreed."

We sheathed our swords and trudged through the garden to the house. Nathan pulled on the door handle and gestured for me to go first. I smiled and thanked him as I walked into the kitchen, Nathan following right behind. Unbuckling our weapons from our belts, we hung them on the hooks adjacent to the door.

"Oh, my package!" I wrenched open the back door and ran through the garden to the apple tree, picking it up.

"Isabelle, your breakfast is getting cold!" Adel shouted from the open door, aiming a wooden spoon at me.

"I'm coming," I said, turning away from the tree, package in hand.

A heavy aroma of eggs and bacon filled the kitchen. I set the package on the kitchen table and sat by Nathan, pulling a heaping plate to me. Adel sat across from us.

"What's this?" Adel asked, picking up the parcel with her thin fingers, her brown eyes probing.

"Oh, it's nothing important. Just a book I ordered." I shrugged.

"Good luck finding a spot to put it." Adel laughed, setting the package on the table with a light thump.

"You too?" I pursed my lips. "Honestly, I expected you both to be better. Don't encourage someone to read if you don't want to have a house littered with books."

Adel lifted her hands up in mock surrender.

I changed the subject. "Do you have Mava's dress ready?"

She nodded. "Yes, and I'm going to need your help with the last fitting and getting her ready. I can't believe that girl is getting married already. I remember holding her as a newborn."

"She's going to be so happy with Carl." I imagined the two of them together. Mava, with amber eyes that danced, an infectious smile, and an overall warm manner. Carl, with his dark brown hair, smooth and friendly face, tall frame, broad shoulders, and toned muscles. He was as handsome as they came in Saren. Mava and Carl were perfect for each other.

"Oh, Gods forbid. Look at the time." Adel glanced anxiously at the clock. "We've got to get ready." She stood, smoothing out the lines of her brown dress. She grabbed some dishes and took them to the washing basin.

I shoveled in a few bites of breakfast, hardly tasting it, and gulped down some milk. I stood, grabbing my plate, and setting it with the rest of the dirty dishes Adel piled up.

Within the hour we loaded everything into the cart.

"I set a dress on your bed, and I want you to wear it. It will bring out the green in your eyes," Adel said. "Hurry up and change and meet me downstairs."

I took my package with me as I headed upstairs to change. I set it on my bed. I'd open it when I had time.

Nathan flicked the reins as I climbed into the cart. Amber trotted at a leisurely pace up the dusty dirt packed road. A warm breeze tickled my face. I breathed in the scent of freshly cut hay from the nearby fields.

Shop street came into view, housing the main row of businesses. On Gods Day, the stores closed midday so proprietors could spend time with their families. Nathan carefully navigated our cart past Mr. Vander while nodding a greeting. I let my eyes trail by Mr. Traver's post, Jensten's butcher shop, and Agatha's bakery. Few people were out trailing the boardwalk, mostly women with baskets in hand and children in tow. Their husbands no doubt toiled in the heat gathering their harvest. It had been a good year for farming.

I reached over and put my hand on Nathan's arm. "Will you let me off at the market? I promised Mava I'd bring her a bag of peppermint sticks. It'll just take a moment."

"We'll wait." He pulled up short in front of the store. I hopped down and hurried inside, taking care to avoid Mrs. Coltrane and her three little ones as I passed.

Mr. Bryder looked up from the inventory book and smiled at me. "Hello Isabelle, what can I do for you today?" His dark brown eyes twinkled underneath a set of black bushy eyebrows.

"Hello Mr. Bryder." I returned the smile as I walked up to the counter. "I'd like a bag of peppermint sticks please."

"Coming right up." He reached for a paper sack and took the lid off a glass jar filled with peppermint.

The door jingled, signaling another customer. Distaste bloomed as I turned my head to see who had come in. Josiah and Ned, my two biggest tormenters. Their eyes scanned the shop before lighting upon me.

Josiah strolled forward, his blue eyes perusing me. Ned followed silently.

Josiah whistled. "You're a vision today Isabelle."

I fought against an eyeroll as I waited for the ensuing barb.

Ned nudged Josiah's arm. "She's missing something." To me he said, "You don't have your gut sticker."

"It's called a sword," I said shortly, unable to help myself.

Mr. Bryder deftly inserted himself. "That'll be three Starlets Isabelle."

I reached into my pocket and pulled out a small purse. I fished around it for the right coins. Aberron had a simple currency system with only three coins to deal with: gold, silver, and copper. All our gold coins were stamped with a picture of a sun. We called them Sundals. Silver coins had the moon stamped on them, called Moonels. Copper coins had a star, called Starlets.

I handed over the Starlets as Josiah spoke. "Of course she don't have her gut sticker, can't you see she's trying to be real lady today? She's got a dress on and everything." His tone said I was anything but.

"Boys," Mr. Bryder spoke sternly. "Unless you have some shopping to do, I suggest you get out." He handed me the bag.

"Thank you Mr. Bryder." I smiled warmly at him.

"Oh, we've come here for business," Ned assured while I skirted around him and Josiah.

Josiah winked. "See you Isabelle."

I shook my head at him, as I exited and climbed back into my seat in the cart. Nathan finished the short drive to Mava's, where we spent the rest of the morning and afternoon getting everything ready. She was beautiful in a white dress and her dark brown hair braided with white daisies.

"You look stunning." I grinned. "Carl's going to be speechless."

"Oh, you really think so?" Mava put her hands on her stomach. "Gods forbid, I'm so nervous, I feel like my heart's going to burst."

I put a hand on her shoulder, standing behind her as she sat in front of the mirror. "You'll be fine. You love Carl, don't you?"

"Oh, more than anything else," Mava gushed. She stood and faced me, a sly grin on her face. "But I'm not the only one who might be in love. I've seen the way you act around Stefan."

I blushed, wringing my hands together, and mumbled, "I don't know what you're talking about."

She pointed a finger at me. "Ha! I knew it. Do you love him?"

"Love?" I gulped and thought for a minute. Did I love Stefan? Sure, I liked him. I liked the way he made me feel, and I really enjoyed his kisses under the maple tree by the creek. But love? I shook my head. "I like Stefan a whole lot, but I don't love him with the kind of romantic thoughts you're thinking of. Not yet."

"Hmm ... maybe tonight you might change your mind. Especially after a little dancing." Mava laughed lightly, a mischievous look in her eyes.

The ceremony was held outside in Mava's backyard. Log benches took up a good portion of the lawn, situated around loaded fruit trees. An aisle littered with white daisies led to a flowery archway where they were to be married. A soft breeze gave some respite from the searing sun and carried the sweet aroma of peaches and apples. Mava couldn't have picked a better day for her wedding.

Nathan, Adel, and I sat near the front, waiting for the ceremony to begin. I kept glancing behind me, searching for Stefan. I hoped he'd see me and sit next to us. I felt a pang of disappointment every time I watched a group show up and didn't see him among them.

"Who are you looking for?" Adel nudged me, leaning around Nathan.

"Stefan," I whispered. "We were supposed to meet here."

"Oh, he'll be here." She pointed to a small crowd walking to the benches. "See, there's Mr. Travers. Stefan should be coming along any minute now."

Right on cue, Stefan showed up. Plopping down, he gave my shoulders a squeeze. By then, Carl and Mava stood at the archway, hand in hand and waiting for the last stragglers to find seats.

"There you are. The ceremony is about to begin." I leaned into his hug.

"Sorry," he whispered. "A small caravan rode into town and needed directions to—"

The temple priest stood, and all conversation hushed. "People of Saren, we welcome you on this joyous occasion where these two in love will be united as one." He spoke with a gentle smile, gesturing to Carl and Mava.

The priest conducted a beautiful ceremony. Carl appeared to be in a daze of bliss as he beheld Mava. Their genuine grins of love and affection were heartwarming as they listened to the priest recite the wedding prayer.

Stefan caught my eye and grinned, then grabbed my hand and interlaced it with his.

Nathan leaned over and whispered in my ear, his beard tickling. "Don't get any funny ideas, like you're gonna be the next one up there." He glanced at the couple repeating the prayer.

"Don't worry, I'm not," I answered. "You still have time."

"I better," Nathan responded gruffly. Leaning away, he wrapped his muscular arm around Adel, pulling her close to his side.

I glanced at them and smiled. As far as adoptive parents could go, they were the best. They treated me as if I were their real flesh and blood, and it made me exceptionally grateful that I had them in my life. Though, I think they needed me as much as I needed them, since they were thus far unable to have children of their own.

A lavish party followed the ceremony. The sun drooped low in the sky. Lanterns hung from the branches of trees and poles stuck in the ground. All the able men got together and moved the benches to the sides, creating a space for dancing and conversation.

The summer air felt warm, breezy, and perfect. Little children ran underneath the feet of adults, fireflies in their closed palms. Tables buckled down with food and drink while musicians played string instruments. The whole town showed up. I lost count how many times I said hello as I navigated through Mava's crowded backyard.

Millie approached and put a wizened hand on my arm. "Sewing circle is at my house this week. I'm taking over for Mrs. Jensten." Her brown eyes crinkled. "Can't rightly host with her hands out of commission."

I nodded. "Indeed." My eyes darted through a break in the crowd to see Mrs. Jensten sitting on a bench chatting with Agatha and Mrs. Brunes. Thickly wrapped linen covered Mrs. Jensten's hands. Adel told me she tripped over one of her children's toys near the hearth and her hands had fallen into the fire.

"How is the treatment going?" I asked Millie. She tended to most of the sick in Saren, using her vast knowledge of medicinal herbs. Occasionally a traveling Healer came through, but he never received much business. Not many, including myself, were willing to trust a mage. The instant healing he purported seemed too good to be true. Who knew what sort of effect magic could have on a person later on? I shivered inwardly.

"Good. With my regimen she should regain full use of her hands," Millie said proudly. She patted my arm. "I best be off, do remember to tell Adel about the change for the sewing circle if I don't see her."

"I will." I smiled after her as she trotted off. For a woman well into her old age, Millie surprised with her strength and energy.

A crowd of well-wishers surrounded Mava and Carl. "Congratulations!" I leaned in and hugged Mava when I got the opportunity.

"Oh, Isabelle, I can't thank you enough for all of your help today." Mava beamed, gripping onto Carl's hand. Carl glanced down and grinned before addressing another guest.

"You're welcome." I smiled.

"Dance with me!" Stefan grabbed my hand, interrupting our conversation.

Mava gave me a knowing look, raising her eyebrows slightly. She shooed me away. "Dance!"

I let Stefan pull me through the throngs and into the swarm of dancing couples and small children bouncing to the lively tune.

We danced through several songs before I said I needed to catch my breath. "I'll get a drink." I let go of his hand and traversed over to the table filled with pitchers, greeting friends along the way.

I poured a cup of cider and leaned against the table, watching Stefan get ambushed by his little twin sisters begging for a dance. He latched onto their hands, and they danced around in a circle. I laughed at the silliness, the joy on the twins' faces infectious.

A man came up beside me and nodded his head in greeting. He had a prominent mustache and dark brown hair that fell slightly over his ears. His clothes seemed scuffed with dirt, but it wasn't a farmer's style of clothing. I guessed he'd been traveling. I didn't recognize him. Maybe he was a guest of Carl or Mava?

"Nice party, isn't it?" he spoke, a smile falling off his lips.

"Yes, it is," I said.

I couldn't explain it, but the man sent a shiver down my spine. I took a deep breath, trying to quell the feeling.

"I wondered if you might help me? This is my first night in town, and I was supposed to meet with the innkeeper about a room, but I'm afraid I don't know who he is. Could you point him out to me?" He stuck his hands in his pockets and glanced around, looking unsure.

"Oh, you came with the caravan?" I asked.

He nodded.

I smiled. "I'd be glad to help. Follow me and we can search together."

He smiled widely. "Thank you."

I tried not to shudder. *Get a grip on yourself, Isabelle*, I thought, blinking slowly. *He hasn't done anything to warrant concern.*

"All the shops close early on Gods Day. We like to spend time with friends and family," I said conversationally.

"Naturally," he agreed.

I peered through the crowd trying to find the innkeeper. The mustached man followed close behind as I walked through the dance floor.

"There." I pointed with my left hand, as I carried the cup in my right. "That's the innkeeper, sitting on that bench under the peach tree. He's the one draining his cup."

"Thank you, miss." The man smiled and stuck out his left hand.

I shook it. As I moved to let go, he gripped harder, staring at the back of my hand. "You wear the Mark of the Gods."

I wrenched my hand free. My juice splashed onto the ground. I cleared my throat and responded stiffly. "Yes, I was born with it."

"Hey, Iz, come dance!" Stefan called to me.

"If you'll excuse me." I turned around and made a beeline for Stefan, happy for any excuse to be rid of the mustached man.

"What's the matter?" Stefan asked, grabbing the cup from my hand. "You look troubled. Was it that man? Did he say something to you?"

"It's nothing." I tried to shrug it off. "He just noticed my birthmark, that's all."

Stefan grabbed my left hand and kissed the back of it, right over the birthmark shaped like the Mark of the Gods. It resembled a sun—fiery red, bright, and burning. The middle coiled in a circle with four large triangle points surrounding and four smaller ones in between them. It looked more like a brand than a birthmark, but I always liked to call it a birthmark since it literally appeared at birth. The same sign represented the Gods of Aberron, and I had spent my entire life trying to forget it even existed.

"Don't be so self-conscious about it. It's not like you put it there on purpose. It's been there since birth," he said, letting go.

I nodded, taking a deep breath, I bounced on the balls of my feet to fight off the shudders. "You're right. It's just I hate the way people react to it like I have some crazy magical power or something. Which we all know I don't."

No one had ever given me a straight answer when I questioned it. I had spent hours of my life staring at the birthmark, wondering why it was there, burned into my skin like a brand. The Mark of the Gods wasn't exactly well received by others. I gazed at the back of my hand, lamenting the difficulty of hiding the birthmark.

Normally, the temple priests and priestesses wore the mark. Tattooed with black paint, they placed it on their upper arms, near their shoulders. The red mark on the back of my left hand reminded me of a beacon. It shone bright and open for everyone to see. I hated it.

Though it never did anything remotely out of the ordinary. It never glowed or tickled or burned. I didn't think I had an ounce of magic in me. I figured something should have happened by now if I possessed any ability. Seventeen made me a young lady. I doubted I'd grow any more than my current height and had finally accepted that I was doomed to be short for eternity.

"Don't worry about it, Iz," Stefan said. "I'm sure he didn't mean any harm. Everyone reacts that way when they first meet you."

"Well, next time I'm going to wear gloves," I said.

Stefan laughed. "And deny me the pleasure of holding your hand?"

I bit my lip and conceded. "Maybe."

I spent the rest of the party trying to forget the man I helped, but every time I turned around, there he stood, staring at me like I was his idea of dinner plans. I didn't have a clue of what to do about it until Stefan started to notice it as well.

"Come on; I'll take you home," he said.

I nodded in relief. "That sounds good. Let me just tell Adel."

I found Adel chatting with a few ladies from town. Stefan and I said our goodbyes.

"I'll be home soon, dear," Adel said. "That is if I can find Nathan." She peered through the crowd, pursing her lips.

"Good luck." I laughed.

I glanced behind me and noticed the unsettling man again, watching my interactions with Adel. His eyes seemed to follow us wherever we went. I casually put my hand on Stefan's shoulder and whispered a plan. We enlisted the help of several unruly boys and Stefan's twin sisters. One of the boys pulled a toad out of his pocket, and they proceeded to chase the twins around the backyard, purposely knocking over the mustached man. Stefan and I quickly ran out of sight.

We strolled hand in hand toward home, chuckling over the spectacular display we had organized. The moon filled up the path with natural light. Stars twinkled like gems in the sky.

"Do you feel better now?" Stefan asked, pulling me closer.

"Much." I squeezed his hand. "Thank you."

"I hope that guy leaves tomorrow. I didn't like the way he stared at you. It wasn't natural," Stefan said.

"Agreed." I nodded vigorously.

"Hey, can I ask you something?"

"Sure."

"Do you ever wish your life were different? That you had never come here?" His tone sounded serious.

I responded with what I suspected he actually wanted to know, cutting straight to the heart of the issue. "Do I wish I had never watched my parents' murders and that I lived with them in Korrun? All the time. But it doesn't change the fact that it did happen, and my life changed irrevocably. I am grateful for Nathan and Adel taking me in and raising me as their own."

"I see." Stefan sounded slightly glum.

I leaned into his shoulder. "Don't worry. I like it here. I don't have plans to leave." I grinned but doubted he could see it clearly in the moonlight.

"I mean where else can I get a cute post boy to deliver packages to me and walk me home?"

Stefan chuckled. "True." There was a little more bounce in his step after that.

CHAPTER TWO

"H EY!"

Stefan and I swiveled around. The mustached man we'd tried to avoid caught up with us. Anxiety crept up. His persistence unnerved me. Couldn't he see that I didn't want anything to do with him?

With the moonlight shining down on us, I saw the man smirk. "You didn't think you could get rid of me that easily, did you?"

"What's your obsession with Iz?" Stefan demanded, taking a step forward. "Why can't you just leave her alone?"

The man pulled an arm back and punched Stefan hard in the face, then threw him onto the ground.

"Stefan!" I rushed forward.

The man snatched my arm as I reached for Stefan, who was lying in the dirt, groaning and disoriented. "You're coming with me." He pulled me into him, pinning both arms to my sides. I stomped on his boot, but he only chuckled. "Nice try, princess."

"Help!" I screamed as I struggled against his firm grasp.

The man wrapped one arm around my chest and covered my mouth with his hand. "None of that." He started to drag me away as Stefan struggled to get up and come to my aid. I kicked at the man's legs, hoping to trip him, but he seemed to expect every move and account for it.

Just when I thought I had no chance of escape, Nathan and Adel rode into view. I thrashed harder; the man's hand slipped off my mouth, and I shrieked. "Nathan!"

"Isabelle!" Nathan jumped off the moving wagon. He sprinted to me. The man moved fast, but Nathan was quicker. He wrenched the man off me using his grizzly bear strength. I scrambled out of the way as Nathan walloped the man, hitting him right over his left eye and cheekbone. The man fell to the ground, gasping in pain.

Nathan turned to me, his chest heaving. "Are you all right?"

I shuddered, tears spilling from my eyes. "I'm fine."

Nathan gripped my shoulders. "Are you sure?"

"Yes," I said, wiping my cheeks. I clutched at my stomach, now coiled in knots, fearing I'd throw up.

Nathan let go and turned to the man he had hit. Except he had disappeared. In the short moment it took for Nathan to check on me, the man had slipped out of sight, running through the tall corn beside us. We'd never be able to find him in the dark.

"Stefan." I skirted around Nathan and fell to my knees beside Stefan. He was sitting up now, Adel crouched on the other side of him. "How are you?"

Stefan clutched his head. "Ouch, Iz."

"Everyone get into the wagon," Nathan ordered. He reached out a hand and pulled Stefan up. Adel and I guided him to the wagon.

Nathan spurred our horse—Amber—into a canter, reaching our house in minutes. Adel and I helped Nathan unhitch Amber and led her into a stall.

"We'll unload tomorrow," Nathan said. "Let's get inside."

We guided Stefan to the house, and all the while I apologized profusely.

"It's not your fault, Isabelle," Stefan said.

I couldn't help but think it was.

We set him on a chair. Adel went around lighting lamps in the kitchen. I took a washcloth and wet it. An ugly bruise had started to appear on Stefan's cheek and jaw.

"No." He protested when I leaned down and brought the rag to his face.

Undeterred, I pressed it lightly to his bruise. He gasped.

"Your face is swelling; this will help." I wished I had some ice, but there was none to be had in summer.

"Can somebody tell me what's going on?" Nathan demanded.

I handed Stefan the rag and straightened. I rushed into an explanation of everything that had transpired between me and the mustached man. I remembered the way his hands gripped me, and I shuddered.

Nathan folded his arms. "You're not leaving this house without your sword from now on. There's no telling where that man is now or what his intentions are."

I nodded, appreciating that he believed I could protect myself with it. "I promise."

Nathan strode out of the room, muttering something about checking windows and doors. Adel started heating water in a kettle for tea. The air had a tense quality to it. I sat next to Stefan and took his hand in mine. His lips curved up as he squeezed my fingers.

Nathan strode in just as Adel set cups in front of us, filled with apple cider tea. "The house is secure, but I've got a bad feeling in my gut."

"I don't think we should send Stefan home considering his injuries, and that man could be lurking anywhere. He could hurt Stefan again," I said with concern.

Nathan nodded as he reached for a mug. "Stefan can sleep in one of the guest rooms upstairs."

"I don't fancy a walk home with my head spinning," Stefan said, gingerly touching his temple.

After finishing our tea, Adel and I helped Stefan up the stairs and into a spare bedroom. Following many assurances that he'd be all right, I returned to the kitchen to retrieve my sword. I would not sleep without it tonight.

As I climbed into bed, my eyes lighted on the package. Needing something to take my mind off the events of the night, I pulled it to me. I started unwrapping it, but instead of the volume I'd expected to find beneath the brown paper, there was a wooden box.

I lifted the lid, revealing a note and a red velvet drawstring bag. My eyebrows furrowed in confusion. I pulled on the drawstring and peeked inside, my eyes growing wide as I stared at the gleaming gold coins. "What in the Gods?" I whispered.

I fished through the pile of gold, pulling out the letter. I opened it.

> **Isabelle,**
> **Gods forbid, I hope this gets to you in time. There is a man traveling in a caravan from Carasmille to Saren. My sources say he is an excellent tracker, cunning and known to harm. His purpose is to retrieve the girl who wears the Mark of the Gods. Your life is in danger. It is imperative you leave Saren and travel to Thimbleton to meet me. I can keep you safe. I've sent enough money for travel, lodging, and whatever else you need. It may be best to have Nathan escort you. Once you arrive, ask the innkeeper to send a message to the King's castle in Carasmille so I know where to find you. I look forward to seeing you again little sister. Be safe.**

Joshua Mirran

The letter fell from my hands and fluttered onto my lap. The mustached man who had tried to grab me after the party must be who Joshua meant. "What have you done brother?" I murmured.

I hadn't talked to or seen my brother Joshua in twelve years. After our parents' deaths, we had been shipped off to completely different locations. He was in the capital city of Carasmille, and I was in Saren—two different worlds.

I looked over the note again. Words popped out at me. Harm, danger, Leave. The thought of facing off the mustached man again made my stomach roll. Resolve formed in my gut. I had to go before he went after me again.

I thought about bringing Nathan like Joshua suggested. Stefan's bruised face flashed to the forefront of my mind. I shuddered. Nathan could get hurt, perhaps even killed, if we were discovered. I could not risk his life. I glanced at my sword lying near my pillow. Nathan had been teaching me defensive lessons since I was five. With a blade in my hand, I trusted my ability to take care of myself.

I set the paper aside. Reaching underneath my bed, I found the extra-large mostly cream-colored bag. I used it so often that I had patched it up at least three times already. Ransacking my room, I shoved whatever I could fit into my bag. Clothes and toiletries, needle and thread, a small box of lotions and medicines. Pulling the drawstring closed, I attempted to haul it over my shoulder.

Gods forbid, what did I put in there? Putting the bag down, I opened it and took out several items. I needed to be light on my feet, and I couldn't go fast with a heavy pack over my shoulders. *That's better,* I thought as I picked it up again.

I hitched my sword to my belt, grabbed my bedside candle, and tiptoed out of my room. I paused by Nathan and Adel's door and pressed my ear against it. Soft snores reached me. Assured they were asleep, I moved to Stefan's door. I couldn't very well tell Nathan or Adel my plans. They'd stop me from going or worse try to come along and potentially get hurt. But I had to inform someone. I turned the handle, not bothering to knock and stepped inside. "Stefan," I whispered.

With a groan, he sat up in bed, hand touching his temple. "What is it Iz?"

Softly putting my bag on the floor, I sat on the edge of his mattress. Quietly, I explained about the contents of the package he'd delivered to me this morning and my plans to leave. Stefan's eyes gradually widened and by the end I expected him to protest. Before he could open his mouth, I pinned him with a steel glare. "I've already made up my mind. There's nothing you or anyone else can say or do to stop me."

Stefan cursed as he rubbed his forehead. "Gods Isabelle."

I stiffened. Stefan only used my full name when he was displeased with me.

His pale blue eyes caught mine. "This is madness, you know that right?"

I took his hand in mine. "I'm the one being hunted, not you or Nathan and Adel. It killed me to see you get hurt tonight. I'm not willing to risk anyone's safety with this journey. You'll all be fine with me gone." I patted my sword.

Stefan nodded slowly, relenting under my determination. "All right Iz. What do you want me to do?"

I breathed a sigh of relief. "Tell Nathan and Adel what I've done in the morning."

"All right. Have you got a map?" he asked.

"I need to get it from the library," I said.

Together we slinked through the house, careful to be as silent as possible. I cringed at every creaky floorboard. I couldn't afford to have Nathan or Adel wake up. In the kitchen, I tucked a bit of food into my bag, jerky, biscuits, a waterskin, and such. Then I retrieved a map.

Stefan quickly went over a route with me, using his vast trail knowledge from his job as a post boy. I felt his displeasure at letting me go off alone. It filled me with a strong sense of determination to prove I could do this. I folded the map and stowed it into my bag. I slung it over my shoulders. "I'm ready."

Stefan stood. "Take the tunnels. You'll have a better chance getting out of here undetected. I'll walk with you to the edge of town."

I quivered, reminded of all the times I'd been down there, huddled together with family and friends fearing for Saren.

Occasionally, tornadoes ripped through our farming community. Often enough for the residents of Saren to construct an underground tunnel system connecting houses and shops together. Ordinary root cellars led into passageways wide enough for two people to walk side by side. Years of work went into this, started by grandfathers long since passed. The passages constantly expanded as new generations worked and maintained it. When a tornado approached, we gathered together in the tunnels until the storm passed. It kept the residents of Saren safe.

Stefan led the way into the cellar. He switched out my bedside candle with a lantern. We pushed back multiple crates of potatoes and opened the hidden door. I shivered, imagining all kinds of bugs that crawled in these shafts.

Hand in hand, we walked through the tunnels, following the markers to the outer edge of town. My throat felt constricted, and I couldn't think of anything to say to Stefan.

He glanced at my worry-stricken face. "You can do this, Isabelle. Don't for one second think you can't."

I nodded, gulping down my apprehension as we reached the end of the tunnel.

I gazed at Stefan, and my shoulders slumped. We were just getting to know each other, just starting to explore what a relationship could mean. Now, I didn't think I had it in me to say goodbye.

He smiled ruefully and nodded, understanding what I couldn't verbally get out. He set the lantern down and opened his arms, enveloping me in a bone-crushing hug. "I'm sorry," I apologized into his shirt. "I wish we could have—"

"I know," Stefan cut me off.

We broke apart, and I took a step back.

He kicked at the dirt wall in frustration. "Gods forbid, I should be coming with you."

I put my hand on his chest. "No, don't. I couldn't bear it if you got hurt again. He's after me, not you," I reminded.

Stefan embraced me once more. "But I can't let my girl go out there alone knowing you're being hunted by some savage criminal. What kind of man does that make me?"

How quickly we switched roles. I found myself consoling him as he had just done for me. "Have a little faith in me, will you? I can do it. I'm an independent woman. I take care of myself." I basked in independence, and Stefan knew it. He couldn't win this fight. My voice took on a bitter edge. "I've got my sword. That man will never touch me again."

Stefan sighed, his shoulders slumping in defeat. "You were always meant for greater things; I knew it from the moment I set my eyes on you." He took a deep breath and exhaled.

I rolled my eyes. "As soon as I get this all sorted out, I'll come home."

"You better." He leaned down and kissed me softly.

Stefan went up the stairs first, opening the hatch and scouting out the perimeter. When he didn't see anyone, he gave me the go-ahead to come up. Taking a deep breath to steady myself, I climbed up the stairs and stepped out into the open. From here on out, everything I knew was going to change.

CHAPTER THREE

HE SUMMER SKY LOOKED gorgeous. The moon filled the night with its luminescent glow and guided my way through many fields of wheat. Although it didn't stop me from tripping over gopher holes and anthills. *Gods forbid, I could use some sun.* It would take me twice as long to get to Thimbleton if I had to spend the entire journey walking in the dark, stumbling over who knows what. *What if I stepped on a snake?* The thought made me quicken my pace.

I heard something lumbering through the wheat field behind me. I couldn't make it out. I crouched and waited, holding my breath, and freezing my position. My hand slid down to the dagger in my boot.

Had he—or they—already found me? My stomach twisted in knots, ramming me with nervous adrenaline. *I can't die now.*

"Woof!"

I jumped, falling backward into the dirt.

"Boomer. Don't scare me like that," I softly reprimanded the big black-and-white dog who had come to investigate. "You stupid dog. You're liable to get hurt sneaking up on people."

He woofed and threw his head into my hands. Laughing quietly, I scratched him behind his ears.

"Good boy." I pulled a piece of jerky out and gave it to him as I stood. Boomer chomped through the jerky, then lay on the ground and started rolling.

"I'm sorry, boy; I don't have time for a belly scratch." I leaned down and patted his head. "Now stay; don't follow me."

Boomer woofed back. He stood and fled back into the wheat, going the opposite direction I headed.

I hope that's the last surprise. Boomer's unexpected visit heightened my senses and anxiety. I touched my temples and took a deep breath. Exhaling slowly, I reigned in my emotions. With every natural sound of the field, I imagined it was the man who had tried to grab me, following my tracks. It became increasingly difficult to differentiate between the buzz of nature and the noise of a possible tracker on my trail.

I reached the end of the last wheat field that opened into an apple orchard. The sweet smell of apples made my mouth water. I plucked one from a low-hanging branch and rubbed it on my shirt, hoping to shake off any bugs I couldn't see in the darkness. I bit into it. The juices ran down my chin. Having something to bite into helped ease the tension I felt.

I fell into a rhythm of steady exercise. To pass the time I focused on the steady beat of my heart and the pounding of my feet against the ground. Occasionally, I thought about different defensive tactics I had practiced, but mostly I kept my mind clear. I hoped that if I didn't think, then I didn't have to worry. Frightened adrenaline would eat me alive if I didn't do something about it. By the time I found the Trivail Forest and entered, dawn approached quickly. I set my bag down next to the first large tree I saw and rested.

I poured a little water from my pouch into my hands and rubbed the back of my neck and forehead. The water felt refreshing going down my parched throat as I took a long drink. My sore feet and ankles throbbed from stumbling through the darkness, and this was only the beginning.

Wary about going to sleep, I watched the area for a half hour, eating a few pieces of jerky and bread to keep me awake. Nothing happened. Not even a chipmunk ran in front of me. *Maybe if I rest a little ... I'd be all right.* I closed my eyes, unable to keep them open any longer.

I dreamed I stood in a field with wheat enveloping me, rising to my hips. Not a single cloud loitered in the azure-blue sky. I turned around in a circle, my hands brushing against the stalks. I stared hard at my surroundings;

everything felt real and clear. Usually, my dreams had a warped sense of reality.

What kind of place am I in?

The field connected to a forest. Its deep green and darkened canopy called to me, and I felt an intense desire to run over to the edge of the wheat. *Why am I compelled to go there?* I moved forward. The tall grains brushed against my legs, but I paid no attention. My thoughts entirely focused on my destination.

Something flashed before my eyes, and for a second I thought I saw a person: a tall, dark-haired man standing at the end of the wheat field. I didn't recognize him. I closed my eyes and opened them again. I saw no one. *What is going on?*

I started running, my breath coming in labored puffs. I couldn't explain it, but I had this inexplicable need to find the man. I knew he stood there a second ago, even if I didn't see him now. I felt excited the nearer I got to the edge of the field, consumed with an intense desire to prove my sanity. When I got closer, he appeared again. The distance between us was too great, and I couldn't make out his features.

I jolted awake. The vision or dream dissolved quickly from my mind. My head spinning from the quick movement, I opened and closed my eyes, clearing the blurriness of sleep. That's when I discovered what had woken me up. Two squirrels dug in my pack; a third crouched on my leg, nibbling on a piece of biscuit.

"Hey!" I shouted, completely forgetting the need to stay quiet. I stood quickly, shaking the squirrel off my leg and snatching my pack. The squirrels ran up the tree chattering angrily.

I peeked in my bag, wrinkling my nose at the mess they had made. Biscuit crumbs covered everything. I pulled the string shut and swung it over my shoulders. I couldn't do anything about it now. I didn't have time to shake out the bag. *Stupid squirrels*, I thought, grumbling.

I took one quick swig of water from my pouch and continued onward, walking deeper into the trees. My eyes scanned the dense forest, looking for any anomaly.

I jumped and fought back a yell, throwing my hands over my head when a bird flew past, its wings brushing my hair.

Get a grip on yourself. You're going to pieces, I thought in reprimanding tones. *You're jumpier than a chased rabbit.*

A gale of wind blew past my face. I heard water rushing.

I smiled. *Right on track.* The map I carried showed a large stream. It ran through the forest and into the outskirts of Thimbleton. The stream was my ticket out of here. I followed the sound of running water until I reached it, discovering that I stood at the top of a waterfall looking down into a ravine. I briefly wondered if Stefan had told me about the waterfall, but I couldn't remember in my hurry. A bald eagle swooped into the stream, coming back up with a fish clutched in its sharp talons. I envied the skill the eagle had. He made dinner seem like an easy catch. I pulled out the map and glanced at it once more, concluding that I needed to head down into the ravine.

The rocky ground sloped downward until it leveled with the water. I found what appeared to be the safest spot and started my descent. The rocks settled loosely among the small crags of grass, moss, weeds, and ferns. It was harder than I wanted it to be. *Why can't I have wings and fly?* I thought wistfully, thinking of the eagle.

"This would be much easier if I hadn't packed so much!" I groaned.

I turned my head sharply to the right midway down the rocky slope, hearing a cracking sound that did not belong in the forest. Fear seized at my heart, and adrenaline surged. Stuck halfway down the rocky slope, my first thought screamed of my vulnerability. I needed to get into the ravine fast.

As I continued my descent, my foot slipped on the loose dirt and rocks. I slid and started rolling. The rocks jabbed, pricked, and banged. Gasping as every rock slammed into my body, I threw my hands out trying to grab onto something, anything, to slow me down. My hands slipped through the silt and rocks, leaving me with nothing to hold.

Going too fast to stop myself, I rolled right off the sloping hill and started to fall.

I'm falling, I thought stupidly, pumped full of pain. It was my last conscious thought.

The sun had almost completely faded when I regained consciousness. I lay flat on my stomach. *Gods forbid, it hurts!* My head pounded, and my legs felt like jelly. Rubbing my head slowly, I felt a patch of dried blood. *Great.* This journey went from bad to worse by the second.

The mist from the waterfall coated my face and body. I fell closer to the stream than I would have liked and onto a bed of smooth rocks, which ended up working in my favor. Jagged rocks could have meant impalement and death.

"Let's see the damage," I murmured. I wiggled my toes and my back, deeming it safe to sit up. I felt around my body, my fingers trailing over the extra sore spots. Miraculously, I hadn't broken anything. Several scratches marred my skin, but nothing too serious.

Groaning, I stood, tired of the mist spraying into my face and onto my bag. I wrinkled my nose, thinking of wet biscuit crumbs. Pain reverberated through my body. It hurt everywhere. I stumbled over the plain of rocks until I found a little patch of grass surrounded by a grove of young oak trees. I set my bag down and rested, accidentally falling asleep.

The sound of something dragging across the rocks jerked me awake the next morning. Cursing at my stupidity for having a head wound and falling asleep, I stared out ahead blearily.

A beaver dragged a piece of driftwood across the rocks. He stopped and peered at me for a second. When I didn't move, he continued his work, scraping the log loudly against the rocks.

Gritting my teeth, I picked up my belongings and trudged onward, deciding on a new direction. I still needed to be close to the stream, but I didn't want to walk on the rocks. I fled back into the trees, close enough to the water to hear it but far enough away to walk on fewer rocks and spongier dirt. My feet and ankles thanked me for it.

Tension rolled off me as I silently padded through the forest, feeling upset over my blatant clumsiness. I entered a clearing overflowing with earthy grass, ferns, and a few patches of open, mulchy dirt. The sounds of the forest muted. What happened to the bird calls? The squirrel chatter?

My answer came quicker than I expected. I dodged to the right, falling to the ground. My hands sunk into the damp dirt as I banged my knee on gnarled roots, but it quickly became the least of my worries. The arrow previously aimed for my heart sailed passed me, lodging into a nearby tree.

Gods forbid! Someone's shooting at me!

I glanced up only to quickly roll onto my side, crushing my bag underneath me. Another arrow flew toward me, narrowly missing my arm. It sliced through a large fern and sunk into the soggy earth. Hastily, I jumped up and ran for cover behind the biggest and closest tree I could find. An arrow whizzed by just as I leaned against the old oak, my chest heaving.

No! This can't be happening. He found me. I hyperventilated as I covered my face with my hands. *What am I going to do?*

I poked my head out from behind the tree to see the attacker. I saw nothing but trees and underbrush. *How am I supposed to come up with a plan if I can't even see them? They're not fighting fair.* Where was their post? I couldn't fight an unseen army, and I had no idea how many people hid themselves.

I poked my head out again and screamed as loud as I could. "Come out and fight like a man, you coward!"

Two arrows zoomed past, narrowly missing my head as I dodged behind the safety of the tree.

Oh, come on ... Stop shooting at me! I balled my hands into fists.

"You come out from behind that tree, and maybe I'll think about it," a rather cocky, yet eager voice shouted back.

I slammed my fist into the tree. Curse that mustached man!

"How do I know you won't shoot me if I come out?" I bellowed. This oak tree had become my safety net. I wouldn't leave it without a good reason. I refused to surrender that easily.

"I swear on this sacred land of Aberron and on its namesake, King Aberron, that you will not be shot," the man drawled, his voice fluid and arrogant. He knew he had the upper hand and milked it for its worth.

"That's not very promising. Lots of people swear on the first King and bail out," I responded.

"Then I swear on the Gods. May they strike me dead if you are," he answered firmly.

I sighed, kicking the back of my boot into the tree. No one ever swore anything on the Gods unless they meant it. Everyone knew the tale of the man who swore on the Gods, then broke the oath. Angering the Gods, he spent the rest of his short life blind, deaf, mute, and unable to walk.

I placed a hand on my throbbing forehead. I slung my bag off my shoulders and let it fall to the ground. Slowly, I crept out from behind the oak tree. My hands tensed, hovering over the sword strapped to my side.

Two men walked into the open. A blonde man, his hair cropped short and sporting a stubby beard. He looked as tall and thick as a tree trunk. What did he do all day, lift hay bales with stones in the middle? He carried a bow and quiver of arrows on his shoulder. The man who had attempted but failed to run off with me once stood beside the blonde, wearing the same traveling clothes that he wore then. He sported a blackened bruise over the left side of his face from Nathan. He smoothed out his mustache. A gleam in his eyes displayed intelligence, and his posture oozed arrogance.

"Ooh, we got ourselves a beauty!" The blonde man grinned.

The mustached man slapped the blonde across the chest. "Manners, Gleason. That's not how we treat a lady."

"Sorry, Boss." Gleason ducked his head, ashamed. When his boss turned back to me, Gleason shot his head back up and winked.

I wrinkled my nose in disgust as I recoiled. "Who are you?"

The mustached man smiled. "I prefer to be unnamed. Call me whatever you would like."

"Call him Boss. He likes that one," Gleason interrupted.

"What do you want with me?" I pressed, shifting my weight from side to side.

"What do I want?" Boss placed a hand on his chest, flashing a bemused smile at my question. He had definitely done this before and reveled in it. "I want everything, dear." His eyes raked over my body.

I unsheathed my sword and pointed it at them, feeling threatened. "Not gonna happen."

"Ooh, you can dance and wield a sword. How very exciting." Boss laughed, rubbing his hands together in excitement while Gleason guffawed next to him.

"I would have skewered you if I had it with me that night," I said with menace. "You're lucky you got away with a bruise."

Judging by the amusement lacing his face, I doubted he considered me a threat. "Well now, I think we match. What happened to you, princess? Can't handle a stroll through the woods?"

"I want her." There was longing in Gleason's voice.

"No," Boss said sharply. "She's already spoken for." He sounded impatient as he tapped his foot.

I raised my eyebrows, taking a step back as the ferns tickled my legs. *Spoken for? I am not their property.* I narrowed my eyes and gripped the leather handle tighter. They might've had a good chance of capturing me, but I wouldn't go down without a fight.

Gleason gestured to me. "She's got a sword; if I have to fight her, I should get something out of it."

"All right, if you capture her, I'll let you carry her back. How's that sound?" Boss conceded, folding his arms.

"I want more," Gleason argued.

Boss pointed at me. "Capture her and we'll talk."

Gleason set the bow and quiver down and surged forward, pulling his sword from his scabbard. "I'll get her."

I put my hand out. "Whoa, stop right there! You're not getting anything!" I took several steps backward.

"I'll shoot you if you try to run." Boss raised a hand and signaled. An arrow came speeding out of the trees, narrowly missing me as I jumped out of the way.

My eyes widened. *There's a third?* Judging by the angle of the arrow that flew, the real archer had probably perched in a tree with a good vantage point. I cast my eyes into the canopy but couldn't see him. No way would I get out of this alive and uncaptured without some miracle. *I'm done for.*

"Gleason will fight you fairly with a sword. But I make no exceptions. You might lose an arm …" He paused, a grin on his face, and stared unashamedly at my legs. "Or a leg."

"You'll never get that close," I told them. My stomach coiled in knots. I'd never actually been in a fight before, even though I practiced fencing nearly every day of my life with Nathan. "Why are you doing this?" I asked, stalling for time. My eyes darted for an escape.

He spoke to Gleason, ignoring me. "Fight."

"Wait!" I held out my hand, taking another step backward. "I have money. Is it money that you wish for?"

"No. I do not care for your petty sum." He wrinkled his nose in distaste, obviously assuming I had a farmer's wage in my bag.

Fine. If he wanted a fight, he'd get one. I took a step forward, swinging my sword in front of me. Already sore from the fall, I hoped the adrenaline and fear pulsing through my veins could keep me going, or else I'd turn into bird food.

Just out of range of the tip of my sword, Gleason charged forward. We circled each other guardedly. I chose my steps carefully, keeping one eye on Gleason and the other on the ground. I couldn't afford to slip. We circled for more than a minute before I started to get impatient.

"Are you going to fight me or not?" I exclaimed in an irritated tone.

"I just wanna get a good look at you," Gleason answered.

I rolled my eyes.

Gleason charged, his sword thrust high. The tip of his blade headed right for my upper shoulder. He wanted to spear me! I swung to the right, blocked, then tried to get his gut. He barely had time to block but hit with brutal strength. *Gods forbid, he's strong.*

I searched for any advantage I could find, while his weight bore over me. I couldn't beat him this way. My mind raced to stay on top of the game. My breathing became ragged, and my body ached even more.

He backed off and surged forward again. I sidestepped to the left, then grazed his arm, slashing through his long-sleeved shirt.

"Gods forbid!" he wailed. Blood stained his ripped sleeve. "She got me."

"Oh, come on, it's just a scratch. Now finish this!" Boss called back. He leaned against a tree, his ankles crossed and his arms folded, watching energetically.

Gleason's eyes bulged. His face transformed into a rage as he realized he had severely underestimated my fencing skills. He howled and spun on his feet, charging like an angry bull. I bit my lip. *Gods forbid, I made him angry.*

I couldn't dodge away in time. Gleason slit my stomach, ripping through my clothing. My skin burned with the shallow horizontal scratch he'd made. The large tear in the shirt exposed the creaminess of my abdomen, now red and irritated with drops of crimson blood. He grinned foolishly, baring yellow teeth. In the background, I heard Boss laughing. I grit my teeth and grimaced.

"There! Now you're even!" Boss clapped his hands together.

I narrowed my eyes, practically dancing from side to side to avoid getting speared. When Gleason came at me for what seemed like the twentieth time, I saw something that I could use. I gripped my sword with every ounce of strength I had and hit the middle of his blade, quickly moving my head in the process to avoid getting stabbed. My blade slid down the steel of his until it reached the hilt. Then I looped the tip through one of the gold spiral designs. His loose grip was exactly what I hoped for as I flung the sword from his hands. He fell to the ground, and I pointed my weapon at his throat.

Wow, it worked. Success! I thought excitedly, my chest heaving from the exertion.

"Well done, my lady," Boss said with a flourishing bow. Then he waved his hand, signaling to the archer in the trees.

He lied!

I took a step backward as the arrow zoomed toward us, impaling the man whom I held at sword point. He fell facedown at my feet, the arrow protruding out of his neck, and within seconds he died. I looked up, horrified.

"What'd you do that for?" I glared at the boss.

"He lost to a woman. No use to me." He shrugged, switching the subject casually. He stepped forward, walking away from the tree he leaned against. "You seem to know your way around a sword well."

Ire flashed in my eyes. "What do you want?"

"I want everything. The whole world." He grinned, lifting his hands and turning around in a circle. "I know you won't come willingly, so I will give you a chance. You win, and I'll let you go." He pointed at himself. "I win, and you voluntarily come to meet my employer."

"Who is your employer?" I questioned, lowering my sword slightly as he spoke.

He chuckled and waved a finger at me. "Tsk tsk," he said disapprovingly. "Answering questions wasn't part of the deal."

"I don't really have a choice, do I?" I asked, putting one hand on my hip.

"Of course not. Now let's begin." He spoke in a lower tone, matching the dark mood.

He unsheathed his sword with a brandished flair, and I knew any tricks I had up my sleeve wouldn't work. This guy had been better trained, unlike the other idiot he paired me with. That poor idiot who died. I felt a little sad about it. Had he suspected imminent death when he signed up?

We both took our stance. I scanned for any weakness I could find, but wasn't seeing anything. *Now I will die; or worse, get taken to his employer.* I shuddered. I could only imagine the horrors that visit would entail.

Before I could regain a good grip on my sword, he charged forward offensively. I hastily sidestepped to the right, stumbling backward and nearly tripping over the same tree root I had banged my knee on.

"You're quick. I like that." He smiled.

I glared and wiped the sweat off my brow with the back of my sleeve.

The boss scaled back on the attack and began again with a few jabs and parries. He got more serious after I grazed his collarbone, and within seconds we engaged in a battle that rivaled any practice with Nathan.

Predator against prey in a fight purely for survival. The steel clashed so strongly I half expected sparks to fly off.

"You are good," he praised, trying to hold his position. "But not as good as me."

I breathed heavily while blocking him, refusing to grace him with an answer.

His strength and agility appeared never-ending, and I quickly felt in over my head. I started searching for any way out. My muscles screamed in pain. The back of my boot backed into the dead guy as I tried to get ahold of my footing as he slammed into me. *That's it! The dead guy.*

I fought more aggressively, fighting on the offense instead of the defense. He didn't expect that, and I could see the surprise on his face. I slid to the left, my feet slipping on the mud and mulch, and forced him to slide to the right. We switched positions without so much as batting an eye. Now the dead guy lay behind him, not me.

He pushed me forward, but I refused to give in. I sidestepped and came back with what little fierceness I had left. I aimed high, then low, and all over the place, pushing him backward without him realizing.

"What kind of swordplay is this?" he laughed.

I jabbed toward his gut.

In his haste to block, he stepped back, tripping over Gleason and falling to the ground. His weapon fell from his hands. I quickly stepped forward and pointed my sword at his throat.

"Well done." He smiled, holding his hands up in surrender. "You have me beat."

"Then you'll let me go?" I huffed, trying to regain my breath. I wiped my brow with the back of my sleeve.

"No. I still need you." He raised his right hand higher and signaled.

Uh oh. I knew what that meant. I tried to dodge, duck, do anything to get out of the way. It seemed like the arrow flew before Boss even signaled.

"Gods forbid!" I screamed. Pure, unhindered pain and shock erupted. An arrow protruded out of my left shoulder. I stumbled backward, nearly collapsing onto the soft ground, but by some miracle, I managed to stay upright. I couldn't buckle under yet.

Boss laughed, moving his legs off Gleason. "Ooh, I bet that hurts." He picked up his sword and stood, pointing it at me, and came closer. He tried to knock my blade out of my hands, but I resisted.

He shook his head and sighed. "Give up. You can't win."

"No," I said icily.

"You're only making this harder on yourself." He took another step forward.

His hand twitched, and I sensed his plan. I jumped to the left, ducking as the arrow he called for zoomed toward me. Instead of hitting me like he had intended, it impaled Boss directly through his heart. He crumpled to the ground, dead.

The archer screamed in anguish.

"No! Brother! No!" the archer sobbed from behind a tree. "You'll pay for what you've done!" He walked into the open clearing, gripping onto his bow so tightly I half expected it to snap. His face appeared red and splotchy from the raw emotion. Glistening tears wet his cheeks, sliding into his scruffy brown stubble.

What I've *done? I didn't shoot him!* I thought angrily.

"I don't care about taking you anymore. I'm gonna make you suffer for killing my brother. You're going to die a slow and painful death. All alone, with no help." He reached behind him and pulled an arrow out. It took him only a second to notch and release. His hands were shaking, tears still streaming down his face as arrows started flying in a steady stream.

I ran for cover but not before another arrow hit the outside of my lower right thigh, just above my knee. "Argh!" I cried out.

I collapsed behind the oak tree, my protector, fighting the waves of pain that engulfed me. Blood blossomed through my clothes. Nauseating to see, I resisted the urge to throw up.

I worried the archer would shoot me point-blank. Fighting back the overwhelming pain, I clawed at the tree, pulling myself up so I could lean against it and peek. He strode forward, a bow in hand, two arrows left in his quiver. My legs buckled under me, and I fell backward, then scrambled until my back hit the tree.

"Please!" I begged for my life.

He reached out and tugged on the arrow wedged in my shoulder. I screamed in pain.

"That should do it," he grinned, shoving me to the ground. "Suffer long, then die." He turned around and sprinted away.

I crawled forward, my fingernails digging in the dirt, intending to see the direction he went. I collapsed onto the forest floor, falling onto my back like a puppet on strings. I closed my eyes, passing out from the pain and physical exertion.

When I opened my eyes again, light still shone. I must not have been out for very long because the sun hovered high in the sky, its rays filtering through the tree canopy. *What is going on?* The sudden spike of discomfort helped me remember the attack and arrows. I stared at my blood-soaked body. *Gods forbid it hurts.*

I choked back the urge to throw up and took deep, steady breaths to calm down. I dragged my useless body over to a tree and leaned against it. I felt around the arrow on my shoulder. It had lodged itself in too deeply for me to pull out. I couldn't even feel the edge of the arrowhead. The one in my thigh was shallow. If I had been a few inches farther away, it would have only grazed my clothing. I could at least see the top of the silver arrowhead. *What a relief.*

I prodded the arrow in my thigh, trying to figure out the best way to get it out. I screamed loudly, not caring if anybody heard. The archer had made it clear he wasn't coming back. The pain became so intense that I wanted to die right then and there. If my thigh felt that unbearable with a little nudging, I wouldn't even try to touch the arrow in my shoulder.

I ripped the bottom half of my shirt off. I used the material to wrap it tightly around the wound and the arrow shaft, going underneath my armpit and over my shoulder to keep it tight and hold it there. Using one hand made it difficult. Blood soaked through it in minutes, but I didn't dare pull it out one-handed. I doubted my ability.

Using material from my ripped pant leg, I wrapped the wound on my thigh. The bleeding slowed to a gradual ooze. Eventually, these arrows needed to come out. I had no idea how to do it on my own. The pain overwhelmed me, and deliriousness set in. Tears trickled down my cheeks. I closed my eyes and focused on even breathing, falling unconscious again.

It was dusk when I regained awareness. My eyes still closed, I took a deep breath and winced, scrunching up my face as the pain came back in full force. I opened my eyes, and the golden sunset filtered through the trees and landed on my head. I squinted against the sun's rays, placing a hand on my forehead to shield the sun, and looked up. Then I noticed the shadow of a man looming over me. I screamed as I tried to pull out my dagger.

CHAPTER FOUR

EY, TAKE IT EASY. I'm not going to hurt you," a young man said, falling back onto his hands and skittering away. He must have been crouched right over me.

I shook my head, trying to clear it to build a mental barrier against the pain. Clutching the dagger tighter, I asked, "Who are you?"

"I am only trying to help. My name is Andrew." He spoke slow and clear. "I thought you were dead."

Help? Help me right into their evil base, I thought, convinced that he worked with the men who tried to capture me. *Maybe he was their employer?* "You're not taking me!"

Andrew raised his eyebrows. "Take you? Why would I want to do that? You're injured, you need help."

He's lying. I had no control over my convoluted thoughts as I tried to fight off the waves of pain. I took a deep breath and tried again. "Who sent you?"

Andrew stood. "Nobody sent me. I just happened to walk into this. Gods forbid, you are a spirited thing."

I gritted my teeth and closed my eyes, trying not to scream out in pain. A single tear rolled down my left cheek. *What am I going to do? I need assistance, but I'm afraid to trust him.*

Andrew bent down and snatched my sword lying in the dirt. He twiddled it between his hands.

"Give it back." I glared at Andrew, pointing my dagger at him.

"No." He stared directly at me, completely undeterred.

I opened my mouth to argue, but a wave of pain hit, and I halted. I gripped onto the dagger, my knuckles going white as I whimpered.

Andrew stabbed the dirt with my blade and let it stand there. I slowly pulled myself up, using the tree as my anchor, and leaned against it. It took every ounce of self-control I had not to cry out. I tightened my grip on the dagger, ignoring the sweat pooling around the handle. Little droplets of blood fell from my wounds. I could feel it sliding down my skin.

"Wow, you have strength." Surprise flitted across his face as he folded his arms.

I let go of the tree and put all my weight on my left leg. *Moment of truth.* I slowly took a step forward, dragging my right leg along through the underbrush of ferns and tall grass.

Tears clouded my vision and I stumbled forward, staring down at my feet. I couldn't afford to slip. My right leg and left arm were practically unusable. I took another slow step, dragging my useless body along.

My strength failed me on the third step, and I started to fall forward. I opened my mouth in a silent scream as I realized my fate. Andrew reacted quickly. He wrenched the dagger from my hand and caught me before I hit the ground.

"Can't you see you need help?" He asked as he held me in his arms.

I blinked slowly to clear my eyes of the tears, so I could see Andrew properly.

He was significantly younger than the men that attacked me, and his tone of voice and manner didn't match the others. He didn't wear plain traveling clothes. His leather jerkin had intricate designs carved into it. I would have fallen without him there to catch me. Maybe he was sincere in his desire to help.

Andrew gently lifted me and cradled me in his arms. I inhaled a strong cinnamon woodsy cologne. My eyes got heavy again. Everything blurred. My throat tickled. I started coughing more. I rubbed my mouth and found traces of blood. I ran my tongue around my lips and realized I had bit it. One more injury to add to the list.

"I'm not helping a murderer, am I?" Andrew asked, moving in long, swift strides. His boots rustled the undergrowth of plants.

Their deaths etched in my memory, I shuddered. "No."

"Good." I heard relief in Andrew's voice.

I closed my eyes, falling unconscious to the sound of Andrew's labored breathing.

When I woke, I heard rushing water and a fire crackling. The sun faded into darkness. I lay on the ground, the soft grass damp underneath me. Andrew had moved me while I slept. I took a deep breath and exhaled, alerting him. He crouched over me.

"I moved us by the stream. We need to take those arrows out now." Andrew's shoulders tensed, his jaw set.

"Water," I croaked.

He handed me a flask and I drank, letting the water soothe my parched throat. The cold water helped clear my head.

"Better?" he asked.

I nodded. "Sit me up please."

He got up and quickly came back with a small log he set behind my back for support. Not the most comfortable thing to be propped against, but better than nothing.

Andrew sat next to me, folding his legs underneath him. "I've had a good look at both arrows. The one in your leg is not as serious; it's just barely lodged into your lower thigh muscle. However, I can't pull on the shaft, or the arrowhead will break off, and I'll have to go searching for it. Which will be more painful." He sighed, rubbing his forehead as he gave me the facts. "Unfortunately, that's exactly what I'm going to have to do with the arrow in your shoulder, since I can't even see the arrowhead. It hasn't gone all the way through, so I can't push it out either." He frowned.

I grimaced.

"I can put a mixture of pain-relieving herbs around the area, but you're still going be in intense pain, and since you've been wounded for so long, I can't patch it back up, or we'll risk major infection. He rested his hands on his lap. "This is the only option I feel I can do."

"What about bleeding out?" I asked.

"You've already lost more blood than I'm comfortable with, but the arrows are also acting as a block, and you will bleed twice as much once they are out. I'll have to hold down pressure for a while at first. Until I can think of a suitable way to bandage it," he said.

My pulse raced underneath my skin. Regardless of what I chose, whether I went with his plan or came up with something new, it would hurt—bad. I cursed at my cruel luck. Then I remembered my box of lotions carried a medicine with healer magic infused in it. *Emergencies only*, I remembered Adel saying when she'd given it to me. I definitely considered this one.

"My bag." I glanced around me, feeling frantic. "Where's my bag?"

"Is this it?" Andrew reached behind him and hauled my bag into view.

I nodded. "There's a box; pull it out."

Andrew untied the strings and opened it. Grabbing the small wooden box, he fumbled with the latch for a second. "What do you need?"

"There's a purple bottle in there. Use it." I held my breath as another wave of pain hit, exhaling slowly.

"There's at least three purple bottles. Which one?" He fished them out and showed them to me before I picked out the right one.

Andrew peered closely at the bottle. "Where'd you get this? This is really expensive stuff."

"Just use it, will you?" I snapped.

"All right. All right." He uncorked the bottle. "Which one do you want me to start on first?"

I gritted my teeth. "My thigh."

He nodded solemnly. "All right."

He poured some of the swirling liquid onto my thigh and a little onto my left shoulder. Immediately I felt some respite to the burning pain. It didn't vanish but became manageable. I sighed in relief.

"Hey, what's your name?" Andrew suddenly asked.

"Sorry. No names." I coughed and grimaced.

"I've got to call you something now, don't I?"

I shook my head. "Make up a name if you must."

Andrew ran a hand through his hair and sighed heavily. He rolled his shoulders back. "You ready for this?" He came closer and resituated, sitting on his knees.

Andrew used the firelight to guide his actions. He held the knife over the fire for a moment, sterilizing it as best he could. He blew on it for a second to cool it down before bringing it closer to my leg. "I'm going to run my knife along the side of this slit and use it to push the arrow up."

I took a quick breath, my hands gripping the dry grass beside me. "Do it."

I couldn't help but tense as Andrew wedged the knife into my flesh. My fingernails dug into the soft dirt around me. I held my breath, fighting the urge to throw up. My stomach tied in knots. I clenched my jaw. After a minute of wiggling and intense discomfort, he expertly pulled the arrow out while simultaneously throwing cloth on the open area. Blood blossomed onto the linen, drenching it quickly.

"It's out." Andrew sounded pleased, and his hand clamped down on the wound, giving it the pressure it needed.

I tried to smile but failed. *One down, one more to go.*

"I'm going to need you to hold the pressure on this one while I pull out more supplies. Can you do that?" He watched me earnestly, leaning slightly forward.

I locked eyes with him, noticing the intensity of his blue eyes. I bit my lip and winced, having forgotten that I'd bit it too hard earlier.

"Hey," he prompted me.

I closed my eyes, trying to focus. "Yes." I moved my right hand onto the blood-soaked cloth and put as much pressure as I could. It wasn't enough.

Andrew chuckled softly, shaking his head. "All right, we're going to have to try something else." He placed his hand on top of mine.

He rummaged through his pouch until he found a ball of linen. Using his teeth and one hand, he unraveled it and wrapped it around my leg, creating the pressure needed to stop the blood flow. He tied it off neatly. "That should hold."

We sat rather close to the fire for light. Andrew sighed and leaned back, wiping his brow with his bloody hand, leaving a streak of blood on his forehead. *My blood.*

"Wow, this is intense. I have a new respect for healers." He wiped his knife and stuck it in the fire to sterilize it again.

"You're not a healer?" I asked, noticing the medical supplies he carried.

He shook his head. "No. I just come well prepared for emergencies." He smiled.

"All right, now for the hard one. Your shirt is in the way. I need to cut it off." He gestured to my shirt with the knife in his hand.

"Go ahead," I said tersely. It didn't cover me adequately anyway.

Andrew set the knife on top of a small cloth he'd pulled out of his bag. Using his fingers, he gently tore my shirt off. With so many tears in it already, it came apart easily, leaving me in torn pants and a breast band. Not exactly what I wanted to show off, but I couldn't help it. The air felt warm on my skin, making me grateful for the late summer season when it got the hottest.

Andrew felt around the arrow wound, and I gasped from the discomfort. I'd need to pour the entire purple bottle over the wound to feel nothing at all. I wasn't willing to do that.

He grimaced. "I'm sorry."

"You can't help it."

He sighed. "I have to make a wider incision to pull it out. It'll take me a few minutes to search for the tip. You ready for that?"

I nodded.

"Perhaps you should lie down," he suggested. He removed the log from behind my back and slowly eased me onto the ground. "That's better. You might want to bite down on something."

I shook my head. "No, just get it over with."

"Suit yourself." Andrew took a moment to steady himself, his hands poised over the arrow.

I closed my eyes tight in anticipation; my heart beat rapidly. My muscles tightened. Sweat beaded on my brow and rolled down my face. I was scared to death, and it showed.

"Hey, look at me," Andrew commanded, lowering his hands.

I opened my eyes and stared into his face.

"You can do this. Just watch my face, focus on something else. If you tense up like that, it's going to hurt worse." He put a hand on my good shoulder. "Just watch my face, and I'll talk to you."

I nodded, whimpering, and slightly relaxed my grip on the dirt and grass.

"All right, here I go." Andrew brought his hands over to my shoulder.

Already nauseated, I could not handle watching him cut into my flesh again. Once was enough.

"Oh!" I sobbed as I felt the knife slide into my skin. I fixated on Andrew's chiseled face, noticing how focused he appeared. His full lips in a tight line, his bloodied brow furrowed in concentration and damp with sweat. His stunning blue eyes darted back and forth.

I bit my lip. *Gods forbid he's gorgeous.*

"So where are you from?" he asked casually while working his fingers into the wound.

I got three words out, tears clouding my vision. "Not—tell—you."

Andrew smirked. "Still don't trust me, do you?"

"Right."

"I'm a good guy if you'd give me a chance," he said.

I narrowed my eyes. *No chance.*

"There, found it," he muttered.

I cried, biting my lip as he worked the arrow out of the muscle, the pain agonizing. He tugged on the arrow a few times and within a minute pulled it out. Andrew quickly held pressure on the wound and deftly wrapped it with the linen. "Whew, glad that's over." He grinned, leaning back.

Tears rolled down my cheeks, but relief flooded my heart. I never wanted to be shot again. I let go of the dirt and folded my shaking hands together.

"I'm sorry," Andrew said. "It had to be done."

"I know." I fixated on my hands, which were stained with blood and dirt.

Andrew grabbed my left hand, which was basically useless with my shoulder out of commission, and squeezed it. "That scratch on your stomach needs to be taken care of." He gazed up and down my body, his eyes roving over the multiple injuries.

He got up and left. I closed my eyes and focused on even breathing.

I opened my eyes when I felt a warm wet cloth against my skin. "What are you doing?"

"I'm cleaning some of this blood off so I can assess your other injuries." He wrung the rag and started cleaning the blood off my stomach. "My, you're covered in bruises. What happened to you?"

"It's a long story." I didn't have the energy to explain it all to him right then.

"I'm sure it is." Andrew started wiping the blood off my left arm. He gripped my left hand. "This isn't blood. You have the Mark of the Gods on your hand."

"I was born with it." I tried to pull my hand away, but he squeezed harder, blocking my attempt.

"Please," Andrew said. "Tell me your name."

I bit my lip, my hand trembling in his as I stopped resisting. I took a deep breath and exhaled, averting my eyes to the fire. I wanted to trust him, but I worried about the ramifications. How much did a name cost?

I closed my eyes and went with my gut.

"Isabelle," I said, opening my eyes. "Mirran."

Andrew let go as though he'd been shocked. My hand dropped with a resounding thump onto my thigh. He gazed at me with eyes wide, mouth open. I cocked my head to the side, my eyebrows furrowed in confusion. He ran a hand through his hair and then got up. "Excuse me." He walked away.

I sat up with some difficulty and covered my mouth with my hand. *Gods forbid, what have I done?*

I didn't understand why my name had caused such a strong reaction. I worried I had put my trust in the wrong person. *Maybe my gut is wrong?* It had never steered me wrong before. I rubbed my forehead as anxiety rocked through me. I shivered and clutched at my stomach as a cooler breeze touched my skin.

Andrew came up behind me and wrapped a blanket over my shoulders. "This will help you stay warm."

I accepted the blanket and pulled it tighter over my shoulders. "Thanks."

He stoked the fire, then added in a few sticks. "You should rest now. Get some sleep."

"Why did you walk away?" I asked.

Andrew rubbed the back of his neck and stared into the fire. "Sorry, I—I needed to relieve myself. In my haste to help you I didn't realize I'd been holding it for hours."

I narrowed my eyes. "So, it had nothing to do with my name?"

He shook his head and cleared his throat. "No. You have a beautiful name, by the way, but that wasn't the reason."

I didn't believe him, but I nodded anyway. As I moved to scooch forward in the grass to lie down, it occurred to me how exposed and vulnerable my position was. What if the archer came back to see if I had died? And when he saw that I hadn't, what would to stop him from killing me then?

I struggled to move, deciding I needed a safer location to hide out until my injuries healed well enough for me to walk to Thimbleton.

Andrew eyed me with concern. "What are you doing?"

I reached for my bag. "I appreciate all your help, but I'm leaving now."

"To stumble around in the dark?" He eyed me incredulously. "You shouldn't be moving at all in your condition."

"The archer is still out there. I don't want him to come back and finish me off when he sees I'm still alive." I gripped the log I'd used to support my back and attempted to use it to stand but fell on my butt with a huff and gasp of pain. I hadn't the strength. *Great*, I'd have to crawl.

Andrew scrambled to stop me. He grabbed onto my right hand. "I can protect you."

I pursed my lips, worry gnawing a hole through my stomach. He'd been capable enough so far, but could Andrew fight off the archer if he decided to come back?

"I'm a light sleeper, and I'll have my sword by my side. You'll be safe," Andrew spoke earnestly.

I relented. "All right, I'll stay."

He let go of my hand. "Good."

"May I please have my sword?" I asked. "I'll feel better with it next to me."

"Of course." He retrieved my blade from the opposite side of the fire and handed it to me. "Now rest. I'll make sure nothing happens to you, I promise."

"Thank you." I lay down in the grass, tucking my sword by my side. I closed my eyes and let the crickets and the sound of the stream lull me to sleep but not before wondering three things. *Why did Andrew react that way when I told him my name? Why is he helping me?* A small errant thought entered my brain before I drifted into exhaustion. *Why are those blue eyes so hypnotic?*

CHAPTER FIVE

T TURNED INTO THE most uncomfortable night I'd ever had. Despite all the work Andrew did, the pain still throbbed strongly throughout my body, making my much-needed sleep difficult and almost unobtainable.

I stared into the night sky, watching the bats flit about and listening to the soothing sound of crickets. I made all those assurances to Stefan that I could handle myself on this journey. My failure stung worse than a bee sting. How could I go back to Saren and say that, despite our best efforts, the man from Mava's wedding found me anyway? I couldn't let my family see me like this, injured and in pain, afraid and confused. It wasn't who I was, and yet it's who I had become.

I had a better handle on my thoughts now that the arrows were out and my injuries patched up. As much as I hated to admit it, even with a clearer head, I still found Andrew striking, with his chiseled face and golden-brown hair that grew in waves around his ears and fell into his eyes. I remembered his hands against my skin, pulling the arrows out. They were large and a little calloused, but his movements were gentle and soft.

I couldn't help but feel attracted to the man who saved my life, and that made me angry. I didn't know a single thing about him, save his name. Yet one look into his blazing blue eyes, and he took my breath away. I sighed, scrunching my face against the throbbing. *There is something seriously wrong with me.* At a time like this, romantic notions should be the last thing on my mind. Even though Stefan and I were not formally courting,

I had kissed him. It made me feel like I headed into betrayal with these thoughts about Andrew.

I sneaked a glance at Andrew's sleeping form, remembering the way he spoke to me. His tone was so commanding and authoritative, he obviously came from high society or had been given adequate schooling—probably both. Where did he come from, and why did he walk in the forest all by himself?

Despite his help, I worried about trusting him beyond what he had already done. Everything about Andrew and his chivalry could be a lie, and I didn't feel ready to rely on someone that could potentially lead me into a trap. My gut twisted with confliction, not wanting to trust him but knowing I didn't have a choice considering the severity of my injuries.

When the sun finally came up over the horizon, I felt a surge of relief. Regardless of having two arrows pulled out of my body, I hoped to be strong enough to continue my journey to Thimbleton. I folded up my belongings as best I could one-handed, shoving what I could into my bag. I snatched a clean shirt and pulled it over my head.

I took a deep breath, knowing my decision rested on how well I could walk. *I can do this.* My determination quickly turned into dismay the minute I managed to stand. I held back a sob as I stumbled to find a place to relieve myself a short distance into the trees. By the time I got back to my belongings, I had an answer. My body betrayed my wishes. I couldn't count on myself to go anywhere.

Then I noticed Andrew didn't lie near the burning embers of the fire. *Where did he go?* I glanced around, peering through the trees and underbrush and around the bank, but didn't see him.

I gasped and put a hand over my mouth. *He left me!* I stumbled backward, anxiety rocking through me. I clutched at my sides, my stomach in knots. How could he do this? I thought he wanted to help. What if the archer came back? What if he brought reinforcements? I couldn't stay here without protection. I'd have to hide until I was well enough to walk to Thimbleton.

A twig snapped behind me, and I reacted before I could think, swiveling around to see Andrew a finger length away from me. I took a quick intake of breath and winced, the pain catching up to the rapid movement. *Gods forbid I shouldn't have done that.*

"You're up. How are you feeling?" he asked casually.

I opened my mouth, but no words came out. Excruciating pain set my nerves on fire. It took every ounce of self-control I had to stay standing. "Thank you for watching over me last night, but I must go now." After thinking he left me once, I didn't want to depend on someone who could leave at any time. I needed more security that I worried Andrew couldn't provide.

Andrew took a step closer. He eyed me all over, his blue eyes so bright and sharp. I gulped, feeling like he could see right through me like a pane of glass. "I said I would protect you from the archer, yet you're so quick to be on your way; it's almost like you're running from the entire Aberronian army. What else are you afraid of?"

"I don't have to tell you everything," I said stiffly. Better to be nestled somewhere safe, then see how long he'd stay.

"I suppose not," he murmured. "But if you're so well, why are you so rigid? You're clenching your fist so tight your knuckles are white." A hint of a smile rested on his lips.

I unclenched my hand, unaware that I'd tightened it, and narrowed my eyes. Andrew toyed with me. I decided to be straight with him. "I can handle a little bit of pain."

He raised his eyebrows. "A *little* bit of pain? I just pulled two arrows out of your body last night." He shook his head. "Walk for me," he commanded suddenly, folding his arms. "Show me you're suitable for travel."

"I don't need to show off to you!" I flared, throwing my good hand out. "If I want to go, I will." I pointed a finger at him. "You can't hold me prisoner."

Andrew smiled mockingly. "So defensive ... I have no intention of making you a prisoner. I'm just trying to knock some common sense into your head. You need rest. Allow your wounds to heal. You still have a very high risk of infection setting in."

"I know that, but I can't stay here. I'm exposed." I bit my lip, wishing I could pace back and forth. The archer could come back at any second, and I would have no way to defend myself if Andrew decided to take off, even just to get firewood. *I'm useless.* My pulse quickened as I buckled under the emotional and physical weight. Big fat tears spilled from my eyes.

Andrew rushed forward and caught me before I fell. Easing me onto the grassy ground, he held me while I sobbed from the surmounting pain, fear, and overall worthlessness I felt. I had spent the last twelve years training to take care of myself, planning for every contingency. I constantly strived to achieve my ultimate goal, to never be left defenseless or stranded because I lacked the knowledge to support myself. In one day, all my walls were torn down.

Once I cried myself dry, I wiped my eyes with the sleeve of my good arm. I cleared my throat. Embarrassment filtered through at my emotional breakdown. I'd turned into a pathetic wreck physically and emotionally. I frowned, thinking Andrew probably wished he hadn't found me.

"Are you all right?" Andrew asked softly, still holding me.

I took in a deep breath, attempting to settle my feelings. "Yes. You can let go of me now."

He released me and sat facing me. I stared into his blue eyes, compassion reflecting back, and suddenly felt like an open book again. Easy to read and predictable. "How do you do that?"

"Do what?"

"See right through me. You make me feel like you can see all my secrets." I frowned.

Andrew grinned, flashing his perfectly straight, white teeth. "Do you have secrets?" he asked casually.

"Stop fishing. Just answer the question," I persisted.

He shrugged. "It's my job."

"Your job?" I raised my eyebrows in question.

"I couldn't be the future king if I wasn't able to discern people's true character now, could I?" Andrew smiled.

"King?" I emphasized, my jaw dropping a little.

"Someday," he answered nonchalantly.

I didn't know much about Court and its affairs. Farmers didn't need to be able to name dignitaries or nobles or their titles—it didn't directly affect them. However, everyone, regardless of their station in life, learned the family line of the King. From King Aberron, our first King and namesake of our country, to our current ruler, King Brian. Most people knew the King's genealogy better than their own.

It suddenly clicked, and my jaw dropped open. "You're Crown Prince Andrew Brian Jason Sorren, son of King Brian?"

Andrew waved his hands down his body. "In the flesh."

That explains his commanding tone and well-bred manner. But how could I be sure he told the truth? I had never seen a painting of him. "How do I know you are who you say you are?"

He pulled on a locket from underneath his shirt. "Would anybody else have this?" He held it out for me to see.

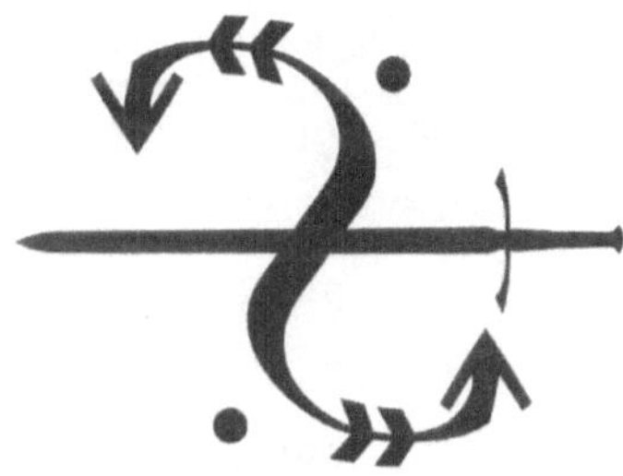

It displayed the King's crest. I had seen it many times before in books and manuscripts, official letters sent to the town. A large backward *S* with a sword through the middle. The tips of the *S* resembled an arrow with feather-like ends. Last, a dot on each opposite side, one on the upper right-hand corner and the other on the lower left-hand corner facing the outside of the curve.

I couldn't deny the crest. Aberron considered it a crime to wear the crest of the King unless you worked directly for the King, like a palace servant or military member. Only royalty could display it in the form of jewelry. It set them apart from everyone else.

I am sitting next to the future King of Aberron.

I could feel my stress levels rising exponentially. I took a deep breath and tried to calm down. "What are you doing out here?"

"I am on my Walk." Andrew brought his knees up and rested his elbows on them.

"Walk? I didn't know that was going on." I gasped. "That's why you haven't used magic on me."

He frowned, his shoulders slumped. "Yes, an unfortunate stipulation of the rules."

The Walk was a rite of passage for the Prince. He couldn't ascend the throne without having done this first. The Prince started out at the palace in the capital city of Carasmille and walked around the entire kingdom without the ability to use magic or take any guards with him. It was common knowledge that the line of the King possessed the strongest magical abilities out there. It never failed to pass down through the lineage and became an integral part of the monarchy.

A Prince got outfitted with the bare necessities and was sent on his way. He was allowed to take a horse, but many people disapproved, thinking a Prince who rode a horse lacked stamina and courage. The point of the Walk was for the Prince to take a good look at his kingdom before taking the throne. To mingle with the citizens, see the needs of the poor, and be humbled.

I placed a hand on my forehead, flabbergasted. Where could I find the time to breathe? Accept? Process?

First my brother told me leave home and traipse off to Thimbleton to meet him. I hadn't heard from or seen him in twelve years. He could have been dead for all I knew. Next, I'd almost been kidnapped and attacked, and now the Prince was my personal healer. *The Prince. Our future sovereign leader.* I didn't think I could handle any more surprises.

"I can't believe this," I muttered, shaking my head and rolling my eyes. Completely blown away, I nearly forgot about the pain I suffered.

Andrew reached over and placed a hand on my good shoulder in pity or consolation; I didn't know which. I closed my eyes, taking in a few deep breaths until it hit me. *The Prince is touching me, and I am attracted to him.* This felt wrong, even worse than feeling like I'd started to betray Stefan. I couldn't let Andrew touch me. I couldn't let him near me. And I absolutely could not let my heart go for him, not even for a second.

"Isabelle?"

Andrew opened his mouth to say more, but I didn't want to hear it, so I cut him off.

"I'm tired. I'm going to rest." Shrugging off his hand on my shoulder, I slowly eased off the ground. I didn't go back to the campfire. Instead, I sat and nestled against a tree trunk. I needed space to clear my head, and, thankfully, it seemed Andrew understood that.

I leaned my head back and stared into the tree canopy, focusing on the rough texture of the bark and the veins in the leaves. My tired body ached, and my stomach rumbled in hunger. I wanted to sleep and forget this whole thing. Forget my wounds; forget that I ever left home in the first place. I shut my eyes and dozed.

I dreamed. The tall wheat rose nearly to my hips. The blue sky had no clouds in sight. A dark green forest hung at the edge of the field. Realization set in. I'd been here before. I started running to the forest. I felt no pain nor saw any injuries. I ran as fast as I could go. Exhilarated freedom greeted me with open arms.

A man blinked into existence. Tall and lean, he kept his black hair long, contrasting with his ivory skin. He wore ornate blue-and-silver robes. He held his long, nimble hands out in welcome.

"Isabelle." His calm voice penetrated deep into my bones, piercing into my very soul. I slowed my pace, preparing to meet the man. What kind of importance did he hold?

Abruptly I felt reality tugging me away from the dream world. I reached out, hoping to anchor myself there, but to no avail. I opened my eyes back into the real world wishing for better luck.

Andrew crouched in front of me. "We need to talk."

I sighed, rubbing the sleep out of my eyes. "About what?"

"About what really happened in that clearing."

I stared at him, my lips pursed. This conversation would happen sooner or later whether I wanted it to or not. Two men died. I couldn't dismiss it or forget it ever happened. I cleared my throat. "What do you want to know?"

He sounded firm. "Everything."

I brought a hand to my forehead trying to rub a headache away and chose my words carefully. "I was running away from a man I met at a wedding."

"Which man? I buried them both." Andrew sat next to me.

I flinched, remembering watching the life drain out of their eyes. I rubbed my face and fought the urge to heave. I swallowed nervously. "The dark-haired man with the mustache." I folded my hands together. My adrenaline picked up, and my heart raced as I explained, the images still clear in my mind. I went over everything from the moment I stepped into the clearing to when the mustached man accidentally got shot. "I didn't kill them," I ended sharply, staring straight into Andrew's blue eyes.

"I believe you," he said. "Please continue."

The memories, fresh and vibrant, made it difficult to explain everything. I could still feel the fear for my life and the shock of death right before my eyes. I shivered and stared at the rushing stream.

"What did the archer look like? Short, tall?"

I gave a brief description of him. Fair skin, medium height, curly brown hair with a scruffy beard, broad shoulders and brown eyes.

"Why did the archer leave you alone? Why didn't he try to take you with him?"

I fixated on his blue eyes. "He was upset. He said he wanted me to suffer long and die for killing his brother. But I didn't kill him. The archer shot the arrow and I ducked out of the way. I didn't know it would hit him."

"What were their motives in kidnapping you? Did they say anything else?" Andrew put a hand on his chin, deep in contemplation.

"They planned on taking me to someone else. I don't know who. They said I was spoken for. I thought it was you at first." I bit my lip, feeling embarrassed for assuming. "When I met the boss at the party, he seemed very interested in my birthmark." I sighed. "That's basically everything."

Andrew cursed under his breath and ran a hand through his hair.

I eyed him sternly. "Do you know something?"

His face immediately changed to one of innocence. "No."

I narrowed my eyes at him. "I don't believe you."

Andrew raised his hands up in surrender. "Honestly, I don't know why they chased after you or what they planned. They were probably some common thieves looking for a pretty girl to profit from."

I nodded, accepting his answer.

He took a breath and locked eyes with me. He casually plucked at the grass as he spoke. "I don't think you're well enough to move; we'll just have watch for the archer and hope he doesn't show."

"You're staying?" I asked.

Andrew sat up straight. His blazing blue eyes flashed. "I'm not leaving an injured, defenseless woman alone."

I flinched at his stern tone and yet I found myself relieved. "Thank you."

He smiled. "You're welcome. You must be hungry. Come back to the fire, and I'll make something to eat." He held out a hand and helped me off the ground. I pulled my hand away from his the second I felt stable. His lips thinned. Had I offended him?

Andrew hardly said a word as he prepared food over the fire. He pulled two potatoes and three carrots from his pack and chopped them up, then put them in the boiling water. From a small pouch, he poured seasonings into the water. I handed him jerky from my bag, and he added it in.

While he stirred, I wondered what roamed through his mind, but I didn't think it right to ask. I told my heart to shut up every time I watched him push a strand of hair out of his eyes or when he glanced concernedly in my direction. I hated his attractiveness. Why couldn't I have gotten some ugly pig farmer to rescue me? Though, I doubted the skills a pig farmer would have in comparison to a prince. *At least I wouldn't worry about my heart or feel like I'm cheating on Stefan.*

Andrew handed me a steaming cup of jerky stew. I thanked him and sipped the broth slowly. It burned my throat as it went down.

"I need to check on your injuries. I don't want to see an infection start, and the only way I know how is to monitor it closely." Andrew's shoulders tensed.

"Go ahead. I don't want to die," I said. I finished eating and refused seconds.

He visibly relaxed. "I'll get things ready." He took the pot of jerky stew and poured what remained into his cup, then went to the stream and rinsed out the pot. He returned with it full of water and set it on the fire.

Andrew helped me out of my shirt, leaving me in my dirty, bloodstained breast band. I felt revolting. *I am disgusting.* I wanted to take my torn, bloodied clothes and throw them in the fire. But the thought of being naked in front of the Prince stopped me.

Andrew nimbly unwrapped the shoulder dressings and set the linen in the boiling pot of water to clean it. We didn't have enough new linen to redress it completely. He poured a little medicine from the purple bottle into a rag and dabbed my shoulder. I gasped as the cold liquid touched my skin.

"Sorry," he murmured, lightly patting the wounded area. "Good news—I don't see any infection."

"Great." I pursed my lips in a thin line, trying to keep from screaming.

Andrew pulled the wet linen out of the boiling pot of water and held it over the fire to dry it quickly. He looked so dedicated holding the linen over the flames, staring into the fire, that I felt my heart soften. I quickly cleared my throat and stared toward the stream, hoping he didn't notice the endearing way I watched him.

Andrew glanced at me. "You don't happen to have another one of those, do you?"

"Another what?" I asked, confused.

"Another, um, what do women call them?" He pointed to my chest.

I followed the direction of his finger and glanced downward. "A breast band?"

"Yes. That one's pretty much done for, and the cleaner you are, the less chance of infection," he explained, shrugging.

"In my bag."

Andrew pushed my bag closer to me, and I pulled items out onto the grass until I found one. I held it in my hands trying to figure out how to put it on one-handed.

"I can help, you know."

I shook my head. "No way. You've seen enough of me already."

"All right, just thought I'd offer." He shrugged, backing off.

"Close your eyes," I demanded.

Andrew rolled his eyes but did as I instructed.

Using one hand to reach behind my back, I unclasped the breast band and let it fall into my lap. I wrinkled my nose in disgust at the sight of dirt, dried bits of blood, and grime. I pressed the clean one over my chest and tucked one side through my useless arm and held it there while I grabbed the other side and pulled it around. The breast band quickly became a challenge while I tried to grab onto both sides and clasp them together.

"Are you done yet?" Andrew asked, his eyes still closed.

I clenched my jaw, annoyed at my lack of dexterity. "No."

"You sure you don't want my help?" he offered again softly.

I sighed heavily. "I need your assistance—please."

Andrew opened his eyes.

"Clasp the back together, will you?"

He took the material from my hands and clasped it together.

"Thank you." I forced a smile, letting my hands fall into my lap.

"You're welcome."

He helped me into my shirt after assessing the cut across my belly and patting it with the medicated cloth. He then moved down to the lower half of my body, unwrapping the linen and following the same procedure he did with my shoulder.

"You need new pants," Andrew said frankly, his expression taut.

I grumbled. No way could I get pants on by myself.

"Just do it quickly and try not to see too much." I grimaced.

Andrew helped as best he could without glimpsing, though I couldn't help but feel red in the face as I felt his hands against my bare skin. However, the prospect of clean clothes and bandages far outweighed the embarrassment.

"There. All finished." He sighed, running a hand through his hair again.

"Thank you," I said with as much gratitude as I could muster.

"My pleasure," he said as he started putting everything he used away. "So, where are you from?"

"Saren."

Andrew frowned for a moment. "Hmm. I don't think I've heard of it."

I waved my good hand dismissively. "Hardly anyone ever has. I am starting to think that maybe your government officials have forgotten we exist."

"No, they can't have forgotten you, surely," he disagreed, setting the medicated rag in the pot to be washed. "They are supposed to receive monthly charters and reports of each town and district in Aberron."

"My town is boring. Nothing ever happens. It probably gets ignored," I said.

"You're a farming community then?" he asked while bringing his knees up and resting his elbows on them, pausing from his work.

I nodded.

Andrew chuckled. "Yes, nothing exciting ever happens in those small towns. They get some lower dignitary to go over the reports. There's usually little to resolve, so they aren't sent up for higher delegates to assess."

"I knew it," I muttered, shaking my head.

"You should be grateful nothing major happens in your little town. How would you feel if you housed the entire Aberronian army?" Andrew asked. "You'd get no rest. People are coming and going constantly. It's always loud and busy." He shuddered.

"Sounds like a city," I said.

"It is a city." Andrew nodded. "Carasmille is enormous and alive twenty-four hours a day every day of the year. Those little towns should be grateful for the peace and serenity they get. You'd never get that in a city with all those busybodies." He got up, taking the pot of dirty water with him. He tossed the water in the grass as he walked to the stream.

I thought about my home in Saren. Would I want it to change? To be loud, noisy, and eccentric? No, I loved Saren for what it was. A quiet farming town where we made lifelong friends. I preferred Saren to stay the same; I just wouldn't be there to enjoy it. Would I ever go back?

CHAPTER SIX

NDREW HELD HIS ROYAL locket in his hands and murmured into it. A blue light glowed around the locket.

What is he doing? I narrowed my eyes, shooting suspicious glances at him. I thought he couldn't use magic during the Walk. By the time I reached the stream's bank, the locket stopped glowing, and Andrew tucked it underneath his shirt.

I lay in the grass, kicking off my boots and letting my feet glide in the water. "Brr." I shivered delightedly. Andrew sat by me, leaning back on his hands and crossing his ankles. I breathed in his cinnamon woodsy cologne.

"What were you doing?" I asked, trying not to sound suspicious or accusatory. "I thought you weren't allowed to use magic."

"I'm not." Andrew faced me. He swatted at a buzzing dragonfly near his face. "My locket has a store of magic, so I'm technically not pulling it from my own source. It's kind of bending the rules but necessary." He turned back to gaze at the stream.

"Why do you need it?"

"I have to check in with my father every couple of days or he gets worried. My father wears an identical locket, and we use it to communicate. I am the heir to the throne, so they are doubly cautious of my whereabouts." He slid his boots off and dipped his feet into the water. A silly grin appeared on his face. "Wow, that feels good."

I smiled, nodding. "It does wonders to offset the pain."

"I'm glad." He casually plucked the grass beside him. "Once you're healed well enough, where are you headed?" He cast his eyes on me.

"Thimbleton," I answered. "You?"

Andrew smiled. "Same. Thimbleton is my last stop on the Walk before I head home to Carasmille. Can't say I'm looking forward to it." He frowned, his bottom lip jutting out slightly. *Gods forbid, he's adorable even when he pouts.* I bit my lip and quickly turned away, hating the fact that my first thought focused on his handsomeness. I needed to work on that. *He's not a puppy, so stop eyeing him like he is.*

"Why not?" I hoped my voice didn't betray my internal struggle.

"I have to find a wife," he said flatly as if the idea abhorred him. "It's my next duty to become King. Mother's going to be shoving girls at me to court until I find one I can live with. It's not a very appealing prospect."

"I'm sorry." I wanted to put my hand on his arm, offer him some sort of comfort, but I resisted. I considered our association tenuous, two people brought together by my unfortunate circumstances. Besides, I already considered getting close to him a bad idea. A farm girl and a prince did not exist in the same circles.

Andrew shrugged. "I've been raised to expect it." He leaned back, resting his weight on his elbows. "What do you seek in Thimbleton?"

Minnows swam around my feet, tickling. Holding back a giggle, I pulled my legs out. "I'm supposed to meet my brother."

"Joshua?" Andrew asked.

I gasped in surprise. "You know my brother?"

"Of course." His brow furrowed at my questioning eyebrow. "My father took Joshua in after your parents died. We grew up together. I consider him family. Surely you knew that?"

I shook my head. "No. I knew he lived in Carasmille but that's it. We haven't spoken in twelve years. I used to write him, but he never responded so I quit."

"Huh." Andrew frowned.

I tucked a stray hair behind my ear. "Is Joshua well?"

"He was when I left for the Walk." He pulled his feet out of the water as he sat up. "Father promoted him to Commander about two years ago. He keeps himself busy overseeing the protection of Aberron."

"That sounds like a lofty position," I said.

"It is," he said. "Only direct royalty like my father and myself outrank him."

"Hmm." I watched the blue dragonfly Andrew swatted land on a tall blade of grass. It made sense now why Joshua said he could protect me. He probably had resources I could only dream of.

Andrew spoke casually, his eyes out on the water. "I told my father what happened to you. He ordered me to stay by your side. I'm not supposed to take my eyes off you. It's for your own protection, considering the circumstances."

"What?" *No!* Being around Andrew made it hard to keep my thoughts straight. Just one glance, and I felt like a bug flying into the light of the fire. Disgusting, but I couldn't help myself. I didn't want to be stuck with him, the biggest distraction of my life, all the way to Thimbleton. I worried about trying to stay true to Stefan if I stayed around him much longer. That very worry made me feel terrible. *Gods forbid, what is wrong with me? What am I going to do?*

"Hey, I'm not the King. I only follow his orders." Andrew shrugged nonchalantly.

I wanted to push him into the stream, grab my stuff, and distance myself from him as fast as possible. If I weren't injured, I could have avoided him altogether. He would have never found me slumped against a tree half-dead, and I would never have gazed into those dreamy blue eyes. Stress made my jaw hurt.

"I'm really not that bad of a guy to be around. I don't know why you're so upset." Andrew watched me with interest.

"I don't belong with you," I said shortly. I grabbed my boots and yanked them on.

His expression hardened. "Why not?"

I went with the most logical reason. No way would I tell him his looks attributed to most of my discomfort. "I am a blacksmith's daughter from an insignificant farming town. You're a Prince. If I wasn't in dire need of assistance in the middle of nowhere, we wouldn't even be conversing."

What was the King thinking? I didn't mean anything to the Sorren monarchy. I stood and started hobbling away.

Andrew scrambled to his feet. In three long strides, his boots matched my steps as he caught up with me. "You think I'm too good for you."

I gave him a cursory glance, noting the irritation on the lines of his face. "Yes."

"You're wrong." He skirted in front of me. I sidestepped him and kept moving. "Joshua is a brother to me." He gestured to us. "That basically makes us family."

I slowed to a stop as my energy started to fade.

Andrew's blazing blue eyes bored into mine. "It doesn't matter that you grew up in a farming town. If you're going to spend time with Joshua, sooner or later we would have met."

I bit my lip, unable to argue with that statement.

He took a step forward. The tips of his boots touched mine. I sucked in a breath at his close proximity. His cinnamon woodsy cologne intoxicated me. "What's your real problem with this arrangement?"

I spoke quietly. "You're a distraction."

Andrew raised an eyebrow and pointed to himself. "I'm a distraction?"

"Yes. You distract me," I confessed, pushing my hair away from my face.

"What part of me distracts you?" He seemed genuinely fascinated.

I gestured to him. "All of you."

Andrew waved his hand up and down his body. "All of this ... distracts you?" he repeated, slowly raising an eyebrow at me.

I could see the humor in his blue eyes, and it made me angry. I had no doubt he was used to girls fawning all over him, but he wouldn't get it from me, even if I found him attractive. It wasn't my job to boost his ego.

I scurried away, completely disregarding the throbbing pain that increased with every step. My face felt hot and embarrassed. I didn't mean to admit that to him, but he had a way of getting information out of me without much effort on his part. "Well not anymore," I murmured. "No more admissions handed on a platter." I sealed my lips. There wouldn't be a single crack he could wiggle himself into. I would be as strong as granite. He couldn't break me. Not now. Not ever.

"Isabelle, where are you going?" He matched my pace.

"Away from you," I responded, stumbling forward.

"I can't help it if I distract you," he said, keeping up with me easily.

"Yes, you can. You can just stay away from me," I answered a little breathlessly.

"No, I can't. I promised my father I would keep you in my sight," Andrew argued patiently.

He stared down at me, his lips in a tight line, his eyes slightly crinkled, and his arms folded across his chest. My eyes widened. He was frustrated with me. *Good, serves him right. He could afford a little frustration.*

I rubbed my forehead. Quarreling was getting me nowhere.

"Is that all we're going to do? Argue?" Andrew inquired, running a hand through his ruffled hair.

I sighed, staring down into the yellowed grass. Is that all I was good for? I couldn't remember the last time I argued like this until he showed up. Now I struck out faster than a rattlesnake. What had come over me? I shouldn't act like this. This quarrelsome nature wasn't me.

"No," I said quietly, feeling guilty.

"Good. Now will you come back to camp?" Relief laced his tones.

I shook my head. I wanted to stay right here and feel guilty alone.

Andrew moved closer to me until he stood mere inches away. He wore a mischievous smirk on his face. I leaned my head back to see him properly, instantly suspicious. Nothing good ever came from smirks like that.

"What are you doing?" I narrowed my eyes.

"Nothing." He grinned.

"No," I said slowly, putting my hands out in front of me as I tried to back away. "You are planning something."

He pulled me into a hug. Taking care to not hurt my shoulder, he wrapped his arms around my torso and held me.

Ooh, he feels comfortable. I closed my eyes and rested my head on his muscled chest, listening to his strong heartbeat and letting all my worries and pain float away.

Suddenly Andrew moved his arms away from my back and gently lifted me into his arms.

"What do you think you are doing?" I yelled at him, struggling to break free but failing miserably as his strength and my injuries made it impossible. "Put me down."

"I'm taking you back to camp." He gazed down at me, not caring to hide the large grin on his face.

"Great," I muttered. *Back to the beginning.*

"This is my body," I said sternly while cradled in his strong arms. "I should be in command of it."

"You can't be trusted right now," Andrew answered firmly.

"Since when did we switch sides? You're the one who can't be trusted." I pouted, my bottom lip jutting out like a petulant child's.

Andrew laughed a deep rumble through his chest. "Oh, really? You still believe that?"

I didn't know what I believed. He turned my world upside down, like the ground became the stars, and the stars, the ground. Nothing made sense.

"Thought so," he said when I didn't answer, and he strode through the grass.

He set me down slowly by the dwindling embers of the fire. He crouched close by, threw some sticks into the embers, and blew on them to get the fire burning again. It wasn't long until a small fire steadily burned.

"I'm going to go get more wood for this fire. Will you please stay put? You need to rest if you're going to get any better. Tomorrow I think we should move, just in case the archer does try to come back. I'd move us sooner if I thought you could handle it." His eyes darted back and forth between the trees and me. "I'll stay close."

I nodded; grateful he felt the same sense of urgency I felt. I closed my eyes, letting the rushing stream and twittering birds lull me to sleep.

I dreamed I swam underwater in a boundless ocean; pebbles lined the bottom of the floor, mixing with the silt and sand. It shimmered and glowed, filtering light from above. I swam to the top, gasping for breath. Waves crashed over me as I treaded water.

A quick flash and suddenly the tall, black-haired man with penetrating eyes stood on top of the water, his hands clasped together. Not a drop of water touched his clothes, but it soaked me to the bone. "Isabelle," he whispered.

I heard it echo throughout every fiber of my being. Abruptly he disappeared and left me alone, treading water. I swiveled around searching for him. *Where did he go?*

He materialized closer and whispered my name again, then vanished. *What's going on?* I started to get frustrated.

The dream transformed.

I stood in the forest, in the same clearing where the attack happened. I couldn't see a creature or man in sight. The dark-haired man appeared in front of me, his hands clasped together. He whispered my name.

"What do you want?" I tried a direct approach as I folded my arms.

He took a step back before vanishing again, not emitting a single sound. I turned around in a circle, my eyes scanning everything in sight. Seeking the man who haunted me. Nothing.

I closed my eyes and opened them again, feeling irritated. Out of the depths of the trees, the two dead men I fought emerged. I gasped, bringing a hand to my mouth. They both appeared alive and whole without a scratch on them. They carried swords in their hands. Evil grins coated their faces with lust in their eyes. I screamed as they started running to me. Their swords aimed to kill. I had no warning. No escape.

As I stood there frozen in terror, the dark-haired man appeared, watching with interest. He waved his hand. The scene dissolved, morphing into the wheat field with the man in front of me.

I considered him captivating, with ivory skin, a goatee, and black shoulder-length hair. His open gaze looked calculating and cold but also entrancing. I suspected he had acquired power—loads of it. He made me feel intimidated and small, as though I would shrink to nothing underneath his gaze. I wished his ice-blue eyes contained more warmth to them like Stefan's or Nathan's, even Andrew.

His voice sounded silky smooth and clear. "You are Isabelle Elaine Mirran, daughter of Daniel and Anne Mirran."

"Yes," I said warily.

He opened his hands in welcome. "I am Haldren, a God of this world."

Unease hit me hard. A God? There were four main Gods that I knew of. The only four in existence, or so I had previously thought. Zadek, best known for his favor of men and war. Men prayed to him right before a battle for strength and guidance. Amora was widely known for her passion for women, fertility, and love. People sought after her most for her guidance in the affairs of the heart. When people wanted to barter, they prayed to Tomas, the God of intellect and negotiations. Last, the Goddess Nachura, commonly recognized for favoring animals, crops, and nature in general, was revered among farmers and farming communities. In many farmers' eyes, she was the crown jewel of the Gods. No other God or Goddess could compare.

I stared at Haldren. *Who is he and what is his role?*

"I have watched you for quite some time," he said.

"Why?" I asked.

He stepped forward and touched my shoulders. I felt a cold thrill run through me. "You are important." He let go and stepped back.

I placed a hand on my chest. "Me?" I shook my head. "No way. I'm just an ordinary girl of no value."

Haldren pointed at my left hand, the one with the birthmark. "So ordinary as to have the Mark of the Gods on your hand?"

I looked at my birthmark, ready to hide it behind my back, and watched the burning red color sparkle. I furrowed my eyebrows in confusion. It had never done that before. I frowned. *What kind of magic did he use on me?*

"I was born with it. I don't know why it's there." I shook my left hand, but it still glowed and shimmered. I tucked it behind my back.

"I do."

Disbelief clouded my features.

He nodded. "I know more about you than anybody else alive."

"Start talking," I demanded.

Haldren laughed softly, slowly shaking his head. "It is not going to be that simple. All will be revealed to you in its right time."

I rolled my eyes. What was the point of even mentioning it then?

"You made the right choice when you heeded your brother's letter. Joshua can provide the protection you require," Haldren said. "Nathan started to come after you, but I alerted him that you had found yourself a worthy protector to help you reach Thimbleton."

My shoulders slumped with my failure. "I ran but they caught up with me anyway."

Haldren nodded. "Joshua warned you about the danger, but you survived, and your family will be safe. However, you are in a great deal of pain in the living world. Your reserves of energy are depleting." He spoke with frankness. I guessed he saw through me, straight to my injuries in the real world.

"It's not every day I get shot with arrows," I muttered.

"How fortuitous for you to have a prince tending to your care," he said lightly.

"Yes." *A blessing and a curse,* I thought.

The corners of Haldren's lips curved up, giving me the impression he read my thoughts. "As a gift, I will send Nisha. He is my most trusted horse."

Surprise flitted across my face as my jaw dropped. "You're giving me a horse?"

"Nisha is not an ordinary horse. He can speak mind to mind with any person he chooses. He may go where he likes and do what he pleases. I believe he will be a good companion for you." He smiled, and for the first time, the smile was not cold.

"A talking horse?" I said, appalled.

He shook his head. "He is more than a talking horse. He is a descendant of man and has the mind to understand human things regardless of his nature."

"How can a horse be a descendant of man?" I didn't see the connection.

"A man once begged the Gods to become a horse; we granted his wish. He physically became a horse but retained the mind of a man. Nisha is a descendant from him and was taught the ways of man," Haldren explained. "Understanding human nature makes them better companions."

That sounded absurd. Suspicion grew within me. I narrowed my eyes. "Why are you helping me?"

"Is it not a God's duty to help whom I see fit?" he asked.

I shrugged, unable to argue or agree. I didn't know enough about the Gods and their responsibilities to make an assessment.

"Take care Isabelle Mirran." He waved his hand. Suddenly the ground disappeared, and I fell. Everything went black.

I jolted awake; the quick movement alerted the pain, and I cried out. Night fell. The stars glittered in the inky black sky. A cool breeze filtered in around us. Trees rustled as birds flew to their nests for the night and bats came out.

I sat up facing the fire; Andrew stirred something in a pot over it. His blazing blue eyes watched me with concern. "You all right?"

I slapped at a bug that landed on my arm. "Fine," I mumbled.

"You don't seem fine to me," he said.

I took a breath and exhaled. "I need to tell you something."

Andrew took the pot off the heat of the fire and set it in a small pile of burning embers. He sat back and brought his knees up. He rested his hands on them. "I'm listening."

"A God has been appearing to me in my dreams," I said.

"A God?"

I heard the skepticism in his voice. "If you're not going to have an open mind about this, then I won't tell you anything."

He sighed. "You're right. I'm sorry." He put his knees down and leaned back in the grass, relaxing his stance. "Please continue."

"Haldren—"

Andrew's eyes went wide. "Haldren?"

"That's correct." I nodded, my voice firm and unwavering.

He muttered something indistinguishable and ran a hand through his hair, appearing thoroughly alarmed. It perturbed me. "What has he said to you?"

I could tell Andrew knew more about this mysterious God than I did. I wanted to question him and demand answers. Instead, I continued with my story. "Perhaps I should backtrack first." Quietly I explained about Boss's kidnap attempt in Saren after Mava's wedding and Joshua's letter telling me to leave.

Andrew raised his eyebrows in surprise. "So it wasn't just happenstance they found you then, was it?"

"No. I was their target." I took a deep breath. "Haldren said I'd made the right choice in going. He said Joshua could protect me."

"Joshua is a highly skilled warrior with many means at his disposal," Andrew agreed. "You would be safe with him."

Andrew's confidence in my brother sent a sliver of relief into my heart. The soft breeze blew the smoke of the fire in my direction. I scooted out of the way.

"What else has Haldren said?" Andrew asked.

"This is where it gets a little strange." I laid it all out for him. "Just now, he said he was going to give me a horse—that talked."

"You've got to be joking." He did not sound pleased at all.

"I wish I was." I rubbed my eyes, frustrated.

Andrew's eyebrows furrowed, his lips in deep frown. The concern on his face scared me.

"You know what? It's my problem. Don't worry about it. I'll handle it myself." Not listening to my protesting body, I stood and started hobbling away, stomping through the grass and into the trees.

I didn't ask for my life to spiral out of control, or for a God to invade my dreams. I definitely did not ask for a talking horse, if one even showed up.

Just like I didn't ask to get attacked or for Andrew to arrive to rescue me. *Gods forbid, why did I have to be singled out like this?*

It made me sick to my stomach over it all. A rage started to boil over the injustices served, and none of it my fault. I peeked over my shoulder to see that Andrew still sat on the ground, his legs folded underneath him. He spoke into his locket; a soft blue glow emanated from it in the darkness. I couldn't hear him. He didn't even try to come after me.

I couldn't squash the feeling of hurt that he allowed me to walk off like that. What happened to not being able to leave his sight? What if I was too wild and insane, and the King voided out his previous order and told Andrew to get out of here before it was too late?

I didn't watch my footing, and in my zeal to get away I rammed my boot into a rising tree root, resulting in a hard fall to the ground. "Ouch!" I cried. Tears sprang into my eyes. I stayed on the ground lying on my stomach, crying softly from the pain. My injuries throbbed, my heart ached so much that I wished for unconsciousness. My head turned to the side; I rested one ear on the damp earth. The rest of my body lay in crooked angles over rising tree roots. I heard Andrew calling out my name, but too much pain and too much pride held my tongue in place. Even in this dire state, I did not want his help.

The undergrowth of ferns and other plants rustled, and twigs snapped. Boots squelched into the dirt. Andrew approached. If I possessed any power at all—a single shred of magical ability—I'd have used it to disappear. Anything to save myself from him finding me stuck in the dirt.

"Oh, Isabelle." He spoke softly and apologetically.

I heard the sympathy in his voice, and I didn't want it. "Go away." I clenched my teeth, fighting against the pain. It wasn't easy to form sentences when I wanted to scream and cry. "I want to be here," I lied.

He crouched down beside me. "You poor girl. That's why you shouldn't run off like you did," he gently scolded. "You're liable to get into all kinds of trouble."

"I don't—" I cleared my throat. "I don't need—your pity. Nor your reprimand."

"No, you don't need anything from me, right?" he responded arrogantly.

I groaned. "That's right."

"So you're just going to lie there all night in the cold mud?" he shot back at me.

"If—" I took a deep breath and held back the whimper. "If I have to."

Andrew cursed. "Gods forbid, you are stubborn."

"Deal with it, or leave me alone," I snapped, the pain making me testy.

"When are you going to learn?" Andrew sounded aggravated as he stood and leaned against the tree I tripped over. "I'm not going anywhere."

"Then take me seriously."

"I am."

"No, you're not," I said with conviction. Forcing back the pain, I explained further. "You have only taken my injuries seriously. This entire time you've never taken me seriously as a person; *an individual,*" I emphasized. "You don't see me as an equal. You see an invalid you're forced to take care of with—" I paused, searching for the right words. "Unexplainable issues," I finished lamely.

Silence. For once I think I made Andrew speechless.

"Take me seriously as a person, and don't look at me like I'm cracked, because I'm not," I finished.

"Are you done?" Andrew asked, sounding exasperated.

"Yes," I groaned in distress.

He didn't speak, but I heard his fist pound against the tree. "You're really testing my patience," he muttered a few moments later.

I believed wholeheartedly in what I said, and I wouldn't back down. Not even a smidgeon. If that meant I'd lie in the mud for the rest of the night, then so be it.

He crouched in front of me, and our eyes locked through the light of the moon and stars.

"All right. You want me to take you seriously? Fine. But you also need to stop assuming," Andrew countered crossly. "Stop assuming that I don't believe you. Stop assuming that I'm out to foil your plans. Stop assuming that I think less of you because of your gender and injuries. I am the *Crown Prince* of Aberron and yes, I have been ordered by my father—the *King*—to stay by your side, but that doesn't mean that I am stuck here out of loyalty. You assume too much."

Not a single shred of cocky arrogance showed in his outburst. He spoke with surety and conviction, laying it all out without looking back. I saw the truth in his words. He needed to own up to his mistakes, and I needed to own up to mine.

"Then show me you believe differently," I said tersely, scrunching up my face.

"Don't run off before I have time to explain," Andrew said crossly. "I shouldn't have to chase after you. Especially considering your injuries. You're going to make them worse."

I gulped, instantly ashamed. I didn't want to hurt myself further. In all honesty, I didn't want to lie in the mud with knobby tree roots digging into me all night either. I mustered up what little courage I had available, completely crushing any ounce of pride I held after our argument. "Will you help me up—please?"

Andrew sighed, sounding weary. "Yes."

He snaked his strong arms underneath my body and lifted me off the ground.

"Ow ow ow!" I wailed. I wondered if I should have stayed in the mud—it hurt less than being picked up.

"Sorry."

Andrew brought me close to the fire and laid me on the soft grass. He threw some sticks onto the fire and blew on it to get the flame burning bright again.

"You're covered in dirt," he commented. "We better clean that off to see the damage."

He took the pot of dinner out of the embers and poured it into two cups. Then he took the empty pot and walked down to the stream. Coming back minutes later, he set the pot on the fire. Once it reached a steady boil,

Andrew grabbed a rag. He dipped it in the hot water and brought it to my face, slowly wiping the grime off.

I closed my eyes and let him work on me. The hot rag burned into my skin at first but soothed whatever injuries I sustained during the fall. I whimpered when he cleaned off a particularly painful part of my face.

"Sorry. You've got a cut over that eye that's reopened from your previous tumble," Andrew explained.

"Right," I muttered.

My mind replayed the argument, and I wanted to apologize for assuming, but I didn't know what to say. I couldn't put my feelings into words. I remembered the way he ran his hand though his hair, the slight shake of his head, and the way he gazed into the sky muttering curses as he digested my seemingly tall tales. His posture had belied his unbelief.

I sighed and wished for Stefan. He wouldn't have acted like Andrew. Stefan would have wrapped his arms around me and said we'd get through this together. We'd probably end up laughing about it. He'd take all my worries and hold them with me, side by side, fully united. But Stefan wasn't here, and I was stuck with a prince who tried to hide the fact that he knew more about my mysteries than I did.

Andrew stuck the rag into the hot water. "I need to wash the bandages again and rewrap them." He helped me out of my shirt to look at my shoulder.

Andrew got out the purple bottle and dabbed it over my injuries. I enjoyed the few minutes of bliss as the pain reliever set in. He took a good look at the cuts and bruises on my upper body. He confirmed it didn't appear any worse and redressed the wounds with the hot linen. He helped me into my shirt.

Andrew resituated, closer to my leg. "Will your pants roll up high enough?"

"I think so." I reached forward and started to tug on the hem of my pants, feeling grateful I thought to pack loose ones.

"Here. Let me help," he offered. He slowly started rolling up the material.

"Ouch." I sucked in a breath, my hands digging into the ground.

"Sorry." He grimaced. "This isn't my area of expertise."

"That's hard to believe, you seem so capable," I said, amusement lacing my tone.

His face went red. He coughed and turned away for a second.

I laughed, a carefree, happy laugh, and it felt good. My heart lightened, and for a single moment in time I felt in control. It helped bolster me for what I saw next.

Andrew frowned as he stared at my thigh, unwrapping the linen, and putting it in the boiling water.

"What is it?" I asked, all laughter evaporated. I clutched at the grass, my fingernails digging deeper.

"This doesn't look so good." Andrew grimaced.

I leaned forward to see. Congealed blood oozed along the wound, the skin around it painted in angry hues of red. If I didn't watch it closely, it would get worse.

"I think all the walking you've done has put a strain on it." He peered over it.

"So what? I've got to become a complete invalid?" I scowled.

"It's what I would suggest," Andrew said softly, taking the linen out of the pot and drying it over the fire.

I clenched my jaw. "I would like to keep my leg, so I'll do it even if it kills my spirit."

He nodded. "Good choice."

He poured medicine on the wound and wrapped clean bandages over it, then he started to roll down my pant leg.

"See, you're becoming a pro already." I forced a smile to hide the wince.

Andrew gave an embarrassed grin back. He grabbed the pot of dirty water and threw it into the weeds, away from us.

He handed me a cup filled with a bean soup and a spoon. "So, can I ask you a personal question?" Andrew eyed me, gauging my reaction.

"You can ask, I'm not sure you'll get a response," I said, taking a bite. Spices hit my tongue, salt, pepper, onion, garlic. Surprised, I dipped my spoon back into the cup, eager for a second taste.

"How many boys are going to be heartbroken when they've realized you've left?" He wore a playful smile, but underneath that his demeanor showed blatant curiosity.

"What makes you think boys would be interested in me?" I tried to keep my voice even, though my heart raced.

"Don't play coy," Andrew said indignantly. "You're beautiful, even with the bruises."

I searched his face thinking I'd see a lie, but when I found none, I blushed. "I scared them away with my sword." *All except Stefan.* I felt a quick pang in my heart.

He leaned forward; his expression incredulous. "Really?"

I laughed and nodded. "I've had several boys tell me that if I'd lose the sword, they would court me, but it's not something I'm willing to give up."

"It's a good thing you didn't since it saved your life." Andrew drained his cup and set it down.

In the distance, a horse whinnied. I glanced at Andrew, my eyes wide, wondering if he heard it too. He quickly grabbed his sword and long dagger and looped it on his belt. He stood, folding his arms defiantly, and stared in the direction of the sound of clopping hooves.

Through the trees emerged a humongous black horse, the biggest one I'd ever seen. His black coat gleamed. The white swirl on his forehead strangely matched the swirl in the middle of my birthmark. *Interesting.*

The horse rocked his head back and pawed the earth, dust pluming around his hooves as he neighed. He lowered his head until his black eyes leveled with mine.

"I can't believe this is happening," Andrew breathed. His muscles tensed as he shifted his weight, seeming unable to stand still.

I addressed the horse, staring up at him from the ground. "Nisha?"

The horse moved forward, avoiding the fire, and stood closer to us. Andrew stepped backward until he stopped just barely in front of me, his hands hung loosely by his sides. I had the stark impression that he would protect me if this meeting didn't go well.

"I am Nisha. I come at the request of Haldren." His deep voice seeped into my mind like cool water spilling over. Thoughts formed unbidden in my mind, sounding decidedly male. *Strange.*

"Welcome, Nisha," I responded out loud.

Andrew glanced at me, his eyes wide and alarmed. "Did you just hear him speak in your mind?"

I nodded.

"I did too." He shook his head and ran a hand through his hair, like he was trying and failing to make sense of it all.

I focused on Nisha, ignoring Andrew's internal struggles. "I need to get to Thimbleton, but I cannot walk on my own. Would you please allow us"—I gestured to Andrew and myself— "to ride you?"

Nisha's response washed over our minds as he neighed. *"I will."*

I shivered, not used to a foreign voice in my head. It would take some time getting used to.

"Thank you," I said with gratitude.

"Can you read our minds?" Andrew asked. "Could you hear us if we responded to you mentally?"

"I can only project my voice into your minds. I cannot hear a response unless you speak out loud," Nisha responded.

"That's a relief," Andrew said quietly.

"I couldn't agree more," I muttered softly back.

Andrew cast his eyes up to the darkened sky. "It's late. Let's rest for the night then begin at dawn."

Nisha trotted over to a patch of grass away from the fire and bunkered down.

I lay on the soft grass and stared into the night sky. The waning moon only lit a sliver of the sky, and the stars glittered like diamonds dancing along the planes of space. It took my breath away. Frogs, crickets, bats, and owls all played their song with the melody of the wind. Tall grass and reeds rustled with the gentle night breeze.

"It's beautiful, isn't it?" Andrew commented, lying next to me, his eyes gazing up into the sky.

"Yes, it is." I sneaked a glance at him. His mouth was slightly open in awe, his eyes darting back and forth as he took in the glory of the night sky. It was so ordinary, so human, that my heart melted. I wanted to forget that he was the Prince and that I shouldn't be feeling this way. So, I turned my face back to the moon and tried to become impassive. Impenetrable.

I spoke quietly. "Good night Andrew."

"Sleep well, Isabelle," he said, voice soft.

CHAPTER SEVEN

THE SKY LIT IN orange and yellow hues, with a few sparse clouds tinged pink and purple. Birds chirped, rustling the leaves as they flew from branch to branch. A chipmunk scurried into the tall grass, clutching onto a snail. Andrew and I worked quickly to clear the remains of camp.

Between the both of us, there wasn't much to carry. Andrew had one pack on his back, and I had my patched bag, plus our swords and daggers. I felt eager to leave, and my heart raced in anticipation. This forest carried too many bad memories.

Since Nisha didn't come with a saddle, Andrew procured a thin rope from his pack and slung it around Nisha's neck for something to hold onto while we rode.

Andrew helped me onto Nisha's broad back as he knelt. I groaned, biting my bottom lip, and winced from the movement, not thrilled about how far my legs spread apart. Regardless, I wouldn't complain. I rode enough horses in Saren to expect this. We put my bag in front of me in between my legs. Andrew securely fastened his pack on his back and swung up behind me. He grabbed onto the makeshift reins, and we set off.

I couldn't ignore his nearness. I could feel his strong chest against my back; his arms rested around my waist, keeping me in place as he held the rope. I felt a blush creep along my cheeks at the closeness, relieved that Andrew kept his eyes on the forest and not down at me.

The forest became a blur of browns and greens. Nisha trotted at a constant pace, weaving through the trees and mossy underbrush. I winced and bit my lip every time he hopped over a mossy log. The constant jostling agonized my body, but Andrew held me steady.

"You hungry?" Andrew held a piece of jerky in front of my face.

"Yes. Thank you." I accepted his offering.

"You're welcome," he said.

I tore into the piece of jerky, relishing in the salty taste of the meat. It took my mind off the pain to have something to chew.

"Isabelle, there is something I want to say to you." He spoke with resolve in his voice.

"Go on." I bit into the jerky.

"I reacted poorly when you told me about your dream and the possibility of Nisha's arrival. You're right, I was skeptical." He spoke with sincerity.

I raised an eyebrow at him, my lips mashed together. *I knew it.*

"I didn't doubt that you believed you had this experience, I just ... I didn't want to accept it." Andrew fumbled with his words as he gripped harder on the thin rope. "I want you to know that I won't doubt you again, and if you said Haldren was bringing you a flying cat, I would believe it." He took a deep breath, his chest rising and falling. "I know you're not crazy, and I'll try my best to act accordingly."

"Is this an apology?" I asked, unsure.

"Yes," he said firmly.

"I was wrong too," I admitted. "I do assume too much, and I'm sorry I yelled at you."

"You weren't too far off the mark this time," he answered drily. His tone softened. "How are you feeling?"

"I'm all right." I sighed. I refused to complain. The sooner we got to Thimbleton, the sooner I could settle in a soft, warm bed.

"Lean your head back and rest. I'll make sure you don't fall off," Andrew gently coaxed. He pulled on my right shoulder until I leaned my head against his beating heart. I expected it to be awkward, but exhaustion ran deep through my bones. I didn't care as much as I thought I would. I fell asleep to the sound of Nisha's hooves snapping twigs and ferns.

The sun hovered high in the sky when Andrew woke me. The forest still surrounded us on all sides, with the stream lazily winding its way through. Andrew slid off Nisha and gently lifted me down. He let go once my feet planted firmly in the ground.

Nisha trotted over to the stream and drank deeply.

"I thought Nisha could use a rest and we could have lunch," Andrew said casually. "Feeling any better?"

"I'm fine." No words could even come close to describe the pain and soreness I felt from the horse ride, but I needed to get to Thimbleton, regardless of how much I suffered.

He appraised me, and I suspected he saw through my lie. "At this pace, we should be there by nightfall."

"Great. I could use a bath and a soft bed." I stumbled over to a tree and leaned against it, putting my hands behind my back.

Andrew smiled. "We sure take our beds for granted until we don't have them, huh?"

I smiled weakly in response. "I need a minute to wake up." I hobbled over to the stream and sat by Nisha. I cupped the cold clear water with my hands and threw it on my face. I shivered as the water brought my senses to life.

I patted Nisha and thanked him profusely.

Nisha neighed and rocked his head. *"You're welcome."*

We ate a quick lunch. Andrew declined to sit and walked around as he ate, inspecting the trees and plant life while he stretched his legs. Once refreshed and our stomachs satisfied, we hopped on Nisha and continued our journey.

I leaned my head against Andrew subconsciously.

"Comfortable, are we?" he murmured, amusement lacing his tone.

"As well as I can be, injured on a horse," I responded drily.

"Oh, come on." Andrew scoffed. "I know I'm not a soft bed, but I can't be that bad, can I?"

"Actually, you're very cozy," I admitted, biting my lip.

"Ha." He sounded satisfied, and his chest rumbled. "Good."

"Your future wife should be very pleased," I ventured.

Andrew groaned. "Don't go there. The last thing I want to think about is what's awaiting me at home." His tone turned thoughtful. "Perhaps I should extend the Walk. I'm sure there's a town or two I haven't visited."

Genuine curiosity colored my tone. "Has no woman ever struck your fancy?"

Andrew's hands tightened on the thin rope, tension apparent in his voice. "I am not immune to a woman's charm."

"Then what—" I started to ask.

"I'm sick of women seeing the crown above my character. They look at me like I'm a prize to be won—even the married and old ones—and the lengths they go to be noticed is revolting." He shuddered.

I spoke with certainty. "I'm sure there's women out there who don't view you that way. Not every woman wants to be royalty." Not me. I abhorred attention.

"You're right." Andrew leaned around me until he could see into my face; a hint of a smile rested on his lips. "I have met one."

I smiled up at him. "See, hope is not lost."

"No," he whispered. Andrew didn't take his blazing blue eyes off mine, and I found it hard to breathe. A mixture of desire and doubt filled me as I got caught up in the depths of them.

"Your eyes are very green, almost like emeralds," he commented softly, moving closer toward my face.

He came near, his lips a fingertip away from touching mine. Nervous tension filled my soul as I realized his intention.

Just when I was about let him kiss me, Nisha neighed, jostling us as he jumped over a fallen log.

Andrew quickly moved his head back up, grabbing onto the rope more securely. His arms closed tighter against my sides as he fought to keep us steady. "Whoa ..."

I blinked, shaking my head slightly. I felt like a bolt of lightning zapped me. *What am I doing?* Hadn't I told myself that I wouldn't give my heart to Andrew? *He is a prince.* I couldn't let him kiss me. I couldn't betray Stefan.

I sat up straighter, moving as far away from him as possible, and stared directly ahead at the thinning trees. My heart beat erratically, and I felt dazed and light-headed. I closed my eyes. *Pretend it didn't almost happen.* He was not going to kiss me. *Nothing happened,* I chanted in my mind. I didn't betray Stefan. Then why did I feel so guilty?

"I think I see some fields coming up." I pointed ahead, peering through the thinning trees. My voice sounded false. I shut up.

"Isabelle ..." Andrew said, completely ignoring my observation.

"Yes?" I tried to sound casual but failed miserably.

"We need to talk about what just happened." He sounded serious.

"What? No, we don't." I feigned ignorance, as if I didn't know he had almost kissed me. "Nothing happened."

"I shouldn't take advantage of you. I lost my head for a minute. I'm sorry," Andrew apologized.

"Don't worry about it. Nothing happened," I answered as if I didn't care, when in truth I cared more than I wanted. A whole lot more.

"It won't happen again," he said firmly. "I promise."

"Good," I answered, taking in a huge breath of air and exhaling slowly. It didn't help me get rid of the gut-wrenching remorse.

"All right." He sounded relieved.

My chest tightened, and I found it harder to take my next breath. I cast my eyes to the ground, feeling ashamed and rejected. My eyes filled with tears unwillingly. Andrew didn't want me. I knew I should feel relieved and that I could focus solely on Stefan and our potential for a budding romance, but it would be a flat-out lie if I told myself that I felt absolutely nothing for Andrew.

Andrew was a prince. He could have any girl he wanted. Someone prettier and smarter than me. A girl who understood what it meant to be around royalty and handled herself accordingly. He would never want an injured farm girl. How ridiculous would that be?

Ridiculous. That's what I'd become. Ridiculous for wishing that I could be more than friends with a prince. I'd be the laughingstock of Court if I showed up dressed like this, loose black pants and a light green cotton shirt, holding onto Andrew's hand. It didn't matter that we had a connection through Joshua. I knew nothing about high society, something he probably considered a requirement.

Andrew's true colors shone with his rejection. Despite saying otherwise, I believed deep down he knew I didn't belong in his world. He just wanted to save me some grief, protect me from diving in waters too deep and drowning. I should feel grateful that he watched out for me. It still didn't make his refusal feel any better.

And yet I wondered, did I really want Andrew, or did I crave the protection that he provided? I couldn't be sure. Perhaps it was better that he didn't kiss me after all.

The afternoon waned, the sun sinking farther into the cloudy blue sky. We emerged from the forest and discovered a dirt road about the width of a large cart. Deep lines gouged the dirt from the many carts going to and fro.

I cast my eyes up to the sky, enjoying the wind dance along my face as Nisha trotted. I breathed a big sigh of relief; staying too long in a forest made me feel trapped.

Along our way, we passed fields of grain and other produce. Numerous orchards and small houses dotted the countryside.

"Isabelle, look up ahead," Andrew whispered in my ear as we reached the top of a hill.

I absentmindedly gazed to the left, watching the tall wheat sway in the wind, reminding me of my dreams with Haldren. I peered above Nisha's mane and through his ears. Nestled in a beautiful valley with the stream running along the side resided Thimbleton. Only a few miles more until we reached the city.

"I see it," I said.

I leaned forward, craning my neck over Nisha's head to take in as much of the city as possible. A large curtain wall of rough, gray stone surrounded the city. Red tile rooftops, spread out in a wide expanse as far as the eye could see, were separated by what had to be hundreds of cobblestone streets running straight and narrow between them. Tall fir trees grouped in bunches rose high above the rooftops. Flickering lights dotted the city, like a million fireflies. In a way, it reminded me of the forest. Dense and crowded, except with buildings instead of trees. I wondered if people felt claustrophobic in there.

"I told you we would reach it today." Andrew grinned, obviously pleased with his accurate assessment.

"So you did."

Nisha picked up his speed from a steady trot to a canter, and I wondered if he sensed my urgency to get to Thimbleton. I leaned forward and patted his neck in gratitude. He replied by demanding an extra portion of oats once we got to our destination. A mile away from the city, the dirt road turned into well-maintained cobbled stone. I didn't see a single weed within the cracks.

A stone wall about three or four levels high surrounded Thimbleton. Judging by the soldiers patrolling on top, I guessed the width wide enough for four men to walk side by side. Plain blue and red flags billowed in the wind along the wall. A large metal portcullis, wide enough for two lanes of traffic, barred the entrance to the city. Nisha's hooves clattered and clopped as he slowed his pace, reaching the end of a line of carts, carriages, livestock, and people seeking entrance into the city.

"There are so many guards." My eyes roamed over the men strolling high above us, the setting sun glinting off their swords and other array of weapons.

Andrew chuckled. His chest rumbled against my back. "It's a big city; we have to take necessary precautions."

"Right." My cheeks flamed from embarrassment, reminding me how naïve I was. Saren was established on open ground, not a wall or gate surrounded it.

The line moved steadily through the portcullis and into Thimbleton. People stopped briefly to speak to the guard before moving on. It took longer if they pulled a cart, as multiple guards skimmed through their belongings or produce.

A large burly guard asked questions at the gate; his loud voice boomed.

"What be your business here?" he asked the balding old man in front of us. The older gentleman pulled a handcart overflowing with carrots.

My mouth salivated as I watched the guards skim through the dirt-caked carrots. My stomach gurgled in hunger. I wanted to sink my teeth into every carrot in the whole cart, dirt coated or not.

"Harvest Festival, selling carrots," the old man answered, wiping his brow with a handkerchief.

Once the guards stepped away from the cart, nodding their approval, the guard waved him on. He trudged forward, groaning slightly from the weight of the carrots in his handcart. I couldn't help but feel a bit nervous and ashamed when Nisha trotted forward, stopping just in front of the gate. I didn't need a mirror to know that I looked downtrodden and bedraggled.

The burly guard's whole countenance changed when he recognized Andrew. He bowed. "Highness." He straightened and grinned. "What be your business here?"

"To safely return this little gem to the arms of her brother." Andrew let go of the rope and, with a feather touch, rested his hands on my shoulders.

"Welcome." The guard bowed low again, opening his hands in welcome.

"Thank you." Andrew smiled at the man. "Ralph, isn't it?"

The guard beamed. "Aye. You remembered."

"Your family, are they well?" Andrew inquired.

"Very well," Ralph said, resting one hand on the hilt of his sword. "My wife is due to have our first child any day now."

"Congratulations." Andrew smiled with more warmth this time. "May the Goddess Amora bless her with an easy delivery and a healthy child."

"Thank you," Ralph said, bowing again. "Enjoy your stay in Thimbleton." He gestured for us to ride through the gate.

Andrew picked up the rope and prodded Nisha into a trot.

"Do you come here often?" I asked as we distanced ourselves from the gate and rode farther into the city.

"Not too often but lately more than any other city," he replied. "If you're wondering about the guard, Ralph used to be a palace guard assigned to one of the side entrances. He relocated to Thimbleton just before I started the Walk."

"Oh, I see."

"I don't remember everyone's names, but I make it a point to try to learn as many as I can when they work at home," he explained.

How thoughtful. I admired that he took the time to do that. It showed he cared for people.

Architects designed the cobbled streets broad enough for two carriages, or carts, and a horseman to ride abreast. Sidewalks lined both sides, leading up to shops built of stone or brick. Signs placed on wooden posts named each road, and I discovered we rode on Thimbleton. Lanterns hung on stone posts placed every ten long strides or so lit the road and the sidewalk. The flames flickered, casting shadows. Grateful for the extra light, my eyes soaked in every part of the city I could see.

The buildings crammed together, so close that a horse couldn't ride in between them, and in some sections I saw no gap in between the different shops. On the bottom of the buildings, large windows displayed wares. Buildings with second levels had smaller windows that reminded me of the ones at home. Perhaps people lived above them? The businesses hung brightly painted wooden signs over the sidewalks. They dangled over people's heads as they ambled up and down.

Even though the sun started to set, the city teemed with life. Women clung onto the arms of their sweethearts, pointing at the window displays. A group of young boys ran up the street, snaking through the crowds, laughing and shoving one another. I felt sorry for one young man when he walked out of a weaver's shop, heavy laden with boxes, while a richly dressed lady snapped open a fan and shouted orders at him. The poor lad seemed ready to collapse under the weight of the packages.

"Don't faint on me yet," Andrew said lightly, whispering in my ear to be heard over the noise.

"What?" I didn't understand.

"Your eyes are so wide, and you're swiveling your head so much to see everything. I think you might faint from all of the exposure," he explained chuckling.

"I can't help it. There's too much to see," I said, my eyes roaming.

"Catch your breath at least. You'll get used to it soon enough," Andrew said nonchalantly.

I doubted it. "Where are we going?" I asked, as Andrew directed Nisha around other carts, carriages, and horses, turning away from Thimbleton Street onto Willow.

"The Blue Willow," he answered. "It's the best inn in Thimbleton."

Near the end of the less busy Willow street, Andrew stopped in front of a large stone building, easily the size of a mansion. My jaw dropped. The masonry work astounded me. I stared at the different sizes of stones layered in a beautiful design. Small shrubs and flowers lined the path leading up to the ornate double doors.

"This is it." Andrew nudged Nisha forward and directed him to the side of the inn.

A hostler stood by the stable and opened it when he saw Andrew coming. Many horses lazily munched on hay and oats. Andrew leaped off Nisha. He grabbed my pack and set it on the ground, then slowly lifted me down onto my shaky and tired feet. He held on to me for a minute, sensing my need to gain my footing, until I gave him a look to let go. I leaned against a stable door as he led Nisha to the hostler and flipped him a coin.

"Make sure he is groomed well and fed with an extra portion of oats. This horse deserves it," Andrew said.

The hostler nodded. "Right away."

"Oh, and an apple too, if you have it," I said, listening to Nisha's requests.

I leaned on Andrew as we made our way to the front steps and into the inn.

Inside, everything was richly furnished in blue and gleaming wood. Long blue drapes with gold edges lined the windows. The carpet was threaded in hues of blue with many colored flowers. A large desk stood center in the room, drawing my attention to it. Many sheaths of paper were stacked high in neat piles. In the middle of the desk lay a small silver bell. We reached the desk and Andrew rang the bell. While we waited for someone to come, my eyes trailed around the luxurious fixtures.

I glanced to my left at the large, ornately carved stairs leading up to closed doors. To the right, a large and spacious room overflowed with tables and raucous laughter. Men, women, and children took up every table available, eating or drinking. A young maiden about my age swerved in and out of the way of tables, handing out steaming blue plates piled with food. I salivated. I couldn't wait to rip into a real meal.

Music flowed from a small piano an old man played to entertain the guests as they ate. Saren certainly did not have this kind of extravagance in their small inn. I felt enthralled watching so many people interact with one another. It reminded me of the parties in Saren—those were the only times our little town got as loud as this dining room.

"It must take many people to run this place," I whispered to Andrew.

He laughed, resting his hand on the desk. "Yes, it does. But they are highly renowned for their hospitality."

A plump woman with flyaway red hair entered the room, though her eyes kept darting back at the dinner room to a group of men who laughed particularly loud. One of them slopped some of his drink down his front when his comrade slapped his back to the amusement of the other men.

"I'm sorry for the wait. May I help you?" She glanced at us, then back at the rowdy table.

"Yes, I was wondering if you had any rooms available?" Andrew asked.

The lady focused on us, then widened her eyes, placing a hand on her heart. "Oh! Your Highness, I'm sorry, I didn't recognize you." She dipped into a curtsy, her cheeks glowing to the same shade as her hair.

"That's quite all right." Andrew's fingers curled into a fist. I could feel the annoyance radiating as the lady fussed over him.

"Rooms. Let me check." She shuffled some papers around and pulled a ledger out. "Unfortunately, I don't have many available. The Harvest Festival is going on, and most people reserve rooms weeks in advance." She muttered something unintelligible. "Drats. I'd assume you want a separate room for your lady friend, but I've only got one room available." She frowned and glanced into the dining room once more, clearly wishing she could kick the rowdy people out.

She cleared her throat. "It's the best room in the house, so you'd get your own bathroom and extra amenities. Perhaps you would take it and make other arrangements for your lady friend at the Silver Leaf across the road?" She peered closer at me, her eyes widening as she fought to hide the disgust at my appearance.

"Absolutely not. She stays with me," Andrew said firmly.

The innkeeper gasped. "But Highness—"

Andrew's tone went from pleasant to commanding within a second. "She is my charge. Her health is precarious at present, and my father, the King, has procured an oath from me to watch over her. Unless you would prefer I take my business elsewhere?"

"She has a point," I said. "I would prefer not to be known as the lady sharing a bed with a prince." I grimaced. "We have our reputations to think of."

The innkeeper appraised me in a new light, as though I'd suddenly become more of lady than some common mistress picked up on the streets. She smiled and addressed Andrew. "Exactly."

"But I still have to keep an eye on you regardless of where we stay. I'm not going to break my promise to my father," Andrew persisted.

"Oh no. Please don't break your oath. I merely thought ..." She paused, seeming to rethink whatever she planned to say next. "Forgive me. You may have the room if you would like," the innkeeper said. "It's five gold Sundals a night, and you're welcome to stay for as long as a month. If you would like to stay longer, we have to draw up a contract. However, I doubt we'll be needing to do that with you." She pulled a piece of paper out of her book and handed it to Andrew. "If you'll sign here please."

Andrew took the pen and signed his name. He fished out the money from his pocket and gave it to the lady, receiving a key in return.

"Your room is at the top of the stairs, number twenty." She paused, glanced ruefully at me, then suggested. "If I might add, we have many kinds of healing medicines and creams that might help your lady. We could send some up if you would like, free of charge."

Andrew nodded. "That would be nice. As you can see, we have been on a bit of a journey and could both use a hot bath and food."

I nodded. "Oh, that sounds wonderful. Thank you."

The lady smiled. "I will send the maid up in a few minutes then. If you have any questions, my name is Joan. I am the manager of this household and will take care of any needs that arise."

I couldn't change the cuts or bruises on my face with a flick of my hand. I didn't have that magical ability. My wounds needed time to heal. Coming to a fancy establishment appearing like I'd had a run-in with a cow stampede was hard to swallow.

I stumbled up two flights of stairs, leaning heavily on Andrew. My breath came in short gasps as my leg throbbed persistently. When we approached the last section of stairs, I groaned. Andrew chuckled and gently swept me in his arms. He effortlessly carried me up, passing people with incredulous stares. I tried not to let my cheeks show my embarrassment.

On the walls, paintings hung in blue frames, and the blue threaded carpet ran like a banner down the hallways over the wooden floor. The whole place was elaborately furnished and the fanciest establishment I could remember setting my eyes upon. If my health had been better, I would have loved to inspect every detail of the craftsmanship.

Andrew stopped in front of a door with a brass number twenty placed in the center. He set me on my wobbly feet and wrapped his arm around my waist to hold me steady. "This is it." He unlocked the door and opened it wide, gesturing for me to enter.

My eyes took in the large room. A four-poster bed made neatly with blue flowered quilts stood in the middle to the back of one wall. Two end tables sat by the headboard on either side of the bed, and above them windows with the blue drapes let in the dwindling sun. A round table and three chairs took up another side of the room, and an additional cushioned chair rested next to an empty fireplace. There were two doors on opposite sides of the room, leading to a closet and a bathroom.

If they made rooms this size in an inn, I could only imagine what Andrew's bedroom at home was like. It'd probably swallow up Nathan and Adel's entire house.

"What do you think?" Andrew asked, shrugging off his pack and setting it on the floor.

"It's nice." I set my bag down and sat on the bed.

"Good." He surveyed the room. "You look dead on your feet. Why don't you rest while I quickly clean up? Then you can take a long, soothing bath, and I'll have dinner brought up. I'll make a fire first to keep you warm."

I nodded and leaned against the pillows. Closing my eyes, I fell asleep almost instantly.

CHAPTER EIGHT

SABELLE." ANDREW GENTLY PRODDED me awake. I opened my eyes blearily. He crouched beside the edge of the bed, smelling strongly of lavender soap. His wet hair dripped into his eyes as he pushed it back. He smiled. "You ready for that bath?"

I rubbed the sleep out of my eyes. "Bath—right." I sat up and used one of the posts to help me stand.

The bathtub was large and deeper than the one we had at home. Andrew turned on a faucet and hot water poured out, tendrils of steam rising steadily.

"Where did all the hot water come from?" I dipped my fingers in the water. I was used to lugging hot water in buckets to our bathtub. Only a few months ago, Nathan developed a pipe system where we poured buckets of water into a cauldron and heated it over a fire. Then the hot water rushed down a pipe and poured straight into the bathtub. It became the talk of the town for weeks as Nathan instructed other farmers on his ingenious plan.

"Don't you know?" Andrew raised his eyebrows in shock. "Every major city in Aberron is situated there for one purpose." He held up a finger. "Hot springs." He pointed to the running water. "Throughout the last three hundred years every king has been working toward expanding the use of the hot springs for our convenience. We have instant hot water in almost every prominent establishment, with many lobbying for more expansion. We even have water experts whose sole purpose is to travel to every corner of Aberron to search for undiscovered hot springs. It's one of the things that makes our country so valuable. I can't tell you how many foreign embassies are jealous of our hot springs."

I pointed to the toilet. "What about the toilet?"

Andrew rolled his eyes. "Oh, come on, I shouldn't have to explain that to you as well."

I laughed. "I understand. The plumbing is Aberron's finest glory."

Andrew grinned. He reached down and turned off the hot water. "Enjoy your bath, Isabelle, courtesy of every past and future King of Aberron."

I smiled. "Thank you."

He left the room, shaking his head and rolling his eyes as he closed the door behind him. I slipped my clothing off and unwrapped the bandages, letting it all pile onto the floor in one heap. I sank happily into the tub and closed my eyes, relishing the steaming water as it soothed all my aches and pains.

I didn't care to see my ravaged body. I didn't think I could handle it, so I lay there in the water until I had the nerve to wash. Then I scrubbed with vigor, stripping off layers of dirt and grime, revealing the many bruises and cuts underneath.

My upper thigh where the arrow wound resided appeared red and angry. It didn't seem any better than when Andrew checked it the night before. Thankfully, it didn't look any worse either. I prayed that no major infection would incur.

When I got out of the water and walked over to the floor-length mirror, I cried. I covered my mouth; my body was an utter mess. Clean of all the dirt and grime of travel, there was nothing to hide the blue, purple, green, and yellow bruises littering my body. I couldn't even recognize my face.

"Look at me," I whispered. "I'm a bruised rainbow of colors."

A sob escaped my throat, and tears slid down my cheeks. I clutched at my stomach. No wonder Andrew stopped himself from kissing me. *I am ugly.* Disgust ran clear throughout every fiber of my being. I shuddered and closed my eyes, afraid to see any more.

"Isabelle, are you all right?" Andrew gently knocked on the door.

I quickly cleared my throat and wiped away my tears. I tried to squash my rolling emotions and hide the fact that I'd been crying. "Yes, I'm fine. No worries."

"Isabelle, you don't sound all right." Andrew's muffled voice sounded concerned.

"No, really, I'm fine." I tried to assure him. I cleared my throat again. "I'm coming out." I pulled on the light blue robe hanging on a hook and wrapped it around my battered body. I'd forgotten to go through my bag to pull out something decent to wear before I stepped into the bath.

"How was your bath?" Andrew stood by the door, his hands in his pockets.

I blinked, caught off guard by his close proximity to the door. His stance reminded me of Stefan, who stuck his hands in his pockets often. I trembled, wanting Stefan, my best friend and confidant, to wrap his arms around my waist and console me. I wanted to cry on his shoulder and listen to his gentle voice encouraging me. He'd tell me I was beautiful regardless of the injuries marring my body. Stefan would do anything to get me to laugh, and I needed him now more than ever.

I didn't want Andrew staring at me with pity in his eyes.

I made an effort to smile, but it was false. "Great."

"The maid brought in some fresh bandages and salves while you were in the bath. I thought we could try them?" Andrew suggested.

His tone and posture implied that he wasn't entirely convinced of my well-being. I would never admit to him that my problem lay with vanity and a desire for Stefan to make it all better.

"Let me get clothes first," I responded, hobbling over to my bag.

"Oh, no wait." He put a hand on my shoulder. I halted. "Go to the closet. I went downstairs and acquired a selection of clothes. I don't know your size so I got several different ones, and you won't need to return them. That way you have something to wear while your travel clothes are getting washed." He directed me to the closet.

"Thanks."

I pulled on the closet door and walked in the tiny room. I found an array of different clothing in multiple sizes, from day wear to nightwear and lots of underwear. I didn't understand why Andrew thought I needed so much underwear. *He obviously knows nothing about women's clothing.* I slipped on the undergarments I thought seemed closest to my size and put the blue robe back on. I decided it was pointless to put a cotton nightgown on when I would just have to take it off for Andrew to bandage me up. I grabbed a nightgown off a hanger and draped it over my arm, intending to put it on later.

I sat on the cushioned chair near the fire that had the best light in the room. Andrew pulled the table nearer, careful not to knock over the bottles and bandages now covering it. He sat and opened a few bottles containing different colored and strong-smelling ointments, then started rubbing them over the cuts. I gasped and winced as I tensed up.

"That stings," I said through gritted teeth.

"I'm sorry," Andrew murmured, undeterred. "We should take you to a healer, now that we're actually in a city."

"No," I protested immediately.

"Why not?" he asked, gazing up at me.

"Because the last time a farmer from Saren went to a healer with mage abilities he died, and all he had was a broken leg. I don't trust them or their magic," I explained curtly. "I don't need anyone else seeing my body either. One person is enough. I shouldn't even mention the cost. I know they are expensive."

"You're with me; the cost should be the least of your worries. They could speed up the healing process," Andrew countered.

"And miss out on the fun of healing naturally? No, thank you." I shook my head, firm in my decision. I wouldn't let Andrew pay for a healer when it should come out of my own pocket if I decided to go to one. Already, I felt obligated to pay him back for the room. I toyed with the idea of slipping coins in his bag when he fell asleep to make up for it.

"All right. Suit yourself. But don't say I didn't offer." He shrugged. "And not every healer is as bad as the one who killed that farmer. They have to be trained and licensed before they're allowed to practice."

I sighed, not wanting to debate. "I don't want to argue, but it's my body and my choice. Please respect that?"

Andrew nodded, consenting. "Fine." He finished wiping the salve over my body as I winced and bit my lip. Deftly, he wrapped clean bandages over the major areas.

I sighed in relief when he finished. I put my hand on his. "Thank you," I spoke with as much gratitude as I could muster.

"You're welcome. Let me help you into that nightgown." He grabbed the nightgown that hung over the back of the chair and helped me slip it on.

A soft knock came at the door. "Your Highness, it's Joan. I've brought you something hot to eat." She called through the door.

Andrew answered the door, and Joan came in carrying a large tray with steaming blue plates of food, followed by another young lady carrying a pitcher of cider and cups. The young maid, easily rivaling my age, gasped, an alarmed expression on her face as her eyes darted between Andrew and me. Joan snapped her head at the maid and gave one deadly glare. The maid mumbled an apology. Her cheeks and mine tinged pink with embarrassment.

Andrew pushed the bottles of medicine and bandages off to the side to make room for the food and drink, completely unaware of the thirty-second interchange.

"Is everything to your liking?" Joan asked after setting the tray on the table.

"Yes, everything is quite satisfactory, thank you," Andrew assured her.

"Good. I'll leave you be. Enjoy your meal." Joan and the maid curtsied as they backed out of the room.

We ate quietly, savoring every taste that dropped into our mouths.

Even though it hadn't been long, my stomach acted like I hadn't eaten a proper meal in months, years even. I pushed the mostly empty plate away from me, feeling full and gratified. I wanted to crawl into bed and sleep forever. Sleep off every pain and worry. I glanced at the bed. The only bed. I would think with a room this size there would be two. What were they thinking when they put only one bed in such a large room?

I felt sure our sleeping arrangement wouldn't be a problem after Andrew's complete refusal of me. Now that I saw myself through a mirror, I couldn't blame him.

I moved away from the table and pulled the covers back, sliding into the soft flannel sheets. Andrew leaned back in his chair and watched me.

"Where are you going to sleep?" I asked him.

"I'm not sure." He rubbed his chin.

"There's plenty of room in this bed," I offered.

"Um." Andrew opened his mouth and closed it.

"What are you worrying about? You made your intentions very clear this afternoon." I couldn't help the coldness that seeped into my voice, still hurt over my appearance and rejection.

He sighed, regret lacing his tone. "Isabelle."

I knew he didn't want to have this conversation, and truthfully, I didn't want to have it either.

"We're both tired and have been riding all day. Just get into bed and don't worry about it," I said.

"Fine." He shrugged and exhaled his breath in defeat.

"Good." Tired and achy, I didn't want to argue anymore.

I rolled over and closed my eyes, hoping sleep arrived quickly to ease the pain. When I just barely started to fall unconscious, I felt Andrew slide into the bed and roll to the edge.

"I don't bite, you know. At least not anymore," I mumbled sleepily through the pillow.

Andrew relaxed a little bit and moved inward. "I know," he whispered.

"Good night," I trailed off, sleepily.

"Night."

I saw glimpses of Haldren in my dreams, almost as if he wanted to remind me of his presence and watchful eye. He never said anything, and neither did I, but I couldn't shake off the creepy and intrusive feeling I got when I saw him flicker into existence and disappear faster than lightning striking the ground.

The sun filtered through the cracks in the blue curtains when I opened my eyes. Andrew had already left the bed, and I could hear him dropping things in the bathroom. *A clumsy Prince?* I smiled at the thought.

He came out a few minutes later sporting a loose white cotton shirt and black pants. His hair was wet and his face freshly shaved.

"Good morning." He smiled. "How'd you sleep?"

"Better than I have since leaving Saren," I said. "And you?"

"Fine." Andrew sat on the edge of the bed, wrapping a hand on one of the posts. "How are you feeling?"

"Do we have to talk about that?" I stared into my lap, not wanting to meet his gaze. I felt sorry for myself, and I hated it.

"Come on, Isabelle. Don't start," he warned.

"Nothing's changed from yesterday. I'm still broken and useless." I gripped the blue quilt in frustration.

Andrew pried my hands away from the blanket and held on to them. "Isabelle, look at me," he commanded.

I shook my head, refusing to lock eyes.

"Isabelle." He let go of my hands and cupped his hand underneath my chin, forcing me to meet his eyes. "You are not broken and useless. You just need time to heal, and the best way to do that is to rest."

"I know, but I feel like a chicken cooped up in a cage. It goes against my very nature." I sighed and changed subjects. "Will you make an inquiry about Joshua?"

Andrew nodded. "I already have. He's traveling to meet us. Unfortunately he probably won't arrive for another two days. Father sent him to oversee the Mariel Outpost on the tip of the southwestern province."

"I see. So what did you have planned for today?" I wondered if he would leave me to my own devices. *I doubt it.*

"I sent a note requesting an old friend to visit me. I have a few items of business to discuss while I'm here, but I'm not going out while you rest," Andrew stated. "My father would kill me if I didn't follow my word."

"So you'll conduct your business here?"

"Yes." He nodded.

"Well if I'm stuck in bed all day, I won't have to change, will I?" I said sarcastically.

Andrew smiled cockily. "You, my dear, won't have to change anything at all."

The morning went quietly while Andrew waited for his guest. We ate breakfast. I emptied my things out of my bag and scattered them around the bed, cleaning up the biscuit crumbs while sorting my belongings. My smoky-scented clothes got sent away and washed. I sent a note off to Nathan and Adel, assuring them I was safe. I hoped they weren't too mad at me for running out on them. By midmorning, I wanted to scream.

I watched Andrew casually whittling a block of wood.

"So who is coming over?" I asked, bored with my thoughts.

"Alzmire," he answered shortly. A pile of wood shavings rested on the table as he worked his knife into the wood.

"What does he do?"

"He's a professor for the Sorrenian in Carasmille." At my confused expression, he further explained. "That's a school."

"Oh."

"When he's not teaching at the Sorrenian, he lives in Thimbleton, managing his vast estate. Half of the residents of Thimbleton work for him," he said.

A loud knock came at the door. Andrew set his block of wood on his pile of shavings and stuck his knife in his boot. He answered the door. "Good. You got my note. Come in." He gestured for the man to enter and shut the door behind him.

Alzmire looked comparable to Andrew's height, with a slight build. His dirty-blonde hair had flecks of gray. He wore laugh lines along his clean-shaven face and had warm brown eyes. His clothing screamed wealth and style. I especially admired the blue embroidery on the cuffs of his cream-colored shirt.

"My Prince." His voice sounded mild. "What calls me to you?"

"I'm long overdue for a visit," Andrew said. "Please sit." He pulled out a chair.

Alzmire stepped forward, taking in the room; he caught eyes with mine. His mouth parted slightly as his eyes widened in surprise. He obviously expected Andrew to be alone. "Almost off your Walk then?" He spoke casually, draping his leg over the other in his seat. He placed a hand on his chin, and I noticed he wore several gold and silver rings on his fingers. Other than his first silent, surprised reaction, he seemed very comfortable with his surroundings, not appearing the least bit deterred by my presence.

"Yes," Andrew said, sitting across from him. "Thimbleton is my last stop before home."

"So, who is this lovely young lady sharing your bed?" Alzmire asked, staring at me speculatively.

I narrowed my eyes at him, my cheeks flaming. My fingers curled around the blanket in anger. Lovely is not what I would call myself at that moment, and sharing beds? It insinuated that something far more scandalous than the truth: that we were two people wearing invisible shackles, chained to each other, with the King as our jailor. I felt insulted, and it showed on my face.

Andrew wore guilty grimace. "Forgive me for not introducing you immediately. This is Isabelle Mirran." He gestured to me. "She is Joshua Mirran's sister." The words tumbled out of him faster than a jackrabbit ran from a fox as he hurried to set the record straight. "Unfortunately, they only had one room available last night, and my father has ordered me to keep my eyes on her until she is safely delivered to her brother. As you can see, she's had a bit of a run-in."

Alzmire, who stared at me unashamedly the whole time Andrew spoke, turned to Andrew. "You should have come to me first. I would have housed you. You know I have a big, empty house."

"Yes, I remember." Andrew resumed his guilty expression.

"Well for the sake of her reputation and yours, you better find separate rooms fast," Alzmire said blatantly. "Come, stay with me," he offered.

"That would be very gracious if it's no trouble," Andrew answered politely.

Alzmire waved a hand. "Nonsense. It's no trouble at all."

"Thank you," Andrew said. His shoulders visibly relaxed.

"How long do you expect to be in Thimbleton?" Alzmire clasped his hands together, slumping lower in his seat.

"Two days," Andrew said. "Joshua is traveling from the Mariel Outpost."

Alzmire grinned. "Excellent. That means tomorrow you can ride with me in the Harvest Parade." His tone of voice gave no room for a refusal. He seemed just as good at commanding others as Andrew. I expected that came from ruling over students as a professor.

Andrew pursed his lips, seeming to mull it over. "You know how I dread those things."

"You're on the Walk. It's a requirement for the people to see you," Alzmire stated.

Andrew nodded. "Right." He sighed. "I'll do it, if Isabelle rides with me. Father's rules."

"Perfect. You'll be the crowning glory of this year's parade." He laughed lightly. "Pun intended."

Andrew leaned back, laughing. "That's a bad joke even for you."

"I've been away from my students for too long. I'll think of something better later." Alzmire shook his head.

They gravitated their conversation to business, discussing land and nobles and merchants and the economy of Thimbleton. It became a little too boring for me, so I closed my eyes and let their voices drone on. They didn't need me to be an active participant in their conversation. I was just the luggage Andrew had to bag around until Joshua came.

My ears perked up when I realized they had finished discussing business and my name slipped from Andrew's mouth. I kept my eyes shut, feigning sleep as I listened in on their conversation.

"So, what are you doing with Joshua's sister? Isabelle, right?" Alzmire asked curiously. "You know in all the years I've known Joshua, he's never once mentioned he had a sister. If I hadn't known their parents previously, I'd think he was an only child. It's like she's never existed in his life."

"That's because she hasn't," Andrew answered darkly. "He hasn't spoken one word to her since the death of their parents."

"Really?" Alzmire's voice shot up in surprise. "I wonder why."

Yeah, me too, I thought bitterly. A memory flashed back. I sat at the worn kitchen table, Adel showing me how to dip a pen into the ink bottle. I started writing a letter to Joshua. It was sloppy, with big fat letters and splotches of ink splattered everywhere. I remembered feeling so worried that Joshua had forgotten all about me. I wanted him to know I didn't forget him. I continued for years after to write letters to him, but I never received one in return. That's when I stopped trying. I needed him, but I guess he didn't need me. Maybe he never did.

I refocused on the conversation between Andrew and Alzmire.

"So how did this companionship come to be, and what happened to her? The poor dear looks on the brink of death." Pity laced Alzmire's mild voice.

Andrew energetically explained our first encounter. I suspected he enjoyed the heroic light it put him in as he spoke about finding the two dead men in the clearing and my injuries.

"It's been a rough couple of days," Andrew continued. "I had to pull the arrows out myself and administer aid without the use of magic. It would have taken me half the time to heal her had I been able to use it."

"Have you taken her to a healer then?" Alzmire asked.

"No." Andrew sounded frustrated. "She refuses."

"That's very unwise given the nature of her injuries," Alzmire said.

"I know, but she's a feisty little thing. She could have ten arrows stuck in her, and I still think she'd survive." Andrew sounded like he genuinely believed it.

"And so your father is aware of all of this?" Alzmire asked.

"Yes, he's made it perfectly clear that I absolutely cannot leave her alone. Not that I would of course, and given the circumstances, she needs someone to take care of her, even if she won't admit it," Andrew finished darkly.

"Won't admit it? What do you mean?" Alzmire's voice held curiosity.

"I believe she is the first young female I have ever met that actually hates me for being a prince. I've spent more time arguing with her than I ever have with a woman," Andrew said, flabbergasted. His tone clearly indicated that he did not understand why. "From the moment we met, she's been trying to run away from me as though I were a plague."

Alzmire laughed. "Sounds like you met your match."

Andrew chuckled. "Hardly."

"Well, it's certainly the most interesting thing I've heard all week. Sure breaks up the drudgery of organizing the Harvest Festival. It's been problem after problem. People are losing their heads over the color of the draperies. It's not like there aren't twenty mages that could change the color in a second." Alzmire pounded his fist against the table.

Andrew chuckled. "Your problem, not mine."

I opened my eyes, not caring to pretend sleep anymore. Achy and tired from lying in one position for so long, I needed some relief. I pushed a few strands of hair out of my way, cringing as my fingers brushed along the bruises. My face felt hot to the touch.

I sucked in a breath as I moved a little to get comfortable. The movement brought Andrew and Alzmire's attention on me.

"You're awake." Andrew got up from the chair and came over.

Alzmire stood as well. "I'd best be going. I trust you know how to get to my house?"

Andrew turned to Alzmire. "Yes. We will be there shortly."

"Until then." Alzmire waved and strode out the door.

Andrew faced me. "No more worrying about our reputations. You can get your own room at Alzmire's." He paused and added. "Right next to mine of course."

"Fine," I agreed quickly, averting his gaze. I gripped onto the blanket, my hands digging into the cloth.

"What's the matter?" Andrew asked, concerned.

"Nothing." I plastered on a smile. "So, when are we leaving?"

"Soon," he said slowly.

"Great," I answered with a false bravado.

I pulled the blankets back and set my feet on the floor. I sidestepped Andrew, who narrowed his eyes in concern, and dragged my feet into the bathroom, shutting the door firmly behind me.

I leaned against the sink, gasping from the pain. I turned on the water and let it run to drown out any noise Andrew might hear. My skin heated up, and I found it hard to breathe. I ripped off the nightgown, leaving me only in a breast band and underwear, believing it contributed to the heat and restriction I felt in my chest.

I couldn't think clearly. I felt like a savage animal ready to bolt. Tears leaked out of my eyes. I gripped onto the sink harder, until my hands physically hurt as I stared into the mirror.

My chest heaved; my eyes darted furtively. "This isn't me," I whispered as I took in every inch of my bruised and battered body. Every bandage, every cut, every mark. "This can't be me. I can't be like this." Anxiety rocked through my frame. I let my hands slip off the marble, and I collapsed onto the floor, curling up into a fetal position as best I could.

I couldn't explain why I suddenly broke down. I felt denied; my mind and body refused to give me the relief I hungered for. I couldn't escape the images that flashed into my head with no warning. I remembered the arrows flying toward me. The way it felt when they pierced my skin. The pain when Andrew sliced into my flesh to pull them out. The blood pooling around me.

I wished I was a stranger to death and the feelings that erupted from the aftermath. I had a front-row seat to death. I knew how it felt to watch my loved ones die, and now I knew how it felt to watch an enemy die. The difference? I felt joy knowing those two men were dead, and it shattered me to pieces.

CHAPTER NINE

"I SABELLE?" ANDREW KNOCKED LIGHTLY on the door.

I didn't acknowledge him.

"Isabelle, if you don't answer me right now, I'm coming in there." He sounded stern.

I heard him ordering me to open the door, but my ears only registered background noise. I couldn't focus. I couldn't move or call out. I'd completely shut down.

The door opened, and suddenly Andrew's face clouded my vision. His mouth moved, but I couldn't understand him. I only heard unintelligible noise. He placed a hand on my forehead and then cursed. At least, I think that's what he did. I wasn't sure.

Andrew got up, and before I could stare blindly at the stone bathtub for long, he came back holding onto a rag. He put it on my forehead, and I gasped from the cold. It shocked me into reality.

"Isabelle?" He tentatively called out to me, taking the rag away, droplets of cold water dripping onto the stone floor.

"Andrew—I—I don't know—what's going on? Everything's—" I shaded my eyes and closed them. Something didn't seem right, but I didn't know what.

"You're burning up. I need to cool you down." Andrew spoke in hard, worried tones. Knowing he worried scared me.

I felt myself slipping back into delirium. It became difficult to discern present reality from disturbing hallucinations. I gazed unblinkingly at

Andrew and watched his face morph into my attacker, the mustached man from the party.

"You're going to hurt me again, aren't you?" I whispered.

I blinked, and the evil man's face vanished, and Andrew reappeared. He lifted my head into his lap and held me tenderly. "No, Isabelle, I'm not."

"Good. I'm so tired," I sighed, closing my eyes.

"I better tell Alzmire we're not going anywhere. It is going to be a long night." He sighed.

Andrew worked tirelessly over me, trying to get my body to regulate. He put me in a tepid bath. My teeth chattered, and I shivered through it. It started to help, but the second he brought me out, I went right back to where he started, burning up and delirious. I fell in and out of consciousness, falling asleep and dreaming vividly, then waking up believing that what I dreamed was real.

My mind repeatedly replayed the day of the attack. Each time it warped into something more sinister than before.

"No. Please don't shoot. Please!" I begged. I tried to move; I yanked on my arms, but they were pinned, trapped in a web of thick, gnarly roots. Absolute horror raced through my system.

The archer, swarmed in shadows, came closer, notching an arrow dripping with bright green slime. A wicked gleam shone in his startling red eyes.

"Too late," the archer said, his voice gleeful and rich as he let go of the string and the arrow zoomed. I watched it come toward me in slow motion, the green slime sliding off the arrowhead and running down the shaft as the wind propelled it forward.

I couldn't break free.

I screamed as the metal pierced my flesh.

I woke up thrashing around the blankets. "Get it out! Get it out!" I clawed at my skin, ignoring the surmounting pain as I ripped at the bandages covering my body.

Strong hands held me down as I flailed. "Isabelle, calm down!"

Hysterical, I sobbed. "Get it out."

"Get what out?" Andrew's voice cut through the disorientation.

"The poisoned arrow," I yelled, frustrated that Andrew couldn't see what I saw and felt. It had to be there; I felt it. I watched it pierce my skin.

"Isabelle." Andrew's blue eyes centered on mine. He spoke slow and clear so there would be no mistake. "There is no poisoned arrow. We got the arrows out a few days ago, remember?"

I closed my eyes and took several deep breaths. That's when truth trickled into my consciousness. There was no arrow or forest. I couldn't move because Andrew straddled me. He held me down to stop me from hurting myself unintentionally. I lay in a bed, blankets brought up all the way to my chin. I was safe.

"I remember," I mumbled, trying to hold on to awareness. "I'm sorry. These dreams are so vivid. I can't get them out of my head."

"That's the fever talking. I knew we should have taken you to a healer," he complained.

"No," I said sharply.

"Isabelle, I've done all I can, but you're still burning up. I don't know what else I can do." Andrew got off me and sat beside me, running his hands through his hair and bringing his knees up.

"Put me back in the bath water," I suggested softly. "Then ask for some peppermint tea. Keep me awake so I don't start dreaming."

"All right. But if this doesn't work then I am calling a healer over whether you like it or not." Andrew's voice gave no room for a rebuttal.

"Fine," I agreed.

He left to get things ready.

A knock came at the door, and Andrew opened it a crack requesting the tea I suggested. Within fifteen minutes Joan arrived with a tray. Andrew set it on the table.

"Everything's ready." He came over to me.

He pulled the covers off and lifted me up. Carrying me over to the bathtub, he gently slid me into the water. It wasn't until I lay in the cold water shuddering that I noticed I only wore a breast band and underwear, and I didn't even care.

"Brr. That's cold." My teeth chattered.

"Sorry." Andrew smiled apologetically.

I sank deeper into the water until only my head peeked out. It helped keep me lucid.

"I'll go get that tea." Andrew left the room, coming back with a cup. Tendrils of steam swirled from the top.

He brought it to my lips, and I sipped some. The hot liquid burned my throat as it went down. The strong smell of peppermint permeated the room and kept my senses alert.

"Thank you." I placed my hand on his arm. Water droplets dripped onto his long-sleeved shirt. "It's helping."

He touched my forehead. "Your fever is going down."

"Good," I sighed, exhausted.

"Gods forbid, Isabelle; you know how to scare a man." Andrew leaned against the bathtub and brought his knees up to his chest.

"I'm sorry." I bit my lip. "I don't mean to."

Andrew ran a hand through his hair and sighed heavily. Dark circles formed around his eyes, and his shoulders drooped, matching the stress in the crinkle of his eyes and taut lips.

"I've worked too hard to keep you alive, and this fever came out of nowhere." He held up a hand. "Just—stop pulling surprises on me, will you?" Andrew said finally. "I can't ... I ..." He fumbled for the right words, exasperation leaking into his voice as he rubbed his temples. "It's not easy."

"I'm sorry," I apologized again, not knowing what else to say.

Andrew put his head in his hands, resting his elbows on his propped knees.

His unhappiness made me want to comfort him. I realized right then and there that my feelings of attraction went far deeper. I truly cared about him. From the moment we met, I shoved my problems at him to deal with. He didn't deserve it nor was it his fault. I resented the fact that after all this time trying to be an independent woman, I couldn't do it on my own. I made him suffer for my shortcomings. I wanted to tell him that everything would be all right and he didn't need to worry so much, but I didn't know if it would be.

I reached forward to put my hand on his shoulder but stopped when I realized he had fallen asleep, I suspected unintentionally. I decided not to wake him. The sky, dark through the small window in the bathroom, indicated that it was the middle of the night. No wonder Andrew fell asleep.

I started feeling better as the fever went down. My mind stayed clear though I shivered uncontrollably in the cold water. Andrew shook himself awake with a gasp. Bleary-eyed, he glanced at me once, then pulled the stack of towels from the shelf. "Wake me if you need me," he mumbled, resting his head on the stack of towels.

"Sure," I agreed.

I went over every experience I had over the past few days. From Mava's wedding, the first attempt to grab me, Joshua's letter, the attack, meeting Andrew, and everything in between. I shoved the hard parts of my journey to a back corner of my mind, hoping that if I worked on the physical, I could get over the emotional. Maybe if I didn't have to see the injuries, I could pretend it was a bad dream.

Dawn approached when I finally felt stable enough to get out of the water. By then, my skin shriveled up until I reminded myself of rotten fruit. Andrew slept without so much as a snore, his head resting on the blue towels. *Great, I'd have to wake him.*

I gently touched his shoulder, and he jolted awake, throwing his hands up. I laughed at his bleary-eyed expression.

"How long was I asleep?" Andrew asked, rubbing his eyes.

"It's almost dawn," I answered.

"Gods forbid. I'm sorry." He ran a hand through his hair, shaking his head as he opened and closed his eyes.

"It's fine. I only woke you 'cause you've been sleeping on the towels." I pointed at the pile of towels on the floor.

"Towel, right." Andrew reached for a blue towel. "How's your fever?" He held the towel in one hand and placed his other hand on my forehead. "You're cool. That's good."

"I feel better. I think it's gone. I'm not delirious anymore at least," I answered.

"Good."

Awkward silence ensued, and I figured he forgot the reason why I woke him up.

"Andrew?"

"Yes?"

"The towel."

"Oh. Right." He quickly stood, holding the towel out wide.

"Look away," I instructed.

Andrew turned his head away and stared at the floor. "I'm not looking."

I stood, trembling, and wrapped the towel around my shivering body. I stepped out of the bathtub. "I'm sorry, you probably saw more of me than either of us wanted, but given the circumstances, thank you for trying to help."

I wanted to clear the air right then and there. It did not bother me that Andrew left me in the breast band and underwear. He did what he could to get the fever down, and being alive mattered more than a little indecency.

"It wasn't that difficult," Andrew said with a tired smile. "The beauty you possess in your face is enough to capture my attention."

I shook my head, disbelieving, having seen the bruises on my cheekbones, forehead, and jaw. "Perhaps we should take you to a healer to check your eyes. Unless you're partial to black and blue."

"Actually, my favorite color is green. The same shade as your eyes, and I have perfect eyesight, thank you." He searched my face. "Those bruises can't hide everything. There's nothing wrong with your smile, and when you're frustrated, you wear the cutest pout I've ever seen. Your bottom lip juts out just a little bit, and your eyebrows crease."

"Oh." I stared at the floor, trembling from his words instead of the cold water.

"Do you need anything else?" Andrew asked as he rubbed his face.

The bandages and jars of medicines were scattered around the bathroom vanity near the mirror. A robe hung on the back of the door.

"No. I think I can do it myself. I need to try anyway," I answered.

"Fine. Let me know if you need anything." He strode out of the room, closing the door softly behind him.

I walked over to the sink and started going through the bottles, reading every label. I picked up a green bottle I hadn't noticed before. *Where did this come from?* The label read, "Blemish be gone! Face cream to hide any unsightly blemish." In small print, it contained an added clause, "Intended for face only. Apply directly over blemishes and wait for results. May cause a temporary tingling sensation."

I gazed in the mirror, saw the ghastly bruises, and grimaced. *Worth a try.* I poured some of the green cream onto my hand and rubbed it into my face. As it suggested, I felt a slight tingling, tickling, sensation, and I giggled. As the green cream soaked into my skin, my face became clear of all cuts and bruises.

"Gods forbid." I touched my face and felt no pain.

Now realizing the bottle had magic as an ingredient, I picked it up to search for indicators. Nothing. I peeked inside the bottle. The cream didn't shimmer like the purple bottle I had. I would have never suspected it. Shouldn't they have put a warning label or something on it?

My eyes darted back and forth in the mirror, seeking out every part of my face. *I can't say I'm not happy with the results.* I bit my lip, deciding not to care. I had bigger problems to deal with than a magical face cream.

I touched my face again and whispered a heartfelt thank you to no one in particular.

Suddenly Haldren's face appeared in the mirror, a smile resting on his lips. "You're welcome." He disappeared before I could respond.

I raised my eyebrows in surprise. His interest in me had definitely started to become unnerving.

Having a clear face gave me courage to tackle the rest of my injuries. I applied salves and bandaged everything. When I finished and wrapped the robe around my body, I strolled out of the bathroom with my self-confidence boosted. I felt like a new woman masking hidden pain.

Andrew casually whittled the block of wood. The noise from the door closing alerted him to my presence. He looked up, and his lips parted as his eyes widened. "Isabelle. Your face. What did you do?"

"Haldren left me a little gift—a magical healing face cream," I explained.

Andrew raised an eyebrow, and his hand tightened on the block of wood that had yet to take on a discernible shape. "Haldren?" He set the block of wood and knife on the table.

I hobbled closer to him. "His face appeared in the mirror a minute ago." I leaned on the table.

He pursed his lips, and his eyebrows furrowed.

"I don't know about you, but I've been taught since birth not to offend a God. I know it's strange and puzzling, but frankly I'm afraid I'll insult him if I keep questioning why he's helping me." I put my hand on Andrew's shoulder. "Unless you're willing to tell me something I don't know." I let go of his shoulder.

Andrew rubbed his chin as he contemplated. "No, you're right. I think it would be a bad idea to refuse his generosity." He held up a finger. "Just know this: Gods are fickle. When they take an interest, you start walking on a narrow plank of wood over a deadly canyon."

"Then I must choose my steps carefully," I said, grateful for the warning.

"Please do." Andrew propped his elbow on the table and rested his chin in his hand. He shook his head, staring at me unashamedly. "Gods forbid you're beautiful."

I slapped him lightly on the shoulder with my good hand. "Don't joke."

He held his hand over his heart, mockingly offended. "I do not joke."

I didn't believe him, not when I knew he could have any girl he wanted. I sauntered past him and into the closet, searching for something to wear.

All the clothes from my cream-colored bag had been hung up. I browsed through my selection of clothes and what Andrew acquired. My fingers skimmed the garments, then stilled at once as my eye caught sight of an azure gown. I rubbed the material between my fingers. Silk with an overlay of lilac chiffon. Diamonds hung like gems at the neckline. I'd never seen anything so gorgeous or expensive.

A note was attached to the sleeve. I unpinned it and read:

**Wear this and you'll be the Belle of
the ball —Haldren**

I bit my lip, worried. Everything else he had given me thus far possessed some element of magic. There was a high chance that this dress had magic in it as well. What would happen if I put it on? I pulled it off the hanger, half expecting something to occur. A minute passed by, then two, but nothing changed. Andrew's warning played in the back of my mind. I needed to stay in Haldren's good graces.

The note from Haldren I held in my left hand suddenly glowed. I yelped and dropped it. As it fluttered to the ground I noticed something else had been written.

**You worry too much, child. The
dress is safe. —Haldren**

"Thank you," I said to Haldren, knowing he could hear me even if I couldn't see him.

I held the dress in my arms, cherishing the soft material. I opened up the closet door, taking it with me.

"What's that?" Andrew eyed the dress warily.

"Another gift from Haldren," I answered.

"Breakfast is coming," he informed me. "You might want to eat before you put on that dress."

"Right."

I hung the dress up on the back of the bathroom door. Joan, the innkeeper, came in with a large tray. A maid trailed behind with cider.

"You're looking better today." She smiled at me.

"I am feeling much better, thank you," I said politely.

They set the tray on the table, curtsied to the Prince, and hurried out of the room.

A soft knock came at the door a few minutes later. Andrew answered it. Returning to the table, he clutched a note. He opened it and chuckled. "Alzmire doesn't miss a beat," he said.

"What did it say?" I set my fork down.

"Don't weasel out. Be ready by nine," Andrew said, sliding the note across the table.

Underneath the words, Alzmire added a drawing of a grinning weasel shackled to a ball and chain.

I smiled and set my fork down. "Andrew?"

"Yes?"

"What if the archer is in Thimbleton and sees me in the parade? What if I see him?" I took a deep breath and exhaled, attempting to quell my worries.

Andrew set his cup down. "Then we will surround ourselves with guards. He'd have to go through them and me before he got to you."

"But he's an archer. What if he perches on some rooftop and shoots down?" I persisted.

"Then I'll have guards in the crowd and on the rooftops," he countered. "If you do see him, then discreetly point him out to me, and I will alert the guards." He reached over and put his hand on mine. "I promise I will keep you safe."

"Thank you," I whispered, my heart gushing with gratitude.

Andrew met my eyes and spoke with care. "Your safety is a huge concern for me, but I also have a duty to my people. I have to abide by the rules of the Walk and mingle with the citizens. Saying no to Alzmire's invitation would be considered a transgression. It would be something people could use against me when I ascend the throne—that I refused my obligations."

"I understand," I said. I wanted Andrew to succeed.

He finished eating before I did and slipped into the bathroom to get ready.

My breath caught in my throat when he came out wearing his best traveling clothes, his hair wet and combed. Even if we were only meant to be friends, I couldn't ignore his handsomeness.

"You look nice."

"Thank you." He smiled lightly.

I brushed past him, breathing in the strong cinnamon and woodsy cologne he wore as I tottered into the bathroom. Slipping on the dress felt delightful. It accentuated every curve, fitting like a glove with no way to tell that I was bandaged and battered underneath it. It hid every mark on my body. For a moment while I stared in the mirror, I felt whole. No pain, no sorrow, just feminine and beautiful. Exactly what I needed after everything I had suffered through.

I braided part of my hair and tied it back, leaving the rest of it down. It naturally curled into little ringlets, giving me less to style. I took one deep breath before leaving the bathroom. *Nothing can stop me today.*

Andrew's back was turned away from me as I closed the bathroom door behind me.

"I'm ready," I said.

Andrew spun around, his jaw plummeting open as he admired me. He cleared his throat. "You—you—"

I smiled. "Yes?"

"You don't look the same," he said lamely. He ran a hand through his hair and muttered something inaudible. Shaking his head, he stared down at his feet.

"Of course I don't. It's the first time you've seen me in a dress." I gestured to my attire. "I am allowed to be feminine now and again."

Andrew's face turned red. He opened his mouth and closed it again, apparently at a loss for words.

"Shall we go?" I asked after we stood there for a minute in complete silence.

He nodded, not taking his eyes off me. He grabbed my hand, and together we left the room.

What's come over him? I thought, perplexed. *It's just a dress.* Could he be rethinking his refusal of me? I dared not hope.

CHAPTER TEN

AND IN HAND WE slowly made our way down the stairs. The maids dusting the framed paintings stared wide-eyed, several shooting me disdainful and, to my surprise, jealous looks out of the view of Andrew. "Please tell me we are going to Alzmire's tonight."

Andrew swiveled his head around searching for the source of my embarrassment. "What am I missing?"

I sighed. "Just get me my own room tonight. Please."

"After the parade. We'll go to Alzmire's," Andrew assured me.

"Good." I tried to straighten out my posture as we walked, but it put more strain on my injuries. I had to live with the limp, but I'd take it. Today I wanted to feel like somebody else. Step into another girl's life without my worries swirling over my head like a mini tornado ready to swallow me up.

Andrew wouldn't take his eyes off me. He beheld me like a boy beholding an array of sweets.

It unsettled me. "Stop looking at me like I'm something you desire out of a window shop."

"I can't help it. You are dazzling." He held up his hands in surrender.

A man opened the door to his room and stepped out, nearly bumping into me.

"Oh, I'm sorry, miss," he quickly apologized.

"It's quite all right," I said demurely.

He gazed at me openly for a minute, his mouth slacking as his eyes raked me over. I wondered if he even noticed the Prince standing beside me. I smiled briefly and pulled on Andrew's hand to start moving again. That was the second person who'd stared at me that way. *What did Haldren put in this dress?* What did they see that I didn't?

At the first level, a little boy ranging around six or seven poked his head out the door.

"Da." He fixated on me. "There's a real fancy lady. I think it might be a princess."

"Quit your yapping. S'not true," a man said from inside the room. "We don't have no princess."

I flashed my best smile and corrected him. "I'm not a princess, but he is a prince." I indicated Andrew with the tilt of my head.

He gawked at me. "Da. She just spoke to me. The princess lady is with a prince," he yelled.

"If I hear one more lie come out of your mouth, I'll make sure you don't go to the parade," the father said sternly. "Now get back in here and shut the door."

The boy reared his head back and slammed the door.

We reached the front hall just as Alzmire strode through the front doors. He beamed when he saw us at the bottom of the stairs. "My, Isabelle, you look perfectly stunning. What did you do?"

"Face cream." I shrugged, quickly hiding my wince. "I found the dress in the closet."

Alzmire turned to Andrew. "You should take lessons from her." He pointed at me. "She knows how to dress for a parade."

"Cut me some slack. I'm on my Walk. I can't wear anything extravagant," Andrew said.

"Fine. At least wear this." Alzmire procured a deep-blue sash from his pocket.

"Agreed." Andrew slipped it over his shirt. "Now there's something we need to discuss before we leave."

Andrew pulled Alzmire aside. I sat on a bench and let them talk in hurried whispers. Alzmire nodded a lot, his eyes darting back to me occasionally. When they finished speaking, Alzmire went to the front desk and asked Joan if he could send a message. Andrew stood by me, resting his hands on the back of the bench.

"What was that about?"

Andrew leaned down. "Guards. I promised I would keep you safe."

A guard marched in ten minutes later. He caught sight of Alzmire and strode directly over to him. "Everything is ready, Lord Alzmire."

"Perfect." Alzmire waved us over.

Outside, an entourage of soldiers on horses waited for us. They bowed, then kept their faces impassive. Not a cloud could be seen in the clear blue sky, and a soft breeze tickled my face.

"You have options," Alzmire said. "You can ride in an open carriage or on a horse."

Andrew turned to me. "What would you prefer?"

"I wouldn't mind taking Nisha," I answered, shielding my eyes from the sun as I tilted my face up to see Andrew. "I can ride sidesaddle."

"Can you handle him on your own? He is a big horse." Concern showed on his face.

I nodded. "I'll be fine. I know how to ride."

Alzmire smiled and clapped his hands. "Great. I have the perfect horse for you, Andrew." He snapped his fingers, and a boy trotted over, holding on the reins of a blinding white horse. "This is Snow. She's a little spirited but loves attention. She's a great show horse."

Andrew nodded. Grabbing onto the reins, he greeted the horse. "She'll do."

Andrew led Nisha out of the stables while I sat on a bench and waited.

"It's not often you have to ask a horse for consent to ride," he muttered as he helped me hop on.

"I'm sure he appreciates it all the same." I rubbed Nisha's neck. "Don't you, Nisha?"

Nisha neighed. *"Yes."*

Guards flanked us on all sides as we rode through the crowded cobbled streets to the start of the parade. My eyes soaked in everything from the throngs of people to the brightly colored shops. I couldn't get enough of the liveliness.

"I want you front and center," Alzmire called over his shoulder. He rode a chestnut mare, her mane and tail braided with flowers and blue ribbons.

We turned a corner and my breath caught in my throat. A horde of people converged together, conversing loudly. Acrobats, jugglers, musicians, animal handlers, and many more acts that I had no name for. Everyone wore bright colors, and I blinked slowly as my eyes adjusted.

"This is what a parade is?" I asked Andrew.

"You've never seen a parade before?" he asked, glancing over at me.

I shook my head. The idea of Saren putting on a parade sounded absurd. I imagined a bunch of farmers walking down Shop Street proudly displaying their favorite farm tool with a little boy juggling eggs as the finale. The thought made me chuckle.

"I have participated in many parades, though I have never actually watched a full procession. They always put me front and center. It's the worst spot because I never get to see the acts behind me perform. One of these days I'll find someone with a resemblance to me and he can pretend to be me while I hide in the crowds and watch the whole thing," Andrew said with a hopeful expression.

"Andrew, how am I supposed to spot the archer with these crowds?" I asked, eyeing the masses doubtfully.

"The guards, Alzmire, and I have a description of him. You won't be the only one looking," he said.

"All right, everyone!" Alzmire cupped his hands in front of his mouth and shouted to the throngs of people. "Prince Andrew and Lady Isabelle are the front-runners, and behind them I want the jugglers and acrobats to line up." He started going down the line shouting orders for everyone to line up in their proper places. After a while of shouting he rode back up to us. "Ready?"

"Yes," everyone shouted in unison.

"Start!" A shower of rainbow sparks flew out of his hands and lit up the sky.

We reached the beginning of the waiting crowd; cheers went up as people waiting on the sidewalks saw the parade rolling forth. Never in my life had I seen so much activity. Bouncing children pulled on their mothers' skirts and pointed. Fathers lifted their toddlers to see better. Lots of laughter and smiles. The noise was incredible.

Every so often Alzmire sent up a shower of rainbow sparks. It never ceased to catch my attention when the sparks dazzled in the air and showered down into the street, transforming into a silver glitter and dusting everything in sight.

We turned down Vendors Street. Between the shop buildings and the road, people set up booths to sell their merchandise. A large aisle ran through the middle for the parade. The majority of the townspeople converged on Vendors Street, taking up every space available. Guards stationed themselves at intersecting lanes, turning away carts, carriages, and horsemen. Shouts rent the air as the townspeople recognized Prince Andrew. People screamed, laughed, and bowed, then laughed some more.

"Highness!"

"Prince!" "Our future King of Aberron!"

I should have expected it, but it still stunned me to see how much love Andrew received. Young maidens literally threw flowers and handkerchiefs at him hoping to catch his eye. Several shouted their confessions of love, and one group of ladies chanted, "Make me your Princess."

A young lady attempted to run out in front of Andrew's horse. Two guards raced to circumvent her and grabbed onto her shoulders. They held her in place as she professed her undying love and adoration. Andrew held up a hand and stopped the procession. He directed Snow over to the lady and slid off. Picking up a rose from the ground, he handed it to her and kissed the back of her hand. His words to her got lost in the noise of the crowd. Andrew hopped back on Snow and beckoned for the parade to continue.

As Nisha trotted forward, I glanced over my shoulder at the lady. The guards held her up by her arms as she sagged, in a daze.

I abruptly felt inadequate riding next to such glory. I lost my smile. *Why am I in a parade, riding next to the illustrious Prince Andrew?* What made me important enough to deserve his attention? Nothing, except the fact that his father forced him to keep an eye on me. I couldn't understand why the King made him in the first place. He didn't know me. I shouldn't be here. My resentment for our situation came bubbling up to the surface.

I felt unwanted and unworthy, a broken farm girl put on display in a fancy dress. I kept my movement minimal and didn't even wave. It hurt too much to try. I stared blithely, not focusing on anything until I saw the little boy from the inn jump out into the road.

"Beautiful lady! It's the princess lady!" He hopped up and down. His father yanked him to the side of the road as we trotted past.

Andrew caught eyes with mine and laughed. "Looks like you got yourself a name. Beautiful Lady." He pulled on the reins of Snow and moved closer. Grabbing my right hand, he lifted it in a cheer. Then he started shouting the nickname the little boy gave me. "Beautiful Lady!"

The crowd caught on swiftly, and they shouted Beautiful Lady with Prince Andrew. Amazed at the power Andrew held, I laughed at his careless smile and the silliness of it all.

As I played along, I wondered about his motives. Wouldn't people see him holding my hand as a unified front? And yet, we were connected by nothing but a barely molded link of friendship. I didn't understand, and I wanted to remove my hand from his.

Andrew leaned closer to me, grinning ear to ear and showing his perfectly white teeth. "Your smile is infectious."

I shook my head and scoffed. Though I couldn't hold onto the gloom and confusion for long, as the atmosphere drew me in. The parade's enthusiasm spread like a wildfire through the people, finally catching up with me.

Behind us the jugglers juggled, and the dancers danced. Imported little monkeys waved flags of Aberron and flags displaying the King's crest. Andrew held on to my hand for the rest of the parade, forcing Nisha and

Snow to ride close to each other. Nisha didn't seem to mind, but I didn't think to ask him.

Showers of color sparkled above us, dusting our heads with glitter, and in that moment riding down a street with hundreds screaming at us, I felt, *dare I say it?* Happy.

The parade route ended at a park. Throughout the parade, my eyes scanned the faces of many people, but I didn't see the archer among them. I breathed a sigh of relief, grateful that I had made it through unharmed. Alzmire thanked everyone who made it possible, and they dispersed into the city.

We followed Alzmire to a pavilion set up in the park. We sat and sipped tea and munched on pastries. with small slabs of ham, cheese, and bread.

"I think that went well; what do you think?" Alzmire beamed, sloshing his cup of tea.

Andrew smiled. "Alzmire, you have officially outdone yourself this time. I have never seen such artistry in a parade. My father will want to recruit you for Carasmille."

Alzmire shook his head, holding up a hand. "Oh no. One parade is enough, thank you. Still, I agree, I really have outdone myself. What am I going to do next year?" he mused, putting a hand to his chin, then burst out laughing, slapping the table.

"You'll think of something. You always do." Andrew picked up a small tart and popped it into his mouth.

"Do you arrange the parade every year?" I asked, fidgeting with the napkin in my lap.

"Yes, I do. It's a little hobby of mine. I put this together during my free time when I'm not teaching," he explained, grabbing a cookie.

I nodded and let the men start up a conversation on their own. Though I tried to hide it, Andrew sensed the weariness I felt. When he said we needed to leave, Alzmire agreed, promising to meet us at his home later that evening. The prospect of getting my own room considerably lightened my mood.

We left the table and ambled to the stables. Two hostlers brought our horses to us. Both had nice things to say about Snow and Nisha, and it made me feel proud that, temporarily, I had a great horse. The guards returned to escort us. I appreciated that Andrew took my concerns seriously. It took us longer than expected to get to the inn because Andrew stopped multiple times along the way to talk to townspeople.

Andrew glanced at me with a rueful smile. "One minute. This will be the last one, I swear." He swung off his horse and approached a group of men. "How are you liking Thimbleton?"

"You really want to know?" one of the men asked, appraising Andrew.

"Yes." He nodded.

"Well, boys, now's our chance. Anybody got concerns?" The spokesman of the group turned around and eyed his friends.

I tuned them out, having heard Andrew ask this question eight times before. Instead, I asked Nisha how he liked the parade. He said he enjoyed the attention. I wondered how long he would stay with me, but I didn't want to ask him, afraid he'd leave sooner than I wanted.

"We work for a man we never see. All of us are tired of the letters telling us how to do our jobs," the spokesperson complained.

"Thank you for telling me your concerns," Andrew said. "Unfortunately, I cannot force Alzmire to leave the Sorrenian, but I will talk to him." He bid the men goodbye and hopped on his horse.

The guards waited outside while we went in to pack.

The morning flurry of patrons had subsided. We saw only the hustle of maids rushing to clean rooms, carrying armfuls of sheets and towels in preparation for tonight's guests. Andrew and I carefully navigated around them as they hurried with their heads buried in the sheets. I enjoyed that they were too busy to stare at me with disdain.

We packed quickly. Andrew took my bag and slung it over his shoulder. He gripped my hand firmly and slowly led me down the stairs. I took them extra slow this time, as I had started to feel the wear on my body.

Andrew led me to the bench. I sat while he informed the innkeeper Joan that we would not be there another night. She fussed over him, asking how he liked his stay and lamenting that he had to leave so soon. Andrew assured her that the accommodations had been excellent.

"Have you found a separate room for your lady friend then?" she asked, glancing at me.

"I have." Andrew smiled.

"At another inn?" Her lower lip trembled.

I could tell the thought of him taking his business elsewhere deeply bothered her. He assured her we would be with a friend.

Andrew tied our packs to Snow, then gave the reins to a guard and rode with me instead. He kept me steady as we trotted through the bustling city. The ride to Alzmire's house tired me. I leaned my head back, and the noise of the city faded to the background. Exhausted, I closed my eyes. I briefly remembered Andrew gently lifting me off Nisha and carrying me into a house.

He lay me on a bed. "Sleep," he whispered.

"Mmm," I mumbled. I decided I was dreaming when I felt Andrew kiss the top of my head.

"Isabelle." Andrew gently prodded me awake.

"What?" I asked blearily, my eyes still closed.

"Isabelle, darling, I need you to wake up."

I stiffened; all sleepiness evaporated within a second. Andrew called me darling. My eyes flew open, and I stared at him, wide-eyed in disbelief. He chuckled. My senses took hold then. First my sense of smell as I breathed slowly in and out. The room smelled … old? I sat up. Dark gray curtains covered most of the windows, shrouding us in a dim light. All the pieces of furniture, save one chair in the large room, had white sheets draped over them. Their silhouettes indicated the type of furniture underneath: tables, chairs, and lounges. A big empty house indeed—empty of people, not furniture. I wondered when Alzmire last had visitors.

"Are you up for a short excursion to Silverdens?" Andrew asked. "I've just got a note from Alzmire. He said there's a man there with information about the archer. Also, there's an arrow lodged in the wall, and he wants us to look at it. See if it's the right man."

I nodded. "Yes. Let's go." I stumbled out of bed and realized I still wore the dress. I bit my lip. "Allow me a few minutes to freshen up before we go?"

Andrew pointed me to the bathroom. He had already unpacked my bottles of medicines and bandages. I would thank him when I came out. I undressed slowly, and my heart sank when I beheld my battered body. A stark reminder of everything I wanted to forget, it felt like a slap in the face.

I unraveled all the bandages and added more healing salves to every cut and bruise I could find. Holding back so much pain while I enjoyed what the Harvest Festival offered had taken a toll. My body begged for the soothing relief of the cold creams. Despite sitting whenever possible, my leg showed minimal improvement. Deftly I rewrapped everything with new linen and slipped the dress back on. I lightly brushed my hair by the mirror. *There, now I can pretend again.*

"I think everything's all right," I said to Andrew, leaving the bathroom refreshed. "Thank you for putting the supplies out."

"You're welcome." He smiled.

"I take it Alzmire doesn't stay here very often, does he? Or have many visitors?" I asked casually as Andrew led me through the large mansion. Just like my room, everything had a white sheet draped over it. I discerned some of the shapes: a table and chairs, a painting, a suit of armor. Every wall had been painted a muted gray, the stones underneath my feet, a light tan.

As we entered the stable Nisha tossed his head at us, then looked away, as if our presence annoyed him. *"I am not leaving. Find another horse."*

"Did you catch that?" I asked Andrew.

He nodded. "We can take Snow." Andrew inclined his head to the stall beside Nisha's. "I won't break up a newfound friendship."

I followed his gaze, noting the pretty, cream-colored mare, its head bent close to Nisha's.

We rode Snow together. Alzmire's house resided a little way out of the main city. We rode alone on a winding dirt path, passing harvested fields at twilight, moving to the flickering lights and noise.

"You sure you're up to this?" Andrew asked, weaving his fingers through mine. His lips pursed in concern.

I stared down at our entwined hands, slightly in shock at Andrew's audacity.

We paused on the front steps of Silverdens. A soft glow emanated from the cracks in the front door, and the windows burst with candlelight. Clinking dishes and raucous laughter could be heard from the sidewalk.

I'd never entered a pub before, and my stomach filled with butterflies. *What would Nathan and Adel think?* They preferred staying home over going out. Though truth be told, our local pub lacked decorum. Farmers went in there to share horror stories of failed crops and complain about their hard labor. I took a deep breath. Now was not the time to think about Saren.

I nodded. "Lead the way."

CHAPTER ELEVEN

NDREW APPRAISED ME, SEARCHING for indecision. I forced myself to keep my face impassive, though underneath I trembled with uncertainty.

"All right." He stopped a man walking up the steps. "I'll give you a Sundal if you find Lord Alzmire and ask him to come out here."

The man licked his lips. "Right away, Highness." He rushed inside and came out two minutes later with Alzmire.

Andrew flipped the man a coin. He snatched it and walked in with a new bounce in his step.

"Good, you got my note." Alzmire smiled.

Andrew nodded. "Sorry to make you come out here. I had to make sure you wrote it."

"Naturally," Alzmire agreed.

Huge, crowded, and noisy, the pub was littered with wooden tables and the men and women lounging about them. The air reeked with stale smoke and ale. Many tables had an overabundance of food that spilled onto the floor, underneath the table and chairs. A band of musicians played a lively tune. People danced, others played cards, but most chatted with sloppy grins and drinks sloshing in their hands.

The entire room quieted and gawked when they noticed Andrew's arrival. Despite not wearing anything that would draw attention to him, he couldn't be missed flanked by Alzmire and me. They'd surely seen us in the parade together. I wondered if he ever got the chance to be inconspicuous.

"Every time," Andrew muttered.

Everyone observed us as we passed, some with interest and others bland-ly, but soon conversations started back up, the music played again, and people danced jovially with drinks leaking out of their hands onto the wooden floor. Andrew, a true gentleman, pulled a chair out and gestured for me to sit before he did.

A young maiden rushed up to us. She curtsied, her cheeks flushed, then asked Andrew what we wanted to drink. Andrew ordered silver water for the both of us, then politely declined the offer of food. I shot him a thankful smile. I didn't think I could eat anything even if I tried.

"What is silver water?" I asked.

"It's just water with peppermint flavoring. It's quite good and clears your mind," he explained, leaning back in his chair.

"Why not a real drink?" I asked, tucking a stray hair behind my ear.

He leaned in close and spoke quickly and softly, his breath tickling my ear. "I prefer to have a clear mind with so many people around. Keeps me sharp if someone tries to pull something."

I nodded in understanding as Andrew leaned back in his chair. Our drinks arrived. I tentatively sipped and tasted peppermint. I lolled it around my tongue.

"What do you think?" Andrew tilted his head and eyed me.

I swallowed. "It's good; different. We drink mostly cider in Saren."

"They don't have mint-flavored drinks?" Andrew asked.

"Why would they? It's a specialty here; full of flavor and not an ounce of liquor," Alzmire said, setting his drink down.

Andrew chuckled. "Sometimes I forget since the chef at home makes every specialty in Aberron." He turned to Alzmire. "Now about this in-formation you have. Who did you want me to talk to?"

Alzmire pointed discreetly to the gray-haired man shuffling cards at the table in front of us. His eyes locked on Alzmire's and he nodded once, his hands blurring around the cards. Alzmire subtly reciprocated the gesture. "His name is Barry. He's a bit of a card shark and known for gambling with anyone with a coin in their pocket."

"And he gambled with the archer, I take it?" Andrew asked, appraising the man.

Alzmire nodded. "Last night."

"How did you acquire this information?" Andrew sipped his drink.

"Oh, I didn't go fishing for it, if that's what you're asking," Alzmire said. "I overheard him talking to his tablemates while I waited for a worker of mine to meet with me. I caught the tail end of his story and then heard him express an interest in playing against you, so I sent the note. He promised to give me the whole story if I brought you along."

A man sitting with Barry tilted backward in his chair, cards in hand. He went too far and fell over. His head hit our table and Andrew and Alzmire gripped the edges to keep it upright as our drinks sloshed unsteadily. His friends erupted in laughter. The man got up from the floor, dusting food and grime off his shirt.

"'Scuse me, Highness." He bowed to Andrew. "My lady." He nodded in my direction. "Lord Alzmire."

"Ah, Trevor, how many times do I have to tell you not to lean back in these chairs? They aren't like the ones at home," a lady said to him. Shaking her head, she made a disapproving noise.

His face turned red. "I know." He bent down and started gathering up the cards he dropped.

"Well, Trevor, since you rudely interrupted the Prince's party, you might as well ask if they want to join our game," Barry said, setting his cards down.

"Oh, right, yeah sorry." He faced us again. "Would you care to join our card game?"

Andrew politely agreed. We joined our two tables together for more room.

"Allow us to introduce ourselves," Barry said. "I'm Barry." He pointed to himself. "This is Melina, Tessa, Jaydon, and Trevor you met already."

I suspected Melina and Tessa might be sisters, with their matching blonde hair and blue eyes. Jaydon had flaming red hair, a thick build, and a handlebar mustache. Trevor contrasted them all with curly, jet-black hair and a goatee. He had a devilish glint in his chocolate-brown eyes.

"A pleasure to meet you all," Andrew murmured. "I assume you know Alzmire, and this is Isabelle." He gestured to me.

I nodded, acknowledging his introduction.

"So you do have a name, Beautiful Lady." Trevor grinned.

I smiled curtly. "Yes."

"So what's the game?" Andrew steered the conversation away.

"Pilfer." Trevor grinned greedily and rubbed his hands together.

We played several rounds of Pilfer, a betting game with cards and dice, and chatted casually with one another. Alzmire nonchalantly brought up the archer. Barry focused his attention on Andrew as he recounted the story, while everyone else watched and listened.

"So this man comes in last night, absolutely filthy. Pine needles in his hair, dirt smudged on his scruffy face and covering his clothes. I asked him where he'd been, and he said he just left the forest of Trivail. I noticed he carried a bow, so I asked if he'd been hunting. 'Yes,' he said. 'I went hunting.' Then he laughed, hysterical. He ordered drinks one after another, something about a tribute to his brother. When I had taken all the money he had to offer, he stood and stumbled over to the musicians."

Barry took a sip of his ale. "First he started dancing, wildly, then he started singing about his lost love in Nistier. His singing was so atrocious that half the room covered their ears. Hank," he titled his head, indicating the large, burly man behind the counter, casually pouring drinks, "was about to escort him out, when he suddenly pulled out his bow and notched an arrow. He started screaming about being a good shot and that it wasn't his fault. Hank tackled him to the ground, and the arrow went flying into the wall. You can see it over there." He pointed to an arrow lodged in the wall above Hank's head. I peered at the arrow and gulped. I recognized the brown-and-white striped fletching. "As he shoved him out the door, he kept screaming about needing to get to Carasmille."

"Good thing we didn't show up last night like you wanted, Trevor," Tessa said.

Everyone in the group nodded.

"I must congratulate Hank on his quick reflexes," Andrew murmured, glancing at the arrow.

"Hank is a good man," Barry said, shuffling the cards. "While most pubs in Thimbleton make you hang your weapons by the door, he lets you carry them with the unspoken promise that you'll behave. He gets more business than the others for that, but sometimes it comes at a cost." He set his cards down. "Now who's up for another round?"

The mood shifted. Barry passed out the cards and dice, and we played several more rounds of Pilfer.

Trevor turned out to be a bit of a character. He laughed carelessly and took high-stake risks. Unfortunately for him, he couldn't mask his intentions, and most of his risks didn't end up in his favor. By the fifth round, he was penniless.

"I think you're out, Trevor," Barry said, his smile gradually bigger as he raked in the coins, adding them to his large pile. A master of the game, his unreadable face nearly beat out Andrew.

"Now wait just a minute, I still got more to offer." Trevor pointed a dirty finger at Barry.

"What can that be? We've taken all of your money," Barry said lazily, leaning back in his chair. The cards became a blur in his fingers as he shuffled them.

I wondered what he would offer. It couldn't be much, considering he had empty pockets and ragged clothes. But that didn't seem to deter him.

"We play for dares." He grinned. "I throw in one dare as the ante. If I lose, then the winner must dare me to do something. But if I win, then I keep the winnings like normal."

"What kind of dares?" Jaydon asked, resting a hand on his chin.

"Nothing that will get me in trouble, of course. No stealing or whatnot." He glanced furtively at Andrew.

"I could use a good laugh," Andrew said.

The rest of us nodded. Barry passed out the deck. Surprisingly, I had decent cards. If I rolled the dice right, I had a chance of winning. It didn't take long for half the group to bow out as the game progressed.

Trevor sat on the edge of his seat. Sweat poured on his brow as he gripped onto the cards with his dirty fingers. I added one silver Moonel to the pile and waited. Barry added three silver Moonels. Eventually, it came down to Trevor and me.

"All right, lay down your cards," Trevor said.

We laid down our cards simultaneously, discovering identical matches. I picked up the dice and Trevor held another pair in his hand. Whoever had the highest roll would win.

"On the count of three, roll your dice," Barry instructed. "One, two, three."

We shook the dice and let them fall. They hit the table and rolled.

"Eight is higher than six. Isabelle wins." Barry picked up the dice.

Trevor cursed and pounded his fist into the table.

I dragged the pile of mostly Moonels and Starlets to me and faced Trevor. "So when do you pay up for that dare?"

"Now I suppose." He sighed heavily. "I really thought I had it that time. Tomas is not helping me tonight."

"I'm pretty sure Tomas has always favored Barry. You know he only loses two games out of ten." Melina smiled.

"You're lucky I control your finances and allot an amount for betting, otherwise you'd be out of home and food," Tessa said.

Trevor grinned and kissed Tessa on the cheek. "My fair maiden saves the day."

I glanced at Andrew. "What should he do?"

He shrugged. "I don't know, but make it funny."

"You're a great help," I said drily.

"How good of a dancer are you?" I questioned Trevor.

"Fair." Trevor fidgeted in his seat.

"Ask if you can clear the dance floor and dance solo for everyone." I smiled. "That's reasonable, right?" I waited a few seconds for someone to disagree, but no one did. "Just ... no singing, and you better inform Hank before you start." I didn't want him kicked out for something I had come up with.

The group laughed.

"A little dance? No problem." He got up and ambled over to Hank. Hank eyed us and nodded. Then Trevor strolled over to the musicians.

The dance floor cleared within a minute. The musicians played a spirited tune. Trevor flailed his arms and spun in circles, dancing with an imaginary maiden. The whole room laughed, and the more belligerent people whooped and hollered.

I observed Andrew watching Trevor make a fool of himself. He chuckled softly, seeming untroubled and carefree. He caught my eye and grinned. I turned away, my cheeks flaming.

Andrew stood and addressed Trevor. "You're doing it wrong."

Trevor paused midstep. "What?"

"It's three steps to the right and two back, followed by a heel turn," Andrew corrected.

Trevor bowed. "Care to demonstrate?"

Andrew stood and faced me, his deep blue eyes gently gazing into mine. He held out his calloused hand. "Dance with me?"

I wanted to refuse. What happened to our agreement? Dancing had to be more strenuous than hobbling. Could my leg handle it? And yet, Andrew asked so tenderly that I couldn't deny him. I put my hand in his and let him lead me to the dance floor.

"Just watch me," he told Trevor.

Andrew held my waist and clasped my right hand in his. I put my left hand on his waist. My injuries made it impossible for me to reach his shoulder. The music shifted to a slow melody. I let him twirl me around slowly and gently. In the back of my mind, I registered the strain, but it wasn't enough to make me stop. Andrew glided me across the dirty and drink-stained floor effortlessly, demonstrating the moves that Trevor had tried to do on his own.

"You dance so well," I murmured.

He chuckled. "I should. I've had lots of practice."

Right. I smiled without warmth as I cast my eyes to the floor. I imagined he had danced with dozens of girls, if not more. No doubt it was all part of his princely duties.

Andrew moved in closer, pulling me into him as we danced. I trembled as I tried to steady my beating heart. Just a dance. *It doesn't mean anything,* I struggled to remind myself.

He moved fluidly, as though we danced on air. His chest pressed up against mine, his arm tightened around my waist.

"Do I still distract you?" Andrew spoke softly as his lips brushed against my ear.

My breath hitched, knowing I couldn't take back what I would say next. I took a deep breath and exhaled slowly, then I tilted my head back until I could stare into his beautiful blazing blue eyes. "Every second."

Andrew grinned like he knew all along, and in part, he probably did. We'd suffered through so much together that he had to have some inkling or suspicion of my feelings. Despite trying to smother my feelings for him and hold onto Stefan, it was a lie to say that I felt only friendship for Andrew. A lie that I told myself over and over, hoping I would eventually consider it truth.

"Ready to take a chance?" he asked, cutting through the noise of the crowd and music.

"A chance on what?"

He smirked and twirled me away from him; the world spun before my eyes. I felt dizzy. Suddenly, he drew me close.

"Whoa," I breathed, my eyes going wide. He chuckled as the crowd applauded and cheered.

Andrew's large hands held on to my waist, pulling me so close I could feel his body heat radiating. He bent his face toward mine and gently caressed my cheek with the back of his fingers. "I think I'm falling in love with you."

What? He can't be serious. I reared my head back to get a better look at his face. My instant reaction was anger. How dare he toy with my emotions? He'd made his intentions very clear on the ride to Thimbleton. This couldn't be true.

I searched his face, seeing only tenderness and warmth reflecting back. I'd seen a similar expression on Nathan when he beheld Adel. I froze. Passion and deliberation showed in Andrew's countenance. He tilted his head closer until his forehead rested on mine. Our noses touched. His arms wrapped snug around my waist. I closed my eyes and breathed deeply, taking in the scent of cinnamon woodsy cologne and peppermint. Tentatively, his lips met mine.

And so it started, the sweetest kiss I had ever experienced in my life. The first and only kiss that felt like fate. My heart, body, and soul lit on fire. His lips, fueled by desire, felt soft and sure against mine. I didn't know a kiss could feel this good; it was a blissful oblivion that I never wanted to end. Who cared about tomorrow when we had today, now, here, forever?

But even a kiss of pure perfection couldn't last forever. We broke apart, and Andrew loosened his hold on me. I touched my lips and stumbled backward in utter shock. Andrew smiled bashfully, and a red blush tinged his cheeks. He shuffled his feet, seeming genuinely nervous and uncertain. The crowd whistled and cheered around us, but it sounded muffled. My skin flushed hot. I couldn't breathe. I needed air.

"I'm—" I cleared my throat and tried again. "Please excuse me." I turned on the balls of my feet and stumbled out the door.

"Isabelle, wait!" Andrew called after me.

My breath came in heaving gasps when I finally slowed down and leaned against a nearby building, Andrew not far behind me. My body throbbed. I cried out in pain and put a hand over my mouth to stifle my cries.

Why did I let him kiss me?

I placed a shaking hand on my forehead. Mixed emotions flooded through me to the point that I feared I'd drown. *Andrew rejected me!* He promised he'd never kiss me! I shuddered, and tears fell freely down my cheeks as my legs gave out underneath me. I put my fingers to my lips, remembering the way his soft lips meshed with mine. I sighed and stared listlessly at the stars. I felt branded. Andrew's kiss swept my heart out from underneath me, and it suddenly wasn't mine to keep. It was his.

Why did I feel so miserable?

CHAPTER TWELVE

SABELLE!" ANDREW CAUGHT UP with me, his breath coming out in labored puffs. He leaned down until his face leveled with mine. "Are you all right?"

I closed my eyes, biting my lip. Emotionally, a thunderstorm raged over a sea of high and low waves. Half of me soared over the kiss. I danced on air, only to be shot down with an arrow tainted with anger and mortification. *Why?* Why did he have to make it so complicated?

With tears still clouding my vision, I rounded on him. "How could you?" I stood, waving off his hands offering to help. "You said you would never kiss me. You made it very clear that you did not want to go down that path."

"I know, and I was wrong." Andrew straightened.

"You can't do that," I said angrily. "You can't play with my emotions like I'm some child's toy. It's not right." I shook my head and leaned back against the brick wall. My body felt on fire again, but not for love. Pure fury raced through my veins. He'd taken advantage of me after I admitted a truth, knowing I wouldn't refuse him. I balled my fists and tucked them behind me. "Did you even think about the cost before you kissed me?"

"Did I even—" Andrew ran a hand through his hair, curling his fingers into a fist. "Gods forbid, Isabelle, I just told you I was falling in love with you! Of course I wasn't thinking. I've never said that to anyone before." He took a step back and muttered under his breath. He kicked at a stone flower pot in frustration, then hopped on one foot, gasping in pain.

His theatrics eased my anger. I tried not to laugh. "Did you mean it?" I asked softly, unclenching my hands and letting them hang loosely at my sides.

"You are so infuriating," Andrew said. "Come here." He grasped my arm and pulled me into him. He cupped my face in his hands and locked eyes. Our noses brushed against each other's. "I know it's fast, crazy, unexpected, and Gods forbid I'm terrified, but I mean it, Isabelle Mirran. I love you." His voice was clear and unmistakable.

His lips tangled with mine, and my world exploded. He kissed me with passion and desire. It wasn't soft or gentle but a need, a thirst to prove his honesty. In that instant, I knew with absolute certainty that I loved him.

When we broke apart, both gasping for air, Andrew hugged me and rubbed his hand up and down my back. "Do you believe me now?"

"Yes," I said breathlessly. I leaned my head against his muscled chest. His heart beat fast and strong, matching mine. "I believe you."

"Do I need to ask how you really feel about me?" he asked with some uncertainty.

"No. You already know." I cinched my arms tighter around his waist.

Andrew chuckled. Squeezing me softly, he sighed. "Come on, let's get out of here."

He wrapped his arm around my right shoulder, and I snuggled up close as we walked back to Silverdens.

Alzmire stood on the front steps. "Everything settled then?"

"Yes," I said. "We worked it out."

Alzmire smiled. "Great. Andrew, your mother will want to hear about this."

Andrew rubbed his face and nodded. "I know. It's late; I think Isabelle should rest. Joshua should be here tomorrow. Can we meet you back at your house?"

"Of course," Alzmire answered. "I was just about to take my leave as well. We can ride together."

"So was I right about the archer?" Alzmire asked as we rode in the darkness to his mansion. Alzmire had one hand on the reins, and his other hand glowed blue light, enough for us to see the road.

"Yes," Andrew and I said simultaneously, our voices taking on the same hard tone.

"I'm going to pass this information off to the patrol guards in Carasmille. If we know he frequents pubs, we might have a chance of finding him there," Andrew said.

"What would you do if you found him?" I asked.

"It's a process, but the gist of it is he would be arrested, then put on trial and sentenced for his crimes. Same as any criminal in Aberron," Andrew explained.

We reached Alzmire's place. Andrew carefully helped me off Snow and set me on a large log while he unsaddled and led the horse into the stall. Alzmire did the same with his chestnut mare. Not one of us mentioned the kiss between Andrew and me, though it weighed heavy on my heart. It wasn't every day a prince admitted feelings for a farm girl.

We said our good nights to Alzmire, and Andrew led me back to the room I had woken up in earlier. When we arrived, Andrew lit several lamps, and we sat on the bed. Our backs leaned against the headboard. He held on to my left hand and rubbed it softly with his thumb, right over my birthmark. I turned my head and stared at him, a question forming in my mind.

"What?" He stared back at me.

"Why me?" I blurted.

His blazing blue eyes met mine. "You make me feel more than I ever have in my entire existence."

My mouth parted in surprise. "Seriously?"

Andrew nodded. "I don't fully understand it but it's undeniable."

"Oh." Never in my craziest imaginings had I dreamed a prince would declare feelings for me. I bit my bottom lip, casting my eyes to the quilt.

Andrew tilted my chin up with a finger. "What?"

My cheeks flushed. I opened my mouth, but nothing came out.

He leaned forward, pressing his forehead against mine. "You can tell me," he encouraged gently.

My heart pounded as I squeaked the words out. "Are you sure you're not using me to get out of courting girls your mother may have lined up?"

Andrew drew back. "Absolutely not. I have never bestowed my attentions with ill intent in mind."

I flinched at the severity of his tone and gaze. "I believe you."

Andrew's expression softened. He cupped my cheek and rubbed with his thumb. "I run the risk of getting flayed alive when your brother finds out. I do not take this lightly."

"Nor do I," I responded in kind. "You have made a great impact on me."

"Because I'm a prince?" he asked.

I wrinkled my nose. "To be honest, I do not find that favorable."

Andrew surprised me with a smile. "That is what drew me to you. You're not falling over yourself to please me because of my station. You face me head on. I want someone who has the guts to hold me accountable."

"You think I'm it?" I asked.

Andrew's eyes raked over my face, causing my cheeks to heat. "I'm willing to stake my heart to find out."

I reached up, letting my fingers trail across his cheek and alongside his jaw. Andrew sucked in a breath, his eyes wide. I closed the distance between us, pressing my mouth to his. He groaned. His arms snaked around me, pulling me closer. His mouth plunged mine, seeking, tasting, devouring. Blood rushed to my head. Passion ignited my heart. My limbs weakened to mush.

Andrew broke the kiss, his harsh breathing matching mine. His arms around me were the only thing keeping me upright. His blazing blue eyes were wild and pleading. "Court me."

"Yes." The word spilled out of my mouth before I had a chance to fully think it through. I did not have the power to resist him.

"Thank the Gods." The wide grin he gave me sent my stomach tumbling as though flying through air.

The way Andrew looked at me made me feel more alive next to him than ever. He set my heart on fire in a way nobody else did. Not even Stefan, my best friend. My heart stopped and slowly restarted. *Gods forbid, what am I going to do? This will crush him.* I cared deeply for Stefan.

I shivered and glanced at the empty fireplace, not realizing how cold the room had gotten, or maybe it was just me? I couldn't be sure.

"Are you cold?" Andrew's grip tightened around me.

"A little," I admitted.

"I'll make a fire." He got off the bed and went to the fireplace.

"I've got to check on my injuries," I said. I grabbed a lamp and headed into the bathroom.

Alone, my emotions got the better of me when I rewrapped the bandages. Letting go of Stefan felt like letting go of Saren and everything in it that I loved. I wasn't ready to do that, but I couldn't hold onto two men. I needed to make a choice. I gripped the edge of the sink, willing myself to make a decision. I pictured Stefan and Andrew standing side by side. Stefan, a wry smile on his face, hands in his pockets, his blonde hair falling into his pale blue eyes. His leather post bag slung around his shoulder like always. Andrew, his muscular arms folded, his head held high and regal, a sword tied around his belt. His blue eyes blazed. I put my face in my hands, gripping my hair in frustration. "I can't do this," I muttered. "I can't make a decision." I felt two different kinds of love for them. I couldn't compare the two. I felt stupid for even trying. I sighed, deciding not to choose altogether. For now, I would love them both. Fate would lead me to where I needed to be.

The fire burned steadily when I walked out of the bathroom wearing a cotton nightgown.

"Everything all right?" Andrew asked.

"Fine."

"Good." He wrapped his arms around me, and I snuggled in close.

"I could get used to this, you know," I murmured into his shirt.

"You're not the only one," Andrew said, rubbing his hand along my back. Closing my eyes, I breathed deeply, enjoying his cinnamon woodsy cologne. "It's late; we should probably go to sleep." He let go of me. "I'm in the room right next door. If you need something, don't hesitate to knock." He led me over to the bed, kissed the top of my head, and swiftly left the room.

I lay down and closed my eyes. For once, the injuries were not the center of my focus. Andrew Brian Jason Sorren, Crown Prince of Aberron, was.

Andrew gently caressed my face. "Isabelle."

I opened my eyes. He crouched next to the bed, meeting my eyes.

"I'm sorry, did I oversleep?" I asked, suddenly aware of how bright the sun shined through the windows. I rubbed the sleep out of my eyes.

"No, darling. I thought you would want breakfast and time to get ready before we meet Joshua." Andrew rested his arm on the bed. "I've just received word, we're to meet him at the Statue of Aberron in Thimbleton park in an hour and a half."

I put a hand on my forehead, trying to clear my head from the fogginess of sleep. "Right. Joshua." I'd slept so well, without waking once, that I completely forgot about Joshua.

My nerves picked up as I got ready and ate. Alzmire had apparently enlisted the help of one maid and a cook to stay year-round in the house. Two older ladies with no prospects of ever leaving. In a smaller house out back lived a young family that kept up with the maintenance and grounds. Andrew said Alzmire left early this morning to ride to Carasmille. I wished I could have thanked him for everything.

I methodically packed and unpacked my bag. After redoing it for the third time, Andrew put a hand on mine and told me to calm down.

"You'll be fine," he assured. "Joshua's family to you and me."

"What's he like?" I asked, realizing Andrew had hardly spoken about his personality.

"Well, he's—" Andrew put a hand on his chin as he thought of ways to explain Joshua. "Kind of explosive to be honest."

I raised my eyebrows.

He amended, "He reacts quickly to situations, sometimes jumping in before his brain catches up with him, but he has a kind heart. He's a little rough, but the soldiers love him. Kind of like you at first." He tacked on a smile.

"Under normal circumstances, I am not rough; I'm as smooth and creamy as butter," I retorted.

"Hmm, I'd like to see that." Andrew grinned as he pulled me close, pressing his lips against mine.

I laughed and pushed him away. My nerves faded. That's what I liked about Andrew—his ability to distract me from the major issues that I was too afraid to deal with. I needed a stable anchor in my life, someone to reassure me and keep me calm in troubled waters. He fit perfectly.

"You ready?" Andrew asked as I finished pulling on the drawstring of my crammed patched bag.

"Yes."

He slung his pack over his shoulder and grabbed my bag. Once we explained our plans to Nisha, Andrew led him out of the stall and borrowed a saddle from Alzmire.

"My time with you is still needed. I will stay with you until Haldren calls me home," Nisha said as Andrew finished the last straps.

Andrew rode with me on Nisha. My heart felt full as he directed Nisha to the city park. I stared at the stone and brick buildings, memorizing the vibrant colors, the people, the smells, and the noise. My first experience in a big city; I didn't want to forget it.

After Andrew's debut in the parade, many townspeople called out to him as he rode. He waved and nodded to them as he navigated around carriages and carts. We passed a group of soldiers heading to the main entrance. Andrew paused for a minute, thanking them for their service.

Ralph, the guard stationed at the entrance of Thimbleton on our arrival, sped to us on a brown gelding. He slowed down as he saw us. "Healer's just informed me. It's a girl!"

"Congratulations!" Andrew called as Ralph spurred his horse into a canter, grinning from ear to ear.

The statue of Aberron was positioned in the middle of a grassy park strewn with large oak and maple trees, shrubs and flowers. Several families laid patchwork quilt blankets on the grass. Food spilled out of their baskets. Children ran around, chasing squirrels up trees. Three little girls had a tea party with their dolls under a large maple. Andrew helped me off Nisha, and I stood before the chiseled stone statue, seeking a likeness between Andrew and Aberron.

"Trying to see any resemblance?" Andrew asked with a wry smile. He let go of the reins, and Nisha trotted off into the grass. Several men strolled over to admire him.

I nodded. "I see some."

"What do you see?" He snaked his arms around my waist. I leaned my head on his chest.

"You have the same broad shoulders, strong and muscular. I think," I tapped a finger on the bottom half of my lip, "but I could be wrong, you have the same nose?" I glanced up at him.

Andrew chuckled. "Yes, I've been told that many times. People always want to see a likeness between past kings and future ones." He let go of me as an older couple stopped to greet him.

I glanced behind me once to see a line of people queuing up to meet the Prince. The corners of my mouth lifted, knowing that if Joshua didn't come soon, we would be here for a while.

I stepped forward and touched the statue, remembering the history of our first great King. A uniform government didn't exist before King Aberron. The townspeople chose one man to be their leader called the Orate Judge. He made up the rules for them to live by and posted them outside their city gates. No sense of order or law governed the land in between the cities. It forced many people to spend their whole lives in one place, fearing they would be overtaken by thieves and ruffians if they journeyed. When the Dregans from Dregaitia invaded, a brazen traveler called Aberron united every city. Together, they defeated the Dregans and remained a free people. After the war, the survivors banded together to become one. They changed the name of the land from Fraison to Aberron, then made Aberron ruler over it all. In many eyes, he was the greatest King to ever live.

The artist sculpted him to appear strong and undefeated. He carried a sword in his clasped hands. The sword pointed outward while he gazed into the distance at some unknown enemy. The Dregans perhaps? His beard and shoulder-length hair made him seem wiser and more important.

"You ready for this?" Andrew asked. Miraculously, I saw no line of people. Had he spoken to them all already?

My smile faltered. "No. What if I don't like him?" The floodgates unlocked, and every emotion and every thought I had about Joshua came bubbling up to the surface, my anger for his silence and absence at the heart of it.

Andrew opened his arms and wrapped me in a hug. I rested my head on his chest. "You can do this. I'll be right by your side." He kissed the top of my head.

"Andrew, what are you doing with my sister?" a man's deep voice cut through the air behind me.

Andrew quickly let go of me and took a step back. He held his hands up in surrender. "Joshua." The wariness in his voice alarmed me.

I swiveled around and stared at my brother. He was slightly shorter than Andrew. Dark brown, wavy hair fell to his shoulders; he wore a few days of stubble over his strong jaw. His bulging muscles showed through his burgundy shirt. However, his narrowed green eyes and cold expression caught my attention more than his warrior's build. The sword he pointed at us only made it worse.

"I was told you would be with her, but I didn't expect you to be kissing her!" His voice, cold and merciless, sent a shiver down my spine. His nostrils flared as he tightened his grip on the pommel of his sword. He looked ready to turn Andrew into mincemeat.

"Calm down, Joshua," Andrew said, his hands still raised to his chest. "There's a lot you don't understand."

"Oh, I think I understand perfectly," Joshua said shortly. He took a step forward, brandishing his weapon.

"Don't make me fight you." Andrew started to pull out his sword.

"Why? You think you can beat me?" Joshua snorted in derision.

"All right, enough of this!" I shouted as Andrew started to make his rebuttal. "Joshua, put down that sword." I glared at him, hands on my waist. When he didn't move, I inflated my lungs, taking in a big gulp of air. I used all the commanding tone I possessed and pointed my finger to the ground. "Now!"

Joshua sheathed his blade. He wore an array of weapons on his belt. His hands twitched beside his hips, ready to grab something else if our meeting didn't go well.

Fury boiled in my veins, pumping me with adrenaline. I stormed over to him and did the unthinkable. I swung my right arm back as far as it would go and slapped him hard in the face. Joshua's eyes bulged as his face swayed to the side.

"How dare you?" I screeched as I shook my stinging hand out, realizing I probably looked pathetic. "How dare you point a sword at us—at me—and treat Andrew with so much disrespect."

"Isabelle, he is the Crown Prince of Aberron. Do you realize what you've got yourself into?" Joshua straightened his posture and rubbed his red cheek. An imprint of my hand started to form.

I stared at my brother coldly. "I know exactly who he is and what's at stake."

"You can't know that surely." Joshua shook his head. "You've never spent a day at Court."

Joshua tilted his chin up, focusing his attention to Andrew. "Andrew, surely you realize what you've done. You're effectively feeding her to the vultures!" He started to pace, clenching and unclenching his fists.

Joshua acted like Andrew had ruined me. He muttered curses under his breath. Distress lines appeared on his forehead. I furrowed my eyebrows, confused. Why did Joshua suddenly become so protective when he hadn't bothered with me before?

"I can't change what I've done or how I feel," Andrew said resolutely. Grabbing my hand, he planted his feet firmly beside mine. "I love Isabelle."

Joshua gripped the pommel of his sword. His eyes bulged wildly, and his whole face took on a red hue, matching the mark on his cheek. "You what? You barely know her!"

Andrew's word choice when describing my brother rapidly made sense as the conversation continued. Joshua *was* explosive.

Andrew held his ground. "I know her better than you do. Gods forbid, you shouldn't even have the right to call Isabelle family after your behavior. A *real* brother wouldn't have ignored his sister for twelve years!"

Joshua took a deep breath. His shoulders slumped, and I didn't know if was because he felt ashamed or he attempted to reign in his anger. "You're right, I haven't been the brother I should have, but I'm here now. I wouldn't have ridden for four days straight if I didn't care about Isabelle."

I studied Joshua's face harder, noticing the bags underneath his eyes, the tired lines across his forehead, and the overall gauntness in his cheekbones. "How did you know I was sought after?"

"A God appeared to me." Joshua's tone and expression indicated he didn't wish to talk about it.

"Haldren?" I asked, undeterred.

Joshua's eyebrows rose. "Yes ..."

"Perhaps you're involving yourself for the sake of not angering *him* over any care for me," I challenged.

Joshua flinched. *Figures.* I let go of Andrew's hand and sat on the edge of the statue of Aberron. Standing for so long had started to hurt. Joshua stared after me with regret in his expression.

"What are your plans with Isabelle?" Andrew asked my brother.

Joshua's gaze flicked from me to him. "I'm taking her with me to Carasmille. Haldren said she is attracting trouble with the Mark of the Gods on her hand. I aim to protect her."

"Make her a priority. She's had a few run ins already," Andrew said.

"What happened?" Joshua asked sharply, taking a step forward, his hand still resting on the handle of his sword.

"Didn't Father tell you?" Andrew's expression showed confusion.

"He only said that you would be with her. He didn't say anything else." Joshua raised his eyebrow, perplexed. His eyes roved me all over, searching for an anomaly. I scowled at him.

I watched their interchange, their postures near mirror images of each other. They were quick to interrupt as they spoke. Andrew was right. They acted like brothers even if they weren't blood related.

"Isabelle fought off attempted kidnappers on her way to meet you." Andrew folded his arms, fixing his eyes firmly on Joshua as he waited for a reaction. "She barely escaped alive.""Unscathed?" Joshua asked as he glanced at me.

I wore a long-sleeved shirt and long pants with boots that rose to my knees. Since my face was clear of bruises and cuts, he couldn't see the damage underneath.

"No, I pulled two arrows out of her body," Andrew said.

Joshua's eyes widened. He turned to me. "Did they take advantage of you in any way?" He spoke to me in a sharp voice like a guard getting answers out of a vagabond. His tone offended me. I was his sister, not some common thief.

"Don't talk to me with that tone of voice. I am not a criminal," I snapped at him, still seething over his complete rejection of Andrew and I as a couple.

Joshua balled his fists in irritation and fidgeted. I didn't care. I wouldn't make it easy on him. He didn't deserve it.

"I'm not—" He paused. For once I could tell his brain worked faster than his mouth. "Just answer the question."

I sighed and rubbed my forehead. "No. They were more interested in taking me to their leader. No, I don't know who," I added at Joshua's queried expression.

Joshua's lip curled as if frustrated for the lack of information. "Why didn't you take Nathan with you like I suggested?"

I lifted my chin. "I wasn't about to put his life on the line for my sake." No doubt the archer would have shot him dead on sight.

Joshua wore disbelief. "Nathan agreed?"

"I didn't give him a choice," I admitted.

Joshua and Andrew spoke simultaneously. "You left without telling."

"What's done is done. Haldren told Nathan I had a worthy protector so he knows I'm safe now." I shrugged, then winced.

Joshua's eyes flashed with concern. "Have you been to a healer?"

I shuddered. "I am not letting a healer touch me with their poisonous magic."

Joshua turned to Andrew. "You seriously want her?"

Andrew lifted his hands. "I can't help how I feel."

Joshua muttered something under his breath, clearly unenthused. My immediate feeling toward Joshua was one of complete distaste. I folded my arms and crossed my ankles, the petulant child in me coming out. Andrew came up beside me and put his hand on my good shoulder.

"How bad are your injuries? Can you ride?" Joshua eyed me up and down again as though something had changed within the last few minutes.

"I'm fine." I stood and stormed off to Nisha, leaving them both standing there gaping.

Nisha knelt, and I slid onto his back. Only then did I notice the townspeople leisurely enjoying Gods Day in the park, watching our interaction with interest. I felt too angry to feel embarrassed.

"I never expected my sister to be so ..." Joshua stumbled to find the right word.

Andrew spoke. "Like you? Temperamental, passionate, demanding?"

Joshua scowled. "All of the above."

CHAPTER THIRTEEN

NDREW SWUNG UP BEHIND me. Joshua whistled, and a gray and white speckled stallion trotted out of the trees.

"I just dropped off some men at the guard tower. More are stationed right out of town for me to escort them to the barracks in Carasmille," Joshua said as we trotted out of the park.

A group of soldiers on horses waited by the side of the road, just past the main gates under a line of oak trees. A few hung onto the reins of pack horses ladled with supplies. Joshua directed them to follow behind us. He kept them just out of earshot of casual conversation.

As we rode north, the cobbled stone turned into worn dirt. To the left and right of us I saw many fields, mostly through with harvesting. Small houses dotted the open countryside. The road to Carasmille appeared well journeyed, and we passed many travelers coming to and fro. What if we passed the archer traveling to Carasmille as well? I shivered, and Andrew wrapped his arms tighter around my waist.

The wind became stronger as we rode, blowing my hair into my face. Clouds drifted in and out of view as the day wore on. Andrew gave Joshua all the facts I'd given him concerning the archer who'd tried to kill me. Joshua planned to make inquiries in Carasmille.

We stopped in the late afternoon near a creek and a grassy plain to rest and eat a little before continuing. My body ached, and I needed the respite.

"How are you feeling?" Joshua asked, concern on his face as he watched me wince in pain when I moved my leg into a better position. He grabbed a piece of bread.

"I'm fine," I answered, tight-lipped.

"She'll continue to say that until she keels over," Andrew said drily, taking a drink from his water pouch.

I lightly slapped Andrew's arm. "Cut it out, will you? Stop telling him all my secrets."

"How old are you, Isabelle?" Joshua changed the subject.

"Seventeen," I bit into an apple.

Joshua furrowed his eyebrows, seeming deep in thought as he scratched the stubble on his chin.

"What does my age have to do with anything?" I wondered what went on behind his eyes.

"I need a place where I can keep you safe but not have to keep an eye on you all the time. It wouldn't be right for you to traipse around with a bunch of soldiers and me," Joshua explained, glancing at the men sitting in the grass a little distance away.

The soldiers laughed and shoved one another in jest.

"I don't know, they look kind of fun to me," I quipped, watching a soldier chase after another into the creek.

Joshua glanced at the men. "Not all men can be trusted around a pretty girl."

"You're thinking about the Sorrenian," Andrew said softly.

"Sorrenian?" I turned my attention away from the guards and back to Joshua. I briefly remembered Andrew mentioning it, but I couldn't remember its significance.

"It's a school," Andrew reminded gently.

I wrinkled my nose in displeasure at the thought. Adel tried to put me in Saren's community school when I was a child. I was too new and different. Reeling from the loss of my parents, I didn't speak. My birthmark made me an oddity. The other children—all but Stefan— bullied and threw garbage at me. Adel opted to tutor me from home to avoid further confrontation. I quivered to think of that experience happening again. "No thank you. I learn better on my own."

"Why not? I'm sure they didn't teach you much in that backwater town you were in." Joshua looked away from me at the guards as he said it.

I squeezed my apple in anger, and the juices ran down my fingers. "Don't insult Saren. We may be farmers, but we're not ignorant."

My outburst didn't faze Joshua at all. He calmly set his bread down and explained. "You may know how to read and write and count to one hundred, but you do not know how to navigate your way around the capital city of Carasmille. I want you to be in a place where you can meet people your age and get some friends. It will be good for you."

I looked at Andrew. "What do you think?"

He shrugged. "It's not exactly my place to say, but I don't think it's a terrible idea."

I glared at Andrew and briefly contemplated throwing my apple at him.

"Hey, don't get mad at me. Just think about it," Andrew said. He took the apple from my hand and bit into it.

I didn't want to think about it. "I think you underestimate my abilities," I said, forcing my voice to sound even.

"I don't doubt your book-learning ability," Joshua counterargued. "But you don't know a thing about city life. Particularly the lives of nobles and rich merchants." He pointed to Andrew. "Every person who has a young daughter is vying for Andrew to marry one of them. These people are not only going to be your peers, but your competition. You need to associate with people in your own bracket, especially if you want to have a relationship with Andrew." He took a breath. "There's more at stake with courting a prince than you realize." He picked up his piece of bread again.

Joshua's frank expression left no room for a rebuttal.

"Joshua's right," Andrew confirmed, entwining his fingers with mine. "As soon as the Court realizes I'm back from my Walk I'm going to have a horde of girls paraded in front of me." He shuddered. "They know my next step to obtaining the throne is to marry. I expect the contest to gain notice will be ruthless."

Joshua's emerald green eyes glinted. "You can count on it."

"Great." I let go of Andrew's hand and rubbed my forehead to fight off the oncoming headache. *What did I get myself into?* I didn't want this. Though I didn't have a clear picture of what I *did* want, I knew this wasn't it. There were only three things I believed to be absolute truth right now: One, I loved Andrew. Two, danger sought after me. Three, I couldn't go back to Saren and have the ones I love get hurt trying to protect me.

Andrew wrapped his arm around me, tucking me close against his body. "Hey, don't worry, you have me claimed."

I glanced up at him, giving him a small smile. I wanted to believe him wholeheartedly, but a little doubt crept in. A blacksmith's daughter from a farming town against a host of rich, probably beautiful, cultured women. Andrew may have wanted me now but would that change in the near future? Would he see a quality in another girl and wish I had it? Perhaps I should go the Sorrenian to view what I was up against and learn what I needed to not be ignorant in Andrew's world.

I took a breath and exhaled slowly. A small sense of determination cloaked in an abundance of trepidation filled me. "All right, I'll go." Joshua's face melted into relief. Andrew grinned at me. I held up a finger. "But if it's completely awful, I reserve the right to find a new situation."

"How about we make a deal? You stay three months, and if you still hate it after that much time, then I will find a better option," Joshua offered.

"Two months." I held up two fingers. "That's plenty of time for me to decide if I hate it or not."

Joshua rolled his eyes. "Two and a half."

"Agreed." I held my hand out, and Joshua shook it. Andrew tried handing the apple back to me, but I waved him off. He shrugged and bit into it again.

We mounted our horses and continued north to Carasmille. The grassy plains stretched on with nothing else in sight. I learned they had named the path we traveled on Capital Road since it led directly to Carasmille. Every path intersecting ours had a stone post with names and directions to other towns. We passed a sign that said Korrun with an arrow pointing left. I felt a pang in my heart as I remembered that's where we'd lived with our parents before their murder.

I leaned on Andrew, wanting to forget Korrun and my parents for the moment. "What's the Sorrenian like?" I decided I better learn as much as I could about it since I had agreed to go.

Andrew navigated Nisha around two men and a wagon filled with potatoes that was pulled by two oxen. We rode over a small bridge as the path wove into a grove of trees.

"It's not bad; rigorous," Andrew answered simply. "Though I must admit I took on more duties than the normal student, so my view might be a little skewed." He spurred Nisha into a canter, catching up with Joshua, who rode ahead and scouted for any brigands hiding in the trees. Apparently this section of Capital road got ambushed often. "The school has been around since the start of Aberron. I believe Aberron himself began the construction in his old age, and his daughter took over when he died. Every royal down the line has gone there."

I frowned. "A simple blacksmith's girl is going to fit in great."

"You're not a blacksmith's girl," Joshua said sternly. "You have everything all of the other young people have. You have money and an estate and connections to the crown."

"No, I don't!" I protested. "I don't have anything."

"You're a co-owner for the estate in Korrun. I've been managing it, but eventually you are going to take that over," he explained, staring into my surprised expression. "We have lands and titles, farming operations and the like." He loosened his grip on the reins. "You have money, Isabelle; it's just been in safekeeping."

I narrowed my eyes, wishing I would have known that earlier. I never envisioned leaving Saren because I didn't think I had anything else out there for me. Why didn't Nathan and Adel say anything to me? Did they even know? I scoffed. Of course they knew. Before they'd moved to Saren, they led a life in Court when Nathan worked for the King as a knight. Why had they kept so much hidden from me?

The stars twinkled like diamonds in the sky, shining against a bright moon, when we reached the outskirts of the city. It had the same gate entrance as Thimbleton did: a huge curtain wall with many guards surrounding it. Although it appeared to be twice the size.

After getting through the city gates, we rode onto the cobbled streets. Joshua took the lead, cantering past darkened houses and candlelit windows.

"A little bigger than Thimbleton, don't you think?" Andrew leaned down and whispered in my ear.

I widened my eyes, taking in what little I could see in the darkness. Lanterns lined the main road, with many dim streets shooting off. Everything from the squished brick and stone buildings to the smell and noise of the city reminded me of Thimbleton. The only difference I saw was size.

"I'd say so," I breathed.

We stopped for a couple of minutes part of the way through the city while Joshua rode behind us to tell the soldiers where to go.

As we rode farther into town, additional lanterns lit up the night, lighting the roads and buildings. More people loitered about. The city appeared live with commerce, busier than I ever saw Thimbleton during their Harvest Festival. Saren closed shop an hour before the sun set. Carasmille seemed truly a city that never slept.

Toward the center of town we passed a large, shallow pond with a marble statue of Aberron in the middle, depicted in the same stance as the one in Thimbleton. His hardened glance shone brightly against the moonlight and lanterns. I wondered if Thimbleton's was a copy of lesser quality.

"This statue is more magnificent than the one in Thimbleton," I told Andrew.

He chuckled. "It's the nicest one I've seen."

I took it all in—whatever I could see through the blackness—as we rode farther on through the city, passing houses and businesses, stray animals, and the occasional city folk. Away from the center of Carasmille, it became quieter, with slumbering people and closed doors. The road started to slant upward, unveiling a massive building made from white marble. I counted ten exceptionally large turrets just in the front alone. It easily rose ten levels high, if not more, and wider than I could see in the darkness. I yearned to see it in the light. The moonlight and stars accentuated what they could. I found it breathtaking: a beacon in the darkness.

"That must be the castle," I stated.

"That's home." Andrew sighed, glancing up at it on the hill.

"It's huge!" I exclaimed.

Andrew chuckled, squeezing my hand gently but tight. "Yes, and very easy to get lost in. I've often wondered about petitioning for a directory."

I laughed. "Surely you don't get lost."

Andrew shook his head. "No. But I get tired of everyone else asking me for directions. The castle not only houses us, it also houses many court and governing proceedings, and there are rooms for everything under the sun."

The road curved away from the castle, and we turned east to a smaller, but no less grandiose building made of regular gray stone. I turned my head around to gauge the distance between the castle and the Sorrenian. Due to its enormous size, I could still see the castle in the moonlight.

Andrew caught my intention. "I'm only a ten-minute ride away. I'll still be close."

"Good." At least I could look at the castle and imagine Andrew.

We rode up to a large iron gate, and Joshua spoke quickly to the sentry who opened the gates to let us pass. Joshua led us to the stables. A large torchlight flickered in the wind, lighting our way.

Many horses poked their heads out of their stalls at our arrival.

"There are many horses," Nisha said, trotting forward. He eyed them, turning his head left and right.

I patted his neck. "Will it be all right?"

"Yes," Nisha answered.

"Good." I rubbed his neck some more.

Andrew slid off and lifted me down. He led Nisha into a large stall. A hostler came by to take care of the horses. Andrew gave him quick directions, making sure Nisha got an extra portion of oats and a sugar cube if available. Judging by the way Nisha rocked his head, I guessed he had requested it.

"Joshua, I better take my leave now," Andrew said.

Joshua nodded. "Your father will want to see you immediately."

"Give me a minute to say goodbye to Isabelle." Andrew clasped my hand in his. He didn't make it a demand, but he wasn't asking either. "I'll see her to the door in a minute."

"Fine." Joshua stalked off, shaking his head in disgust.

Andrew waited until Joshua marched out of sight before he held open his arms and crushed me in a hug.

"Careful," I squeaked.

"Sorry." Andrew loosened his hold. He rested his forehead against mine, breathing deeply. He held my face in his hands and tangled his lips with mine, kissing me with gentle passion.

"Don't go," I whispered, suddenly terrified. "I don't know if I can do this."

"I told you I'd keep an eye on you until you were safe with your brother, and I've done that now," he said, caressing my cheek. "You'll be fine. I'll come visit you as soon as I can, but it might be a while." He rubbed a hand on my back as I leaned my head on his chest and listened to his strong heartbeat. "I've been gone for some time on the Walk, so there is much I have to catch up on. I promise to write you. It would be unbearable to not hear a word from the lovely, courageous girl I'm courting."

I smiled, loving that he wanted me as much as I wanted him.

"I won't forget either," he added.

"You better not," I mumbled into his shirt.

I would miss the warmth of his body close to mine. The smell of his clothes—wood and cinnamon. His soft kisses and the way he kept me grounded.

"How are you feeling?" Andrew asked. "You must be hurting from the ride."

I smiled. "You know my answer."

"Yes, I know, you're fine. Don't forget to change your bandages tonight, and if you start to feel the least bit off, then get a healer. I won't be there to take care of you." He kissed the top of my head as he let go of me and stepped away. I trembled; my stomach knotted.

"I know. I'll be fine. Don't worry." I didn't want to admit to him that fear filled every crevice of my body and soul, though I suspected he knew already.

"Well, make sure you get some rest before you start anything," Andrew said.

"I can handle it."

"I know," he said. "Come on; I better walk you up to the door. Joshua will be waiting."

Andrew intertwined our fingers as we ambled up the hill to the daunting school that I couldn't see all of in the darkness.

"Took you long enough." Joshua leaned against the double doors, his arms folded.

"Just give up already. I'm not ending my courtship with Andrew because you think I should," I said hotly.

He muttered something unintelligible and shook his head.

"Well, I'll leave you in the capable hands of your brother." Andrew let go of my hand, and I worked hard not to grasp his again.

"Thank you for rescuing me. You saved my life. I don't know what I would have done without you." I spoke with gratitude and sincerity that flowed in my heart for him.

"I'd do it again in a heartbeat." He smiled and faced Joshua. "I expect I'll see you soon."

Joshua nodded slowly.

Andrew gave one brief wave and strode down the hill to the stables.

Reality hit me like a brick. *Andrew's gone.* I shivered and took a deep breath, then exhaled, hoping I could bear whatever came next.

I focused on even breaths, trying to clear my head as we entered. Overwhelmed with Andrew's departure, I barely noticed where I walked as

I followed Joshua down a torch-lit hall. I waited next to him while he knocked on a large, thick wooden door.

"Enter," a man said through the door.

Joshua turned the handle and gestured for me to go first, following behind as I entered.

"Ah, Joshua, I was wondering when you'd show up," the man said behind a book, his voice mild with tired patience. He set it down and smiled. He had a long face, a few wrinkles, and graying, short hair. His eyes appeared sharp and clear, despite seeming in his late fifties and ready for a few years of rest. Folding his hands together, he rested his elbows on the armrests of the chair.

Joshua prearranged this without my consent? I sneaked an accusatory glare at him. How dare he pretend to come up with the idea on the ride to Carasmille! I fought against an urge to smack him again.

"Lord Leavesden, this is my sister, Isabelle Mirran," Joshua introduced me.

Lord Leavesden smiled, resting his eyes on my face. "A pleasure."

I smiled weakly back.

"I know a little of your situation, but please enlighten me once more." He gestured for us to sit.

Joshua pulled out a chair for me, and I sat, grateful to rest my legs after a long ride. I bit my lip, attempting to focus on the conversation and not my tired and aching muscles.

Joshua sat in the adjacent chair and crossed his ankles "Isabelle's birthmark has recently garnered some unwanted attention. I've taken her under my care to keep her safe. However, with my duties for King Brian, I can't keep an eye on her as much as she probably needs. I think the Sorrenian will give Isabelle the necessary education to enter court society and suit my requirement for a secure location."

Lord Leavesden scratched his head. "Unwanted attention over a birthmark?"

Joshua nodded at me. "Show him Isabelle."

I lifted my left hand, turning it so he could see the back. "There's nothing special to it, but people keep thinking there is due to its resemblance to the Mark of the Gods."

Lord Leavesden's eyes widened. "I see." He blinked. "Well, we have many protections on this school that I think would keep her safe for a while. But we don't want to run the risk of bringing trouble into the Sorrenian."

"Of course," Joshua agreed good naturedly.

Lord Leavesden's brown eyes sought mine. "Where are you from?"

"Saren," I said softly.

"What kind of education have you had?" he queried.

"They have a school there, but I never attended," I told him. "I studied out of old books with my adoptive parents tutoring me."

"And who were they?"

"Nathan and Adel Whysten."

Lord Leavesden smiled. "I know them from their days at Court. How are they doing? It's been years since I spoke to them."

"They are well, enjoying the comforts that a small town has to offer." I felt a pang of homesickness as I spoke of them. I missed them so much already, and it had only been a week.

"They always wanted a quiet life." He tapped his fingers against the desk. "So, Joshua, what do you want us to teach her?"

"Put her with the boys and girls her age, let her take all the classes they do." Joshua shrugged. "If she struggles, then reassess."

"What about the afternoon block?" Lord Leavesden raised his eyebrows.

Joshua spoke firmly. "I want her in the defensive classes."

"Are you sure? Most girls take up needlepoint, art, or music lessons for those two hours. It would look better on her list of accomplishments for future relationships." Lord Leavesden moved a stack of papers on his desk and pulled out a fresh sheet of paper.

"No, I want her to be in the fighting classes." Joshua sounded decided. "She must be able to defend herself if more trouble comes. I hope it doesn't, but I'd rather she be prepared anyway. She already has some experience with it."

Lord Leavesden nodded as he pulled a pen from a jar. "Of course. Just be aware that she'll be the only girl there."

"Fine," Joshua said, not seeming the least bit deterred.

I sat back and listened to them negotiate my future and the costs. It sounded like more money than Saren had combined to stay at the Sorrenian. Under normal circumstances, I would have protested the expense. However, Joshua had made his decision clear. I believed I couldn't change his mind, regardless of how much I objected.

"One more thing," Lord Leavesden said as they finished discussing living arrangements and classes. "Do you know if you have any magic?"

"Magic?" I questioned, making sure I heard him right.

"Your brother does." He nodded at Joshua.

"Nothing has ever manifested, so I don't think so, but there isn't anybody in Saren that checks for that sort of thing," I said.

"Then we will have Professor Slystream check, just to be sure you're right." He scribbled something down on a paper and handed it to Joshua. "Here's her class schedule." He looked at me while fiddling with the pen in his hand. "If any of this is too hard for you, let me know, and we will work out something else."

I gave a short smile. "I'm sure I can keep up. I am quite capable." Slim chance of them teaching me something I didn't already know. I expected to be bored with the course work more than anything else.

Lord Leavesden set the pen on his desk and stood. "Let me direct you to your rooms so you can get settled in." He grabbed a lantern as we exited. "Breakfast starts at seven a.m. sharp, and your first class is at eight. Lunch is at noon, and dinner is five p.m."

Tired as I felt, my mind whirled around the information as I tried to process.

Lord Leavesden smiled. "Don't worry, we have a bell to signal the times, and there are clocks in every room. Tardiness is not accepted." He took a breath and continued. "Everyone meets for the meals. You are allowed to take your food up to your rooms if you have a lot of studying to do." He held up a finger. "But if your room becomes too untidy, we take away those privileges. We routinely check rooms unannounced throughout your stay. Most of the time when you're in class." He talked rapidly as he led us up a staircase and down numerous hallways.

By the time we arrived at our destination, I was completely lost. The nearly pitch-black hallways didn't help.

Lord Leavesden faced me and pointed at the door. "This door is password protected. To open it, say *passiflora*." He pulled open the door. "Enjoy your stay at the Sorrenian."

With that ending statement, Lord Leavesden took his leave and walked down the hall, carrying the light with him. Joshua walked inside. It was too dark to see much, so Joshua threw his softly glowing red hand out toward the fireplace, and suddenly a fire roared, lighting up the room.

"You used magic." I set my bag down.

"Yes." He shrugged. "It's easier that way."

"When did you find out you had it?"

"When the King took me in. Our parents had planned to check but never got around to it." Joshua's tone took on a bitter edge. "A lot of things they planned on doing got neglected. They weren't home much."

"I remember." I wrung my hands together and wondered if we'd ever get past the small talk stage. It felt easier to speak to him with Andrew by my side.

"Most kids are tested when they're seven or eight, when they're old enough to understand the consequences of magic. Unless they show manifestations—then they're tested and trained at a younger age." He glanced around, hand on his hip. "Check out your room and tell me what you think." He gestured for me to move around.

I roamed around the space, taking it all in. Two red chintz chairs with a small table in between them faced the fireplace. A desk resided underneath a large window that the moonlight shone through. Red drapes, pulled back and tied with a red tasseled cord, surrounded the window frame. The door to the right led to a fully functioning bathroom with a rack of shelves stocked with towels and toiletries. The door on the left revealed a large four-poster bed. A quilted blanket with red and white square patches lay over it with matching red and white pillows. One end table resided at the head of the bed. A fireless lamp rested on top. Against the left wall farthest from the large window were two large dressers. Each room had a clock but no pictures. I guessed the occupant chose the final touches.

"It's nice." I shut the bedroom door behind me. "A little bare, but I can fix that."

"I'll send over some paintings from the castle that will liven the place up," he offered.

"That would be nice, thanks." I tried to smile.

"I'll bring some supplies, paper and such, tomorrow morning before your classes start." Joshua surveyed me. "You should get some rest."

"Yes," I agreed.

He headed to the door and paused, his hand on the handle. "I know you're not eager to stay here, but thanks for putting up with it."

"You're welcome," I said, surprised at his effort to patch things up between us.

"Good night."

"Night."

Joshua opened the door and strode through, closing it behind him.

I held my lips in a thin line. *Guess that's it. I'm on my own.*

CHAPTER FOURTEEN

 SPENT SOME TIME EMPTYING out my bag and rewrapping the bandages before slipping into a nightgown. I crawled into bed and fell asleep almost instantly. After a long day, my body gave out, mentally and physically.

I stood in the wheat field with Haldren.

"I should thank you for the dress and face cream," I said.

"It worked wonders, didn't it?" He smiled, seeming pleased. "The Sorrenian is your new abode then?" He plucked a strand of wheat and twiddled it in between his fingers.

I felt sure he already knew that. "For a while."

"The Sorrenian boasts of a strict regime and their ability to produce strong, educated leaders. It is not for feeble minds or the faint of heart." He grinned coldly, dropping the piece of wheat. He must have seen something in my expression, for he added, "Don't worry, you will survive—eventually."

"Eventually? What's that supposed to mean?" I folded my arms.

Haldren's eyes twinkled. "You'll see."

"If you're just here to taunt me, then send me back. I could use some real sleep," I grumbled.

"Rest then. You need it." Haldren waved his hand, and suddenly the world disappeared.

I woke up to complete darkness, irritated with Haldren for giving me more puzzles to work out. I couldn't tell the future, but he obviously had some idea of it. Frustrated, I closed my eyes and willed myself to fall asleep.

It wasn't easy; every waking moment reminded me of how sore and alone I felt.

The sun shone brightly through the window when I woke to a loud bell ringing. I shivered, realizing I had kicked the blankets off while I slept. I sat up and winced. *Ouch.* Every part of my body ached. I took a few deep breaths, inhaling and exhaling, trying to stanch the steady flow of pain.

It took me a while to get out of bed; I leaned heavily on one of the posts before moving slowly to the bathroom to clean up. I ran hot water and soaked my bruised and ached muscles. I didn't have much time to enjoy it. The clock neared seven.

I slipped into tan pants and a loose, light-pink long-sleeved shirt. Lord Leavesden never gave me a paper on dress standards, so I hoped this would be acceptable. I braided my hair and pinned it up. A knock came at the door when I slipped in the last hairpin.

I opened the door. Joshua walked in carrying several cloth bags. "Good morning. Here are the supplies you need. The paintings will be here tonight." He set the bags on the table, then grabbed one with a pink floral pattern out of the mix. He handed it to me. "I had this one made up with everything you need for today. You can switch it out with what you want when you have time."

"All right." I pulled the straps of the bag onto my good shoulder.

"Come on; I'll escort you to breakfast." He tried to smile, but it came out weak and half-hearted.

I searched his face, noticing the bags underneath his tired, bloodshot eyes. I put a hand on Joshua's arm. "You need some sleep. When was the last time you rested?"

Joshua chuckled. "Sleep is a fantasy given to those with idle pleasures and pastimes. You doing all right?"

"Yes, I'll be fine," I said, my go-to answer for everything. My issues shouldn't be someone else's to bear.

Windows lined the hallways on one side, lanterns or torch brackets in between them. Paintings, depicting nature and various people, took up the empty space on the other side. Brass numbers a little higher than eye level gave directions when one hallway connected to another. I attempted to commit the numbers to memory so I could find my way back. This place was a maze.

Joshua led me down the stairs and back to the entry hall. I sneaked a glance inside the connecting dining hall and saw a bustle of tables filled with kids ranging from barely in their teens to my age, seventeen to eighteen. The smell of breakfast and loud conversation permeated the air.

I hesitated, having absolutely no desire to go in.

"Oh, come on, you'll be fine. Just sit on the left side of the room. That's where the older students sit." Joshua pushed me gently toward the open doors.

I stumbled forward and froze when two older boys passed by.

"Looks like we got a new girl," one of them said. His eyes, silver I think, roamed me over, and a smirk fell off his full lips. He lightly nudged his friend who hadn't been paying attention.

His blonde friend turned his head, and our eyes locked. My eyes widened. He had the exact same shade of blue eyes as Andrew. My stomach tied in knots.

The boy smiled briefly and waved before strolling into the eating hall. He didn't see my half smile, half grimace in return.

I swiveled around and faced Joshua, knowing this would be futile, but I couldn't stop myself from trying. "Joshua, do I really have to do this? Can't we figure something else out?" I didn't want to go anywhere near that blonde boy. As if I didn't feel Andrew's absence already, he would be a stark reminder of what I missed.

"No, we can't. Remember what we talked about? If you want a chance with Andrew, then you need to be here. Now go." He pushed me a little harder toward the dining hall, and I reluctantly walked in. I glanced back once over my shoulder. Joshua grinned and waved me on.

Large windows let in natural light by the breakfast buffet, and chandeliers hung down from the ceiling. Paintings of food and scenery decorated the walls. Long tables and benches covered the room. On the right, farthest away from the food, the younger students sat, ranging from what appeared to be about twelve to fourteen. Toward the middle were students from fourteen to possibly sixteen, and on the far left, the students of seventeen and eighteen lounged. At the back of the room professors sat and chatted. I guessed there to be one hundred and fifty students and professors in all, give or take a few.

The students hushed as they saw me. The new girl. My cheeks felt hot as I hurried to find a seat. For the first time in ages, I felt truly intimidated by individuals my age and even those younger, knowing these were the children of the great and powerful in Aberron. Gradually, the conversation picked back up, a little louder than before. No doubt they discussed my arrival.

My appetite had vanished the second I walked through the double doors. I thought I would be sick if I tried to eat anything.

I did a quick sweep of the room with my eyes. Each section of students appeared lost in their own little world of friends and foes, except that they kept one eye on their tablemates and one eye on the older students. I wrinkled my nose at the show of jealousy and desire.

My eyes trailed over the group of older students and locked onto the boy who reminded me of Andrew. He laughed, showing an array of gleaming white teeth, and shoved his friend in jest. Even the older students watched him with hawk-like eyes and adoration. He was their leader. The student version of a God.

Before I could assess how I felt about it, Lord Leavesden trotted by and glanced down at me.

"Good morning, Isabelle. Not hungry?" he asked.

"Not so much," I answered softly.

He smiled warmly. "You're just nervous. Come with me; I'll help you get settled." He beckoned for me to follow.

Reluctantly, I got up and followed. He led me to the food and handed me a tray. I piled pieces of fruit on it and got a cup of water.

"My son is about your age; I'll introduce you," he said.

We went directly to the top of the food chain, where the boy I wanted to avoid sat among a group of worshipers. Once they realized Lord Leavesden and I loomed over them, they quit laughing and throwing grapes at one another. I fought against a strong desire to bolt.

"Henry, come introduce yourself to our new student." Lord Leavesden directed his attention at the God.

"Hi, I'm Henry." His voice sounded bright and exuberant; he flashed a smile.

"Isabelle," I murmured back.

"Would you care to sit down with us?" He gestured to his already-crowded table.

"Yes, thank you." I sensed I didn't have a choice to say no. Not with Lord Leavesden standing beside me.

Everyone quickly made room, shoving their trays against the others, squeezing closer to their tablemates. I set my tray down and sat on the bench.

Lord Leavesden smiled. "Thank you, Henry. I'm putting her in your care for the day. Help her get to her classes all right. She's in every one of yours."

"Even the defensive ones?" Henry asked, his eyebrows raised.

Lord Leavesden nodded. "Yes, Henry. Even those." He rested his brown eyes on me. "Enjoy your breakfast, Isabelle." He meandered off to the front of the room, greeting people along the way.

I eyed the pile of fruit on my plate. It looked as appetizing as a piece of manure. When I glanced up, I noticed all eyes rested on me. My stomach rolled.

Henry grinned. "Isabelle, huh?"

I nodded slowly, not wanting to gaze into his eyes that painfully reminded me of Andrew.

"Does that come with a last name?" he asked, his grin not faltering even once.

I suspected he tried to be charming, but all I saw was self-assured cockiness.

"Mirran. Isabelle Mirran," I responded.

The boy who first noticed me in the entry hall sat across from me. He leaned over and whispered something to Henry. Henry nodded.

"You don't happen to be related to Joshua Mirran?" Henry asked. "I thought I saw him in the entry hall with you this morning."

"He's my brother," I said lightly.

"I thought there was some resemblance," the boy who whispered said, pushing his black hair away from his face.

"I couldn't say." I hadn't been around him enough to find many resemblances except the same shade of green eyes.

"Allow me to introduce my other tablemates." Henry took the lead in conversation effortlessly. "This is Dominic." He pointed to the boy sitting across from me. "Next to him is Aliyah." He pointed to a girl who smiled prettily, curiousity showing in her lightly painted face. "And then there is Falden."

Falden grinned but not cockily; an overall gentleness wafted off him. Henry named off a few more people down the line of the table, but I couldn't remember their names.

"A pleasure," I mumbled meekly. I brushed some of my hair away from the left side of my face. Eyes suddenly widened as they caught my birthmark. Inwardly I cringed. I hated introductions for this reason.

"Hey, you wear the Mark of the Gods," Henry said with obvious interest.

"It's just a birthmark eerily similar to the Mark of the Gods," I clarified. "It means nothing."

I received a bunch of subtle eyebrow raises and dubious expressions. I fought against a scowl. *I really should invest in a pair of gloves,* I thought.

"So why haven't we seen you before?" Dominic peered at me. "Your brother went here. Why not you?"

"I've only just reconnected with Joshua. I've been living in Saren." At their confused expressions I added, "It's a small farming community in the south."

"Farming?" Henry sounded amused.

My face went cold. I didn't take kindly to anyone who looked down on farmers. Without them and their hard work and sacrifice, no one would have food on their plates. Farmers made up a big portion of Aberron, since the soil was particularly good for growing. They didn't have fancy lives, but they worked hard for them. Harder than I bet any of these people ever did.

"Yes." I tried to keep my voice civil, but I knew it had a cold edge. "Farming."

Henry put his hands up, backing off. "I didn't mean to get you upset; farmers are an integral part of our community. Without them, our country would crumble."

I relaxed a little. "I'm very passionate about farmers and the hard work they do to put food on our table and keep our economy going."

"So are you a farmer then?" Aliyah asked.

I shook my head. "I only gardened. My adoptive father is a blacksmith by trade."

"Blacksmith." Henry's eyebrows raised, a soft smile gradually appearing. "That's a noble profession." He laughed and leaned closer to his tablemates. "I guess even farmers need a blacksmith."

I didn't know whether he meant his joke to be condescending or not. I couldn't read him very well, so I just nodded and kept silent. They eventually moved on to other topics and left me alone. I didn't even try to understand who or what they talked about.

Henry had a charismatic, slightly intoxicating personality. He drew people in effortlessly. I couldn't help but compare him to Andrew, and it left me with a pang in my heart. Henry had the same blue eyes and strong jaw. I noticed some differences: hair color, ears, not as muscular. His hands appeared smoother and not as calloused either.

Henry glanced at me toward the end of breakfast. "You didn't eat anything."

"I'm not actually hungry," I said.

Henry cocked his head slightly to the side and raised his eyebrows but didn't say anything. A bell rang. I cringed, the shrill sound ringing in my ears. Everyone in the dining hall got up, grabbed their bags, and slung them over their shoulders.

I took a breath and stiffened. Nervous anticipation consumed me. For the first time in forever, I prayed to the Gods that they would help me get through this day.

"Just follow us. You'll figure it out soon enough," Henry said casually.

"Sure," I agreed.

I felt like a blind lamb in a crowd of sheep following Henry and his group to the first class of the day. I hadn't even bothered to check the class schedule, and at this point I figured I didn't need to.

A small plaque next to the door of the classroom we entered read "Professor Ventreast. Mathematics."

A decent-size room, small desks, and chairs faced a large blackboard with math equations written in dusty white chalk. Framed equations hung on the wall next to charts with helpful math hints. I ambled over to a large desk littered with papers. The professor watched me as I reached him. His hard mouth and crooked nose caught my attention. His broad shoulders were hunched over, most likely from time spent leaning over his desk.

"Isabelle, right?" he acknowledged me. "Lord Leavesden informed all of us that we were getting a new student today. Seems rather strange that you're coming here so late, though."

"I wasn't expecting to be here," I explained.

He leaned back in his chair, fiddling with a pen, and eyed me. "I've learned never to expect anything. Therefore, I'm never disappointed."

"Might be a good idea," I said lamely, shoving my left hand in my pocket.

"Well, just find any empty seat and try to follow along; I'll come talk with you once the class is started." He pointed in the direction of the desks.

I nodded and took a seat near the front of the room. I set my bag on the floor next to me like everyone else had done.

The professor snaked his way through the desks until he faced us. "Get out your homework. I am going to collect it." His voice carried across the room well.

Students scrambled to shove papers and books aside. Professor Ventreast went around the room and collected everyone's papers. He set them on his crowded desk and walked to the front of the room.

"Today we are focusing on probability." He turned around and wrote the word on the blackboard.

I listened intently as he taught the class. He scribbled equations on the board and made the class solve them while calling on random students for the answer. He never called on me once.

"All right, open your books, and write down these numbers. I want them done and ready to hand in tomorrow." He put the chalk down and dusted off his hands.

I had barely opened the front of the book when Professor Ventreast marched over.

"Did you understand any of that?" He sat in the empty desk beside me.

"Yes." I nodded.

"What kind of schooling did you have where you came from? Or did you go to school?" he amended his first question. Schooling wasn't a requirement in Aberron, so it wasn't out of the ordinary to ask.

The soft chatter suddenly ceased as the whole room waited for my response. I felt a flash of annoyance at their open curiosity but tried to stifle it. "I studied out of books we had at home," I explained.

Professor Ventreast pursed his lips and furrowed his eyebrows. I didn't know what it meant.

"Name a book you studied out of," he commanded, rubbing his chin.

"A math book?" I queried.

He nodded.

I raised my eyes to the ceiling as I thought. "*Math and Logic: An Integral Part of Our Lives* by a Sheridan—Sheridan something or other, I can't remember the last name."

Professor Ventreast got up and grabbed a book off a shelf, then shoved it in my face. I leaned back to avoid a collision with my nose. "Is this the book you used?"

I stared at the old green velvet cover and nodded. "Yes, that's the one. By Sheridan Grades."

"This is more advanced than the one on your desk." He pointed to the book on my table. "I might have to switch yours out with another one."

"You mean this isn't basic math?" I pointed to the book I had studied out of growing up.

Professor Ventreast shook his head.

"Oh."

"Do you mind if I test you?" He set the old book on the desk with a thump; plumes of dust rose.

I shrugged and held back a wince.

Professor Ventreast wrote out an intense equation on the blackboard. I recognized it from the book by Sheridan Grades and had an answer within one minute.

He raised his eyebrows at me when I gave him the correct answer, his thin lips in a slightly amused smile. "Well then, you do understand this."

"Yes, Professor," I said meekly. My skin flushed hot as I watched the other students stare at me in amazement. Several scratched their heads, appearing thoroughly confused as they focused on the equation on the blackboard.

For the remainder of the class, Professor Ventreast tested my knowledge of mathematics, becoming exceedingly delighted throughout the hour as I solved each problem. By the end of the class, Professor Ventreast said he would search for a different book for me, something I had never studied out of before. He seemed thrilled to have a student able to understand harder concepts.

"Well, lady, looks like I should come to you for help with my math homework." Henry grinned as we walked out of class.

I shrugged and winced slightly. Gods forbid I needed to remember to stop doing that. "Oh no." I fumbled for the right words to say. "I mean—I didn't—"

Henry shrugged. "Don't worry about it."

The next professor stood by the door greeting everyone as they walked in. Short for a man, he took on a rather frenzied appearance with a balding head and a black mustache. The stain on the front of his shirt, shaped like a cat's paw, made me think he was often clumsy.

"Isabelle Mirran, right?" he asked while shaking my hand. "I hope you're not allergic to cats."

"I'm not," I said, glancing at the name plaque to get his name.

Professor Breldian grinned. "Good, because the only seat left is Ginger's favorite." He pointed at the desk where a large fluffy orange cat loafed. One green eye opened, she eyed the students as they settled in. "You can push her off, but she'll just climb back on. Don't worry, she's very nice and loves to read."

"That's fine." I ambled slowly over to the desk. "Hello, Ginger." I rubbed her ears. She purred. Her claws jutted out as she stretched and pushed her head back into my hands. I smiled, taking that as an invitation to sit down. I petted the cat leisurely while the professor made his way up to the front to address the class.

Professor Breldian picked up an old, worn leather-bound book and thumbed through a few pages before finding his desired location. He cleared his throat a few times and read.

> **"The senseless wonder,**
> **Lost through time.**
> **Questions unanswered,**
> **Alone they chime.**
> **The past relived,From g**
> **reat men of old,**
> **The future disguised,**
> **Their stories told.**
> **Given as a gift,**
> **'Tis present here.**
> **Each moment vivid,**
> **So close ... disappears.**

A universal paradise,
Lost in our minds.
Life unceasing.
A never-breaking bind."

He set the book down on his desk and folded his arms, staring speculatively at the class. "Now who can tell me who wrote those famous words, and where we can find them?" He leaned against the desk.

Dead silence. Not a single student raised a hand or spoke up.

Professor Breldian tapped his foot on the stone floor, thoroughly disappointed. A minute passed by. "Come on, you should all know this."

Unable to stand the silence any longer, I raised my hand. Professor Breldian smiled, seeming relieved that someone, at least, ventured a guess. "Yes, Isabelle?"

"It was King Elan, fourth King of Aberron," I said.

"Yes!" he shouted, raising a fist in the air.

I flinched—his exuberance caught me off guard.

"And where can we find it?" He paced back and forth, his shoes slapping against the stone floor.

"On his tombstone," I said, folding my hands together under the table.

"Which is located where?" he shot back.

"In the Hall of the Kings, deep in the Fraison mountainside," I answered. Ginger swiped her paw at me, so I petted her some more.

Professor Breldian paused midpace and asked a totally unrelated question. "Where are you from?"

"Saren," I answered.

He put a finger on his chin, tapping it as he stared at the ceiling, contemplating. "Saren—that's south of here right?" He glanced at me.

"Yes," I answered, surprised he recognized the name.

"The south is mostly made up of farmers. Am I safe to assume that is the case for Saren?" He started pacing again.

"Yes," I said, wondering why he asked in the first place. If he recognized the name, wouldn't he know it was farming community? Perhaps he memorized maps in his free time.

Ginger stood and stretched. I leaned back to avoid her long, bushy tail swatting my face as she hopped off the table.

Professor Breldian raised a finger in the air and paused, completely misconstruing my answers. "Take note, class: a farmer knows more than the descendants of the rich and royal."

My cheeks flamed as muttered grumblings started among the other students. I slumped lower in my seat, feeling stupid for answering the question. The professor had just ruined what little social standing I could have had. Among my peers, I sensed I sunk faster than a rock thrown in a pond.

We spent the rest of the class writing down what we thought King Elan meant when he wrote that poem and why he thought it important enough to put on his tombstone. Ginger hopped back onto the desk, forcing me to write in my lap.

As I followed Henry to the next class across the hall, I froze. Alzmire stood near the open door, greeting the students as they marched in. With everything else going on, it had slipped my mind that he taught here.

"Isabelle!" Alzmire held out his hand and enclosed mine in his. "Lord Leavesden said your brother enrolled you, but I couldn't quite believe it." He let go. "Why?"

"It's a long story." I sighed and rubbed my forehead. "I'll explain it when you have time."

"How are you feeling?" He put a hand on my left shoulder and eyed me up and down.

I winced at the pressure he put on my bad shoulder. "I'm fine."

"The Sorrenian has its own personal healer, so don't take on too much if you don't think you can handle it," he advised me, moving his hand away.

I nodded. "I'll be fine."

He smiled. "All right, but we must chat soon. I want to know what's going on."

"Yes," I agreed.

I sat in the only empty seat left and waited for Alzmire to start the class. From the pictures of maps and old artifacts lying across the room, I expected it to be history. I was wrong.

"It's First Day, and you know what that means. Foreign language. Please get out your Nistieran books. Turn to page twenty-four and practice sounding out the vowels," Alzmire directed, striding through the desks and to the front of the room.

Great. I already knew how to speak the language fluently. It helped that Adel's mother was Nistieran. We often spoke it at home, though Nathan always hated it. He understood it well enough but had issues with pronunciation. He said he felt silly when a gruff man like him spoke a fluid and flowery language. Unlike our native tongue that sounded harsher when spoken. As a child, I loved it when Adel would sing me lullabies in Nisterian. For a while, it became the only thing that helped me sleep.

Alzmire came over to my desk and leaned against it. "I don't suppose you know any Nistieran, do you?"

I answered in Nistieran. "I am fluent in the language."

Alzmire beamed and responded in the same tongue. "Really? Who taught you?"

"My adoptive mother Adel is half-Nistieran," I explained. "Also, we do more trade with Nistier than anywhere else, so my adoptive parents thought it would be good to learn."

"Perfect. Most of these dimwits can barely say hello in Nistieran, so I can test you and have our chat at the same time." He grinned and pulled a chair over. Sitting down, he crossed his legs and spoke. "So how did your meeting with Joshua go?"

"Poorly," I admitted. "We argued. My brother disapproves Andrew as a suitor. I don't think Joshua's opinion matters. He's never shown interest in me before, I don't care for him to start now."

"If he's been so indifferent why are you now under his care?" Alzmire asked.

I lifted my left hand and dropped it. "My ridiculous birthmark is causing unwanted attention. I swear I don't have a magical bone in my body but people keep thinking I'm special or something. Hence the attempted kidnap that nearly cost me my life." I waved my right hand flippantly. "Joshua can protect me better than my adoptive parents in Saren."

"Joshua certainly has the skills to keep you safe," Alzmire agreed mildly. "So why the Sorrenian?"

"Joshua thinks the Sorrenian will teach me the proper culture to enter court society." I paused, then added, "A look into the lives of the rich and noble, if not a book-learning education."

"How old are you?" Alzmire leaned his elbow on the edge of my desk and rested his chin in his hand.

"Seventeen."

"You meet the age criteria," he mused. "Hmm. . . now that you're in my class, I don't know what to do with you. You already speak Nistieran so eloquently." He cocked his head to the side and eyed the ceiling, his lips pursed as he contemplated. "You could easily work as a translator." His eyes flashed to mine. "We've had a recent shortage of them, which is why everyone's learning Nisterian. We just made this class mandatory. Maybe you can be a tutor to the others." He gestured to the class.

I scoffed. "Do you see the expression on their faces?" I cast my eyes around the room and saw the other students eyeing me with scowls. "I'm pretty sure the last professor ruined my chances of having friends when he insulted them using me."

He raised an eyebrow. "Oh? What did he say?"

"A farmer knows more than the descendants of the rich and royal," I said drily.

Alzmire laughed, shaking his head. "That's a good one."

I grinned; his laugh infected me. "If only they took it as a joke."

Alzmire nodded, his smile evaporating. "The children of the rich and powerful think they rule the world. Don't let it bother you. I warn you, though, they will search until they find a flaw and will most likely, no—" He raised a finger. "Undoubtedly—exploit it."

I gave him a half smile. "I'll keep that in mind."

Alzmire grinned and patted me on the shoulder. "So you should. I better check on the others." He stood. Putting his hands behind his back, he stretched, then started directing students in the class, helping them sound out the vowels in the book.

Falden, who sat in front of me, turned around. He spoke in our native tongue. "Hey, how'd you get so smart?"

"I grew up with this language. We spoke it often at home," I said.

He nodded and closed his lips into a tight half smile, half grimace. I didn't know what to make of it.

Henry caught up with me as the class ended. "Speak another language as well? What else are we going to learn about you today?"

"Guess it depends on what the subject is," I said meekly, gripping onto my shoulder bag.

The next class turned out to be land and business management. Many potted plants strewn about the room, forcing the tables to be scrunched together for space. It reminded me of home, and I loved it.

I ambled over to the teacher. She leaned over an aloe vera plant.

"Hello," I said. "I'm new to your class."

She turned and smiled, revealing warm amber eyes, a small nose, and a pointed chin. "I heard about you from Professor Breldian. You must be the first farmer to ever step through these doors as a student. It's quite a surprise." She held out her hand, and I shook it. "I'm Professor Morel." Her voice sounded slightly brusque for a woman. "Have a seat over there, and we'll get started." She pointed to a seat.

Once sitting down, I tuned into the muttering around me.

"Wonder if she's any good here. She's good at all the other classes," Falden said.

"She's basically a farmer, remember?" Aliyah said hotly. "Of course she'll know about agriculture."

I quit listening.

Professor Morel tapped a stick on a table to get our attention. "Before we start, I believe an explanation to our new student is in order." She angled herself to me. "In this class we discuss the inner workings of Aberron. We cover everything from being a merchant, fisherman, farmer, logger, miner, and the like. We also discuss hot spring expansion, treaty negotiations, and how to maintain the upper hand as a leader or diplomat. Most of the students attending the Sorrenian will be taking on leadership roles in their family's profession. It is my duty to make sure no one shames their family with a lack of knowledge or propriety."

I nodded. First class of the day that might hold my interest.

Professor Morel took a deep breath and centered her eyes on me. "Currently we are studying the lives of farmers. Now I realize, as a farmer yourself, there is little I can teach you. The others, however, have much to learn." She faced the rest of the students. "In fact, raise your hand if you have ever spoken to a farmer, excluding our new student of course."

Out of the fourteen or so students, only three people raised their hands. What kind of sheltered lives did these people live?

Professor Morel smiled and cast her eyes back on me. "See what I mean?"

I nodded. "Yes."

She clapped her hands. "Great. Now we can get on with the lesson."

We spent the rest of the time going over mundane facts about farming. Professor Morel's voice droned on and on about the prices of harvested crops. First wheat, then carrots, corn, and so on. My hope to learn something new dwindled into nothing.

CHAPTER FIFTEEN

 KEPT HENRY'S GROUP IN my sights just to get directions to lunch, but as we got to the eating hall, they gave me a sidelong glance before brushing past. Already I felt a rift between the other students and me.

As I grabbed a little food, I listened to the students at Henry's table converse. They didn't bother to keep it quiet.

"Did you see that new girl? She practically waved her hand, and suddenly all the professors were worshipping her like a Goddess." A girl—Amarilla, I thought—leaned over their table asking.

"Come on, guys; she can't be that impenetrable. There's a chink in her armor somewhere. So what if she's book smart? That doesn't mean she's good on the field. We'll see how she does then. Don't judge too soon," Henry said, his blazing blue eyes catching mine.

"Field? You mean she's not in sewing or art class?" Amarilla's jaw dropped.

Henry broke eye contact and responded to the girl. "Yes, she's supposed to be in our defense classes." He picked up a grape and popped it into his mouth.

"But it isn't proper for a girl to fight," Amarilla protested, throwing her hands up in confusion. "She'll be the only girl there!"

It's what the Lord ordered." Henry shrugged, eating another grape.

I felt eyes on me as I left the dining hall and made my way to my room. I only took one wrong turn as I followed the markers.

I lay on my bed and closed my eyes. Alzmire was right. Already the students searched for something against me. Why did they feel the need to be smarter and superior? I sighed and rubbed my temples. This would be more frustrating than I thought.

I ate quickly and checked on my injuries, applying more salves and a little more than a smidgeon of the purple bottle. Just enough to take the edge off. My skin felt hot and bothered, but I refused to let it get to me. I wanted to be in control of my body. Regardless of how much pain I felt.

I spent a minute going over my schedule and read the little notes that went along with it. I had class First through Fifth Day. Kings and Gods Day were meant for studying and relaxing. They held the first defensive class, fencing with a Professor Trisgeld, outside in the practice fields.

I had mixed emotions about practicing. The last time I gripped a sword in my hands, I used it to defend my life. It wasn't easy to forget the fear and adrenaline pulsating through my body when a sword had crashed down on me. I shuddered and felt a shiver go down my spine at the memory. I took a deep breath and reminded myself that practice saved my life. I would lose my skill if I didn't keep it up.

The other more pressing problem I faced was my injuries. I wasn't fit to practice. I would only injure myself further. I bit my lip, deciding to go down there anyway and tell the professor my problem, hoping he would understand. Maybe he'd let me sit and I could observe the class?

I grabbed my sword and hitched it to my belt.

"There," I said softly. "Ready to face the nightmare."

The sun hovered high overhead, and a soft breeze blew in my face as I caught up with the other students in defensive classes. The boys met me with open glares and hostility. I understood immediately. I overstepped in a man's world.

I couldn't be the only girl that wanted to learn defensive skills, could I? What about the women who wanted to be soldiers? Nathan told me women could join the Aberron army and could even train to become knights if they gained favor with the King. He told me some of the best fighters he ever saw were women. Where did they learn? I wondered how many men stopped women from studying. There'd never been a law banning women from holding a sword, but the unspoken rule was widely kept.

"What's a girl doing in a fighting class?" I heard one of the boys mutter to another named Ethan. I hadn't caught his name yet.

"Beats me." Ethan shook his head in disbelief.

"Look at her—she's such a tiny thing she probably can't even hold a sword properly. My younger sister is bigger than her, and she's barely fourteen," the boy continued, examining me. "Girls aren't made for fighting. It's not right."

I curled my fingers into fists, trying to keep my anger in check. I took a breath. I'd prove these boys wrong, regardless of the toll it took.

"All right, gather 'round all!" The professor called, striding forward. He had silvery blonde hair and a grizzled beard. Scars covered his face. His most prominent feature was a crooked nose. "You know the routine. Stretches! So grab a partner and get going!"

Everyone scrambled to find a partner. I didn't even try. With an uneven number of people, I would be the odd woman out regardless.

"Mirran, right?" The professor called as I nodded. He glanced at me up and down without even a hint of judgment. It caught me by surprise. "Heard about you." He rubbed the whiskers on his chin. "I've heard you know your book learning better than these dolts." He gestured to the boys with his thumb. "We'll see how well you can handle a sword. It's not often a girl wants to learn how to fence." He pointed to Henry and Dominic. "Work with these two since you're new. They're the best."

I glanced at Henry and Dominic. Both wore sly grins on their faces from the compliment. I wondered if Professor Trisgeld gave them out very often. *Probably not.*

"All right, get going!" The professor yelled. He stomped over to Henry and Dominic. "Teach her the ropes. She's new."

"I've noticed," Henry quipped, turning to me. He wore a silly grin as he eyed me all over. He pointed at my sword hanging on my belt. "You've got a sword. You know how to use it?"

"Of course." I unstrapped it from my belt and laid it next to me in the grass while I stretched.

Henry and Dominic laughed, obviously not believing me. *Just wait; they'll see.*

"We'll soon find out," Dominic said with a smug grin, pushing his black hair away from his eyes.

"All right, stretches." Henry jumped up and down and shook out his arms and legs. "Shouldn't be too hard for a girl like you."

I raised an eyebrow. *Like me?*

Henry caught my expression. "You look limber enough."

"I disagree," Dominic folded his arms and faced Henry. "With her small size, she might not have the stamina."

I furrowed my eyebrows. Since when did my size become an issue? I didn't remember Andrew ever remarking on it.

"So we'll go easy on her." Henry shrugged.

"No need, gentlemen," I interrupted. "I'm sure I can keep up."

Henry and Dominic laughed. "Right." They said simultaneously.

"Hey, get moving!" Professor Trisgeld yelled at us.

Henry wasted no time after the professor reprimanded us. He moved his leg forward and into a stretch; I watched for only a second before realizing the direction he took. They were the same kind of stretches I used to do with Nathan every morning. Hoping my body would cooperate, I moved into the same position as fluidly as I could. I cringed briefly at the intense pain but hid it as soon as I realized I was making a face.

"You know that one." He raised his eyebrows, switching into a new move that I copied.

I nodded. "I've done these before."

"Is there anything you haven't done?" Dominic muttered.

I paused and bit my lip, trying to stay composed. "Yes."

"Like what?"

"School," I answered shortly.

"School's nothing," Dominic responded casually.

"Maybe for you," I said. "Not for me."

"I doubt it." He shook his head.

I stopped following their moves and reverted to my old routine. Only slightly different and just as effective. Sweat beaded on my brow at the pain as I stretched, but I refused to give up, not wanting to let them believe that men were superior. Stupid, but I couldn't stop myself.

"What are you doing?" Henry asked. "Those aren't the moves we're supposed to be doing."

"Does it matter all that much?" I gritted my teeth.

"Stretching time's over!" The professor called, stomping among the students. "Pick up your swords and start the blocking routines. Stay in your same groups."

I moved out of the stretch, sighing in relief. *Gods forbid this hurts—this hurts!* Tears leaked from my eyes, and I quickly wiped them away, pretending that I wiped the sweat from my brow. My mental barrier against the pain crumbled into a fine powder. I felt an ooze of blood mix in with the salves and bandages that I had pasted on my shoulder. I grimaced and stared at it. It hadn't showed through my clothes yet. I sighed a breath of relief. *I should quit now before it gets worse.*

I picked up my sword while the others walked over to a small shed to grab theirs. The professor marched over.

"Where'd you get this sword?" He eyed it.

I unsheathed it and handed it to him. "I made it."

"No you didn't." He lifted it up and down and tested the balance.

"Yes I did," I argued patiently. "With guidance."

"With whom?" He narrowed his eyes at me.

"Nathan Whysten." I folded my arms.

"Whysten, the knight?" he queried.

I nodded. "He's a blacksmith now."

Professor Trisgeld rubbed his chin, seeming to remember. "His father was an expert sword maker. Supplied the very finest to the King. Didn't know Nathan made swords, though."

"Only on occasion," I said.

"So I can safely assume you know how to handle this?" He indicated my weapon.

I nodded. "Of course."

"We normally use blades with less of an edge to them. Don't want someone to make a mistake and kill their partner." He handed it back. "But seeing as you're new, would you mind showing me what you can do?"

I bit my lip, ready to tell him that I was injured. "Actually ..."

Henry and Dominic walked past, catching the last part of our conversation. Henry turned to Dominic and said, "She's going to back out. Can't bluff Trisgeld."

"I hope she doesn't. I would love to see Trisgeld expose her as a fraud," Dominic answered.

I clenched my jaw and refocused on Trisgeld. "I would love to." I ignored the nagging thought in the back of my mind that I was making a serious mistake. These boys would learn that a woman has just as much a right to hold a sword as a man.

Professor Trisgeld unsheathed his blade. I moved into position. Unexpectedly, a memory flashed before my eyes. I stood in the forest. Gleason charged at me while his boss laughed. I flinched and shook my head to clear it. *Get a grip. Dead men can't hurt me,* I thought firmly.

I didn't know if Trisgeld noticed, but all the boys huddled together to watch.

"Begin," Professor Trisgeld said, falling into position.

I gripped my sword with my right hand, deciding to forgo using both, which I normally did. I wanted to avoid using my left arm as much as possible so I wouldn't strain my shoulder. Trisgeld started off slow with a few jabs and parries, testing my defenses. I blocked them easily, letting him attack while I defended. Gradually we switched stances. *Not so bad,* I thought.

Professor Trisgeld grinned. "Why don't we set aside the little games and see how good you really are?"

"Are you sure?" I bit my lip. *Not a good idea,* my mind argued. Yet despite feeling chained to my wounds, I also felt revitalized. From the moment

Nathan placed a sword in my hand, fencing had been my escape. The best relaxation technique I had in my arsenal. I lived for it. I knew it was stupid, but I didn't want to stop. I didn't want to give up the one thing that helped me breathe.

"Yes, I'm sure." His expression betrayed annoyance. "They wouldn't have made me the defense professor unless they thought I could handle myself. If it gets too intense, I'll just say stop." He moved on his feet like he'd waited forever for a student to challenge him. It momentarily reminded me of the attack in the forest. I cringed.

We moved into position. The boys stood rock still, their eyes glued to Professor Trisgeld and me. *My audience awaits.*

True to what Trisgeld wanted, we made it as real as possible without actually killing each other. He charged at me, his sword high; I ducked and swiped at his legs. He jumped back and parried my attack. It became a blur of motion. Sweat poured off Trisgeld and underneath my clothes I felt blood. Surprisingly, I found it easy to detach my brain from the pain. Instinct or survival kicked in as I narrowed my eyes and focused only on the oncoming threat. He pulled moves I hadn't seen before, and I had to stretch to get out of the way in time. The bandages now seeped. I prayed the blood wouldn't show through my shirt.

After a couple of intense, agonizing minutes, I moved into an offensive position I thought could get me ahead of the game. Trisgeld feinted to the right and swiveled around, locking my sword with his with a sound of screeching metal. I fought to hold onto my position, but I couldn't match his strength. Not with how much pain I held back.

He twirled the swords around until he hooked the handle and flung it out of my hands. He used the same move I did to defend myself in the forest. I fell to the ground, and my hands dug into the dry grass and dirt as I held back a cry. Trisgeld pointed my sword back at me, a grin on his scarred face.

I cursed at my luck. I didn't expect to win, but I hoped I wouldn't lose so poorly either. He held out a hand and pulled me up to my feet. I cringed against the aching throughout my body.

"Thank you," I said breathlessly, wiping my brow with my sleeve.

He handed me my blade. "I haven't had a match like that with a student since Prince Andrew. You weren't joking when you said you knew how to fence."

"In Saren I practiced every morning before breakfast." I sheathed my sword.

"It shows." The professor finally noticed the boys standing still. "Hey, get to work! No gawking!"

Everyone scrambled into positions and started jabbing half-heartedly at their opponents.

Professor Trisgeld faced me. "I'll reward you with a rest. Why don't you watch Henry and Dominic? Maybe you can give them a few pointers." He walked away, shaking his head and muttering something about girls I didn't quite catch.

I stumbled over by Dominic and Henry; afraid I'd collapse if I had to stay upright for much longer. *Gods forbid this hurts!* I sat in the grass and dug my hands in the dirt. I glanced at my shoulder and noticed a spot of blood showing through. I quickly unpinned my hair and fanned it around, hiding my injury from view.

"Looks like this girl tells no lies. She handled that sword like a trained soldier." Henry whistled. "Hey, you ever seen a girl fight like that, Dominic?"

Dominic shook his head. "No."

"Don't get on her bad side." Henry grinned wolfishly.

I kept my eyes on Henry and Dominic as a distraction from the pain coming at me in full force. Compared to the other boys, they excelled. By the time class ended, the bandages felt soggy with blood. The spot on my shoulder gradually increased in size. *Thank the Gods for long hair*, I thought, sweeping all of it over to cover the blood.

I took deep breaths, trying to manage walking without limping like an old woman. I imagined Andrew eyeing me with disapproval.

Following the class, I entered a large building adjacent to the school. Cloth tapestries pinned to the wall depicted warrior poses. A young man came out of a study. He had fluid features that all blended evenly. I couldn't see a single flaw in his face. No blemishes or scars. Was it magic or luck? I decided on magic. No one could look that good without some help. He glided across the floor. I suspected the girls here favored him.

"Good afternoon, class!" he greeted us, his voice as smooth as his face. "Professor Trisgeld better not have run you ragged, because we have heaps to practice today. Line up and stretch." He eyed us over until he caught sight of me and stopped.

"Ah, Isabelle." He smiled. "The new student. Mind if I have a word?" Using his index finger, he beckoned me forward.

I ambled over, hoping he wouldn't test me.

"Well, my dear, you seem to have a bag full of tricks up your sleeve."

The comment caught me off guard. I cocked my head to the side. "Excuse me?"

"I watched you fighting Trisgeld. You're just as quick with a sword as you are with your mind, or so I'm told." He flashed a charming smile.

"Oh, I guess so." I didn't know if I should feel embarrassed or grateful. All I really wanted to do was curl in a ball and cry.

"Have you ever tried using a staff?" he queried.

"Staff?" I shook my head. "No. I've only practiced with a sword and occasionally a bow or crossbow." I didn't see the point in trying to use a stick as a weapon. It couldn't cut anything.

"There are many things you can do with a staff. It is a good tool to use when you're left without a weapon of choice. That is what I teach. How to use unconventional weapons as a means to defend yourself," he explained, clasping his hands together. "Right now, we are working with staffs. So, say you were in the middle of a fight and you lose your sword—an old man's cane can knock someone out."

I nodded. Truthfully, I didn't see how a cane could beat a sword. I could chop it up.

He smiled, completely oblivious to my inner monologue disagreeing with every word he spoke. "Stand by Henry and follow along. I will come back and observe in a few minutes."

"Back over here again, eh?" Henry eyed me as I meandered over.

"Apparently, they think you are a great teacher," I said, frankly.

He grinned. "I am a fantastic teacher to a willing student."

"I'm sure," I murmured.

"The stretches are the same as the last class, so you shouldn't have any problems." Henry reached down and touched his toes.

"Move into a new stretch," Professor Lildren called out to the class.

I didn't follow my own routine this time. Instead, I copied Henry's moves exactly and fought against the surmounting agony.

Professor Lildren came over. "I don't think we're going to have a problem with you keeping up in class."

"I hope not," I said a little breathlessly.

"All right, grab a staff and get into groups of two. Henry, work with Isabelle; Falden and Dominic, you two work together." Professor Lildren called out people's names and put them into groups.

I saw a sour expression on Henry's face. No doubt he thought I would show him up again, but I had no idea what to do with a staff. I wondered if it would make a difference if I told him.

Grabbing a staff, I waited patiently for Henry to return. He walked at a snail's pace.

"I'm sorry you're partnered with me. I know you'd rather be with someone else." I tried to ease the tension.

"The professor makes the decisions, not us," he said, throwing the staff back and forth in his hands.

"Right." I shut up.

"I'm sure I don't have to teach you anything." He gripped the staff tightly.

I lifted the staff awkwardly. "I haven't used a staff before. I've mainly worked with swords or a bow."

He gawked at me. "It won't take you long to learn then, will it?"

He seemed to enjoy showing me where to place my hands. I asked questions, copying his hand movements as best I could. Despite feeling skeptical, I took the opportunity to learn.

"Not so tough now, are you?" Henry nearly smacked my hand with the staff.

"Never said I was tough." I gritted my teeth, pushing off an outward attack. My stamina began to fail. A headache I tried to block out felt like a pounding sledgehammer. Stress built up faster than I could control. Every move with the staff exerted more energy than I had available. I shook my head and closed my eyes for a second to clear it. I didn't see Henry's staff coming at me. He knocked me right off my feet and onto the ground.

My breath whooshed out as I slammed the back of my head into the wooden floor. I bit my lip hard, and blood spilled into my mouth. My vision clouded.

"Hey, you were supposed to block that." Henry stood over me, concern on his face.

I squinted, seeing double. I gripped my forehead, hiding my face in my hands as I mentally cried out.

"You all right?" He held out a hand and lifted me off the ground with ease. His strength surprised me.

"Fine." I shaded my eyes, fighting the tears of pain forming. I didn't want him to see.

"Hey—is that blood?" Henry pointed to my leg, sounding wary and concerned.

I glanced down. "Gods forbid." Blood showed through my bandages, staining my clothes. My hair had slipped off my shoulder, revealing the injury I tried to hide. I didn't see a point in moving it back. Henry had already seen everything.

"You're bleeding," Henry stated, aghast. "Everywhere." He dropped his staff. It clattered to the floor as he stumbled backward.

"Don't worry about it," I snapped.

Henry's expression turned incredulous. "Don't worry about it?" He rubbed his temples. "I know you fell kind of hard, but I didn't do that."

"You didn't. Don't worry about it," I repeated.

"What kind of person are you? You shouldn't be fighting if you're injured." He balled his fists, eyeing me like I was cracked.

Maybe I was.

"All right, what's going on?" Professor Lildren strode over. He stood in between Henry and me. Everyone stopped practicing and watched our interaction. They held on to their staffs with their mouths open and eyes fastened on me. Once again, I became the main attraction.

The professor's sharp gaze eyed me up and down. He raised an eyebrow and balled his fists. "Henry, what did you do?"

"I didn't do anything!" Henry held up his hands and took another step backward.

"She wasn't bleeding before," Professor Lildren said, his voice cold.

"All right, I might have accidentally knocked her over, but I did not do that," Henry amended, gesturing to me. "You gonna come to my defense or what?"

"Henry didn't do anything." I sighed, rubbing my forehead. "I was injured before."

I saw frustration flash in the professor's eyes. "And you didn't think to mention that before you launched into physical activity?"

I shook my head. "It's not an issue." I didn't want it to be a problem. I wanted it to go away.

"Oh, I think blood is a very big issue." He seemed to think for a moment. "All right, Henry go practice with Dominic." He tilted his head in Dominic's direction. "Isabelle, go to Malsin, our healer. He needs to have a look at you."

"Fine," I lied.

"You know the way?" he asked.

"Yes," I lied again.

I wouldn't protest, but I had no intention of going to any healer. I picked up the staff and handed it to Professor Lildren as I limped out of class. I headed to my room.

I was met with a few open stares as I stumbled to my room, but thankfully no other professors. I feared they would personally escort me to the healer. I collapsed onto the floor in the bathroom, tears of pain leaking out of my eyes.

"I can't do this," I cried softly.

It was too much. The open hostility and my competitive nature, stupidity, and injuries. I lost track of time, crying on the bathroom floor until every ounce of energy evaporated and I fell asleep. My last thought was one of pity. I felt sorry for myself crying on the floor covered in blood once again.

I couldn't be turning into a blood-soaked lunatic ... could I?

CHAPTER SIXTEEN

SLEPT THROUGH THE NEXT class: horseback riding. Another lesson I didn't need. When I awoke, dinner was nearly over, and I still needed check in with the professor who taught magic. I briefly contemplated not going but then thought it wouldn't take long. They would see I possessed no such gift and send me back to my room to rest. Better to get it over and done with. I peeled off my stained clothes and took a quick bath, washing off all the caked blood and grime. I applied a generous amount of salves and wrapped fresh bandages on. I wrapped them tighter and thicker this time. I slipped on fresh clothes and stepped out the door.

I walked slowly throughout the halls, not sure where to go. I searched out the numbers on the walls and compared them to the numbers on my schedule. I nearly bumped into Lord Leavesden when I glanced down at my wrinkled note. Great, he probably heard what happened this afternoon.

"Isabelle, how is your first day going?" He smiled kindly.

I pasted on a quick smile. "Fine." *Wow, maybe he doesn't know.* Better keep it that way.

"Where are you headed? You look lost," he asked, noticing the note in my hand.

"It says on my schedule to see a Professor Slystream to test for magic." I shoved the note in my pocket.

Lord Leavesden nodded. "Right. Follow me and I'll take you there."

I trailed behind Lord Leavesden as we journeyed through the maze of hallways to the classroom.

"Here we are." Lord Leavesden pointed to a room. He gestured for me to enter and followed behind.

The room had a strong stench I couldn't quite make out, but it smelled awful. Kind of like fire and salts, I thought after a minute of breathing it in. Shelves bursting with glass vials filled with different color liquids lined most of the walls. The tables appeared soot stained and scarred.

The professor busily scribbled in a small black book as he held on to a blue vial of liquid. A smattering of freckles showed on his light skin. He appeared tall and lanky beneath the black clothes he wore.

"Euan." Lord Leavesden addressed the man.

The professor looked up. "Oh, I didn't notice you come in." He set the blue vial and pen down, then closed the notebook with a snap.

"No matter. This is Isabelle Mirran. I want you to test her for magic. She doesn't believe she has any gift, but her brother Joshua has it. I thought we better do it out of precaution. She's never been tested before." Lord Leavesden placed a heavy hand on my bad shoulder.

I winced.

"Sure, sure." The professor leaned back in his chair and cast his pale blue eyes on me. "Do you mind waiting until I get class started to test you?"

I shook my head.

"Great." He gestured to an empty desk and chair spaced a little farther away from the others, near the single dingy window. "Have a seat, and I'll be back in a few minutes."

Lord Leavesden let go of my shoulder and smiled. "Thank you, Euan. Good luck, Isabelle." He strode out of the room like a man on a mission.

The class filed in minutes later. I noticed there were significantly fewer students. My eyes narrowed when I saw the duo of Dominic and Henry followed by Aliyah and Falden. Quartet, maybe? Five more students came in, but I didn't remember their names. Two girls and three boys.

Henry didn't even sit down. The second he spotted me, he made a beeline to me. "Don't tell me you're a mage as well?"

"I'm pretty sure I'm not, but they still want to test me." I paused and added. "Don't worry—I'll be out of your way soon."

Henry smiled and leaned a little on the desk until his eyes leveled with mine. *Don't get too close,* I thought. I'd lose my head if I stared at them too long.

"You made quite an entrance in the field today," Henry said casually.

"Wasn't intending to," I answered briskly.

He pointed a finger at me. "There's something strange about you—and I'm not talking about the impressive skills you've got."

I raised an eyebrow.

"So did you go see Malsin?" He switched subjects casually, straightening his posture.

"Yep, I'm all patched up." I bit the bottom of my lip, wishing I could lie better.

"You never went, did you?" His eyes widened in shock, then narrowed.

"What does it matter to you?" I tried not to sound cynical. Something about Henry unnerved me, and not just his eyes.

Henry shook his head and placed a hand on the back of his neck rubbing it. "You are one crazy girl ..." His eyes moved down to rest on my birthmark.

I shrugged.

"All right, in your seats." Professor Slystream clapped his hands to get everyone's attention.

Henry stepped away and took a seat to the left of me. As he sat, he gave me one cursory glance. He had a great vantage point of everyone in the room.

The professor directed the class to open their books and start reading about their new subject. Once everyone got started, he came over, pulled up a chair, and sat.

"If you don't have any magic, you won't have to see me ever again." He smiled crookedly and crossed his legs.

I smiled half-heartedly and folded my hands in my lap, hiding my birthmark. I had no desire to possess a single ounce of magic. Every farmer in

Saren said more times than I could count that magic couldn't be trusted, and I believed them. It wasn't natural.

Professor Slystream cleared his throat. "Magic is very simple. Either you're born with it, or you're not. It usually follows your bloodline. For example, if your mother was born with magic, then it is likely you could have it as well. In your case, Lord Leavesden reported that your brother is gifted, so the chances of you having it are significantly greater. Do you understand?"

I nodded.

"Good." He uncrossed his legs and leaned forward a little. "Now, magic is very much connected to your mind and emotions. You have to have a will for it to work. You cannot say half-heartedly that you want to move the paper. You must want to move the paper. Magic can sense your indecision and if you're scared of it. It might not work properly if it senses fear. It likes to be desired." He spoke rapidly like he'd discussed this many times before.

"All right," I answered tentatively when I realized he expected a response.

"All right, I guess we'll just get to the testing part. There is a word I'll have you say. If magic is present, it will recognize the word and should fill you up with a sensation. It is different for each person. Some say warm light like the sun is beating on them, and others say cool water like they jumped in the lake. I do not think there is any difference in the kind of magic you will have; it's just how your body reacts to it." He paused for a moment, situating himself better in the chair.

"Now I'll explain the word that reveals the magic. It is called Spintry. The root of the word, spin, is like weaving an illusion. It is the creator of magic. Try is your part. It's where you're given the materials and it is your turn to mold it into what you want. You have to *try* to have it. Have a desire and a will. That's why it is called Spintry. You try to spin the magic into the thing you desire." He leaned back and smiled, seeming pleased with his explanation.

"Oh, I forgot to add one more thing." He held up a finger. "If you possess the gift, light will glow around you. A flame will appear in your hand. Only one color, maybe two, will shine, but it could be a range of colors from blue to red, green, or yellow. It won't burn you but will help in figuring out where you're properly placed."

I nodded.

"Here, I'll show you." He put his hand out palm facing up and recited the incantation. "Spintry." A small red flame appeared and flickered in his hand. A soft red glow emanated from his body. He closed his hand, and the flame disappeared. "See? Not that hard." He smiled warmly.

"All right, hold out your hand," he ordered. "Wait, what is that on your left hand?" he asked, grabbing it and looking at the birthmark. "That's the Mark of the Gods." He stared at my face incredulously.

"I was born with it. Don't ask me why it's there because I don't know," I explained, trying to keep the irritation out of my voice.

He let go. "Strange."

"I know."

He cocked his head to the side and eyed me over. "All right on the count of three I'll have you say the word 'Spintry.' Ready?" He held up three fingers and slowly counted down, putting down a finger as he counted. "Three ... two ... one."

Taking a deep breath, I spoke the word as clearly as I could and willed for any magic to come forth. "Spintry."

Instantaneously, an intense feeling of cool water trickling started from the top of my head, running down my body. "Oh," I gasped, shivering against the cold. It felt as if I had jumped into a lake in the heat of summer. As soon as I felt the cold dribble down to my toes, a new feeling emerged. A warm heat ran through my veins like a fast burn. I felt on fire. I took a deep intake of breath and cringed.

Wait—I'm only supposed to feel one of these. What's happening?

Strong, exotic senses and feelings I had no name for overpowered me. I became blind to the classroom. I felt wind on my face and breathed in a pungent smell of roses. In my mind's eye, I saw myself passionately kissing Andrew, and an extreme desire for him erupted. I craved his presence like a drug. I trembled and shook.

Within seconds the magic struck me with another scene. I sat on a hard, marbled throne in a room full of strangers. The lighting dark, faces loomed in front of me, coming in and out of focus. I eyed the richly dressed people with mistrust and cold calculation.

Quickly the picture dissolved, swirling around like a tornado. I opened a book, memorizing the pages, learning secrets long forgotten. Then I rode Nisha, galloping through the grassy plains, then I fell into a boundless ocean. Flailing in the water, I started to sink. Fearing for my life, I pushed my way through, digging and kicking at the sea with my hands and feet until I found my way to the surface. When I reached the top, starving for breath, rain fell hard on my face. I inhaled, filling my lungs with air.

The scene changed. I saw myself sleeping on a four-poster bed; my face had hardly any color as though I was the verge of death. My chest rose and fell slowly.

Abruptly my vision cleared, and reality resurfaced. I stared right into the professor's shocked and terrified face. Fear permeated the room. I looked down at my hands, then understood why. I glowed. My entire body glowed bright colors like the flame I held in my shaking hand. It sparked blue, green, yellow, red, changing colors with a blink of an eye.

Gods forbid! Fear grappled me. Tremors went up my spine. I couldn't stop shaking.

"How do you stop it?" I asked the professor. The flashing bright colors hurt my eyes, and I wanted it to go away.

The professor's jaw dropped open with no sound.

I took a more direct approach. "Make it stop!"

I couldn't stop it if I didn't know what to do. The horror on the professor's face made me think I had turned into a monster. Behind him the students huddled together against a shelved wall, watching me with the same amount of terror as Professor Slystream.

"Findel!" Professor Slystream said hoarsely, finally coming to his senses—at least a little bit.

I wasted no time and shouted, "Findel!"

At once the glowing colors and the flame in my palm extinguished into nothing. I couldn't handle the surge of magic leaving so abruptly. I fell forward, smacking my head into the corner of the singed wooden desk. "Ouch!" I gasped.

A smarting pain surfaced and stayed. I stayed hunched over in the chair, gasping, and shaking. A trickle of hot, sticky blood started to slide down my face. Tears leaked from my eyes that I couldn't stop.

Not my face—again. I closed my eyes and gritted my teeth.

"Isabelle?" The professor asked after a minute. He gently put a hand on my bad shoulder. I cried out in pain and he quickly let go.

I lifted my head. My whole body quivered from the withdrawal of magic. *I'm fine. I'm all right.* I tried to reassure myself. *It's just a little bit of blood and agony. I'm used to that, right?* I can handle it. *I have to be all right.*

"I'm—I'm—" My speech slurred. It became increasingly difficult to put words together. "I'm sorry—" Blood dripped down the side of my cheek and onto my shirt. I wished it would quit so I could focus on an explanation for the professor. "I must—have—have—done something—" I closed my eyes and opened them again. "Something wrong."

I was disoriented, and pain shot out of my head like arrows rapidly shooting into a stuffed dummy. My body felt weak and useless. Bile started to rise to my throat. I coughed and clamped a hand over my mouth hoping I wouldn't throw up on the professor. I needed to get out of here, clean up, and assess the damage. I wanted Andrew. He would have jumped into action, not sat there looking dumbfounded.

Leaning heavily on the desk, I stood. My legs wobbled underneath me. Professor Slystream made no move to help me. He sat there like a useless piece of petrified wood. Still trembling, it took every ounce of effort I had to stay in command of my body. Tentatively, I put more weight on my unsteady legs.

"I'll just—go," I managed say. No one rushed forward to help; all had frozen in place, eyes wide open and unblinking.

I took one step forward using the desk as my anchor. I needed something to hold me steady while I thought up a cautious plan to get out.

The door opened and a middle-aged man walked in. "Euan, I know you have class right now, but I need your opinion on something." He didn't notice the scene at first. He didn't see all the students backed against the bottle-crammed shelves or the professor fastened to his seat staring blindly out the window. Then he stopped and blinked, taking in the scene for the first time. "What in the name of the Gods?" he exclaimed.

My strength failed. I collapsed onto the stone floor. Unable to lift my hands out before me, I felt and heard my right arm crack beneath me. More blood spilled from my face, pooling onto the floor. *Great, it's not a shallow wound.* My voice constricted. I couldn't cry out.

I shut my eyes and consciously lay there on the cold, hard floor. Time moved fluidly. I felt cool hands on me, and someone gently lifted me. I opened my eyes, hoping for a split second to see Andrew. But it wasn't him. It didn't feel like Andrew. Instead, the man who had just walked in carried me. He smelled of peppermint and lavender, not cinnamon and woods.

I wanted Andrew.

"I'm taking her to the healing room. Euan, I suggest you dismiss your students and come with me. Henry, you come along too," the man holding me commanded.

I peeked with blurry eyes into the clean-shaven face of the man holding me. He looked on the edge of becoming middle aged, thirty to thirty-five at most.

I didn't follow the flurry of words suddenly spoken by the professor, but I did notice the flash of skin colors as the class hurried out. A breeze hit my face as the man moved with me. I closed my eyes, wishing fervently that I would not throw up. I bit down on my lower lip against the splitting pain engulfing me.

I listened to the steady footfalls of the men surrounding me. No one uttered a single word.

"Malsin! What in the name of the Gods?" a man exclaimed.

"Follow me if you want to know," Malsin said shortly, never breaking his pace.

Malsin was the name of the man who held me. *Who is he?* Then I remembered. *Healer.* Guess I ended up in his clutches after all.

Another set of feet walked briskly with us. He muttered unintelligible words underneath his breath. I finally recognized him. Lord Leavesden.

"Lord Leavesden, I—what happened?" a woman cried out.

"Emilia, just come with me if you've something to say," Lord Leavesden said tiredly.

I opened my eyes for a second and saw a door opening. A pile of professors spilled out of it.

"Gods forbid!" a man gasped. "What's happened?"

"Come along," Lord Leavesden said shortly.

The world became a blur before me. It was hard to focus on anything; I couldn't or didn't want to think about the fact that all my professors plus Henry and Lord Leavesden followed Malsin. His strength astounded me. He carried me like I was a sack of flour. I felt jostled as we went up a small flight of stairs. I fought to keep my mouth closed, still wrestling with the overpowering urge to throw up.

"Quick, get the door!" Malsin shouted.

Professor Morel pushed open the door, and Malsin laid me down on a soft padded table. My eyes darted around blurredly as professors lit numerous lamps and a crazy amount of light shone throughout the room. It hurt to keep my eyes open. Every person in the room surrounded the table and stared down at me with a mixture of queasiness and concern.

I leaned my head to the side as my stomach heaved. Several professors jumped out of the way.

"Get a bucket or something," Malsin ordered. He shoved a bowl underneath my face, but I didn't have anything to throw up. I'd skipped dinner and barely ate a morsel for lunch. I coughed and wanted to wipe my face with the back of my hand, but I didn't really have a hand to use.

I briefly wondered when I would pass out. Hadn't I suffered enough already?

"I'll have to clean her up before I can assess the damage," Malsin spoke. "Get me water and a washcloth." He directed to the crowd. "Who is this girl?" I felt him place his now-warm hands on my forehead.

"You don't know?" Professor Lildren said. "I sent her to find you earlier today."

"I have never seen this girl before in my life," Malsin said, frankly.

I flinched when a cool, wet cloth touched my forehead.

"It's all right, I'm just cleaning it," Malsin said gently as he patted my head.

I knew that, but it didn't stop me from cringing every time he brought it to my face. I didn't like the cold.

"Head wounds always bleed profusely, you know. There can be the tiniest bit of a gash, and it will pour out blood till you think you're dying," Malsin said while wiping my face. "There, I see the wound." He made a tsk noise with his throat. "Quite a gash. I'm guessing she hit the corner of the table?" He glanced at Henry and Professor Slystream for confirmation. "It will have to be stitched up."

"You're a mage. Just heal it," someone suggested. I couldn't tell who.

I glared, my eyes darting furtively at everyone. Magic had nearly killed me. I would never let anyone touch me with that vile stuff. I wanted to go back to my room and nurse my wounds myself. I tried to lift myself off the table while cradling my right arm. I needed to get out of there before they made it worse.

"Hey, what do you think you're doing?" Malsin stepped forward, placing a hand on my bad shoulder.

I gasped, and a pained expression flitted across my face. Malsin removed his hand as though I had shocked him. He eyed me with alarm.

"Don't touch me," I snarled, fighting to be heard over the professors' side conversations. "I don't—need—anyone's help."

"Isabelle, you're not thinking clearly right now." Lord Leavesden pressed his hand on my right shoulder, trying to hold me in place. I wiggled out of his grasp.

"What are you talking about? She hasn't been thinking all day!" Henry interjected, running a hand through his hair. He stepped away from the table and started pacing back and forth.

I looked Lord Leavesden squarely in the eyes. "I know exactly—" I paused and took another deep breath. "What is going on." I gritted my teeth. "My head—is cut—my arm—is broken." I took another deep breath and spoke quickly. "I can handle it."

"We're only trying to help, not hurt you." Malsin offered a warm smile, an attempt to show friendliness. I didn't buy it.

"Don't you dare use any of your magic on me." My voice started to come back in full force. The very thought of them using magic to heal me knocked me into sense. After the experience I just had, I wanted nothing to do with it. I glared at them all. "I don't need you."

Malsin held his hands out in front of him. "Fine. No magic. Everything I do will be completely conventional."

I narrowed my eyes at him. "How do I know you're telling the truth?"

He sighed, dropping his hands to his sides. "Magic would be my first choice in healing you right now. The gash you have on your forehead is significant, and I could fix it in a matter of minutes compared to days. But, if taken care of properly and routinely cleaned, the wound will close with a few stitches. You'll barely have a scar there by the time it is fully healed. It will take longer, but I *always*," he held up a finger, "put my patients wishes above my own."

I hardly listened to what he said—the pain became too intense. I scrunched up my face and fought the desire to bolt. Would my arm ever be the same? Would I be able to use it normally? Sometimes, when a farmer broke an arm or leg, he complained it didn't feel like it used to. Cold air bothered it, the rain, exercise became too strenuous. This was my good arm, the one I held my sword in. *I need it.*

I believed magic to be the true evil. This wouldn't have happened without it. I refused to let anyone touch me with that vile substance. Next, I would figure out how to get rid of it. Magic could not be trusted. Ever. *Gods forbid I should have never left home.*

"I don't care." I paused, trying to get a new breath. "What you think magic can do. I don't want any part of it."

Malsin frowned. "Fine, then you will endure more pain."

My breathing turned ragged. I trembled and shook. "It can't be worse than what I've already been through."

"What's that supposed to mean?" Malsin asked, furrowing his eyebrows.

I shook my head, not wanting to go through the details of my recent attack while in this state.

"I told her to come to you earlier," Professor Lildren said. "She said she knew the way."

"Why?" Malsin turned his sharp gaze toward him.

"She was bleeding all over! That's why!" He threw his hands up in the air and paced a bit, then rubbed his forehead.

Alzmire held up a hand. "Wait a minute—she was in defensive classes?"

There was a chorus of yeses from the defensive professors, Henry, and Lord Leavesden.

Alzmire put a hand over his mouth, then lowered it slowly. "Gods forbid, if I had known, I would have intervened. I figured she would be in needlepoint or something for the afternoon like all the rest of the girls." He shook his head and balled his fists, looking like he mentally berated himself. He took a step forward, his eyes darting back and forth as he searched my face. "You didn't say anything, did you?"

I shook my head.

"Isabelle, what in the name of the Gods ever possessed you to think that you could handle this?" He sounded exasperated and lifted his hands like he wanted to strangle something. "There's no way you're healed enough to start training again! Do you have a death wish or something?" He leaned forward and got right in my face. I leaned back quickly. "Do you want to die?" He threw his hands into the air and then pointed a warning finger at me. "This is not acceptable behavior."

I kept my lips shut tight. I wouldn't explain my reasoning to him. Sure, I acted reckless and stupid. I knew I made a bad decision before I started, but I wanted to feel alive. I wanted to feel like I could pick up a sword and defend myself after what those attackers did. That I still had what it takes. That I wasn't broken, useless, and needy. I wanted to feel like I had a handle on my life, that I didn't need to rely on anyone but myself. I wanted my independence back.

Everyone in the room frowned in annoyance that I hadn't been forthcoming. I didn't care. My life, my body, my pain. I decided what I could handle, not some stupid professor or healer.

Malsin cleared his throat. He held on to a nightgown and stared me down. "Everyone turn around or leave while I change her into this nightgown," Malsin ordered, meeting everyone's eyes in the room. He faced me again. "Don't even try to fight me on this. You will lose."

His tone of voice intimidated me. I didn't protest. He pursed his lips in disapproval once my shirt was off and he could see the damage underneath. He slipped the nightgown over my torso while I cradled my broken arm and helped him shimmy me out of my pants.

"All right, we're good now," Malsin said.

Everyone turned around, and multiple sets of eyes zeroed in on me. I felt too much pain to care that a bunch of professors, Lord Leavesden, and Henry waited to hear the chain of events leading up to this bloody moment.

"What have you been up to?" Malsin whispered. His intelligent hazel-green eyes narrowed in on me.

I glowered, feeling spiteful as I continued to cradle my arm.

Malsin reached for a cup. "Drink this. I promise there is nothing magical in it. It'll make it easier for me to work on you—might dull your senses for a while." He handed me a cup with green liquid in it. Hesitantly, I brought it to my lips and drank. I tasted spearmint. Malsin helped me lie down on the table as I felt the effects of the liquid start working. I was still lucid, but the pain dulled. I stopped shaking and became as still as a statue.

Malsin went straight to work on the gash marring my face. "This girl is a patchwork quilt of bruises and dressings. Why wasn't she sent to me when she arrived?" He accused everyone in the room.

"We didn't know," Lord Leavesden said. "No one said anything."

Alzmire spoke. "I did, but she refused to see a healer. I wasn't aware she would be in defensive classes, or I would have insisted she stay out of them."

I felt like dead weight as I listened to their conversation. My view consisted of a white ceiling.

"I'm going to need someone to work up a history so I know what I'm dealing with," Malsin said as he hovered over me, poking and prodding the wound. "Does anyone know if she's allergic to anything?"

There was a chorus of nos.

Malsin sighed. "All right ... what do any of you know?" He threaded a needle.

"On her way to meet her brother, three men ambushed her in the woods," Alzmire said. "In the process of fighting for her life, she got shot twice. I don't know if she had any other major injuries. However, when I first met her a few days ago you could barely recognize a face underneath the bruises."

Murmurs from everyone went around the room as they processed the information.

"Well, that explains the dressings," Malsin muttered. "Euan, what happened in class?" Malsin's tone demanded answers. His hand moved in and out of view as he started to stich the wound closed.

"I'm not sure; it was just a routine check for the presence of magic. I do them all the time. Except she just faded out, and suddenly she glowed all different kinds of colors," Euan responded. "I've never seen anything like it before."

"How did she get hurt?" Malsin asked.

"The magic left her body too quickly. She slammed her head into the side of the table. That's where she got the gash. I was too stupefied to do anything to help," he confessed. "It was so bright—the colors blinded me. I've never seen magic react that way in a person before."

"What do you think this means?" Professor Trisgeld stepped forward asking everyone.

"I don't know, but it might have something to do with the Mark of the Gods on her hand," Malsin answered.

I wanted to say something, but my tongue felt thick and heavy. Instead, I was forced to let them guess over my body. I closed my eyes. *Let them speculate*, I decided. *What do they know?*

They continued to discuss what happened in the magic class, getting Henry to confirm what Professor Slystream said. When Henry finished speaking, they allowed him to leave. I expected he left eagerly to tell his classmates about my demise. One more thing for them to pin against me.

I heard the snip of scissors, and Malsin's hands moved away from my face. I felt it safe to open my eyes again.

"All right, Isabelle, I'm going to have to set your arm before we can wrap it. This is going to hurt, so brace yourself." Malsin put a hand on my shoulder and gazed at my face, pity written all over his. I hated that look.

I nodded briefly, relieved I had a little bit of movement left.

"All right, on the count of three." Malsin gripped onto my arm with both hands. "One … two … three." I held my breath as he pushed hard on my arm, setting it back into place. I opened my mouth in a silent scream.

Malsin wrapped my arm deftly and put it in a sling.

"There, I've fixed those two problems at least," Malsin said, wiping his brow. He turned around and addressed the crowd. "There's obviously more going on here than meets the eye, but for now, we're left to speculate."

"I'm going to send a letter to Joshua immediately. He needs to know what happened," Lord Leavesden said.

"But this doesn't make any sense," Professor Trisgeld said, scratching his head. "How could she have fought so well in my class today with these kinds of injuries? She wielded that blade better than I've seen any student do in the last couple of years."

"This is obviously no ordinary girl," Professor Morel said.

"Let her rest. We'll try to get answers later," Lord Leavesden said. "If any of you have other matters to discuss, then follow me to my study."

Multiple feet shuffled, and the room emptied except for Malsin.

"Well, little warrior." Malsin smiled. "I think rest is exactly what you need." He lifted me gently and moved me over to a small cot in the corner.

He gave me another small cup filled with liquid to drink, promising it held no magical properties, and within a few minutes I fell asleep.

Haldren swept me away into his field at the edge of a dark green forest. I sat on a large stone boulder. Haldren sat a few paces across from me on a carved throne molded out of a boulder like the one I sat on. His shoulder-length black hair blew in the wind that he created.

He eyed me like Malsin did, diagnosing all my problems.

"Isabelle." He sighed. "You attract trouble like flies to a horse."

I glared at him; not that I disagreed with his statement, but I didn't want to hear it. I'd heard it enough from everybody else. "It's not like I go searching for it. It finds me."

He smiled quickly. "Yes, I see that danger is very attracted to you. But what's not to like in a beautiful young maiden?" He put a hand to his chin, musing.

I averted my eyes to the golden wheat. I recalled the events of the magic room, of the lights flashing around me and the images in my mind. What did they mean?

"Spit it out. I know you have a question." Haldren eyed me and rested his hands on the arms of his throne.

"What happened in the magic class?" I asked, propping my legs up to my chest, I wrapped my arms around them.

He shrugged. "You are gifted with very powerful magic. Sometimes those who have magic are not aware of it for quite a while. It lies dormant in their bodies just biding its time until awakened. Once roused, it gets so thrilled that it will ..." He paused and crossed his legs, then waved his hand airily. "Act out in some form or fashion." He folded his long, nimble fingers together, bracing his elbows on the throne. "Magic is like a pet. It gets excited and always wants to please the master."

"I want nothing to do with it," I said immediately. "How do I get rid of it?"

"You can't," he responded simply.

"But it nearly killed me!" I shouted. "I don't want it."

"You have no choice," Haldren said firmly. "Magic is simple. You just need to learn to control it." He cocked his head to the side, seeming to contemplate. "Like a dog." He grinned. "Don't shy away from it. It will be your greatest ally." He must have seen something in my expression because he said, "magic has lain dormant in you for seventeen years. You cannot blame it for what it showed you. Don't be afraid to open it up and see where it takes you."

"I don't need a dog. I've got enough problems already," I grumbled. "What did I do to deserve this?" I put my face in my hands and shuddered.

"You'll get used to it." Haldren shrugged. "Accept that life throws you swords when you're not looking. It's your job to catch them before they stick."

"But I feel out of control like I don't even know my body—myself. Magic is terrifying." My shoulders slumped in despair. I rocked back and forth, clutching my knees.

"Look at me, child," Haldren ordered softly.

I lifted my head.

His piercing eyes fixed upon me. "There is only one person in this world that you should trust, and that is you. There will come a time when you will understand why you have been given such powerful abilities. Remember it is a gift, and you should treat it so."

I sighed. "This is all so confusing."

"Confusion and injuries often go together." He spoke lightly. "I've said enough already. Go rest." He raised his hand in farewell, and I felt the world spinning underneath me until I woke up in a cold room lying in a cot.

I placed a hand on my forehead, unable to stop the tears of pain from forming and spilling out. I felt caged, trapped in a body and circumstance that I didn't want. I wished I could melt away and vanish into the darkness. I wished I were someone else. A farmer or simple merchant perhaps. Anyone who wasn't me.

CHAPTER SEVENTEEN

THE CLOCK NEARED SIX a.m. when I woke. Gaining my senses, I assessed how much pain I endured. *Trampled by a stampede of horses would be an understatement,* I thought drily. Sleeping on an old cot had done me no favors. I wrinkled my nose. The roomed smelled strongly of herbs and chemicals.

I wore a white cotton nightgown that Malsin had put on me last night. It didn't fit me as well as I would have liked. The sleeves were too long, so only the tips of my fingers showed, and the hem fell past my ankles. I sat up with some difficulty and waited for my head to clear before I stood, groaning as I did so. Barefoot and not caring, I ambled out of the healing room, using one hand to hold up the bottom of my nightgown so I wouldn't trip. I walked slowly and carefully due to the light-headedness and overall weak feeling of my body. The hallways were eerily quiet. I didn't see a single soul except for Professor Breldian's cat Ginger. She rubbed her head against my leg, her bushy tail tickling me.

"Not now, Ginger." I leaned against a wall, afraid she would weave in and out of my legs and I'd go sprawling. She stood on two paws, shoving her head in my hands. I scratched her head absentmindedly. In the distance, a door opened and closed, catching her attention. She ran down the hallway presumably searching for the source. I continued slowly to my room.

I leaned heavily on the doorknob and whispered the password to enter. "Passiflora."

My foot brushed against a folded piece of paper as I walked in. I bent and picked it up. I sat in a red chintz chair and opened the note.

Someone had drawn a picture of an arrow with words underneath.

**You're proving to be a fighter. I love
a woman with spirit—Employer.**

My blood went cold. Frozen, I struggled to understand how I'd been discovered. The archer had obviously returned to his employer and given him the details of our meeting. But the archer had meant to kill me. How did the employer know I hadn't died and where to find me? He—I assumed it was man based on the bold strokes in the note— knew exactly which room I'd been placed in.

Fear spurred me into action. I wasn't safe here like Joshua thought I would be. I had to leave, now. I eased out of the chair and hobbled to my room. I reached for my cream patched bag on top of a dresser and brought it to the bed. I returned to the dresser and started pulling clothes out. My head spun. My stomach churned. The rest of my injuries throbbed. As much as it grated me, I took it slow.

My heart leapt into my throat at the pounding on my door. I snatched my dagger and slowly padded to the door. Gathering nerves of steel, I opened it. Malsin stood there looking very annoyed. He had a bag slung over his shoulder. My breath whooshed out. I tucked the knife behind my back.

"Finally," he muttered, striding into to the room. "What do you think you were doing?" He paced back and forth, clearly agitated. "Leaving the healing room without telling anyone? I had no idea where you were or if you had gotten into more trouble." He stopped midpace and faced me. "Do you know how serious head wounds can be?"

He was right on all accounts, and I should have expected this, yet I was momentarily caught off guard by his reprimand. "I was uncomfortable. How am I supposed to get better in an ill-fitting old cot?"

"At least leave a note or something." He threw a hand in the air as he started pacing again. "It's policy that you are not allowed to leave the healing room until I have discharged you. I understand you're new, so I'll let it slide, but try to have a bit more common sense." His eyes grew wide and his face stern. "I am the healer. I know what's best for your body." He pointed a finger at me. "And don't argue unless you've spent a lifetime learning human anatomy." He sighed and pinched the bridge of his nose, his tone softer this time. "Taking on too much, too soon is a death wish. Even if *you* think you're all right, chances are you're not, and you're just being reckless and stupid. We still need to take extra precautions."

As I listened to him rant and rave, my eyes widened in surprise. His genuine concern for me was the last thing I expected. He didn't know me, yet here he stood, passionately advocating for my health—for me. "I'm sorry," I said, my voice small and insignificant as I fidgeted with the dagger I hid. "Where I come from, we don't have a healer. They aren't well received. If you had a problem, you dealt with it yourself, however best you could."

"And how many people die when they could have been saved?" he shot back at me. "That's what's wrong with those foolish villages. They're too mistrustful, won't even go a mile near us. Well, it's their fault if they want to die. Not mine." He lifted his hands in the air and dropped them to his sides.

I didn't know what to make of him.

"Now I need to examine you. Please sit down." He gestured to one of the red chintz chairs.

I didn't have time for this. I had to leave, contact Joshua for a safer place. The employer could catch me any second. I took a step back.

Malsin's mossy green eyes narrowed. "What are you hiding?"

"Nothing," I lied.

He strode over and yanked on my left arm. He plucked the dagger out of my hand. "What are you doing with this?" he demanded.

I huffed. "Protection."

"Against?"

"The archer and employer," I explained. "They've found me already. It's not safe. I must go." My eyes darted to my bedroom door where I'd left my patched bag.

Malsin evened his stance. "You're not going anywhere until I've examined you and gotten some answers."

I stared at him. He held my dagger. I couldn't very well fight him, not in my condition. Not seeing another choice I moved to the chair.

Malsin tucked my dagger in his belt. He turned around and started a fire in the fireplace. Once he got it going, he checked me over. "Any pain? Dizziness?"

"It's nothing I can't handle," I answered, meaning the pain. "No dizziness when I'm sitting."

Malsin sat in the adjacent chair and opened his bag. He retrieved a notepad and a pen. He started scribbling, his hand flying off the page, and glanced up once. "Are you allergic to anything?"

"No," I said, then clarified, "but there's not much variety in Saren."

He nodded and scribbled some more.

"What are you doing?" I felt compelled to ask.

"I'm writing down a case history," he murmured. He finished his thought and met my eyes. He took a breath. "All right, I want a full account of every injury you have received in the last two weeks."

I sighed and rubbed my face. "The list would be extensive."

"I don't care." Malsin stared me down, his jaw clenched. "Start talking."

My voice sounded caustic as I spoke. Starting with the fall down the rocky ravine and the attack in the woods. Malsin wrote furiously, taking down every word I said. He paused briefly to ask how I got the arrows out. I then launched into the tale of Andrew's arrival. Malsin's eyebrows shot up in surprise at the mention of the Prince, but he didn't comment on it. I finished with the fever in Thimbleton.

"That's everything, unless you count what happened last night with the broken arm and head injury," I said slowly, resting my arm on the armrest.

Malsin set his pen and notepad on his lap and folded his hands together. He crossed his legs. "And you've had no pain medications?"

"I've been using different salves. One of them has a smidgeon of healing magic in it that dulls the pain, but I use that very sparingly. You can take a look if you would like." I gestured to the bathroom.

"I would like that." He put his notepad and pen back inside his bag and strode into the bathroom. He came out a few minutes later. "Well, at least you had something to work with."

"They've kept me alive so far," I commented drily.

He sat. "Yes, but I think your zest for life helped more than those simple concoctions." He pursed his lips. "Mind over matter so to speak. Still, it's better than nothing." He shrugged, then changed the subject. "Now, I have something with me that should really do the trick."

I watched him with curiosity.

He pulled a medium-size jar out of his bag. The contents were near the same shade of purple as my bottle. More of a lilac than deep violet, I decided as I examined it further.

Malsin smiled. "A little bit of this on a regular basis and you'll barely remember you were injured."

"That looks nearly identical to what I've been using."

Malsin nodded. "They might have a few of the same compound ingredients, but I assure you, this one is much better. I made it myself. It's a recipe healers have been trying to get from me for years." He opened the lid, and an overwhelming aroma of lavender hit my nose.

"Wow, that's pungent." I reared my head back.

"Are you willing to try it?" Malsin eyed me perceptively.

"Will it get rid of the pain?" I countered.

He pursed his lips, seeming to mull it over. "Most of it, yes."

I nodded. "All right then. Go ahead."

It became a bit of a challenge as I stood and Malsin helped me take off the nightgown. I slipped my arms out of the sleeves, and Malsin pulled it up over my head as I held my breath. Next he unraveled every bandage except my arm. I tried not to think about how much he exposed to help. Malsin applied the salve; it was cold to the touch at first, then quickly soothed. He talked as he worked, attempting to make it less awkward. "You're very brave to handle this amount of trauma. I mostly heal minor things with the students, a small cut or cold. On the rare occasion I deal with something bigger, they come in sobbing like a toddler. Here you are full of injuries, and you just take it. No hysterics."

"I've grown accustomed to it." I grimaced.

"Nobody should ever become accustomed to pain," he said softly while wrapping up the last bandage. "There, finished. Feel any better?"

I nodded, suddenly hit with emotion. His statement resonated deep within me.

Malsin smiled. "Good."

I walked into my sleeping quarters and put on soft cotton clothes.

Stepping back out, Malsin retrieved my knife from his belt. "Tell me why you thought you needed this."

I retrieved the note and showed it to him. "This was under my door when I walked in this morning." Malsin pursed his lips as he eyed the note. "Whoever it is thinks I'm important because of my birthmark. I thought he was wrong but now that I know I have magic I'm not so sure anymore. In any case, I don't know how to stop him from coming after me. I must leave, contact my brother, and find a safer place to stay."

"Before you do anything, I think this calls for a meeting with Lord Leavesden," Malsin advised. "We take the security of this school very seriously. If someone is sneaking in undetected, he will want to know about it. We can contact your brother from there."

"All right," I agreed.

He set my dagger on a table and extended his elbow. "Come, I'll escort you to his office. If we take it slow, I think you'll manage."

"Thank you." I took his proffered arm.

The hallways were sparse, the final bell for class having rung. Malsin walked at a slow sedate pace, taking extra care down the stairs as we made it to Lord Leavesden's office. Malsin rapped three times on the wooden door.

"Enter," Lord Leavesden called from within.

Lord Leavesden's eyebrows shot up upon our arrival. "What brings you here? Shouldn't Isabelle be resting?"

"So she should but we've run into a bit of a problem," Malsin said as he helped me into a chair.

"Oh?" Lord Leavesden gave us his full attention.

Malsin looked to me to explain with an encouraging smile.

I spoke quietly. "You're aware my birthmark has caused undue interest and is the reason I was a victim of an attempted kidnap on my way to meet my brother. Hence my sorry state." I casually waved a hand at me.

Lord Leavesden nodded; his brow drawn together. "You both should've been more forthcoming about that in our first meeting."

"I apologize." I slid the note over to him. "This appeared under my door this morning. Somehow I've been discovered. I do not believe I am safe here like Joshua hoped. I wish to contact my brother and find a new situation for myself."

Lord Leavesden read the note with a deep frown. He reached into the folds of his shirt and pulled out a locket. It glowed blue as he spoke into it. "Lily, would you be a dear and tell Brian to send Joshua over? I have a situation that requires his immediate attention."

A soft cultured voice floated out. "Of course darling."

Lord Leavesden rang for tea. A few minutes later, Lily reported that Joshua was on his way. I'd just taken my third sip of chamomile when he walked in.

His green eyes perused me as he took a seat beside me. "Gods Isabelle, one day and you've caused more trouble than a rampant pack of wolves. Look at the state of you!"

I scowled at him. *Some brother you are.*

Joshua faced Lord Leavesden. "What seems to be the problem?"

Lord Leavesden handed Joshua the folded paper. "Isabelle says she found this under her door this morning." Joshua's expression hardened as he read. "Need I remind you, I don't care to bring trouble into this school."

Joshua stuck the paper into his pocket. "I understand."

Lord Leavesden took a sip of tea. "What course of action do you suggest we take?" He inclined his head at me. "Isabelle believes she needs a new situation."

Malsin spoke up. "I do not believe she is fit to make much of a journey. Her health at present is too precarious. She must be supervised by a healer."

"I'm not staying here to fight off kidnappers again," I said firmly.

Joshua scratched his beard then spoke. "I suggest we try increasing security first. I will send over men to guard the entrances to the boys and girls dormitories and add more people to watch the perimeter."

I opened my mouth to protest. Joshua pinned me with an emerald stare. "I am your guardian, as such it is my duty to make these decisions. You still have a lot to learn here, academically and socially." He inclined his head at Lord Leavesden. "I'm told you possess magic. That's something you need to get a handle on quickly. An untrained mage is dangerous. The Sorrenian can help you with this."

I couldn't help my surly tone. "I don't want magic. It's not natural." If I ever returned to Saren, I suspected they'd oust me from the community.

Joshua straightened; his green eyes flashed. "You don't have a choice. Magic is in your blood."

I curled my hands into fists while Joshua worked out the arrangements with Lord Leavesden. Malsin flashed me a sympathetic smile, but I could tell he was pleased with the decision.

When they finished, Joshua turned to me and said, "you'll be happy to know, a man matching the description of the archer was delivered to Carasmille Prison yesterday for a number of crimes. I plan to interview him today to ensure he is the same man."

A sliver of relief pierced my heart. "How did he get caught?"

"I'm not sure. I aim to find out." Joshua pushed his wavy hair back.

"Will you let me know, please?" I asked.

Joshua's expression softened, probably at the anxiety written all over my face. "I will, promise." He patted my hand in a brotherly fashion then stood. "Listen to Malsin and get better little sister."

The bell rang as Malsin and I stepped out of Lord Leavesden's office. The halls filled with students' voices. Malsin pulled me over to a nearby bench in an alcove to wait it out. When mostly silence reigned, he escorted me slowly back to my room. Dizziness claimed the whole journey. A worker in dark blue attire already stood at the entrance of the hall, eyes alert. He nodded at Malsin and me as we passed.

Malsin tugged three vials out of his bag: two blue ones and a green. "I have few vials I'm going to leave with you. One should help you sleep. The other is just vitamins to boost your immune system. The green one is for sleeping, and the blue are the vitamins. Take the green one whenever you feel like it. Take the blue vial before you eat. Once a day." He set them on the end table by the chair. "I don't want you leaving your rooms for anything. I'll have meals brought up to you."

I nodded.

"I'll check on you later, but for now, rest." He pointed to the open bedroom door.

"I will. Thank you," I said with gratitude.For a healer—a profession I spent my whole life suspicious of—Malsin was incredibly gentle and accommodating.

He grinned as he slung his bag over his shoulder. "You're welcome."

The door closed softly behind him. I grabbed my dagger and padded to my bed. I pushed my bag to the end and crawled in. I slid my knife under my pillow and closed my eyes.

Malsin came by that evening after dinner to check on me again. "How are you feeling? Any changes since this morning?"

"No. Nothing new," I answered.

He checked on every single one of my injuries, applied creams where he thought I needed them, and bandaged me back up.

He pulled a note out of his pocket. "Oh, I was supposed to give this to you."

"Thank you," I said, taking the letter. I wondered who it was from, but I didn't think it polite to open it front of Malsin.

The corners of his mouth lifted in a smile. "I'll leave you alone and check on you tomorrow." He strode out of my room, closing the door gently behind him.

I unfolded the note. Splotches of ink mixed in with the letters, making it difficult to read the scrawl.

The man in Carasmille Prison is the archer. Guards say he arrived unconscious with no memory of who delivered him. He says his employer never revealed his face or name. I will continue to hunt down any leads that come up. Keep your strength up and stay safe.

Joshua Mirran

I clutched the note to my chest, relieved. The archer couldn't hurt me anymore. I frowned. If only I could say that about his employer.

Malsin checked on me periodically throughout the week. He handed me a book to read titled *Controlling Your Fate: Stories of Invalids Learning to Make Better Lives for Themselves.* I raised my eyebrow with an acerbic expression as I caught the hidden meaning. Malsin only laughed and told me to read it anyway. I convinced him to hang up the paintings that had been delivered. Joshua had chosen cheery landscapes—a blossoming cherry tree, a flowering meadow, and the like. I hid the waterfall painting behind my bed. I couldn't look at it without remembering my tumble down the ravine. I never got a single word out of the lady who brought me food. Either I scared her to death, or she was mute. I hoped it was the latter.

By the fifth day of confinement, I wanted to pull my hair out. Even though I hated the thought of using magic, I seriously started to consider using it to fix my injuries.

I voiced my concerns when Malsin looked in on me later that day.

"If I stay in here any longer, I'm going to scream." I clenched my jaw, my posture rigid.

"How's your head feel?" he asked, evading my comment.

"Fine," I said rather quickly—too quickly.

He eyed me, reflecting disbelief. "No pain? Dizziness or light-headedness? How is your vision?"

"All fine," I chirped back.

He narrowed his eyes at me, searching for a lie, but I kept my face as impassive as possible and stared him back down. I *would* die if I had to stay in here any longer.

"Well, it's Kings Day; you'll have to wait till First Day for classes again, and I don't want you to go to any physical activity classes." He held up a finger. "That includes business and land management since you're on the farming section. No lifting plants or swords."

"I can't live like this," I complained, slamming my fist into the chair. "You're torturing me!"

"It's going to be torture if you don't want it healed magically," Malsin said casually, folding his arms.

I cocked my head to the side and eyed him with my no-nonsense look. He baited me like a well-experienced fisherman, trying to hook me into the purported splendors of magic. He knew that I knew it. Malsin laughed brightly, throwing his hands in the air. "Nothing escapes that pretty head of yours, does it?"

I shook my head, the corners of my mouth lifting into a small smile. "Hardly."

"Still, it is the only option you have if you want to ..." He paused, seeming to choose his words. "Escape the torture I'm putting you under." He placed a hand under his chin and rested his elbow on the armrest.

"You saw what magic did to me. There's no way it can be trusted," I said firmly.

"Oh yes, I agree." He nodded, crossing his legs.

I raised my eyebrows in surprise. "You what? But you use magic on a daily basis. You shouldn't be agreeing with me."

"Why not?" Malsin countered.

I narrowed my eyes at him. Leaning forward, I asked, "What are you getting at?"

Malsin cut to the chase. He waggled a finger at me. "Magic cannot be trusted with you. You are a complete novice. A person possessing a great amount with absolutely no idea how to use it can be very dangerous." He rubbed his chin. "However, magic can easily be trusted with me." He pointed at himself. "Just as you said, I use it daily. Armed with knowledge and experience, I know how to control it."

He lifted a finger to his mouth, tapping it slightly against his lips. "Now if you had to choose between an experienced or apprentice baker to bake you some bread, whom would you choose?"

"The experienced of course," I answered without a second thought.

Malsin smiled. "Why not the apprentice?"

"Because I'd have a better chance of it coming out wrong," I said, knowing he was baiting me again. I played along anyway. "Nobody likes burned bread."

Malsin nodded, accepting my answer. "All right, say there was an injured student, and he was given the option to be healed by you or me."

I opened my mouth to protest, but he held up his hand to stop me.

"We both have magic. So, it's not out of the question," he continued. "Which should he choose?"

"You."

"Why?"

"Because you know what you are doing," I said tersely, tiring of his game.

"Would you be willing to stake his life on it?"

"Yes," I said, unwavering.

"Ha!" Malsin lurched forward and pointed his finger at me, acting like he had successfully lured me into his web.

"What?" I furrowed my eyebrows, confused.

He leaned back in his chair and crossed his legs again. "Without hesitation, you willingly put another student's life into my hands to be healed with magic. Yet when it comes to yourself, you are absolutely against it.

What's the difference?" Malsin grinned, obviously pleased to be spider of his game.

I opened my mouth and closed it, realizing that anything I'd say could be used against me and would be ultimately futile. I placed a hand on my forehead and sighed. He had weaved a perfect counterargument, and I couldn't see how to untangle myself from his web of truth.

"Isabelle, you're acting more out of fear than for the safety of your health. I am one of the most skilled healers in Aberron. Do you think these rich nobles and merchants would choose some half-wit to watch over their children?" He uncrossed his legs and leaned forward, catching my eyes.

I shook my head.

He held his hands out in front of him. "So you have options. I could use magic and heal you now, and by First Day you'll be able to return to your full schedule without any inhibitions; or you can continue to suffer in pain and wait weeks, months even, before you're able to lift a sword." Malsin leaned back and folded his hands together, letting me stew.

I rested my head against the back of the chair and stared at the ceiling, weighing my options. Trust Malsin to heal me or wait and suffer? My stomach rolled at the thought of months without the ability to grip my sword. The choice was easier to make than I expected.

"I can't live like this any longer," I whispered.

"So?" He raised an eyebrow.

My voice came out soft, with a tremor. "Heal me, please," I surrendered.

"About time you asked." Malsin's smile reached all the way up to his eyes. "I wondered how long it was going to take before you conceded."

I rolled my eyes at him. "Just do it please."

"All right, all right." He rose from his chair and crouched on the floor beside me. "I'll start with your arm and move on from there. Once my magic takes hold, I'll be able to sense where every injury is and knit them back together."

I took a deep breath. "All right."

"It may take a while; nothing about you is superficial," he added.

"Fine," I agreed.

Malsin moved out of his crouching position and sat on the floor. "All right, here I go then." He latched onto my broken arm.

Instantaneously, I sensed a foreign power seep into my veins. I perceived my own magic rise out of the darkness. With my eyes closed, I envisioned myself standing inside a glass sphere. Smoky streams of colored ribbons—red, blue, green, and yellow—enveloped me in their glow. I put forth my hand and touched a yellow ribbon as it swirled by. My breath caught in surprise as it melded with my skin, making my hand glow bright yellow. I shook my hand out, alarmed, then curious. I felt no pain. In fact, I didn't feel any physical ailments at all. *Interesting.* I reached out and touched a blue one with my index finger. As it disappeared into my skin, my hand radiated in hues of deep blue. *What is this?*

I walked around the glass ball randomly stroking the smoky ribbons, enraptured as my hand shone the color I touched. Was I in another world? A different plane of existence?

Before I could learn anything else about this mysterious orb, it dissolved, throwing me back into my normal plane of existence. I opened my eyes to see Malsin staring at me curiously.

"What—just happened?" I shivered and blinked slowly to regain my bearings.

"How do you feel?" Malsin's eyes probed me.

I lifted my broken arm and swiveled it, examining every inch. I felt nothing, no throbbing. I put both my hands on my chest and patted myself down. "I don't feel pain ... anywhere." My jaw dropped as I marveled at the feeling of being whole.

He grinned toothily. "Good. It worked."

"How did it work?" I asked, curious.

"When my magic is activated, it allows me to see and feel everything, inside and out. Then it searches for the biggest problem, infuses itself to the injury until it is healed, then races on to the next," Malsin explained.

I blinked slowly, impressed. *Wow.* I pushed my hair back, tucking it behind my ear. "Something strange happened while you were healing me."

He sat in the other red chintz chair. "What?"

"I went somewhere, or at least my mind went somewhere." I shaded my eyes, feeling ridiculous for mentioning it.

"What did it look like?" he asked, leaning back and clasping his hands together.

"A glass ball with ribbons of different colors swirling around. When I touched them, they penetrated my skin, and my hand glowed." I bit my lip, feeling and, I guessed, reflecting, bewilderment.

"Oh, that's nothing to be worried about." He shrugged with indifference. "You entered your mage core. Or in other words, the place where your magic is stored. It can happen when someone is using magic on you. Your body naturally responds and wants to help by using its own stores."

"So you've been in something like that too?" I felt somewhat relieved but still rather dubious.

"Yes, except mine is a little different than yours. I've only got one color swirling around, as do most people," Malsin answered. "You're quite a conundrum to the magical world, I'd say. I'm interested to see what color you actually possess."

"What's your color?"

"Green of course. For healing." He leaned forward and gazed at me earnestly. "Look, there's a lot to learn about magic and how to use it properly, but for now don't be alarmed. Just—try not to enter your mage core until you're a little more informed on the subject."

I nodded solemnly.

Malsin stood and stretched. "Well, I think my work is finished. By tomorrow you're free to leave your room as you please. Explore the school, go to the library or stables or whatever ... and try to make friends."

I forced a fake smile. Making new friends seemed out of the question. Not after my disastrous first day. "Thank you."

I went to sleep that night grateful to have a body that was completely healed. Magic slowly started to change my outlook on life. Maybe it wasn't so bad after all. Maybe it had value and worth. *Maybe the farmers' superstitions are wrong.* I wondered what else I grew up believing was wrong too.

CHAPTER EIGHTEEN

REEPING INTO THE DINING hall for breakfast the next morning was unquestionably embarrassing. The entire room of students and professors hushed and stared. I frowned, passing students with pieces of scrambled eggs and toast falling out of their mouths. What did they expect? I had to come down here at some point. I couldn't starve. Andrew would never forgive me for that.

"Good to see you are well, Isabelle," Lord Leavesden called from his seat at the end of the hall, I guessed in an attempt to break the tension that had now fallen upon everyone.

I nodded. "Yes, thank you."

Abruptly not feeling so hungry, I grabbed a pear and a roll, then scurried out of there like a chased rat. The chatter rapidly started up after I walked through the doors, out of view but still within hearing distance. I could only assume it would be all about me and my unexpected—possibly frightening to them—appearance.

I could feel the sting of embarrassment course through me as I walked up the stairs back to my room. I tried to shove it into a dark corner. I didn't want them to see me as insecure, despite feeling that way. I wondered if any of this would blow over. I pursed my lips, doubting it. I saw the fear on their faces when they fixated on me in the dining hall. I didn't think anyone would willingly approach me again.

Two and a half months, I thought silently. I could survive two months and a half month, right?

Wrong.

I spent that Gods Day in the library searching for anything that might help me solve my problems. I couldn't find anything remotely close to what I needed. Not a single book on the Gods mentioned Haldren, and there were no books on criminal mastermind tactics. I didn't really expect to find a book titled that, but with a library as huge as they had, I hoped to have something close to point me in the right direction. How could I help Joshua eliminate the employer if I didn't know anything about how villains worked or their habits or patterns? I couldn't believe all criminals acted out of ignorance and stupidity. Who would break the law without a solid reason? How did guards learn to spot thieves? Trial and error?

I tried once to ask the librarian—a tiny, mousy lady nearly as old as the aged, decaying books—for help. The second she noticed me coming to her, she squeaked and ran away. Surprised at her quick shuffle, I quickly gave up that avenue.

Students of all ages carefully avoided me. I lingered in one aisle searching fruitlessly for something. Out of the corner of my eye, I noticed a chubby boy hovering at the end of the aisle. He watched me, his face white as a sheet. I deliberated for a moment, deciding if I should leave and let the poor boy get the book he needed or stay and see if he could muster up the courage to walk past me.

My answer arrived when a girl probably around fourteen sauntered up to me. I saw no fear in her brown eyes, just open curiosity. She wore a light blue dress, her red hair was braided, and freckles smattered across her cheeks. She carried a stack of books in her arm. Behind her, the chubby boy's eyes grew wide, and he froze in horror. I suspected he feared for the girl.

She smiled exuberantly. "Hi, I'm Helda. I just wanted to tell you that I don't think you secretly lure people out of their beds at night, blind them with your rainbow powers, and steal their souls."

"Is that what they're saying?" I whispered.

She nodded. "The boy in my class said he heard it from an older student—I don't know who—that was in the magic class with you last week."

I wouldn't put it past Dominic or Henry to come up with it. I pursed my lips. "I see. Well, it'd be a shame to prove them wrong."

She smiled, gripping onto her stack of books tighter. "If it weren't for my sister Amarilla forcing me not to, I'd talk to you more. I heard you speak Nistieran really well, and I'm having a hard time with it. I could use a good tutor."

"Helda!" a young girl around Helda's age hissed. Standing by the chubby boy, she waved frantically for her to come over.

"In a minute," Helda hissed back, her expression annoyed. She faced me again. "I'm sorry, I've got to go. I'm going to get in trouble if they see me talk to you again."

"If you feel like getting in trouble sometime, I'd be glad to help you with Nistieran," I said, resting a hand on my hip.

"Thanks." Helda turned, but I stopped her.

"Hey, what's that boy's name?" I discreetly pointed at the chubby boy.

"Oh, that's Ellis." She glanced at him and smiled.

Ellis gripped the side of the bookshelf for support, his face shining with sweat.

"Can you please tell him that I will not unleash my—what did you call them?"

"Rainbow powers," she answered.

I nodded. "Right. Please tell him I will not unleash my rainbow powers on him if he chooses to walk by and get the book he needs." I added for good measure. "His soul is safe."

She grinned. "I'll tell him." She hurried away, stopping briefly to whisper to Ellis before meeting her friend. They fell into a whispered argument.

I started perusing the books again, shaking my head at the ridiculous rumors spreading around. Ellis didn't walk down the aisle until I moved over to the next one. Once I learned I could take books back to my room, I did. Though it made me feel like a rat, scurrying out to grab treasure before running back to my hovel.

Gods Day evening, I carried a stack of unhelpful books to the library. On my way, I passed a man wearing the attire of a worker—dark blue shirt and pants—leisurely polishing an old suit of armor. His brown eyes caught mine, and he nodded, acknowledging me. I gave a short smile and nod in return. I hurried past, getting the same feeling of uneasiness that I got when I first met the boss at Mava's wedding. My gut told me not to ignore that feeling. Whomever that man was, my instincts said he was up to no good.

I deposited the books and turned to leave, wishing the library wasn't about to close and I could stay there until the man had finished polishing the armor. As luck would have it, the library had only one entrance at the end of the hallway. I would have to pass him again to get to my room.

Taking a deep breath, I walked out and took quick, hurried steps. I didn't dare meet the man's eyes again and stared straight ahead, catching him in my peripheral vision. My heart leaped in my throat when he picked up his bucket and rag and followed about ten paces behind me.

Stay calm, Isabelle, I told myself.

Once again, I found myself in a situation where I lamented that I carried no weapon. When I turned right, he did. My stomach coiled in knots. I made another right turn and then a left. All the while, the man followed, silent as death except for the thump of his boots on the floor. I came upon an intersecting hallway with three options: left, right, or forward. I went left, and to my utter relief, the man walked forward. Once he was out of sight, I sprinted down the hallway to the girl's dormitories, only slowing when I passed the guard standing attention.

An hour or so later, as I sat by the fireplace skimming through a book, I distinctly heard my doorknob rattle. I turned to it and watched it shake. I hopped from my chair and grabbed my sword. I hovered by the door, weapon in hand, for ten straight minutes, but nothing happened. Perhaps it was just a student having fun?

I went to sleep that night with a dagger under my pillow, my sword by my side, and paranoia wrapped around me like a blanket.

First Day morning arrived faster than I wanted. I dreaded going to class now, powered with the knowledge that they believed I turned into a soul-sucking monster at night.

I shuffled into class at the latest possible moment and hid in my seat with my head down.

"Look, she's back in class again," a boy whispered. Ethan, I remembered.

"Watch out; she might curse you or something," a girl responded. Amarilla.

I felt my face flush. A warm heat dusted my cheeks as I tried to steel myself against their stinging barbs.

I slouched low in my seat, not volunteering any answers. I only engaged in conversation when professors asked me a direct question, which they frequently did when no one else ventured a guess.

Alzmire stood in the doorway of his class greeting the students as they shuffled in. "Isabelle! You're back. How are you feeling?" Alzmire leaned in and gave me a shoulder hug, squishing my shoulders against him.

I smiled wistfully. "Fine, thank you."

He took a closer look at me. He waved his hand up and down, pointing to my muted clothes. "You look like you're trying to fade into nonexistence. Is everything all right?"

I shrugged. "Just trying to avoid attention."

Alzmire made a tsk noise with his throat and frowned. "Feel free to lie low, but don't disappear on us."

I dredged up a smile. "I won't."

Alzmire smiled back. "All right, Beautiful Lady."

"Don't you mean hideously scary?" Dominic interjected loudly, strolling through the door. He dodged out of my way to avoid a collision course.

"That's out of line, Dominic." Alzmire's voice turned cold. "Apologize or face detention."

Dominic's jaw clenched; he clearly worked hard to keep himself in check. He caught eyes with me for the briefest of moments. "Sorry."

I could tell he didn't mean it, but I nodded, pretending to accept his apology.

I slid into my seat quickly and kept my head down. I focused on the grains of the wooden desk, attempting to build up an internal stone wall against the insults. It didn't stop me from hearing the approving hand-shakes and soft clapping at Dominic's remark.

A boy, two seats in front of me and to the right, got out of his seat and came over to my desk. His brown hair was unkempt, and acne covered most of his face. Glasses obscured his eyes.

"Hey, I wanted to thank you." He rested a large, hairy hand on the edge of my desk.

I raised my eyebrows. "Thank me?"

"Yes. Because of you, I'm not bullied as much." He grinned.

Dominic, listening in on our conversation, said, "Don't worry Rodger, we still haven't forgotten about you, you clumsy oaf."

Rodger's shoulders slumped. He removed his hand from my desk and pushed his glasses higher up on the bridge of his nose. His nostrils flared, his fingers balling into a fist as he ignored Dominic and spoke to me. "I think you're the best thing that's ever happened to me. Please continue whatever you're doing to make them hate you." He turned around and sat back down in his seat.

During lunch, a boy around fourteen, possibly fifteen, marched up to me. He wore his light brown hair short around his ears but long on the top and had it combed over to the side; a few strands fell into his muddy brown eyes. A nasty sneer marred his face. "Just because the professors think you're all right doesn't mean we do. We're watching you." He pointed to his eyes, then folded his arms, smug.

I cocked my head to the side and furrowed my eyebrows. "Do you hear that?"

Confusion and surprise flitted across his face. He struggled to hide it as he took a step back. "No. What?"

I smiled coldly. "That's the sound of me not caring. Do what you want." I sidestepped him and waltzed off.

"Hey!" he called after me, but I forced myself not to look back.

I grabbed a cup of apple juice and bread stuffed with ham and cheese. As I wrapped the food in a napkin, Rodger ran up to me, spilling lettuce out of his sandwich. "You're doing great. Keep it up."

I briefly wondered if he was the one who had come up with the soul sucking rumor and spread it among the younger students. Though I didn't remember seeing him in the magic class that night, and Helda said the one who came up with it had been there. In fact, I didn't remember seeing him at all that day. I would have remembered his face. I sighed. Regardless of who it was, Rodger must really want someone else to be the focus of the bullying. I couldn't blame him. It wasn't nice.

I strode to my room for a moment of peace, passing by the worker who'd followed me the night before. He sent a shiver down my spine as he smiled at me, pausing briefly with a mop in his hand.

"Careful, don't slip; the floor is wet," he said.

I nodded. "I'll take care."

When I arrived for Professor Trisgeld's class he folded his arms, adamant that I take a day off. He refused to let me go near a sword, even though I curtly explained that Malsin had healed me. At his insistence, I leaned against a tree near Henry and Dominic and watched. It reminded me of my days of confinement while I healed. Being outside was the only difference.

"Have to sit out of class today, huh?" Henry asked me.

"Not by choice," I said slowly.

Henry smiled. "Good. No one will be skewered today."

I scowled. "You think I'm out to kill someone?"

"Not intentionally," Dominic joined in.

I turned away from them. I focused on the other students blundering their way through class. Professor Trisgeld yelled at Ethan. "You have to get close enough for your swords to touch!"

Henry paused midstrike, gripping his sword in an offensive position. "What, no response?"

I held my lips in a tight line and shook my head.

"Oh, come on, don't you have anything to say to defend yourself? Where's your counterargument?" Henry probed for a reaction.

I didn't want to play his game. Anything I said would be twisted into what they wanted to think of me, not the actual truth. Yet Henry's blue eyes, while actively baiting, reminded me so much of Andrew that I couldn't handle it any longer.

I spat out a response. "You know if I do want to kill someone, I'll make sure you two are my first targets."

"You couldn't kill us. We can outsmart your magic," Dominic said derisively as he pushed his black hair out of his eyes.

I raised my eyebrows, wondering why I gave in to their taunts. I propped my knees up and wrapped my arms around them. *They are absurd.* "You might know more about magic than I do, but I know more about sword fighting than both of you put together. For example, that last move you guys have been working on is completely wrong." I gestured to them. "Henry should be standing a few paces over to the right in the low guard position. The sword should be held point down and centered. Also work on keeping your elbows bent and close to your body. Try it and you'll see."

"Why should we trust you?" Henry asked.

"You shouldn't." I shrugged. "But I know what I'm talking about."

"Let's try it," Henry said to Dominic. They moved into the position, trying the block and attack again. I watched Henry's face change as he realized the difference.

"I think my work is done," I whispered.

"Hey, just 'cause you know more about fencing—that doesn't mean anything." Dominic fumbled with the end of his sentence, failing to get the right smart-aleck comeback.

I rolled my eyes. *Pitiful.* I frowned. "I never said it did. Now please stop pestering me. I don't need it." I turned my eyes away from them. In the distance, I watched a group of horses lazily picking at the grass. It reminded me that I had yet to spend time with Nisha.

Professor Lildren had the same attitude and mindset as Professor Trisgeld: he refused to let me anywhere near a staff for that day. I wondered if the two defense professors made the decision together before I came to class.

I sat out and watched the boys lazily practice, whacking one another aimlessly. Their complete languor and indifference bothered me. Did they think they were immune to attacks? Just once, I wanted to see one of them fight off a real criminal and see how they'd fare then. Maybe then they would take it more seriously.

My mood lightened considerably when I strolled to the stables for horseback riding.

"Isabelle, right?" Professor Hailenne greeted me. Late twenties, I guessed. She had black hair, olive toned skin and large brown eyes. "You fit to ride?"

I nodded.

"Great. Do you have a horse of your own?" she inquired.

"Yes." She followed me over to Nisha. He poked his head out of the stall, blowing a huge puff of air. I rubbed his nose. "This is Nisha."

"Oh, you're the one with the great beauty." She patted Nisha on his neck.

A saddle hung next to Nisha's stall, intricately made with flowers carved into the leather. A hostler came up to me. He pointed to the saddle. "This came for you. There's a note in one of the saddlebags." He lumbered off before I could say thank you.

Reaching into a saddlebag, I pulled out a note and unfolded it.

Isabelle,
You'll ride better with a good sad-
dle. Hope this fits.

Joshua Mirran

"Welcome to class," Professor Hailenne said. "I expect you to saddle him. If you need help, ask a hostler until you can do it on your own."

I nodded, and she walked to the other students.

I rubbed Nisha. "Hello, dear friend. I've missed you."

"Hello," Nisha greeted me.

"You all right if I put on a saddle?" I asked.

Nisha neighed and rocked his head. *"Just put it on correctly."*

I smiled. "Don't worry, you're not the first horse I've saddled." I opened the stall door.

Professor Hailenne didn't require me to do much. Nisha trotted casually around the field. I apologized for not visiting, and he said Haldren had informed him of my injuries. I sensed an undercurrent of concern from Nisha as he asked how I was doing. It comforted me to spend time with him. I spoke freely with him, steering clear of everyone else. I told him about the about the rumors spread around the school and the constant rudeness I got from everyone.

"Let me get close and I will stomp on their feet," Nisha encouraged.

I laughed. "Oh, Nisha if only I could."

I felt revitalized with Nisha, and my spirit was considerably lightened as we parted. From then on, I looked forward to horseback riding more than any other class.

When I got to my room, I found a large box waiting for me from Joshua. I lifted the lid to find dresses, cotton shirts, pants, and undergarments. A short note apologized for the delay and said he hoped the clothes fit.

Even if I didn't enjoy staying at the Sorrenian, I knew Joshua was only trying to do what he thought was best. He did try to take care of me.

I put the clothes away and sat on my four-poster bed, exhausted from being the center of unwanted attention. I still had magic class to contend with. I dreaded going down to dinner.

I grabbed something light to eat and sat at the only empty table. I listened to the hum of chatter and laughter ring throughout the room, but I didn't focus on one specific conversation. My stomach tightened, and I felt homesick. The stark reality of having no one and nothing pierced my heart.

I flinched when the bell rang. I had yet to become accustomed to the powerful shrill ringing.

"Isabelle, you're back!" Professor Slystream exclaimed in a false-sounding cheery voice. He held his hands out in welcome.

I nodded slowly.

"How are you feeling?" He leaned against the doorframe, genuine concern showing on his face.

"I'm fine." I faked a smile.

His smile also seemed forced as he folded his arms. "Isabelle, I've been thinking about what happened, and I want to apologize for how I acted. I should have been more assertive and protective."

"It's all right. It wasn't expected." I shrugged.

"Nevertheless, I need to be more careful. I was thinking that I would rather like to work with you one-on-one for the next few class periods. I have something else planned for the rest of the students, but considering the ... circumstances of your magical ability it might be better to approach it unconventionally. Besides, most of these students have been working with magic since they were twelve or younger, and you've only just discovered your talent."

I felt relieved at his suggestion. My stomached uncurled slightly. "I would like that very much, thank you."

He smiled. "Good."

When the rest of the class filed in, I watched the mixed emotions play out on their faces. When the last student, Dominic, arrived, Professor Slystream stood at the front of the room. A few raised their hands.

"Yes, Dominic?"

Dominic put down his hand. "Some of the class have been talking, and we have decided that we do not want to be in the same room practicing magic as Isabelle—" He paused with one quick glance of disgust in my direction. "As a precaution for our health and safety."

The entire class nodded in agreement, several pounding their fists. "Hear, hear!"

The professor frowned. "Now really! She wouldn't be here if I thought there was going to be a danger to your health and safety."

"I don't trust her," Amarilla said, her arms crossed over her chest. She shot me a dirty look. "Any girl willing to pick up a sword is out to kill."

Professor Slystream folded his arms, evening out his stance. "Do you all remember when Henry iced over the whole classroom? Several of you had to be treated by Malsin. Did you kick him out of class for it?"

"That's different," Dominic said, shaking his head.

"How so?" Professor Slystream raised his eyebrows.

"It was an accident. We knew he wasn't trying to kill us." Dominic glanced at Henry. "Right?"

Henry nodded.

"Well then, how do you account for Isabelle? Is it possible that what she did was an accident as well?" he suggested, gesturing to me.

"It doesn't matter. I won't be in the same room with her if she's to practice magic." Dominic sat up straight and glared as if that would help.

"Fine. Everyone who does not want to be in the same room, will you please stand?" He gestured for everyone to rise.

Everyone but Henry stood.

"Henry—why aren't you standing? Don't you agree?" Dominic whispered loudly to him. Hurt flashed across his face.

"No, I'll take my chances. The professor's right. I iced the room and it was an accident, but we don't know if what she did was an accident as well. No one has asked." He spoke casually, one leg draped over the other. "Besides, the only thing she hurt with her magic light show was herself. Not us."

"Fine. If you get killed, it's not my fault. I warned you." Dominic shook his head in disgust or disappointment. I couldn't quite tell.

"Stay standing," the professor told them. He pulled a locket out of his pocket and started speaking into it. It glowed subtly in hues of blue. Within a few minutes, Lord Leavesden arrived.

"What is this I hear? You don't want to be the same room with Isabelle?" Lord Leavesden queried, his eyes roaming over the faces of all the students.

"No." Dominic became the spokesperson for everyone.

"Why?" Lord Leavesden narrowed his eyes on Dominic.

"For the safety of myself and others. I don't want to be killed," Dominic said, his posture stiff.

"No one is going to be killed, Dominic," Lord Leavesden said crossly.

"You don't know that. We don't know what can happen," Dominic said, smug as he presented his argument.

Lord Leavesden narrowed his eyes. "You may all sit while I discuss the matter with Professor Slystream."

I felt I needed to intervene. I raised my hand and cleared my throat. "Excuse me."

Everyone in the room cast their eyes on me.

"Yes, Isabelle?" Lord Leavesden addressed me, his face entirely impassive.

"As much as it pains me to say it, I think Dominic has a point. I don't think the magic I have is normal." Surprise flitted across Dominic's face at my admission. "I have no wish to hurt anyone while I learn how to control this unwanted power. Might there be a different option?"

Lord Leavesden pursed his lips, seeming deep in thought. "All right, Isabelle, come with me and we can discuss this in further detail." He faced the other students. "Dominic, this is the second time today that you have caused mayhem. I will be writing to your parents. If you cannot behave, a harsher course of action will be taken."

Dominic nodded with an unreadable expression.

Lord Leavesden continued. "I need not remind you all that this is your last year here. Your actions toward one another count." He turned his head to me and beckoned me forward.

I stood, slinging my bag over my shoulder, and exited the room.

Lord Leavesden smiled. "I think I have a solution. Let's hope he agrees."

I wondered who he spoke of and fervently wished we would get along. I followed him to the end of the hall, turning left then right, and up a small flight of stairs passing old tapestries and paintings and a few glass cases containing awards and medals. The school was well stocked in heritage. I recognized the doors as we moved to them. The healing room.

Malsin sat hunched over a small table, holding a vial of pink liquid, muttering to himself.

Lord Leavesden coughed lightly to alert him to our presence.

Malsin looked up, confusion on his face for a second before registering our arrival.

"Lord Leavesden, what brings you here?" He leaned out of his chair, noticing me standing a little behind Lord Leavesden and to the right. His shoulders slumped as he frowned. "Oh no, you haven't hurt yourself again, have you?"

I shook my head.

Malsin grinned. "Good." He set the vial down and folded his hands over his stomach, leaning back in his chair. "So what's going on?"

"We have had a mutiny on our hands; started by Dominic and his cohorts of course," Lord Leavesden stated drily.

"Who else," Malsin said with a quick shake of his head as he rolled his eyes.

"They don't want to practice magic alongside Isabelle. Some health and safety nonsense." He tilted his head, gesturing to me. "Isabelle actually agreed with them and asked for a different situation."

He pointed to himself. "You want me to teach her, don't you?"

Lord Leavesden smiled. "I knew you'd catch on."

Malsin sighed. "Why else would you be here?"

Lord Leavesden nodded. "You've already gained her trust, considering she let you heal her with magic. She at least needs to know the basics." He faced me. "Are you all right with this?"

"Yes, of course." I liked Malsin. I preferred him over Professor Slystream, who clearly couldn't handle unexpected situations. If something went wrong, I had complete faith in Malsin's ability to fix it.

Malsin smiled. "All right, I will take on the task of teaching Miss Isabelle magic." He held up a hand. "But don't expect me to teach a full class. The whole reason I took this job is so I could have time to tinker."

"Just Isabelle," Lord Leavesden reassured.

"Well then, shall we start tomorrow at this time?" Malsin asked me, picking up the pink vial again.

"That would be fine," I said.

"Thank you, Malsin. I appreciate it." Lord Leavesden patted him on the shoulder.

"You're welcome. Tomorrow then." He waved us goodbye, swirling the pink liquid around with his long, nimble fingers.

Lord Leavesden left me in the main hall as he headed to his office. I meandered back to my room. I felt relieved, grateful even. I wasn't the least bit mad about Dominic's revolt. He helped make it possible to learn something about magic without feeling the pressure from others.

CHAPTER NINETEEN

THAT NIGHT I DREAMED I was back in Saren, my hands dusted in flour as I rolled out the dough for an apple pie. The sweet smell of cinnamon-sugar-crusted apples wafted throughout the kitchen. Adel stood beside me and we talked animatedly in Nistieran about the town's upcoming festivities. She smiled, full of encouragement. The back door opened. Stefan and Nathan came in, each loaded with a bundle of firewood. They dropped them in the bin beside us. Stefan sneaked up behind me and wrapped his arms around my waist, pulling me into his chest. His soft lips gently trailed down my cheek and the hollow of my throat. I shivered and laughed. Stefan's eyes lit up as I turned slightly in his arms and dropped a sugared apple slice into his mouth. I was happy.

The dream changed.

Barely any sun filtered through the dark and misty forest and into the clearing. I sensed familiarity and froze. The mustached man charged at me with a sword. I tried to run, but I was glued to the spot. I couldn't lift my feet. I threw my hands over my head and crouched.

His boots skidded to a stop in front of me. "Give up. You can't win."

My voice came out small, wavering on the edge of hysteria. "No."

My jaw clenched in defiance as I looked up. The corners of his mouth lifted into a smile as he raised his sword, taking the killing swipe.

I awoke in a scream; tears trickled out of my eyes and down my flushed cheeks. A sheen of cold sweat covered my body. I shook and trembled as I clamped my hand over my mouth.

"Just a dream, Isabelle," I said, clutching my racing heart.

I couldn't go back to sleep. The dream shocked my senses into high-intensity alertness. I ran a hot bath and soaked, washing off the sweat and grime. I had yet to receive another note, but I still couldn't shake the feeling that the employer was only biding his time, waiting for the right opportunity to strike. Could a guard at the entrance of the girl's dormitories really make that much of a difference?

The next day dragged. All the students who did not attend magic class were quickly informed of last night's triumph. The gloating on their faces made me sick, but I let them have their little laugh over it because, unbeknownst to them, I actually felt I owed them a debt of gratitude.

Rodger handed me a card during Professor Breldian's class. Inside he painted a red heart with a little note congratulating me on last night's success. I crumpled it up and stowed it in my bag, intending to throw it in the fireplace later.

I knocked softly on Malsin's door that evening and entered.

"Isabelle, how are you?" he asked. A smile rested on his lips.

I held my arms out. "Fine. No aches anywhere."

Malsin grinned. "The power of magic is a beautiful thing."

I rolled my eyes and he laughed, slapping his hand on the table.

"Professor Slystream explained a little bit of magic to you, right?" Malsin asked.

"He tried, but I don't remember a lot of what he said." I shrugged and leaned against the doorframe. "Something about it passing down through generations. He didn't go into much detail."

Malsin pulled a chair over and gestured for me to sit down.

"So magic is rather simple to begin with. Usually, out of a group of one hundred people only five or so will have it, so checking for it is not regularly enforced. Most of the time parents will suspect that their child has magic based on a few simple ideas." He talked with his hands.

I interrupted. "If it's not very common, why do so many people here have it?"

"Magic is highly valued, so naturally those with rich lineage would seek after it—marry into families that possessed the ability in hopes of giving it to future generations. The Sorrenian is a school for the rich and pampered, so you see more students possessing the ability." He shrugged.

I nodded.

"These are some of the ways people suspect you might have a magical ability." He held up his index finger. "One, you have it in your blood. A family member has magic. It can skip generations, but it is always important to record it in your family history." He held up a second finger. "Two, the child or person acts out in some way. They make a chair move unexpectedly or the cup they're holding turns yellow. It's usually something small and insignificant set off by an emotion of some kind."

"I only recently found out Joshua has the ability and I certainly never made anything happen out of the ordinary." I crossed my legs, a slow pronounced frown on my face.

Malsin rested his hand on the desk. "Yes, well … that is strange. By your age, you should have done something to indicate that you had the ability. I don't understand why nothing happened."

"What was it for you? Did you get tested first, or did you make something happen?" I bit my lip, realizing I might have asked too private of a question. "Sorry, that's probably too personal."

Malsin shook his head and smiled. "No, it's fine." His eyes crinkled as he remembered. "I was six when my sister, two at the time, fell out of a chair. She got a good scrape on her knee and wailed. While mother went to get the box of medicines, I went over and put my hand on it. My hand glowed green, and suddenly her knee was healed. I was tested right after and immediately put into training."

"Oh." I didn't know what else to say. My mind searched for something, anything, that I did that could have indicated I had magic, maybe something I passed over. I couldn't think of a single instance.

Malsin took a breath, seeming indifferent to my internal struggle. "Now, the first thing is to figure out what category you fall into. There are four colors of magic, and each color is associated with an element. You know what the four elements are, don't you?" He eyed me.

"Earth, water, air, and fire," I spouted off.

Malsin smiled. "Good. Now this is important, so try to remember." He held up a finger. "Red is associated with the element of fire. Blue is water. Green is earth. Yellow is air."

I repeated the colors and their associated element, remembering that all of those colors had shone in my hand. *What did that mean?*

"You have a mage core. It's where you store your magic. You renew your magic by immersing yourself in the element that you are associated with. Once we figure out which category you fall into, then I can go into further detail on how it works," he explained. "And once you know how to replenish your core, you can start using it."

"Do you know what Joshua is?" Maybe we belonged to the same category.

"Red," Malsin said indifferently.

"Red. So his element is fire," I answered, folding my hands together. "That explains how he made a fire appear with his hand."

Malsin nodded. "Yes. Reds are notorious for being lazy fire starters. They never make a fire the conventional way."

"So how does the magic class here work if everyone is associated with a different element?" I asked, curious about the class I would never be in.

"Oh, Professor Slystream puts them into groups. Those with the same element work together learning and creating magic. We haven't had a yellow in quite some time." He waved his hand in a nonchalant way.

I nodded, letting it all sink in.

"What category do you think I am?" I asked.

Malsin put a hand to his chin and eyed me speculatively. "I'm not sure. From what I've heard described, it sounds like you have multiple colors." He shook his head. "The odds of that happening are, well—" He stared at the ceiling as he thought. "Very improbable." He clapped his hands. "Well, I think the next course of action is to start."

"Great," I answered in a fake, cheery voice as I sat down in the chair he offered me.

"Now my best theory is that when you previously tried to open your magic, that it got overexcited and didn't know what to choose. I'm hoping that when we try it again it will have calmed down enough to choose a color and a direction, and we can go from there." He folded his hands together. "Or I could be entirely wrong and you *are* all of them. But I think that's highly unlikely."

"All right." I took a deep breath.

"Is there any color you particularly want?" He asked as an afterthought, scratching his head.

I shook my head. "No, I just want answers. Any color is fine."

"Just a reminder, the word that opens your magic is *Spintry*." He held up a finger. "Eventually you won't need to say it but will be able to open your mage core mentally, like this." He held his palm out, and a green flame appeared. He made a fist, and it disappeared. "Now open your hand, palm facing up," he directed, using his hand as an example.

I copied the movement.

"Simply look at your hand and say 'Spintry' with a desire to bring magic forth."

"All right." I took a deep breath in preparation for whatever came next. Nervous tension left my thoughts jumbled. A shiver went up my spine. *What if I become the light show everyone is so terrified of again?*

I put my hand down. "I can't do it."

Malsin folded his arms. "Why?"

"What if the same thing happens again?" I voiced my fears as I gripped onto my thighs, becoming as rigid as a statue.

He rested his big hand on my mine in reassurance. "Isabelle, if something happens, I will be right here to fix it."

I eyed him, my fear still controlling my actions.

"Unless you never want to know … ?" Malsin pursed his lips, egging me on.

My answer came out too quick. "No. I need to do this." I took a deep breath, squashing my fears into a fine powder.

"You ready?"

I nodded. "Yes."

I lifted my hand and turned it, palm facing up. Taking a deep breath, I said the word as clear as I could and willed for any magic to come forth. "Spintry."

I felt the difference in my body the second the magic activated. The distinction was night and day, like groping in the darkness and then suddenly a light appears, and everything comes into sharp focus. My veins thrummed and pulsated wildly with power.

Instantly a red flame appeared in my hand, not hot or cool. It felt … comfortable. I kept expecting pain, but there wasn't any. The flame flickered, and it tickled against my hand. I resisted the urge to close my palm against the tickle.

"Now we see what color it shows." Malsin leaned forward to get a better look.

The red flame rapidly changed to blue. Within a matter of moments, it went through all the colors available—red, blue, green, and yellow—changing with every blink of the eye.

Malsin frowned.

"What is this supposed to mean?" I asked, feeling a bit put out.

"I'm not sure. It's almost like it can't decide what it wants to focus on. Maybe I am wrong and you're all of them." He rubbed his chin, and his brow furrowed. "But I haven't heard of that before." He held up two fingers. "Two colors, yes, but not four." He tapped his finger against the side of his cheek. "Why don't we give it another minute and see if it will decide."

"All right." I stared at the tiny flame in my hand, wishing it would just choose a color and be done with it. The flame never stayed put. It flipped incessantly between all of them. Blue, yellow, green, and red. I sighed heavily. Why did everything have to be so difficult? Why couldn't I just be normal?

"Hmm … It just doesn't want to decide, does it? All right, let's close it. Put your hand into a fist and say 'Findel,'" he directed.

Disappointment echoed in my voice as I closed it. Instantaneously the flame went out, as did the thrumming in my body. "I'm sorry I'm so difficult." I felt sorry for myself; pathetic, really.

"Don't be sorry, Isabelle." He put his hand on mine, his voice sincere. "We'll figure this out together. Maybe your magic needs time to decide what it wants. It's been dormant for so long it's probably still overexcited. For now, I'll just teach you a bit of everything, and we'll go from there."

I nodded grimly.

"You know, Professor Slystream is the real magic professor here. He might know better than I do. I'll talk to him tomorrow and come up with a list of things we can try." He scratched his head, deep in thought, then smiled ruefully. "You're the first magic student I've had. I'm not actually sure what to do. Why don't we quit for the day? I'm afraid I'll steer you in the wrong direction without some guidance from Professor Slystream."

I smiled wistfully "Sure." I left his office feeling glummer than ever.

When I got to my room, I noticed a bouquet of red roses and delphiniums perfectly arranged in a beautiful crystal vase resided on my desk. A card leaned against the side of it. I picked it up and opened it quickly.

Dear Isabelle,

Gods, I miss you. Joshua told me you had a bit of a rough start at the Sorrenian. Please tell me you are all right. My father won't let me out of his sight—all of this preparing to take over Aberron when he's retired. Frankly, I don't think it's going to happen for quite some time. He enjoys being King and still has loads of life left in him. You're in my thoughts so often that my father keeps asking who the girl is. I haven't told him yet; I enjoy get-

ting the best of him. He pesters Joshua for an answer, but all he does is scowl. Joshua won't tell either. I want you to know that you are always in my heart and on my mind. Please enjoy the flowers as an apology for not being able to come in person. They reminded me of you: red for your soft lips and blue and purple for that beautiful dress you wore when we first kissed. Father is calling for me again. Hope to visit soon.

Love,

Andrew

My heart soared. Andrew gave me exactly what I needed to get out of this depressing mood. I buried my nose in the soft rose petals and breathed in the floral smell. I carried the vase to my bedroom and set it on the small end table next to my bed.

I clutched the note tight to my chest after reading it repeatedly and tracing my hands over the inky letters. Finally, I felt like I mattered in someone's eyes. I went to sleep with a dreamy smile on my face for the first time in what seemed like forever.

Two weeks had passed since I arrived at the Sorrenian. Every day blurred into the next—a drudge of misery to get through. The students either carefully avoided me, the chubby boy Ellis going as far as running in the opposite direction when I walked down a hallway, or the brave ones crafted insults and gave them out judiciously. Helda came up to me again in the library. She said she managed to convince several other people that I was not a soul-sucking monster but no one would go against Henry and Dominic, who actively shunned and persecuted me, to be friends. Since

Lord Leavesden's reprimand to Dominic in Professor Slystream's class, nary a word was said to me with a professor in sight.

I promised if we met again that I would slip Helda a study guide to help with her Nistieran. Her sister, Amarilla, quickly pulled her away after that and scolded her for approaching me. Rodger had gone as far as leaving flowers at my door with a note suggesting how to get more attention centered on me. The least harmful suggestion said to throw food at Henry's head in the dining hall.

The morning classes became a fog. I sank into my seat and hardly spoke. Generally, every professor gave us the last twenty minutes of class to work on homework. Because I already understood the concepts they taught, I usually finished before the hour was out in each class.

Professor Trisgeld finally decided to let me have a partner in his defensive class.

"Henry!" he barked. "Work with Isabelle today. Dominic can work with Falden."

Henry nodded, showing no signs of regret or disappointment. It surprised me at first until I remembered that he shunned, and Dominic instigated.

"So, you're finally ready to fight someone real, are you?" Henry spoke casually as we stretched.

"I've always been ready," I said coolly, stretching my arms out to grab my feet. I hadn't come to chat. I only wanted to fight and get through this class.

"Someone's in a mood," he muttered.

I stopped and looked at him. "I know you don't want to talk or work with me, so what's the point in casual conversation?"

Henry's blue eyes lit up. "That's true. I wouldn't pair us up together if I had the choice, but now that I don't, why can't we chat a little?" He sat in the grass and grabbed his foot, stretching his limber body.

"Because any information you get will be used against me in some way, I'm sure." I brought my arms high above my head and leaned to one side.

"Oh, you think you've got us figured out? Not everything we do centers around sabotaging you." He shook his head, seeming offended.

"I'm sure you manage to squeeze other things into your schedule as well, but give me one example when I've been around that someone hasn't said or done something disrespectful to me." I held up a finger. "Just one. Shouldn't be too hard, right?"

Henry pursed his lips; I could almost see his mind revolve. "All right, I see your point."

Just this morning Dominic had drawn a picture of me run through with a sword and placed it on my desk. Rodger suggested I stick my foot out and trip him in retaliation.

Henry didn't talk to me again while we practiced, and I tried not to think about his startling blue eyes. By now I had concluded that he had to have some relation to Andrew. Not brothers—Andrew was an only child. He had to be a cousin, but how close of a cousin was he? First or second? I didn't dare ask, fearing he would make a connection between Andrew and me.

I worked with Professor Lildren in the staff fighting class. He praised my quick reflexes, but it didn't make me feel any better. Nisha became my only comfort. His quiet talks in my mind gave me the courage to continue.

During our riding class, Henry rode up beside me. "You talk to your horse like it can talk back."

"What does it matter?" I asked. My stomach knotted as it did anytime another student approached me.

"No one else talks to their horse the way you do," he observed.

"Because they have people willing to listen to them," I spouted off, wondering why he chose to break his silence and speak to me.

Henry frowned.

"Rodger talks to you." He patted his beautiful painted mare. "That's someone."

"Rodger only talks to give me suggestions on how I can become the sole focus of your antagonizing," I said drily, my expression no doubt acerbic. "He's become my personal coach on how to get bullied."

"Oh." Henry scratched his head.

Dominic trotted alongside us a minute later on a dark brown, almost black stallion. He kept his distance but rode within earshot. "Henry, I thought we had an understanding."

"I know, I know. No talking to the crazy girl unless we have to," he said, waving him off.

Unexpectedly, Nisha reared back. He whinnied loudly and kicked his front hooves up toward Henry. I nearly fell off. I gripped onto the reins with all the strength I had in my upper arms as my knees dug into Nisha's sides.

"Nisha!" I shrieked.

"Hey!" Henry yelled. He yanked on the reins to pull back his whinnying mare, who had also become startled and pawed the air.

Nisha did not want to obey. He touched the ground for a second, then kicked his front hooves out again. He rocked his head back and forth, his nostrils flaring.

"It's all right, Nisha. It's just a stupid boy." I rubbed his neck, but I could hear him yelling at Henry, and I worried that Henry could hear as well.

How dare he insult my lady. I'll trample him! Nisha screamed.

Henry narrowed his eyes. "Hey, did your horse just yell at me? I could have sworn I heard someone."

"No, he didn't," I lied quickly. I leaned down and whispered in Nisha's ear. "Nisha, don't worry about it." He backed up and shook his head from side to side as he pawed the ground. Dirt flew around his legs. I worried he would charge.

"What's going on?" Professor Hailenne cantered over on a white horse.

"Come on, Nisha; now you've got the professor's attention. I'm going to get into trouble." I urged him to calm down.

Nisha stomped his hooves a couple more times but eventually calmed down, snorting heavily.

"What happened?" Professor Hailenne demanded.

"I think something must have spooked Nisha," I lied, not telling her that he intentionally directed his outburst at Henry. "I'm sorry."

"You need to contain your horse. If you can't control him, then I don't want you riding in my class," she said sternly, eyeing Nisha.

Once Nisha heard those words, he acted completely innocent. He stepped forward and lightly lipped the back of the professor's hand, then stepped back and bowed his head. Professor Hailenne's stern composure broke. She smiled.

"I'm sorry. It won't happen again." I focused directly on Professor Hailenne, attempting to show sincerity. I desperately hoped she wouldn't see through my lie. Controlling a horse with the mind of a human would not be easy.

She nodded. "Class is over. Ride back to the stalls."

I turned Nisha around and started trotting back to the stalls, leaving everyone else in the dust. Once out of earshot, I rounded on him. "Nisha, you can't do that. You're just going to make it worse for me."

"I will not listen to you getting insulted. He deserved that," he retorted, rocking his head back in defiance.

"He might have deserved that, but it isn't going to win any medals," I said darkly.

I hopped off Nisha and fished out a sugar lump I'd been saving for him. "Try to be nicer, will you? I don't want to make it worse here than it already is."

"I make no promises," Nisha said stubbornly.

I sighed, rubbing the front of his nose. "All right. I'll see you later then." I gave him the sugar lump and kissed him on the nose. A hostler came forward, a brush in his hand, and took the reins.

By dinnertime, the school buzzed over Nisha's outburst in the field. It gave them more proof that I was out to get them. I had now trained my horse to be a savage attacker. Several students blocked my way to the buffet of food, demanding that I put my horse down. I gave them one cursory glare and sidestepped them. Multiple girls fawned over a delighted Henry—stroking his hair, touching his arms, asking about his health, while equally sneaking daggerlike glares in my direction over the potential damage my horse could have done to him.

Honestly, the whole show disgusted me.

I barely touched my food. I couldn't stand to watch one more girl pop a strawberry into Henry's mouth. He glanced at me occasionally, gauging my reaction, but I looked away before our eyes could meet. I left before it could get any worse, grateful that I didn't see Rodger around to congratulate me.

CHAPTER TWENTY

TEPPING ONTO THE TRAINING field the following day, I caught Henry in a heated discussion with Dominic. Henry clutched a rumpled note. "If she thinks she can drag me to this dinner party, she's wrong. I'm not going to sit there and watch her fawn over Andrew while encouraging me to be his replica. I swear she wishes he were her son over me."

My curiosity piqued. I worked hard not to appear like I actively listened while we waited for Professor Trisgeld to arrive.

"That's right, take a stand," Dominic encouraged. "Show her you're your own man. Sooner or later she'll see Prince Andrew isn't perfect."

Henry snorted. "Right." He stowed the paper in his pocket.

Professor Trisgeld called us to order, effectively ending their conversation. He made Henry become my designated partner. When Professor Trisgeld endeavored to pair me with someone else, they pretended to be sick and requested to see Malsin. Henry was the only one good enough to keep up with me anyway. He went into shunner mode and spoke only when it became necessary for practice.

As we worked, I couldn't dislodge Henry and his unhappiness out of my mind. The shunner, as I often thought of him, had been the most civil out of the group of haters. And yet, he could still be just as mean as the rest of them. One moment he seemed interested in me as a person and the next he spouted insults. I knew I shouldn't be bothered by what he did or what he thought, but he intrigued me; or rather, his blue eyes intrigued me. Like Andrew, but not. Henry strived for distinction.

When I got to the riding class, Nisha still appeared heated about yesterday. He complained that the gray gelding in the stall across from him got a better view and cleaner, fresher air. Next, he went on a tirade about the hostlers.

"They are slow and lazy." Nisha snorted. *"They did not clean out my water pail. I will not drink out of a murky bucket. No matter how thirsty I get."*

"I'm sorry, Nisha. I'll clean it out for you when we get back," I promised.

"Don't bother," Nisha said, hopping over a fence in the course lain out by the professor. *"I am going to drop it on one of their heads."*

I chuckled. "That'll teach them."

Nisha then pointed out horses he did not like. The gray gelding ridden by Falden at the forefront. *"They are pompous and light-headed."*

"They aren't warhorses," I told him as we trotted over the finish line.

After dinner Malsin had a list of different things to try when I got to the healing room.

I opened the magic and immediately it started switching colors.

"Try focusing on one color. Say, blue." He paced around the room, finger tapping his chin.

I stared at my palm and thought vehemently. *Stay blue!*

The red flame switched to blue and stayed still.

I smiled. "Hey, it worked."

"All right. Now think green," Malsin directed.

I stared at the small blue flame and wished for it to turn green. Immediately the flame transformed into a deep-green flame and stayed still.

Malsin had me repeat the process for red and yellow.

"This shouldn't be happening," he muttered, completely dumbfounded. He put his hand on his forehead. "Even if you wish with all your might for a different color. You can't change it."

"What's wrong with me then?" I asked. "Why am I able to change the color?"

He ran a hand through his hair. "I think we need to look at your mage core and then start testing you on other things. Things only one color is specifically good at. Then I'll know for sure."

Unexpectedly, a knock came at the door, and Henry showed up. I quickly shut the magic off. For a second he stared, probably not expecting to see me there with Malsin, but he quickly regained his composure. "Sorry to interrupt, but a girl has just tripped down some of the stairs, and I think you need to look at her ankle."

Malsin stopped pacing. "Thanks, Henry, will you lead the way?" He turned and met my eyes. "I'm sorry to have to cut our lesson so short, but duty calls. We will continue this tomorrow."

"I understand." I forced a smile.

I meandered out of Malsin's office, going the opposite way he and Henry did, not ready to go to my room. I felt stifled after spending most of my hours sitting in silence. Few students came out of their rooms at this time, making a leisurely stroll more appealing.

I worried about my magical abilities. I had complete trust that Malsin would do whatever possible to figure it out, but what if the results turned out to be bad? What if my power couldn't be controlled?

I found a bench down a low-lit hallway and sat, hoping my overactive mind would meet in the middle with my tired body. My mind didn't care that in the past month I had been savagely attacked, fallen in love, and terrorized by students. It only wanted to jump to the next new thing.

Unexpected voices carried through the hall. I started, realizing I wouldn't be alone for much longer. How long had I been sitting there?

"Haha, did you see his face?" a boy laughed.

I immediately recognized the voice as belonging to a judgmental and rude jerk—Dominic. The instigator.

"That one will go down in history for sure," another boy said.

Henry. Mr. Shunner himself.

As if I don't have enough problems in my basket, I thought sarcastically. I hopped up, hoping I could run away before they discovered me. *Too late.* They rounded the corner just as I did. I skidded to a halt.

"Hey, watch it!" Henry lifted his arms, stepping back rapidly to avoid the impending collision.

"Sorry," I apologized. My cheeks flushed. I suspected a red blush showed on my face. I thought up several choice words for myself for not heading directly to my room.

It made my blunder feel worse when I noticed all ten students of the popular crowd hovered around me. Henry, Dominic, Falden, Aliyah, Amarilla, Ethan, the twins Roanna and Ryan, Cole, and Marie. Wow, I remembered all their names. *That's new.* But knowing their names didn't solve my problem. How could I get out of here unscathed?

"Well, look who we have here." Dominic sneered.

Everyone chuckled except Henry. He leaned against the wall, his ankles crossed, his arms folded, and just ... stared.

Chills went up my spine, and I resisted the urge to shudder. Instead, I eyed them coldly as I regained the stamina I needed to get through this oncoming attack.

"What are you doing down here anyway?" Dominic continued, sweeping his black hair away from his eyes. "I've never seen you here before."

"Why should it matter to you?" I shot back icily.

"Ooh ..." the twins, Roanna and Ryan said in a low tone, their faces lit up with the possibility of a show. It quickly caught on, and others wore the same expression.

Dominic smirked. "You're right, it doesn't matter; we just want to make sure you're not doing something—" He paused, seeming to search for the right word, then smiled toothily. "Damaging."

I raised my eyebrows at them. "Seriously?"

"You wear the Mark of the Gods and your magic is messed up," Henry cut in. "You do things against your nature. You don't add up."

I heard several mumbled agreements. Amarilla nodded her head vigorously.

I crossed my arms. "Is that it? You'd rather I be one of your dumb sheep?" I gestured to his friends with a tilt of my head. "No thank you."

"Watch it. You're outnumbered." Dominic's eyes flashed like he wanted to fight. He took a step forward, his fists balled.

I leaned back. What had gotten into them tonight? They were mean but never this pushy. I laughed. "Like any of you would be a match for me." I shook my head, knowing full well I bluffed, but I couldn't help it. I didn't even have a weapon with me, except maybe a hairpin that could potentially gouge an eye if I got lucky. Perhaps I should brush up on hand-to-hand combat?

Dominic took another step forward while Falden slid into his previous position, absolving the gap. They closed in on me.

"You want to try it out?" Dominic asked eagerly.

"Go right ahead." I motioned for Dominic to come at me, hoping my boldness would make him step down. I didn't want to fight, but they could never call me a coward. I would take them on if I had to.

"Dominic, come on. You're wasting your time on her." Henry put a hand on his shoulder. "Don't be such a hothead."

Dominic scoffed and stepped backward, backing off. "You're right; I have better things to do than fight a little girl." He shoved passed me, knocking me into the side of the wall. Turning around, he snickered at me and continued on his way. The rest of the group followed, a few eyeing me and muttering insults under their breath. They were sheep all right.

Henry waited until the last boy, Cole, sauntered down the hall to follow. He stared at me for a moment, lost in thought, before shrugging off the wall and saying nothing. If it weren't for him, I probably would have ended up in a fight with Dominic. Henry obviously didn't care for me in any way, but he still reined things in when the situation started getting out of control.

Why?

I believed Dominic to be the loudmouth and instigator of the group, but I had no doubt in my mind that whatever Henry said became a rule.

Eager to leave the dimly lit hallway, I headed to my room; too much drama for me tonight. As I passed the double doors leading outside, I reversed my course. A bit of fresh air might clear my head. My skin felt hot from the encounter.

I went to the stables, intending to visit with Nisha. A hostler came up to me as I entered, a scowl on his face. "You need to control your horse. He threw his water pail at me."

I peered closer, noticing a red mark on his forehead that would be a bruise later. I held back a laugh. *Go Nisha!* "Clean it out more often and he won't do it." I stalked off before the hostler could get another word in.

I found Nisha lying down, his eyes closed. I opened the stall and sat on the ground with him. He stirred. *"Hello, little one."*

I smiled. "Hello. Mind if I sit with you for a while?"

"You may." Nisha agreed. He settled back into the straw. *"Is there something you want to talk about?"*

I sighed, deciding not to unleash all my burdens on him. "No. I just want be with a friend." I settled in next to Nisha, resting my back against his, and raised my eyes to the wooden rafters.

Soft snores told me he had fallen back asleep.

I heard two horses ride into the stables. Laughter rang from a rider—Alzmire.

"And that's how I managed to win her hand," Lord Leavesden said.

Boots hit the ground as the two men dismounted.

"A lot of trouble you went through to persuade her," Alzmire said lightly.

"Yes, but worth it," Lord Leavesden agreed.

I curled against Nisha, feeling like I shouldn't be privy to their conversation, and yet I worried about trying to leave. Surely, they would notice me and I would get reprimanded for being out past curfew. I decided to wait until they left. I couldn't help it if I heard them now.

I cast my eyes to Nisha's saddle hanging up on the wall. Something white peeked out of one of the saddle bags. A note? I crawled over, plucked it out and settled back against Nisha.

Lord Leavesden spoke. "So you heard that Prince Andrew is back from his Walk?"

"Yes, yes," Alzmire answered.

"I heard that his mother wants to match him with Lady Marissa. She is visiting from the southwest corner of Aberron to advocate for a better trading port," Lord Leavesden said.

"Oh; I wonder how they will receive her." Alzmire paused before continuing. "I always found Lady Marissa to be very uptight and demanding. She always has something to flaunt over the others, whether it be a trinket or a new beau."

Lord Leavesden chuckled in agreement.

Alzmire continued. "When I last saw Andrew, he was quite smitten with another girl. More so than I have ever seen him. Though perhaps it was just an end-of-the-Walk romance. Now that he is back in Carasmille, he must focus on taking on the duties of becoming a king. Lady Marissa is on a one-on-one basis with most nobles of the Court. It might be a better choice."

"She is accustomed to the ways of Court," Lord Leavesden agreed. "His next duty before becoming the King is to take on a wife. As I recall, he is supposed to have found one within a year or two after his Walk."

"A year and a half exactly," Alzmire interrupted.

"Right, and there is no way he is going to refuse his mother when she has arranged something," Lord Leavesden said knowingly.

Alzmire laughed. "I don't know of anyone who can say no to Queen Averly."

They moved out of earshot, walking through the doors and up the path to the school.

My heart twisted. My fears that Andrew would find someone better increased. I was an oddity with my birthmark and strange magic. I couldn't be good for him. It was foolish of me to think we could have something special.

I took a breath and exhaled. My hand cinched around the paper. I unfolded it and read.

**The Sorrenian doesn't see your
worth. I do. You are wanted—Employer**

Underneath the words, the Employer had drawn the Mark of the Gods
in red.

Dread filled the pit of my stomach. "Nisha." I nudged him awake.

He snorted and shook his head, eyes blinking back sleep. *"What little
one?"*

I showed him the letter. "Did you see anyone put this in your saddlebag?"

Nisha snuffled the paper. *"No. What is it?"*

"The employer," I answered darkly. "I've got to show this to Joshua. Will
you take me to the castle please?"

Nisha rocked his head. *"Yes."*

I saddled him in record time and led him out of his stall. A hostler tried
to stop me just outside of the door. "Hey! Students aren't supposed to be
taking their horses out this late!" He attempted to step in front of us, but
Nisha kicked up his front hooves, forcing the man to jump back.

"It's important!" I called, nudging Nisha into a canter.

Nisha darted through the front gates as guards held them open for a
wagon laden with supplies.

"Stop!" one of the men shouted after me.

The wind whipped through my hair; a cold breeze touched any exposed
skin. Smoke from burning chimneys tainted the air. Nisha trotted toward
the flickering lights of the city. I made out the sounds of turning wheels,
clopping, random shouts from people going to and fro.

Hooves thundered on cobblestone behind me. I twisted in the saddle
to see three guards hot on my trail. Nisha danced out of the way of a
fast-moving carriage just as we were about to turn onto a business street.

"Watch yourself!" the driver shouted angrily at me, flicking the reins.

The pause allowed the guards to catch up with us. Three red faces glared
at me.

"What do you think you're doing?" The guard with black hair falling into his chocolate eyes demanded.

"I need to get to my brother Joshua Mirran. It's urgent," I explained.

The guards looked at each other. Another spoke up. "Students aren't supposed to leave without the proper permissions from a Professor or Lord Leavesden."

I exercised all the stubbornness I had in my voice. "I'm not going back until I've spoken with my brother. I believe my safety at the school is compromised."

Again, the guards silently communicated. The black-haired guard nodded at me. "We'll escort you then."

I breathed a sigh of relief. "Thank you."

They positioned themselves, one ahead, one at my side, and the last behind. Tall brick buildings soon morphed into sprawling mansions the farther we rode. Traffic significantly lessened as the castle loomed ahead. I bit my bottom lip, anxiety working its way through me over the note. It occurred to me that Joshua could not be home. What would I do if he wasn't? The idea of going back to the Sorrenian without alerting him alarmed me.

I wondered how hard it would be to get an audience with Andrew. Regardless of my concerns of our courtship, I knew without a doubt he would want to see me safe. Perhaps even the king since he had ordered Andrew to remain by my side during my journey to Thimbleton.

Huge torches lit up the iron gates in front of the castle. At least ten soldiers stood attention. The guard in front of me, dismounted and spoke in a flurry of words to a sentry. The sentry picked up the locket from around his neck and spoke quietly into it. After a moment or two he motioned us forward. "Proceed."

The iron fence opened up. Nisha walked slowly toward the entrance. Short, manicured hedges lined the walkway. As we halted near the front marble steps, the doors sailed open. Joshua rushed down, concern on his features. I jumped off Nisha and hurried to him.

Joshua clutched my upper shoulders. "What's the matter Isabelle? Are you all right?"

"I'm fine." I nodded my head at the guards behind me. They had discreetly backed away to give us privacy. "These three escorted me here safely."

"What happened?" Joshua asked.

I reached into my pocket and handed him the note. "This was in Nisha's saddlebag." Joshua brought the note up to the light of the torch and read. His face hardened. "Joshua, he's still watching me."

Andrew appeared, flying down the steps. "Isabelle my darling." He nearly knocked Joshua aside as he reached for me, crushing me into a hug. I inhaled his cinnamon woodsy cologne. My soul sang at his presence. He pressed his lips firmly on my forehead. I shut my eyes, basking in his affection. He leaned back just enough to meet my eyes. "Are you all right?"

I nodded; sudden emotion clouded my throat. "Better," I choked, "with you."

Andrew grinned. "Gods I've missed you." His lips touched mine briefly. Joshua loudly cleared his throat. I sensed strong reluctance from Andrew, mingling my own, as he straightened.

Joshua scowled. "This isn't a social call." His emerald eyes caught mine as he lifted the paper. "You found this in your saddlebag?"

Joshua allowed Andrew to take the note to see its contents. His one-armed grip around me tightened.

"Yes, this evening when I decided to spend some time with Nisha," I confirmed. "Nisha said he didn't see anyone put it in there. I asked."

"This is the only note you've seen since the first one?" Joshua asked. "Nothing inside the castle?"

"Correct," I said.

Joshua rubbed his beard. "Well then, perhaps those guards I've stationed inside are working. If you haven't seen anything in the school then you should still be safe. I don't want you going outside by yourself for any reason."

"Joshua." Anger tinged my voice. I did not want to go back.

Andrew returned the letter to Joshua and wrapped both arms around me. He rubbed my back in soothing circles. I melted into him.

Joshua asked, "how far have you gotten in your magic lessons?"

My shoulders slumped. "Not very far. Malsin is teaching me because the other students are too afraid to be in the same room when I turn it on. We still don't know what I am."

Joshua spoke with conviction. "You need the tutoring. Malsin is a well renowned healer. I'm confident he can help you."

"Unless I get kidnapped first," I muttered.

"That's not happening," Andrew growled.

"You will be safe as long as you stay within a group or inside," Joshua said. "It's much harder to kidnap someone with others around."

"Joshua is right," Andrew agreed. "Safety is in numbers."

"Come on, I'll escort you back," Joshua encouraged. "I'll see if I can hunt up any leads with this note when I return."

"I'll help," Andrew offered. "I want my girl to be safe."

"Did you learn anything from the first one?" I asked my brother.

Joshua frowned. "No. Wait here with Andrew while I get my horse." He strode off.

The second Joshua's back was turned Andrew cupped my face and kissed me hungrily. I brought my arms up to wrap around his neck. His fingers moved to thread through my hair. Passion exploded between us. I clung to him like a balm, not knowing when I'd get another chance to be this close.

My heart pounded, my knees weakened, when we broke the kiss.

Andrew's blue eyes blazed through the light of the torch. "Gods you intoxicate me."

I chuckled. "Same to you."

"How are they treating you at the Sorrenian?" he asked. "You haven't had to fight off any boys, have you?"

The blatant jealousy in his tone warmed my heart. I laughed. "Hardly. They're afraid of me. I wear the Mark of the Gods, my magic is messed up, and I fight like a man." I couldn't help the caustic twist in my tone. "Certainly not winning any medals."

"Well, you've got me." Andrew glanced at Joshua approaching. "And your brother too. Hang in there love." He lightly kissed my lips then released me.

"I'll try," I said as I mounted Nisha.

Joshua spurred his horse forward. "Let's go."

The three guards eyed me with new interest on our return journey to the Sorrenian. My cheeks flamed knowing they'd been privy to Andrew and I's display of affection.

Joshua hardly spoke a word; his brow drew low as if deep in thought. As we reached the gates of the school, I admitted I'd run out without telling anyone and the guards chased me down.

Joshua's tone was severe. "Don't ever do that again. Promise me you'll find Lord Leavesden or a trusted professor should something alarm you."

"I will." I knew it was probably what I should've done in the first place but fear hadn't made me think straight. I still wasn't comfortable coming back, but I chose to trust my brother and Andrew.

Joshua quietly thanked the guards as they returned to their stations. He tied his horse to a post then helped me tuck Nisha into his stall.

My brother accompanied me inside the school. "I'm going to have a talk with Lord Leavesden. You go onto bed."

"Yes Commander," I chirped.

Joshua rolled his eyes at me as we went our separate directions.

CHAPTER TWENTY-ONE

 ORD LEAVESDEN HAD A quiet word with me during breakfast the following morning, ensuring I knew to come to him should I discover anything out of the ordinary. I assured him I would.

After last's night's near fight with Dominic, I noticed some of the popular crowd, particularly Dominic, acting rather smug. Whispers about our encounter went about the classroom. I kept my head down and focused on the math calculations but opened my ears to listen. Bets were being wagered on an imaginary fight, and it seemed, much to my surprise, that we were neck and neck on the scoreboard.

My thoughts were interrupted when Professor Ventreast asked me to solve a math problem. Within a minute I answered him correctly, eliciting a rare smile from him.

"Always right, every time." He chuckled, seeming pleased that at least someone in the room understood what he taught.

Nearly every student in the room made a face. In return, I scowled. It wasn't my fault the professor called me out. All the professors did when no one ventured an answer. What was I supposed to do? Pretend I didn't know?

I took my frustration out on a stuffed dummy during Trisgeld's class, getting so worked up that I accidently sliced the head off. It rolled a few feet away, straw spewing out.

"Isabelle, I think you're getting a bit carried away." Professor Trisgeld crossed his arms. "I'm going to need these in one piece for tomorrow's class."

"I'm sorry, I didn't mean to." I snatched the fallen head and shoved it back onto the body. It's not like it needed a head.

Kings Day and Gods Day fast approached, ending my third week at the Sorrenian. It gave me hope: two full days of hiding in my room.

Professor Trisgeld gathered us together and explained a new tactic: defending ourselves against two or more attackers. He then proceeded to show us several moves that would help. I recognized the moves but hadn't had much practice.

He then paired us up into groups of three—two people against one. As my luck would have it, he put me with Henry and Dominic. Cursing silently under my breath at my misfortune, I walked over to them.

"Here's your chance to finally beat me," I baited, swiveling my sword around in my hands. "Two against one." My irritation at being back at the Sorrenian leaked through.

"You think we're going to fight you right in front of the professor?" Henry shook his head. "No, this isn't a real fight. This is just practice."

"You think so?" I eyed them doubtfully.

"If we want to see who the better fighter is, we'll do it away from the professor's eyes and ears," Henry responded. His eyes darted to Professor Trisgeld currently yelling at Cole, Ryan, and Rodger.

"All right then. Are we going to practice or not?" I started to move into a fighting stance.

"Now wait just a minute." Dominic held a hand up. "I propose we strike up a deal."

"Deal?" I straightened my posture. *What are they thinking?*

"A winner takes all kind of thing." Dominic grinned, twiddling his blade in between his fingers.

"What are you thinking, Dom?" Henry asked, hand on hip.

"I propose we fight in a less open place—tonight after classes." Dominic stabbed the dirt.

"Fight with what?" I asked, curious. If he said staff, then I didn't think I had much of a chance.

He held up his sword. "Simple swordplay, just like what we practice in class. No killing of course, first one to disarm the other wins."

"And what is the prize?" I gripped the pommel harder than I meant to and loosened my hold. What could they want from me?

"If we win, you'll answer all questions in class incorrectly," Dominic said, shifting weight from side to side.

Sounds kind of stupid. Couldn't they think of anything better? "And if I win?"

"What do you want?" Dominic asked.

I spoke without hesitation. "Peace. I want you guys to tell everybody to leave me alone. No rude comments, evil stares, and the like. Either treat me like a lady should be treated or ignore me completely." Dominic turned to Henry. "What do you think?"

Henry shrugged. "Fine, I guess."

"All right, deal," Dominic agreed. He leaned into Henry and muttered something into his ear. Henry nodded in agreement. "You'll fight Henry tonight. He's the best."

"Fine," I agreed quickly. I wondered if underneath Dominic's instigating schemes he was a coward, since he willingly offered Henry to fight instead of himself. Perhaps he was all show and no bite?

"Meet us at the entrance hall at eight." Dominic pointed his blade at my chest. "And keep this quiet. We don't want the whole school knowing what we're up to."

"Right." I rolled my eyes. *Who would I tell?*

I had little doubt that I would lose the fight, but if I did, I could handle their request. It surprised me that they didn't think of something better or at least add that I give them the right answers so they could pretend to be smart. Dominic, for all his instigating, didn't think too fast on his feet. Ultimately, their end goal was to get me to make a fool of myself in front of the professors. Still, I'd take that chance if it meant I could have a little bit of peace.

I paid extra attention in Lildren's class, hoping I could learn something that would give me an edge for tonight. I noticed Henry watching me with intense interest as well, seeming to search for something he could use against me later. I prayed he couldn't find anything.

In riding class, I told Nisha of the upcoming duel between Henry and me.

"I wish I could be there to watch you win." Nisha broke into a canter.

I liked his confidence in me. "I wish you could too."

I kept an eye on Henry's table at dinner, watching Dominic discreetly tell his tablemates of tonight's plan. Henry leveled his eyes at me and nodded in a reminder. I wondered what went through his mind about our upcoming duel. Did he really want to do this? Regardless, I knew he cared about his friendship with Dominic and would support his proposal to the end.

Malsin approached me just as I exited the dining hall.

"Oh, Isabelle, I'm so sorry. I'll have to reschedule our lesson yet again. I've got three students with the stomach flu and a boy with a mysterious rash. I can't risk infecting you." He ran a hand through his hair. "I'm starting to think maybe we should just make this a once-a-week deal, but you do need to practice, and someone has to teach you." He smiled apologetically.

"It's all right. I can put off magic a little while longer," I assured. I wasn't in a hurry to test it out, especially today. What if it messed up my duel with Henry? When would I get another chance like this again?

"All right. I'll get back to you soon to set up a time when I shouldn't be busy," he said.

I nodded. "Sounds great."

"Good." He left my side to eat, and I escaped to my room to get ready.

I spent some time stretching in front of the fireplace. I wanted to be as limber as possible. I made sure I wore comfortable clothes and pinned my hair away from my face. Adrenaline heightened as I pondered over different defense tactics I could use.

The clock in the hall chimed eight as I arrived. Within a minute, the ten popular students reached me.

"Follow me," Dominic said.

I picked up the rear in case someone tried to trip me up on our way to duel. We marched through a series of hallways I'd never been through before and descended a narrow staircase. We stopped at a large wooden door. Dominic muttered something and pulled on the handle; it opened creakily. He threw his softly red glowing hand out and lit the torches in the brackets, lighting up the room.

Large, rectangular, and bare, the room fit all eleven of us easily. Four open metal doors lined the left wall, leading to tiny, darkened chambers. Each door had one narrow open slat at the top and a bolted flap at the bottom. *Prison cells.* The Sorrenian housed more secrets than it let on.

"You're probably wondering where we are." Henry folded his arms. "This school used to house the military. During war times, Kings would haul prisoners down here, lock them up, and torture answers out of them using a variety of magical and nonmagical objects. Now it's just an empty room, and no one comes down here. Most people don't even know it exists."

"See? Perfect place." Dominic's eyes gleamed as he rubbed his hands together. "No Professor will catch us."

"Fine." I didn't care about the location. I came to fight and get them to leave me alone, starting tonight.

I unsheathed my sword and waited on Henry. Everyone melted into the walls to watch. Their faces displayed varying degrees of excitement, ready for a show. *They are going to get one,* I thought determinedly, gripping hard on the pommel.

"You sure you want to do this?" I asked. I wouldn't fight Henry against his will.

"It's about time we had a real battle. One-on-one." He pulled his sword up to him.

"First one to disarm the other wins," Dominic said clearly, watching both of our faces so we understood. "I don't want to cart anyone to Malsin, so don't make this bloody."

We both nodded solemnly.

"All right. Here we go." Dominic, hardly able to stay still, took an excited breath. He raised his hands high over his head and dropped them. "Begin."

Immediately I moved into an offensive position. We circled each other, our feet light on the stone floor, before Henry took the lead. His sword came swinging down at my midsection. Instinctively, I blocked his attack with a flip of my wrist. I scanned for a weakness while he regained his composure. We lunged back and forth, each blocking the other's attack easily, testing strengths and weaknesses between us.

"Come on, quit the child's play. I want to see a winner!" Dominic groaned loudly.

Sweat beaded on Henry's forehead and mine despite the cold temperature in the room. We danced, swinging our blades to viciously attack and block. Henry's eyes flashed, and before I completely comprehended his plan, instinct kicked in. He stomped his foot, feinted to the right, then lunged forward. Sensing the danger, my body reacted before my mind could think. As he charged, I sidestepped him and whipped my sword around. I sneaked the tip into the spires of his handle and pulled. It flew from his grip, and steel hit the ground. I pointed my saber at his throat.

"I believe I win," I said, slowly lowering my weapon.

He looked at me in defeat, his hands in the air. We stood close to one of the open jail cells; the other students leaned against the opposite wall, dead silent in shock. I didn't think they expected me to win.

"You may have won the battle, but not the war." Henry leaped forward, throwing his hands out, and pushed me into the cell.

I stumbled backward in surprise. My sword clattered to my feet as I watched him slam the door shut, encompassing me in darkness.

"There, we'll leave you alone," he cackled.

I rubbed my forehead, feeling stupid. I should have known they wouldn't play fair. My fault lay in the fact that I believed they possessed some integrity, given their station in life. That they were better than the men who attacked me in the woods. I'd never make that mistake again.

I heard their laughter as they shuffled out of the room, closing the entrance door behind them. I took a step forward and pushed on the metal door, but it didn't budge. My stomach twisted in knots. I hated that I couldn't see anything but a thin light that came through the slat at the top. I gripped my hair in frustration and kicked at the metal door. *Ouch!* I gasped and hopped on one foot, my toes throbbing. If only I wasn't so afraid of magic, I could use it to get out of this cell. Then I remembered Professor Slystream saying magic didn't react well to fear. Enveloped in this darkness, that's all I felt. I decided magic was out of the question.

I took several steps backward and froze, distinctly hearing metal drag against the stone floor. Terror glided up to my throat, but I swallowed it down. I thought Henry said there wasn't anything down here. Did he lie?

The sound grew louder—closer. I swiveled around and squinted in the darkness. Stiff with fright, I dug my fingers into my thighs. Metal chains moved of their own accord, sliding across the floor to me at a slow but steady pace, fueled by some unseen power. *Magic.*

I held my hands out in front of me, hoping to subdue them before they found their way to my wrists. A few paces in front of me, they stopped. I exhaled a breath of relief, thinking I had escaped their reach. If I pressed up against the door, maybe I could avoid them.

Suddenly the chains rose into the air. I didn't have time to pull my hands back and watched in horror as they acquired their target. *Me.* I stumbled and nearly toppled, my arms weighed down with the cold metal gripping my wrists. I pulled hard, failing to get out of the manacles. *Gods forbid. I'll never break free!*

Within a minute I felt a pinch on both of my wrists. Then everything went black.

Fire! I dreamed flames engulfed me. I screamed for help, but no one came. It burned—*Gods forbid it burns!* I sobbed. *Make it stop. Please—anyone—please!*

My eyes fluttered open sometime within the night or day. I didn't know when. The torch outside the door had gone out, leaving me without even a sliver of flickering light. I pawed at the cuffs. They burned into my skin. My dream about fire connected. My skin hot, I felt scratchy red welts covering my arms, running upward underneath my clothes.

I cried in pain and pulled on the chains, which only made the manacles cinch tighter. *What magic is this?* I cursed. I didn't know any spells that would undo this.

My throat parched, I wished for water. I ran my tongue around my dry, cracked lips.

"Curse you, Henry!" I yelled.

Another pinch on my wrists, and everything went black.

Images flashed in my mind in a venomous onslaught. I couldn't stop it. Thick nautical ropes wrapped around the base of my neck, chest, arms, and legs, strapping me to an upright pole. I stood on tied bundles of sticks and brush. My arms dug into my sides. I struggled against the binding ropes, but I couldn't move. Blood pounded in my ears. I screamed as flames raced through the underbrush and lit the wood beneath my feet. My eyes burned. I choked as I inhaled the smoke. I pleaded for help, but my voice fell on deaf ears.

In front of me, I saw houses and trees engulfed. Women and children screaming in agony sprinted away from their incinerating homes. Men with hankerchiefs covering their faces threw water on the flames that rose higher and higher, all the way up to the sky. Preoccupied with their houses, the villagers didn't notice me. Or maybe they had strapped me in?

I thought I heard someone yelling my name once, but I could not distinguish reality from imagination. The few times I woke, I felt my body getting hotter and hotter as if I literally blazed. The unimaginable pain scorched with an intensity so forceful that none of my pain management techniques worked. In the few moments of darkened clarity, I eventually figured out that the chains burned my skin and elicited the fiery hallucinations.

Trapped in a weak, fragile body, I couldn't speak. My throat seared. I lay on a cold stone floor that did nothing to relieve the burning.

Hours passed.

I lost count how many times the chains poked my wrists, immersing me in the burning village. Each time they became harsher. I recoiled against my burning pyre, shrieking when a man engulfed in flames charged at me, his fiery arms flailing as he wailed. *Make it stop. Please make it stop!* I sobbed in the darkness.

I sensed my mind rebelling against me, slowly turning me insane, broken. Caught at the hands of jealous students, I had little doubt this would be my death. *So be it.*

I desired Andrew. He loved me once, didn't he? Would he cry if I died? I entertained thoughts of those I loved crying for me. Nathan, Adel, Stefan, Joshua, and others, wishing they had saved me. It comforted me to feel wanted. To pretend like I mattered to someone. That maybe I could have made a difference in the world.

"She would have been so lovely," they would say among themselves. "She would have built Aberron into a paradise. Now she's gone before her true potential was ever revealed."

I pleaded for death.

I slept for a long time, lifeless. The poisonous chains made me drowsy, so I would dream of the burning village and my pyre. I barely had the strength to open my eyes, but I found it useless since the darkness blinded me. I wailed in the pitch black, my voice barely above a whisper. I begged for some way to fix this, to escape—to survive.

With a fleeting strength, I pulled at my hairpins, letting my hair sprawl onto the floor. Feeling around, I shoved a hairpin into the lock of on my left hand. I heard a sizzling sound, and my finger scorched. I quickly dropped the useless half-melted hairpin.

Haldren! my mind cried, praying he could hear me. I believed him to be the only one who could save me now. *Please help me!*

He did not come.

I lay on the stone floor for ages. My mind and body slowly decayed. My tears dried up; I couldn't cry anymore. Even awake, I hallucinated images of the fire incinerating everything in sight. Houses, trees, animals, and people blazed. Loud, soul-crushing, gut-wrenching wailing pierced my ears. It was so real; I woke up screaming with no sound in sweltering anguish.

I heard my name shouted hours, months, years later. It sounded familiar, like ... Andrew. I would have smiled if I had the energy. Death granted me my last wish: to hear his voice call out to me. My heart burst with gratitude.

Except Andrew's voice steadily became clearer, louder. *It can't be.* I released my eyes. *Light.* Light slithered through the crack at the base of the door and the top slat. The torch had lit again.

My strength failed, and I closed my eyes.

"This is where we left her," Henry said. "I called out and didn't hear anything. I figured she got out. She's so good at everything; I thought this would be easy for her. I didn't expect her to be trapped."

"Open this door," Andrew commanded, his tone full of authority and anger.

I heard metal scraping, and light filtered underneath my eyelids.

"Oh no." Henry's voice sounded tragic and muffled, as if he had put his hand over his mouth.

Someone rushed to my side. I felt large, lightly calloused hands on me.

"Isabelle!" Andrew cried.

My eyelids wavered slightly as I tried to open them. I wanted to look into his face, but with no energy, my body denied me the pleasure.

"She's still alive." Andrew's voice flooded with relief. "We need to get these chains off her!" He pulled on the chains, and I wordlessly screamed as they cinched tighter. Blood trickled, oozing onto the already-congealed mess lingering on my clothes and pooling on the floor.

Lord Leavesden crouched beside Andrew. He held one of my wrists and studied the cuffs intensely. "They are magic. See the points digging into her wrists? Only magical chains are made this way."

Who else is here?

"Someone get Malsin." Andrew's voice broke. "He's looking for her in another part of the school. Gods forbid, she's covered in burns."

"Henry, go." Lord Leavesden ordered. "I'm going to find someone to get the chains off."

Feet pounded against the floor.

I couldn't help but think these were my last moments. I wanted them to count. Using the last of my energy, I opened my eyes and stared into Andrew's face.

"You're here," I mouthed.

If I was going to die, I wanted to go gazing into the blazing blue eyes of my heart's desire. The eyes of the blue sky and ocean all rolled into one.

Unshed tears formed in his eyes. Andrew tried and failed to smile. He spoke in a gentle whisper. "Of course I'm here, my darling." He gently lifted me into his arms, cradling me in his lap. "You're going to be all right. We are going to get these chains off you." He rocked back and forth slowly and whispered more to himself than to me. "I have to believe that."

I cherished every second Andrew held me in his arms. Despite the fire burning my skin, I felt peace. I closed my eyes again and listened to his erratic heart beating.

Lord Leavesden came back with Professor Trisgeld. He inserted several different keys into the lock. Every single one he tried started to sizzle then melt. The hot metal dripped onto my skin. I screamed, but it came out as a whisper.

Professor Trisgeld held up his last key. An old tarnished one. "If this one doesn't work, then I don't know what to do." He shoved it into the lock and an audible clicking sound was heard. The chains released, the weight lifted as they clattered to the ground.

Free.

Andrew hoisted me in his arms. My chest rose and fell in barely audible gasps. My body went limp.

"I'm here! I'm here!" Malsin shouted. "Oh, you've found her. Thank the Gods."

"She's in really bad shape." Andrew's voice constricted with worry. He whispered in my ear. "Stay with me, Isabelle, my love. I need you."

"Bring her to my healing room. I'll get to work," Malsin said.

Footsteps echoed. Andrew lightly jostled me as he carried me out of the room and up the stairs. I heard someone trot over to him, keeping pace with his long strides.

"Andrew, I'm sorry. I never meant for this to happen," Henry apologized. "I didn't mean—"

Andrew cut him off. "What were you thinking?" Pure fury clouded his voice. "What did she do to you?"

It sounded as if Henry tried to speak but couldn't get the words out properly. Finally, he answered, his voice melancholy. "Nothing. We were jealous of her."

"I can't believe you, Henry!" Andrew raged. "She's barely alive in my arms. You may have killed her. You're lucky I haven't killed you myself."

Henry didn't speak, but he kept pace with Andrew as we headed to Malsin's healing room. It must have been mealtime because I heard plates clattering and many muffled voices.

I heard a shout from what sounded like a younger boy. *Ellis?* "Everyone come quick! Look!"

I didn't have to open my eyes to know what was happening. Many feet hit the floor. I suspected the whole school came to watch Andrew carry me past the dining hall. Numerous people talked over one another, but they hushed as Andrew raced by.

"What happened?" a student asked loudly, breaking the silence.

"It's none of your concern. Students go back to lunch," Lord Leavesden ordered.

We reached Malsin's rooms. Andrew set me down on a soft cot.

"All right. I want everyone out while I work on her," Malsin directed.

"Let me stay. I can help," Andrew said.

I heard the desperation in his voice. It gave me courage and comfort.

"All right, you can stay," Malsin agreed.

Malsin tipped liquid into my mouth; I coughed but swallowed it down. Within a minute, I felt weightless and free. I drifted off to a dreamless sleep.

Everything seemed hazy when I opened my eyes. The burning pain had vanished, but I felt groggy and disoriented. I coughed; my throat still dry. I stared at the white ceiling, marveling at the miracle of being alive. But how long would it last? I knew nothing about my condition.

Andrew's face loomed in my memory. He saved me. I needed to thank him. I turned my head to the side searching for him. He lay in a bed on the opposite side of the room, asleep with blankets up to his chin. His face appeared pale, haggard, and gaunt as though he were extremely ill. My heart clenched, and I found it hard to breathe. All thoughts of my well-being vanished, and Andrew became my sole focus. What had happened to him? I tried to get up. I needed to go to him, to see if he was all right.

Malsin caught me. "Whoa there, don't try to get up just yet."

"What's happened to Andrew?" I asked, my eyes centered on his sleeping form, anxiety and worry rocking through me.

Malsin sat in a chair next to me. "You were so close to dying when he brought you in here, he nearly depleted his store of magic to bring you back. Completely emptying your store of magic will kill you, you know. He'll be all right, but he needs to rest and recharge. I've been feeding him bits of healing magic here and there to keep him stable."

Oh, Andrew. My heart softened with gratitude as I stared at his still form. He'd nearly died to save me. I wanted to curl up beside him and shower him with love and affection while I lightly reprimanded him for putting himself in harm's way.

Malsin smiled, probably seeing the endearment I suspected shined bright in my eyes. "That boy cares deeply for you. He would not leave your side until he collapsed."

I tried to smile, but it felt funny, like my face didn't work properly. I briefly worried if I had a face left. How bad did I look?

I didn't feel as lucid as I thought I should be. I couldn't place everything that had transpired. My memories appeared unfocused as though I watched them through a foggy windowpane.

"What happened?" I asked Malsin.

"We found you in a cell, chained and burned." He shuddered. "We almost lost you." He muttered insults under his breath at the students who had done this.

I remembered: the duel against Henry. I won. They said they would leave me alone. Henry pushed me into the cell. It was dark; something pinched my wrists. I flinched. Then fire, always on fire. I shuddered as it all came flooding back, my desire for death still fresh in my mind.

"How bad is it?" I needed to know. I didn't have the heart or stomach to look at myself.

Malsin grimaced. "It's not great. We've healed you enough that you're not on the brink of death. I have a protection layer on you that's keeping you from feeling anything. Otherwise you'd be writhing in agony."

I asked for a mirror.

"It won't do you any good," he said as he reached for one. "You're in so many bandages you can barely see yourself. The only parts I didn't cover are your face and fingers."

I gazed at Malsin's handiwork. He'd shrouded me in bandages underneath the cream-colored nightgown I wore. My face was singed with red welts but surprisingly whole. My emerald eyes stared back, bloodshot and watery. My chest tightened. I can't look like this!

"I've got to send a note to Joshua. He came by while you were asleep. I promised to alert him when you awoke. I'll come back soon, and we can discuss some treatment options." Malsin started to rush out the door.

"Wait!" I called. "What day is it?"

Malsin paused. "It's Second Day morning. You were trapped for nearly three days." He hurried out.

I set the mirror on the chair Malsin had just vacated. Tears sprang into my eyes. I shouldn't have agreed to the duel. I closed my eyes, trying to order the tears to reverse. *Stupid.*

Lord Leavesden arrived five minutes after Malsin left. I assumed Malsin let him know of my awakened state as well. He sat in the chair next to my cot and asked for a full account of what happened down there. I didn't know what to say.

"It's all right, Isabelle. You can tell me what happened. You're not going to get into trouble. The Gods know you've been through enough already." He put his hand on the side of the cot, as if wanting to put a comforting hand on my shoulder but resisting due to the bandages peeking out of my nightgown.

"I'm sure you've noticed the obvious dislike for me around this school," I said bluntly.

Lord Leavesden frowned. "I am aware of it, yes."

"I got tired of getting tormented, so we struck up a deal. I would duel Henry, and the winner would get what they wanted." I cleared my throat, which was scratchy from disuse.

"What was the prize?" He put a hand on his chin, looking at me intently.

"If they won, I would give the wrong answers in class, act like a fool in front of the professors." My voice sounded caustic in my ears.

"And if you won?"

"They would leave me alone." I despised myself for falling into their trap. "I guess they did when Henry shoved me into that cell."

I saw anger behind Lord Leavesden's eyes as he listened to my account. He smiled weakly and left. I wanted to ask what he planned to do, but I faltered. He wasn't easy to talk to.

My eyes continually trailed over to Andrew deep in slumber. I yearned to sit beside him. With Malsin gone and not able to stop me, I struggled to sit up. Malsin had wrapped the bandages around me so tight that I found it hard to move with ease. I pushed against the side of the cot, using what fleeting strength I had and pressed my other hand against the wall. Once in an upright position, I dragged my legs over the side and let my bandaged feet touch the stone floor.

Now what? I doubted I had the strength to rise, and yet I couldn't stop myself from trying. I reached for the chair, using it as my anchor to stand. I scooted forward, took a deep breath, and lifted myself off the cot. The chair tipped. I gasped as I went sprawling to the ground with it. I lay on the ground, my face pressed against the cold stone, waiting for the pain to come at me in full force. But I couldn't feel anything. Malsin's protection field stopped it.

I launched into a slow crawl, pushing against the floor to propel me forward. I could barely raise my head high enough to see the base of

Andrew's cot. I didn't know how long it took me—ten, fifteen minutes? I had to stop and rest multiple times, but I managed to make it to Andrew. I rolled onto my back, my breath coming in short gasps, feeling pleased with my efforts.

Malsin found me not long after, lying on the floor with one arm underneath Andrew's blanket gripping his hand with a feather touch. He'd barely stirred when I touched him, and that worried me, despite being able to feel the life thrumming throughout him.

"Oh, Isabelle, you reckless, stubborn girl." An exasperated yet slightly amused smile graced Malsin's lips.

"Please," I begged. "Let me stay. He needs me."

"Andrew is going to be fine. I promise." He crouched beside me. "We should be worrying about you."

I believed Malsin; he'd never steered me wrong before. And yet I couldn't bring myself to worry about me—only Andrew. As long as he was all right, I knew I'd be, regardless of what happened.

"Now come on, back to your cot." Malsin gently lifted me in his arms, forcing me to let go of Andrew. For a moment, I resented Malsin for taking me away from my love, but I knew he had my best interests at heart, and the feeling quickly passed.

Malsin picked up the chair I'd knocked over and sat. He took my hand in his. "Try not to move. I need to use my magic to see if anything has changed."

I closed my eyes, feeling tired straight down to my bones, and fell asleep as his magic took hold.

When I awoke, Andrew was sitting up, quietly chatting with Malsin. Concern showed in every fiber of his face. I noticed a hollowness in his eyes I'd never seen before, as though he'd been given a deathblow. His hands curled around the blanket covering his lap.

I had to avert my gaze. I couldn't spend another second staring at Andrew without it breaking my heart. Instead, I focused on Malsin, knowing his words were what made Andrew appear racked with grief.

Malsin placed a hand on Andrew's knee. "The poison is slowly burning her from the inside out. It's attacking all of her major organs." He took a breath and exhaled slowly. "She's dying."

Andrew opened and closed his mouth as though he had a hard time speaking. Gods forbid, I had a hard time breathing. *I'm dying?* I didn't want to hear any more, but I couldn't stop myself from listening even if I wanted to. Some part of me needed to know my fate.

Andrew tried again, fighting to speak through the despairing emotions seeming to choke him. "Is there no way we can stop it?"

"I need more information," Malsin said. "I need to know everything there is to know about those chains. Perhaps then we can find a way to save her." He ran a hand through his frazzled hair. "Judging by the way the poison eludes my magic, I doubt even multiple healers will be able to heal her unless we know exactly what the creator intended." His fingers curled and uncurled with obvious frustration. "At this point, she's only going to get worse. I'm stuck doing damage control until we know more."

"What can I do to help?" Andrew asked.

"I've asked the Healers Guild to be on standby. They're having another one of their blasted conferences, so we shouldn't have a problem getting healers to come to our aid. I've got Professor Trisgeld searching through his vast war collection to see if he can find any mention of the chains." Malsin shook his head with a bewildered expression. "It astounds me that he had a key that worked. 'Pure chance,' he said. On one of his walks around the school he found it half-buried under a rosebush and decided to keep it."

"Thank the Gods that he did," Andrew said. He reached underneath his shirt and pulled out his locket bearing the King's crest. A blue light glowed around it as he spoke into it. After several minutes of assuring his father that he would be all right after some rest, Andrew listed off his demands. "I want every available person you have searching through the records for information about the military and the Sorrenian during King Falan's time. Send everything they find with Joshua." His eyes found mine, and his face softened, but I saw the worry hovering on the edge. "Time is of the essence." The blue light vanished, and he tucked the locket under his shirt.

Malsin stood and patted Andrew on the shoulder. "We'll heal her. I'm not ready to give up."

Nor am I, I thought. Suddenly a very pressing need presented itself to me. I wondered how far Malsin had gone with the bandages. I tried to filter out the embarrassment in my voice as he approached me. As I opened my mouth to speak, I started coughing. Malsin handed me a glass of water. I drank a few sips, then cleared my throat. "Would you mind helping me to the bathroom?"

Malsin took the glass from my hands. "Of course." He set it on the table and gently lifted me in his arms.

As I passed by Andrew, he reached out and brushed his fingers along mine. "Stay with me, Isabelle."

"Always," I said.

It turned out that Malsin had lied. He hadn't wrapped my entire private area, and all he had to do was raise my nightgown and set me on the toilet.

"Just call for me when you're done." Malsin swiftly exited the room.

Pressing issues taken care of, I called for him.

"Better?" he asked with a small smile.

I nodded. "Thank you."

My eyes sought Andrew as Malsin carried me out of the bathroom. Except someone was beside him, blocking my view of his face. I raised my eyes and discovered Henry. Pure unhindered terror gripped me. I shrieked, causing Malsin to jump and nearly drop me.

Unable to stop the screams ripping through my chest, I clawed at Malsin, fighting against his hold with a zeal to bolt and cower.

"Isabelle, calm down!" Malsin shouted struggling to hold me still. With a mad rush, he dropped me onto my cot.

I scrambled against the wall and covered my head with my arms while I wailed and shook. "Don't hurt me! Please!" The hallucinations started playing in my mind. A sea of fire rose to engulf me.

"Isabelle." Andrew's voice cut through the nightmare.

My eyes snapped to his. He lay on the ground as if he'd fallen out of his cot. I moaned as the fiery visions threatened to pull me under. They hovered on the edge of my sight, and I knew if I closed my eyes I'd see it all. Incineration with me at the core.

"Isabelle. Focus on my voice. Focus on me. Do not let your fear win." As Andrew spoke, he pushed himself off the floor and slowly crawled to me, revealing how weak he actually was. He cursed, seeming frustrated with his lack of strength. "Help me to her."

Malsin and Henry grabbed Andrew by his arms and hoisted him to a standing position. With their support on either side, Andrew walked to me. They gently eased him onto my cot. He pulled me into him. I buried my face into his chest and sobbed.

"Henry, we will continue this later." Andrew's tone was clearly dismissive.

"All right." Footsteps echoed as Henry left.

"Shh ... it's all right. I'm here, my darling. I've got you." Andrew kissed the top of my head.

"I can't—I—don't let him near me. Please," I begged, panic flooding my body.

"Henry?" Andrew asked.

I flinched as a memory swam before my eyes: Henry pushing me into the cell. "Don't let him hurt me again." A coughing attack hit. I covered my mouth with my hand, and when I brought it away, I saw blood.

Andrew gripped my hand, concern evident on his face. "Malsin!"

"I'm right here. There's no need to shout." Indeed, Malsin sat right next to us in his rickety chair.

Taking my hand in his, Malsin closed his eyes. A green light glowed around him as he used his healing magic. Several minutes of silence passed. A sheen of sweat appeared on his face. He grimaced as if in pain, and I found myself wanting to pull away, believing me to be the cause of his discomfort.

Another minute passed. A groan escaped through Malsin's clenched teeth. *No.* I freed myself from his grasp, unable to watch him suffer any longer at my expense. Malsin opened his eyes and stared with confusion and anger. I curled into Andrew, afraid for us all. What had I done to him?

"Malsin?" Andrew asked tentatively. "Are you all right?"

Malsin blinked and shook his head, snapping out of whatever dark emotion held him. "Yes, I'm fine." He leaned back in his chair and rubbed his face.

I didn't believe him. My eyes darted between Andrew and Malsin. "No one is touching me with magic."

They both opened their mouths to argue, but I held up a hand.

"No. I've hurt you both. I won't do it again." I glared at them, hoping to make myself clear. I took a deep breath and exhaled slowly. "Malsin, how much time do I have before the poison kills me?"

Andrew's breathing caught, but I paid him no mind. Malsin didn't seem the least bit surprised that I had overheard his conversation with Andrew.

"Two days." Malsin sighed in defeat.

I stiffened with a quick intake of breath. My heart crushed at the news. I had too much to live for, I didn't want to die! I wanted to wallow in despair. *It won't help*, my mind argued. *Being proactive will.* I clenched my jaw, refusing to let that number deter me. "Then let's make the best of it, shall we?" I turned my head to Malsin. "Go rest. Andrew and I will be fine for a few hours. When Joshua arrives with the papers and whatnot we can search together for a cure." I raised a finger. "Only then—if we find a solution—will I allow magic to be used on me." I knew I'd only get worse from here on out, and I wanted to spend this moment of mental and physical clarity voicing my desires while I still could.

I half expected Malsin to argue, but he didn't. "As you wish." He stood, running a hand through his ruffled hair, stress apparent on his face. "I'll instruct the kitchen to bring some food up. I'll be back in a few hours."

"Thank you, Malsin," I said.

He half smiled. "You're welcome." He strode out of the room, leaving Andrew and me alone.

I buried my face into Andrew's chest. "Andrew, I'm so sorry. I never should have—" He cut me off. "I know. Don't blame yourself for this. It's taken all the self-control I have not to lash out at Henry." Andrew's fingers curled into a fist. "If he weren't my cousin and second in line to the throne, I'd have him thrown in a cell of his own."

I flinched at the word *cell*. The fiery hallucinations took hold of my mind then. I closed my eyes, whimpering as the flames raced to me. A child no older than two, choking from the smoke, stumbled and fell in the grass. The fire reversed its course and headed for the boy. I screamed.

Andrew shook me gently as he called out my name. I could feel his arms around me, hear his voice in my ear, but I couldn't snap out of the vision. I stood transfixed with utter fear and anguish for the boy as he struggled to outrun death.

"No," I cried. "No. Please. Stop, please."

I had no power over my mind, as if some foreign entity had assumed control and forced me to watch. As if the chains still held me captive. I became trapped within two worlds: the hallucination and the healing room.

"Oh, thank the Gods, Joshua." Andrew struggled to hold me as I shook in his arms.

Strong new arms held me. "Isabelle!" My brother shouted my name, fighting to be heard above my pleading screams and convulsions. "What's wrong with her?"

"I don't know." Andrew's fist pounded against the wall. "Gods forbid, I'm going to kill Henry."

Abruptly as it came, the hallucination melted away. My chest was heaving, my breath came in gasps. I stared into my brother's emerald-green eyes, seeing them properly for the first time. "Joshua."

"I'm here, Isabelle." Joshua held me to him. "I'm here."

"Good." I sighed and closed my eyes. I didn't have the strength to keep them open any longer. I doubted I could lift my head at this point. I felt Joshua place me back in the cot as exhaustion drifted me off to sleep.

I woke up to muted voices, shuffling papers. Andrew held on to one of my hands and rubbed it softly with his thumb. I felt a difference in my body. Weaker, my heart beat erratically out of my chest. Malsin's protection field started to show cracks, and I felt the pain jabbing at different points in my body.

I moved a little to get comfortable, alerting Andrew to my awakened state. He smiled. "Isabelle. You're awake."

"How long did I sleep?" I asked.

"Four hours," Andrew said.

I took a deep breath and exhaled, trying to settle my emotions. Four hours less to be with Andrew. "Any news?"

He shook his head. "Nothing yet. There is much to sort through."

"Can someone help me sit up?" I asked.

Joshua pulled me into an upright position. I leaned my back against the wall, breathing heavily from the exertion.

Malsin handed me a blue vial. "Drink this."

I brought it to my lips and drank, then clamped a hand over my mouth to keep it down. After a few minutes, I felt marginally better. I pulled at the papers in Andrew's lap. "Let me help."

Andrew placed a hand on mine. "Isabelle, there's something else we should do first."

I furrowed my eyebrows in confusion. "What?"

Andrew stared at me with patience and love in his eyes. "We need you to tell us everything you can about the chains. What they did to you."

I pulled away from him, trembling. "No." My voice wavered as I shook my head. I clutched at my stomach and attempted to bring my legs up to my chest, but I hadn't the strength. "I can't—" I gasped as a sharp pain rocked through me and cut off my voice.

Malsin rushed to my side. "The protection field is slipping. She's starting to feel the effects of the poison."

"Fix it," Andrew demanded.

"I think I've found something." Joshua held up a diary. All eyes snapped to my brother as he read it off. "I have enlisted the help of Macaius to make me a devious set of chains. I have asked that they be unbreakable and filled with an insidious poison. It is no less than they deserve." Joshua turned the page. "Macaius tells me they will be ready soon. I am anxious to see, but he will not permit me one look. For now, I continue the search for the traitors, knowing justice will soon be at hand." Joshua flipped through several more pages, a scowl appearing on his face. "There is nothing more." He closed the book.

"That's a start." I tried to sound cheery, but it sounded fake to my ears. "We have a name."

Professor Trisgeld walked in. "I thought I would check in; see how it's going on your end."

Malsin spoke. "Have you ever heard the name Macaius in connection with King Falan?"

Professor Trisgeld rubbed his chin. "Macaius Roaken?"

"We don't have a last name, but we believe he is the creator of the chains," Malsin said.

Trisgeld cursed. "If he is indeed the creator, then we should fear the worst." He pulled up a chair and sat. "The man had no soul. He lived for destruction, and only King Falan could control him. He built many weapons in his time. After the King's death in the merchant uprising, they found him testing one of his contraptions on an innocent maid, and he was put to death. It is said he twisted the mind of the King to allow him such liberties."

The air felt heavy and strained as everyone let that sink in. It didn't surprise me. I couldn't imagine anyone less sinister would have been able to make the chains.

Andrew spoke first, breaking the silence choking us all. "Something is plaguing Isabelle's mind. It's as if she's here with us one moment and the next she's trapped in some kind of nightmare. I have yet to make sense of what it is."

I shuddered but didn't correct him.

"Isabelle?" Malsin turned to me. "Can you tell us what this is about?"

I held my hands out in front of me as I cowered. "No." My voice faltered. "Please."

Professor Trisgeld stood, watching me with interest as Andrew and Malsin placed comforting hands on me, attempting to calm the rampant terror I assumed showed on my face.

Trisgeld stood behind one of Malsin's long tables filled with medical supplies. "I bet I can tell you what it is." He shook his head and raised his eyes to the ceiling. "Macaius Roaken. I should have known."

"Known what?" Joshua asked, his tone wary.

Trisgeld struck a match. "They called him Cinders behind his back."

I screamed.

CHAPTER TWENTY-TWO

ODS FORBID, DID YOU have to do that?" Andrew scolded Trisgeld as I convulsed in his arms, trapped once again in a mind of fire.

Trisgeld spoke without remorse. "You wanted to know and she wasn't telling. This confirms that Macaius was the creator."

"What do you think she's seeing?" Joshua asked.

"Look at her," Andrew said through gritted teeth. "Do you really want to know?"

"No. I guess not," Joshua finally said.

I heard them plainly. A minute section of my mind paid attention to their voices, hoping to plant myself in their world. I couldn't, though; the flames had me, ravaging their way through the sticks, greedily licking their way to my feet.

"From now on, you've got to avoid certain trigger words and sights. Fire is one, obviously," Professor Trisgeld said. "Think back on the other times she has done this. See if you can pinpoint what set her off."

"Henry," Malsin said. "She was fine until she saw him, then nearly clawed me to death."

"Yes, Henry is one," Andrew agreed. "We cannot allow her to see him."

"Let's all just tread very carefully here," Malsin said. "Keep to light topics around Isabelle while we search for a solution."

And with that, the nightmare vanished, and I found myself gasping in Andrew's arms, staring into his piercing blue, worried eyes.

For the next few hours, Joshua, Trisgeld, and Andrew buried themselves in paperwork. The name Macaius appeared several more times in the documents, but no mention of the chains went with it. I watched the range of emotions on their faces when they caught his name: excited at first, only for it to turn into disgust or frustration.

"They should have done away with that man a lot sooner than they did." Joshua scowled as he set a book down.

I tried to offer my assistance. My eyes weren't broken, and I still had the mental capacity to read.

At once, everyone in the room said "No" in a most forceful and firm voice, causing me to flinch and cower.

Andrew placed a hand on my bandaged one. "All we need you to do is rest and hold onto your zest for life."

Malsin sat with me while the others read through papers. He unraveled the bandages on my forearm and applied healing creams to the ravaged skin. When one didn't work, he tried another.

"I don't understand," Malsin said, after the tenth attempt. He put the lid back on the green cream with a snap. "That last one should have done it. It's specifically for burns." He gripped his forehead, clearly agitated. "What the Gods did he put in that blasted poison?"

"What if you got a sample from the chains and studied it?" I asked.

He shook his head. "I tried. There's none left. All of it is in you."

"So no one else will get hurt?" I wouldn't want anyone, friend or foe, to suffer as I did. If I didn't have Andrew by my side, I doubted I would be sane enough to keep fighting to stay alive.

Malsin smiled. "With the poison gone, we were able to remove them. No one will ever be hurt by them again."

"Thank the Gods," I breathed.

When dinner came, Andrew took it upon himself to feed me. He held a spoon to my lips. "Just try a few bites, won't you?"

I eyed him dubiously but opened my mouth. He managed to get three spoonfuls of food into my mouth before I started coughing. Malsin quickly threw a bowl under my face as I vomited vegetable soup and blood. Eating became out of the question.

With the mirror still beside my cot, I used it and noticed that, within a matter of hours, I had gone from singed and pasty to gaunt and unrecognizable, wasting away to nothing. I refused to let Malsin strengthen the protection field that kept me from feeling pain.

"No magic," I gasped, clutching my stomach as a wave of pain hit. "I won't—hurt you." I'd never forget Malsin's face, full of some dark emotion the last time he put his hands on me with his magic opened. I wouldn't make him suffer for me.

"Isabelle." Malsin sighed. "I can't in good conscience let you languish when I know I can fix it. All healers feel a ghost of their patient's pain when they heal. It helps them know where the problems are. My pain will only be for a moment, but you will suffer for much longer than I." He put a hand on mine. "If we're not able to heal you—if nothing we do works—at least I'll know you couldn't feel it. Couldn't you give me that small measure of peace?"

I surrendered. "All right."

I watched him closely as he strengthened the field. His jaw clenched, sweat beaded on his brow. I suspected he fought against something I couldn't even begin to imagine. I wondered what was worse for him—feeling the injuries or knowing he couldn't save me on his own.

When Malsin finished, I took a deep breath and exhaled slowly as my muscles visibly relaxed. "Thank you."

"It's the least I can do," Malsin said as he also loosened his stiff posture.

When Lord Leavesden walked in, Malsin hurried to apprise him of what we had learned so far. He finished with, "Now that it's your turn to speak, if you've got something important to say, perhaps it would be best if it was said outside."

All eyes darted to me with varying degrees of anxious worry, but it couldn't be helped. I couldn't control the hallucinations or myself when they took over.

"I must speak with Andrew," Lord Leavesden said.

"Joshua, help me up." Andrew turned to me, a soft smile on his lips. "I'll be right back, darling." With Joshua supporting him, Andrew ambled outside to speak.

I knew he wouldn't be long, but I couldn't help the ache that formed in my chest when he left my sight. I relied on him—my anchor—to keep me calm, to remind me that I had a life worth fighting for. I'd drown without him.

Andrew's voice carried into the healing room. "Absolutely not. I don't care if he wants to apologize. I will not permit him to see her."

A minute later, Andrew and Joshua came back in the room. "Let me sit by Isabelle, please." Joshua led Andrew to me and gently eased him onto my cot. "Thank you, Joshua."

"No problem," Joshua said with a tired sigh.

Andrew pushed a few strands of hair away from my eyes. "Told you I'd be right back." He smiled, and I saw love reflecting in his eyes, causing my breath to catch in my throat.

"So you did," I whispered.

As the sky darkened, Joshua, Trisgeld, and Malsin moved to an adjacent room to continue their search. They needed the light I couldn't bear to see.

Andrew refused to leave my side. "Forget propriety. I am not moving." No one had to worry about our intentions, given our current afflictions.

"That's fine," Joshua said. "But at least give her some room to stretch. You're taking up most of Isabelle's cot."

"I don't mind," I quickly said. In truth, I hadn't noticed how little room I had.

"Then bring the other cot over here." Andrew pointed to his on the other side of the room.

Joshua and Malsin carried Andrew's cot and pushed it against mine. It was decided that Andrew should take the one closest the wall and I the other, so Malsin could get to me quicker if need be.

As we settled in, Lord Leavesden and many professors arrived to help. We heard murmurs and shuffling paper from the adjacent room as they searched for something that may not exist: a set of directions for the chains Macaius had created a little over one hundred years ago.

I turned my back against the light from the open door. Alzmire's voice floated from the other room as he asked Joshua about the book he held in his hand. It reminded me of the conversation I overhead between Lord Leavesden and Alzmire. I found myself, in my weakened state, asking Andrew some very pointed questions.

"Andrew?"

"Yes?" His blue eyes held mine. He'd casually been rubbing his thumb over my bandaged hand, seeming lost in thought.

"I overheard Alzmire and Lord Leavesden talking the other night. They said your mother wanted to match you with a—Lady Marissa." I paused to gather strength before continuing. "They said she is familiar with most nobles and might—might be the better choice."

Andrew shook his head. "She most definitely is not. My mother did try to speak to me about Lady Marissa, but that was before I had the chance to tell her about you. I told my mother to put away any foolish notions of finding a girl for me because I already found the one I want."

"And who is that?" I asked softly.

"You. It will always be you." He kissed the top of my head. "So you better make it out of this alive because I will never want anyone else."

"I want you too. Every minute away from you has been a struggle—" Tears started to fall. Andrew held me close as I wept over the cruel injustices life had served.

Andrew spoke to me in soothing tones. "We'll get through this. The Gods cannot be so cruel as to let us find love and lose it so quickly."

I wanted to believe him, but I had doubts. Haldren, the one God I had come in contact with, had yet to make his presence known throughout this ordeal. Perhaps he'd decided I wasn't as important as he had previously believed? I pushed such thoughts away, knowing I could never understand a God's intentions.

Instead, I listened to Andrew's steady heartbeat, breathed in the scent of the cinnamon woodsy cologne that lingered faintly on his clothes, and reminded myself that no matter the outcome, I was wanted and loved.

I awoke sometime in the early hours of the morning to Andrew's voice. "I thought I made myself clear. You're not welcome here." He sounded angry as he clutched me to his chest, as if he wanted to protect me from something I couldn't see.

There was only one person I knew that Andrew would react that way to right now. My suspicions were confirmed when he spoke.

"Punish me all you want. I'll take it, but don't stop me from apologizing to her. She needs to hear it while she still lives," Henry said with conviction.

"Then say it and get out," Andrew spat. His eyes met mine. "Isabelle, love, Henry wants to apologize. Do you think you can listen to him?"

Fear and anger clutched at my heart. "I don't want to."

"Isabelle, please," Henry pleaded. Desperation and anxiety clouded his voice. "Please let me look at you and apologize."

I stiffened. *Face Henry?* "You don't know what you're asking," I said.

I heard him sit on the floor by the cot. He sounded defeated. "I probably don't, but I'll never be able to live with myself if I don't try. I've been sitting outside of the healing room. I know you're going to die if they can't find what they're searching for."

His bluntness took me off guard. Some part of me—the morbid curiosity part—wanted to see if Henry was sincere. Using what fleeting strength I had, I rolled over and faced him. I recoiled at first as pure terror gripped me, but Andrew pulled me into him and held my trembling hands in his.

"It's all right. I'm here, love. You're safe." Andrew tried his best to calm me, but it took several deep breaths and a constant mental reminder that Andrew would keep me safe before I could look at Henry for longer than a second.

Henry's features contorted in pain. "I—am—sorry." He rubbed his face. "Gods forbid I am so sorry. I thought all the war relics were removed years ago. I didn't think there was anything in there that could hurt you. I thought you would be able to get out." He closed his eyes as if he attempted to rein in his emotions. When they met mine, I saw glistening guilt. "Nothing I say will ever be able to make up for what I did, and I will spend the rest of my life wishing I could take my actions back. I just—" He ran a hand through his hair. "I don't know if I'm asking for your forgiveness—I—I needed you to know that I'm sorry and I mean that from the very depths of my soul."

I didn't think he merited a response, even after pouring his apology out. And yet, I found myself speaking to him anyway. "I won't tell you I accept your apology, because I don't." I paused, gathering strength. The poison heartily working its way through my body made me insubstantial and weak. Henry trembled, appearing racked with remorse. "But ... thank you for apologizing." It was more than he deserved. I coughed. Blood slid up my throat, pooled in my mouth, and trickled down my chin.

Henry flinched and scooted backward. He brought his knees to his chest and buried his head. Without a word, Andrew softly dabbed at my mouth with a napkin. I thanked him with my eyes, and his returning smile was so full of tenderness I could have died right then and there and felt complete.

Malsin shouted from the other room. "Yes!"

I stared into Andrew's face, knowing I mirrored the same confusion and sliver of hope.

Joshua strode out of the adjacent room and for the first time since coming, he wore a smile on his face, despite appearing haggard. "I have good news. We found Macaius's diary that tells us everything we need to know about the chains and the poison. We know how to cure you. I'm going now to get healers from the Guild. It will take more than one to do it." He crouched beside the cot and grabbed my hand. "Hang in there, little sister. We'll heal you yet." Joshua stood. "I'll be back within the hour." He rushed out the door.

"Thank the Gods," Andrew breathed.

I closed my eyes as relief flooded my heart. I took a deep breath and exhaled. I could feel my energy gradually slipping away. It became a conscious effort to stay awake and not let the darkness hovering on the edge consume me.

One hour and I would be healed. I prayed I could make it.

"We need to get things ready." Malsin strode out of the adjacent room, a huge grin on his face. He paused when he noticed Henry, his grin faltering. "Henry, what are you doing here?"

"I needed to apologize," he said, lifting his head to meet Malsin's gaze.

"You've done that. Now leave," Andrew commanded.

"Please, can't I stay and help?" Henry pleaded.

"I think you've done enough already." Malsin glared.

Henry cringed. "Please don't send me back to my room. I can't—I have to know if she'll be all right."

Malsin faced Andrew. "What if he stayed outside? He can be a lookout for Joshua and the healers."

Andrew nodded. "Agreed."

Malsin pointed a finger at Henry. "Under no circumstances do I want you in here, unless you have been specifically asked for. Do you understand?"

Henry nodded. "Yes."

"Then go." Malsin pointed to the door.

Henry rose slowly and walked out. I found my fear abated with him out of my sight.

"Where are the professors?" When I went to sleep, I remembered there being many. Now I saw only Malsin.

"They've gone to rest," Malsin said. "They went out the other door so they wouldn't disturb you."

"Oh," I said. "I must thank them when this is over."

"May I see the diary?" Andrew asked.

Malsin retrieved a book from the other room. He eyed Andrew. "If you want to read the whole entry, you may, but I suggest we do not let Isabelle read it. He explains many gruesome acts in detail." He shuddered. "I believe the passage most vital to us is acceptable for Isabelle to hear."

"Go on then," Andrew said.

With the sun on the rise, Malsin had no need for a lamp. He cleared his throat and read. "I fear the King grows weary of me. As I make these chains

I wonder if they are meant for me. He has asked that they be filled with an insidious poison that would break the mind and the body. The images it shall create will be harmless to me for I share a love of all that burns. Once I escape, I need only find my three healers: Tiberius, Mathew, and Mary. Together they can use their magic to undo the damage the poison will inflict on my insides." Malsin handed Andrew the book.

"Three healers will cure me?" I asked.

Malsin nodded, a smile returning to his lips. "Yes."

"He's written a saying all over the margins. Almost like he wanted to commit it to memory," Andrew said, peering at the diary. "Rescind the flame for the innocent."

Without warning the world went dark before my eyes. I gasped as the fiery hallucinations filled my mind. Fire encircled me. I could feel the heat burning through my nightgown. I screamed in pain as the fire touched my skin.

"It burns!" I sobbed as I convulsed.

Andrew and Malsin shouted at me, but I couldn't make out their words or respond to them. My screams rose higher in pitch as every image the chains had ever created flashed before my eyes. My pyre, the sea of flames, families, animals, houses, trees, villages—all incinerated. I choked on the smoke and ash; it filled my lungs until I couldn't breathe.

"She's choking!" Andrew's voice assaulted my ears.

"Quick, turn her on her side," Malsin instructed.

I felt strong hands on me. Liquid expelled from my lungs. Trapped in the illusion, I couldn't tell what it was. I only knew I could breathe again.

As the last image filled my mind—the stumbling boy attempting to flee from the inevitable—it changed. The advancing fire withdrew.

I gasped in wonder as the scenes accosted me once more, except the flames that extinguished life retracted. I gasped as the buildings and trees I watched topple over rose from the dust, appearing whole and untouched. The fire that once devoured an entire village disappeared without a trace. I found myself back at the beginning, strapped to a burning pyre. The blaze under my feet rescinded until I could see it no more.

My vision cleared, and I stared into Andrew's anxious eyes. "Isabelle?" He sounded panicked.

I tried to smile, to reassure him I was all right, but exhaustion dominated me. I turned my head slightly to see Malsin scrutinizing me. I saw blood on his clothes. *My blood?* I frowned.

My body now still, my breathing had become soft and shallow, and I found myself wishing for a reprieve. It would be so much easier to give in and stop fighting. With Malsin's protection field it wouldn't even hurt. I only needed to close my eyes and surrender.

Malsin's eyes widened. "Isabelle, I know what you're thinking. I can see it." He shook his head, his expression firm. "Don't do it. Don't give in."

Andrew's eyes darted to Malsin and back to me. "What?"

"She's thinking about ending the fight," Malsin said through gritted teeth.

"But we're so close. Joshua should be here any minute now with the other healers." Andrew's expression showed confusion and hurt.

Malsin's gaze never left my face. "I know that look. It's the one every person gets on their face when they feel too tired to go on. When surrendering would be easier than fighting through the blackness that seems so inviting." His eyes narrowed. "Don't do it, Isabelle. Not now. Not when we're so close."

But death already held me in its clutches, and try as I might, my time slipped away like grains of sand in an hourglass.

Henry shouted. "They're here!"

Joshua and the healers strode into the room. I used the last reserves of my energy and spoke to Malsin, Joshua, and Andrew, the three men I had grown to love in different ways. My friend, my brother, and my heart's desire.

"I love you." I closed my eyes and took in one last breath, then exhaled slowly.

Death had come to greet me.

CHAPTER TWENTY-THREE

WALKED BAREFOOT ON AN old cobblestone path. My feet pattered against the cold, wet rock. I shivered. Dark stone walls closed in around me, and I could see no sky above. The lighting dim, I was alone, but not afraid. In the distance I saw sunlight. I headed to it, wanting to bask in its warm rays.

I chose my steps carefully, my hand trailing along the cold walls dripping with icy moisture. I felt a long, nimble hand latch firmly onto my arm and jerk me away. Before my eyes, the light at the end of the tunnel dissolved, and suddenly I stumbled into the wheat field with Haldren. He stood before me with cold, penetrating eyes, his hands now clasped together.

"Haldren?" I put a hand to my forehead, feeling disoriented. "What happened?"

"You were heading in the wrong direction. I pulled you away from it. Once you reach the light, you cannot come back. Not even I can reverse it," he explained.

"What was at the end of the tunnel?" I asked, curious.

"Death." Haldren shrugged.

"What's happening with my body now?" I paced back and forth. Did everyone think I had died? Were they still trying to save me?

"A number of healers are working over your unconscious body and drawing the poison out." He cupped his hands together and moved them in a fashion that made me think he molded an invisible snowball. When he held his palm out, a large bead of water covered it. "Take it. Look into the water. You will see."

Haldren dropped the sphere of water, similar to a glistening dew drop, into my hands. I expected it to burst and found myself surprised when it did not. Cautiously, I brought it up to my face and stared.

A picture formed. I looked at the scene from above as if stationed on a high shelf. At least ten healers, both men and women, touched some part of my body. Their eyes were closed, but their mouths moved and their hands glowed green as they worked. No sound came out of the water. I found Malsin by my heart, his face determined. I fixated on my body and shuddered. I slept, my body rigid as a statue. I had a gaunt, pasty, and singed face. My lips, usually bright, appeared pale. I reared back in disgust. I couldn't stomach any more.

I concentrated on another part of the room and saw Joshua pacing off to the side. He watched but didn't get in the way. His hands balled into fists as he paced, his wavy, dark brown hair falling into his face. Sweat beaded on his brow and slid into his beard. Tension rolled off him in waves.

I searched for Andrew and found him sitting in his cot, leaning against the wall. He'd brought his knees up to his chest and buried his face in his hands. He appeared so vulnerable and defeated. Not the Prince I had known him to be.

The ball slipped from my hands and burst at my feet, spraying me with water. "Is it working?" I clutched my rolling, nauseated stomach. "Are they going to be able to heal me?"

Haldren smiled. "Yes."

I let out a huge sigh of relief. "Thank the Gods."

Unexpectedly, Haldren chuckled. I tilted my head to the side and eyed him inquisitively.

Still grinning, and for once his grin did not seem cold or unfeeling, he said, "You're welcome."

My cheeks flushed, and I smiled sheepishly. I had forgotten I stood in the presence of an actual God.

"I owe you now, don't I?" I asked, letting my hands fall to my side. "You saved my life and helped me on more than one occasion."

"Owe me? What an interesting thing to say." Haldren's long, nimble fingers tapped the side of his cheek. His eyes flashed.

"Well?" I crossed my arms. "I don't like owing a debt."

Haldren's cold blue eyes gleamed against his pale face. "There's nothing you can give me right now that I would want … Later perhaps."

"So are we good for now?" I wanted to go home with a clear conscious. I'd worry about what he'd ask for when the time came.

Haldren nodded, clasping his hands together again. "For now, we are … good. As you put it."

"Thank you for pulling me away." I shivered, remembering the damp, icy darkness. The fear finally caught up with me.

"You're welcome," he said. "You're out of danger now. The healers have managed to draw the poison out. Your burns are disappearing. You can go back now."

"I'm ready," I said with conviction, balling my fists.

Haldren waved his hand, and the wheat field dissolved.

My eyes fluttered open to the morning light. I groaned and gripped my forehead. I felt like I had been trampled by twenty horses. My head pounded like a hammer swung at it incessantly. Despite the pain, it made me feel alive, and my heart burst with gratitude.

"Isabelle?" Malsin's gentle voice wafted over.

I let go of my forehead and stared into Malsin's face as he leaned over me.

He smiled. "You're awake. How are you feeling?"

I cleared my dry, scratchy, throat. "Like I've been trampled." I rubbed my eyes.

He frowned. "Here, I can help with that." He put his hand on my head, and the throbbing decreased.

I sighed in relief. As I struggled to sit up, I noticed I wore a light blue nightgown embroidered with pink roses and buttons down the front. It fit me perfectly. Malsin usually carried plain white nightgowns two sizes larger than I needed. I could only assume Andrew had procured this. I doubted Joshua gave much thought to what women wore.

Malsin grabbed some pillows and put them behind my back.

"Thank you. How long have I been out?" I asked.

"A day. Today is Fourth Day," Malsin said as he sat in the chair beside my cot. "With the help of many healers, we were able to draw the poison out and repair the damage."

"So I'm whole?" My mouth dropped open slightly.

Malsin grabbed a mirror from a bedside table and handed it to me. "Take a look for yourself."

I stared into the mirror. My color had come back. I had full, rosy lips and clear cream-colored skin. My eyes seemed a little tired and sunken in, and my cheekbones jutted out more prominently than normal. I wore no bandages underneath the nightgown. I patted myself down and felt no pain ... anywhere. I handed the mirror back to Malsin. He set it on the end table.

"Your body suffered tremendously. It took the combined abilities of ten healers to heal you. You will still need several more days of recuperation." Malsin rested his hands on the bed. He grinned suddenly. "It's good to see you alive." He patted my hand.

His infectious grin took hold, and I smiled. "It's good to be alive." I scanned the healing room in search of Andrew, but I didn't see him. "Andrew?" I asked.

"He's here." Malsin pointed to the closed door of the adjacent room everyone had continued their search in. "He's been conducting business with his father using his locket. Andrew made it very clear that he would not go home until he was assured of your well-being."

"And Joshua?"

"With Andrew of course." He shrugged.

The closed door I had my eyes trained on opened. Joshua strode into view, followed by Andrew, who used a cane to help him walk. My heart softened at his predicament. Both had changed into a new set of clothes, though I noticed Andrew hadn't shaved. The stubble on his face reminded me of our days in the forest.

Malsin stood. "I'll let you visit and check on you in a little while."

I smiled at him. "Thank you."

I met Andrew's gaze, and my heart stopped and restarted as I watched his grin form. *Gods forbid he's gorgeous, inside and out.* I wondered if he felt the same pull I did—the insatiable need to be close, touch, connect—for he moved faster than I thought him capable of to reach my side.

I moved over, creating space for Andrew to lie with me on the cot. Joshua took the chair Malsin had vacated.

"You gave us a scare, little sister," Joshua said, his normally gruff voice softer. "I thought you died."

"I thought my heart had ripped out of my chest." Andrew shuddered and added with all seriousness, "Please, don't ever make me feel that way again."

"I shall try my very hardest not to." I spoke with conviction.

Andrew wrapped his arms around me and pulled me into his chest. "Thank the Gods you're going to be all right."

Andrew's words brought back a remembrance of Haldren. Without him, I wouldn't be alive. "Giving thanks to Haldren would be appropriate. He found me walking down an icy tunnel toward a bright sunlight—death—and pulled me away."

I felt Andrew stiffen, and an expression of horror flashed across my brother's face.

"Well, all that matters is that you're alive and safe." Joshua seemed to force a smile.

Andrew nodded. "Indeed, we owe him a debt of gratitude."

I narrowed my eyes, sensing that any questions I'd ask about Haldren would be squashed before it could fly out of my mouth. "Next time I see Haldren, I am going to ask him why he causes such a strong reaction out of you two."

"Next time?" Andrew's tone had a hint of hesitancy. "How often does he visit with you?"

"Often enough," I said evasively.

Joshua and Andrew shared a look, communicating silently, but I couldn't make out the meaning behind it.

Joshua rested his hand on the bed. "What do you talk about?"

I shook my head, a soft chuckle escaping my lips. "Don't expect me to be so forthcoming when I doubt you'll be. I've said enough already."

Joshua scowled but didn't disagree. "Just be careful. Gods are fickle."

"Of course," I agreed. "Were you able to find any news with the second note?"

Joshua shook his head. "No. The paper has been spelled against getting a read off it. I'm no closer to finding out the source than I was with the first one."

I frowned, wishing Joshua had something better to tell me. "What does that mean for us?" I asked.

Joshua sighed. "It means I have to keep you safe for a while longer and hope that something new turns up."

"You still want me to stay here, even after what the others did?" I asked, appalled.

Joshua shrugged, his lips thinned. "I'm thinking about it."

My eyes widened. "No." I threw the blanket off and started to crawl over Andrew, but he caught me and held me in his lap, facing him.

I would have blushed at the position it put us in if I hadn't felt so angry.

Andrew's eyes danced. No doubt he would be delighted to hold me there forever. "Where are you going?"

"I'm going to my room to pack," I said tersely. "I'll find my own way to keep myself safe."

Joshua held a hand out. "Wait Isabelle. Hear me out."

"No." I struggled to extract myself from Andrew, but he only pulled me closer and tightened his grip. I didn't have the energy or strength to outmatch him, despite him not being in perfect health.

I took a deep breath and exhaled slowly, attempting to rein in my rolling emotions. "Let me go—please."

Andrew grinned. "No. I rather like where you're at."

Heat rose to my cheeks, causing him to chuckle. He glanced at my brother. "While I have her, you better talk. This might be your only chance." He wore a playful smile as he planted his eyes firmly on me.

I could feel the excitement pulsing through him, reminding me of a little boy who'd just been given the toy of his dreams. Except I knew I was much more than that to him, and for a moment I could see it—feel it. A full, encompassing love coupled with a ripple of desire.

I turned my head to stare at Joshua, knowing I'd lose my head if I gazed at Andrew any longer.

"Right." Joshua scowled.

I couldn't tell if he glowered because I straddled Andrew or because I didn't want to listen. *Probably both,* I decided.

Joshua took a breath, and his green eyes met mine. "The Sorrenian is still the closest place to me and one of the safest locations in Carasmille. Lord Leavesden has assured me that they have searched for any unaccounted relics of war. The school is clean. The students responsible for this unfortunate event have been duly punished—"

"Unfortunate event?" I shook my head. "They nearly killed me, Joshua. We're lucky Haldren deemed me important enough to save, or I would be dead."

Joshua and Andrew grimaced.

"Regardless, you're alive now and on the mend. Until the threat against you is absolved, I must keep you safe. I still believe you will be if you remain inside and with other people. Henry came to me and pledged his support to keep others from bullying you. He said he wanted to get to know you and perhaps be your friend if you'll let him."

"Unbelievable," I scoffed.

Joshua shrugged. "He seemed sincere."

I clenched my jaw, and a coldness seeped into my voice. "I don't trust him—and I *don't* want him near me."

Andrew removed his arms from around my waist and clasped my hands in his. "Henry made a serious mistake, and we're not trying to make light of it. But before you completely swear him off, you need to understand where he comes from and ultimately what caused him to react so negatively toward you."

I sighed. "Does it really matter?" I wanted nothing to do with Henry. I doubted anything Andrew said would change my mind.

"Yes, it does." Andrew's tone left no room to argue.

I pursed my lips. "Fine. Am I to stay on your lap while you tell me, or can I move?" What would others think if they walked in and saw us like this?

Andrew grinned and wrapped his arms firmly around my waist once more. "I'll let you go after I have said what I need to."

I raised an eyebrow at Joshua. "Why have you let Andrew hold me captive so?"

Joshua leaned back, crossed his ankles, and rested his hands on his stomach. "He's not harming you, is he?"

Andrew made my heart beat faster, my palms sweat, and my stomach flutter. None of that qualified as painful. "Well, no."

"Then consider me your chaperone," Joshua said.

"And a great one you are," I said sarcastically.

Andrew chuckled. "I think he's great."

"Of course you do." I sighed. "All right, tell me what you must."

"Henry has royal blood. He is second in line for the throne. When you have that kind of power and lineage, people flock to you. They want a piece of that power. They inflate your ego because they want you to like them. They'll do anything to keep you infatuated with them. On the other hand, a lot of pressure is put on you to perform well. Making a mistake or not finishing in first place is a serious offense in many people's eyes. Henry has the possibility of ruling Aberron. They don't want a second-place finisher or some half-wit."

"Naturally," Andrew continued, "it produces a cocky, arrogant, inflated ego with a serious fear of failure. I know this because I've been in Henry's place. I would still be him if my father hadn't taken me aside and knocked some hard truths into my head."

Joshua chuckled. "I remember that. It was a good lesson for me too. 'Perfectionism can lead to ruin. Perform to the best of your ability, accept that not everything you do will be top notch and please others, and we'll get along fine.'"

Andrew nodded. "That's right." He grabbed my hands once more. "When you showed up and, through no fault of your own, made Henry appear incompetent, I'm sure he felt he had to discredit you, to keep others from wondering if he was incapable."

Ire came flooding back. "Right. Because putting me down to curb his feeling of inadequacy is perfectly acceptable behavior."

"No it's not," Andrew said patiently. "Henry should've been given the talk Joshua and I had already. Perhaps things wouldn't have escalated the way they did if he'd had. It's an oversight on my part."

I sighed. "I can accept that." My eyes darted to Joshua. "I still don't want to stay here."

Joshua leaned forward and rested his hands on his knees. "Technically you don't have a choice. I am your guardian until you're twenty."

"Seventeen is legal marrying age," I shot back. "That should give me some rights to choose for myself."

Joshua shook his head. "You're not married yet."

"We can remedy that." Andrew winked at me.

My breath caught in my throat. Andrew chuckled at my crimson heated cheeks.

Joshua's face took on an angry red hue as his eyes bulged. "No." He held his hands out in front of him as if he warded off a plague. "That is not up for discussion."

"Why not? I've got to talk to you about it sometime." Andrew spoke casually, but he wore a cocky grin. "You know I have a limited amount of time, and I can keep her just as safe as you can."

Joshua scowled and stood. "My decision is final. Isabelle, you're staying here for a while longer." He stalked out of the room muttering angrily under his breath.

I slumped my shoulders in disappointment and turned to Andrew. "Can't you do anything about this? You're the Prince."

He smiled and swept my hair away from my forehead. "Sorry, love, Joshua is fully within his rights to make this decision. Only my father could move you without his permission, and I doubt he would without Joshua's consent."

"Then perhaps we should start changing some of these laws," I said.

"What laws?" Malsin strode into the room.

"Guardians," I said darkly. "It appears I am to stay at the Sorrenian against my wishes."

Malsin smiled. "I was hoping you would stay. I can't imagine going back to healing headaches and sniffles with you around."

Andrew faced me and grabbed my hands. "As the Prince Heir of Aberron and the man you're courting, I absolutely forbid you to be sick ever again. You must solemnly swear to be on your best healthy behavior."

I worked hard to keep a straight face. "I swear I shall try my best."

Andrew pressed his forehead to mine and breathed deeply. "I shall hold you to it," he whispered. "Forever."

"Forever," I agreed as we brought our lips together in a kiss of desire.

Andrew's strength improved with a little healing magic, and he abandoned the cane. Regrettably, it meant he had to return to the castle.

"I'm going to be miserable without you." I couldn't stop the pout forming on my face.

Andrew smiled wistfully. "I won't be away for long. You've consistently displayed a talent for finding trouble on your own. I worry what state I'll find you in the next time we meet."

I grimaced. "I don't mean for it to be that way."

"I'm just stating the facts as I see them, love." He reached for a small white box resting on a table. "I have something for you that I hope might ease the loneliness you'll feel while I'm away." He lifted the lid, revealing a dazzling bracelet. Silver with blue sapphires and purple amethysts intertwined like a braid. I had never seen anything more delicate and precious in my life. My heart flooded with warmth and love for him and his thoughtfulness.

Deftly Andrew clasped it around my wrist. I stiffened at the feeling of something wrapped there, and a memory of the chains briefly flashed in my mind. I took a breath and pushed the picture out. A bracelet given to me out of love had nothing to do with the pain-inflicting manacles.

"I had this specially made for you," Andrew said. "May it serve as a reminder of my love and affection."

"I wish I had something to give you," I murmured. "I'm afraid all I have is my heart."

Andrew's blazing blue eyes met mine. "That is worth more to me than the treasures of the world. I shall never want for anything else."

"Then take it," I said with boldness. "I give it freely." I leaned forward and kissed him.

Andrew groaned as we broke apart. He ran a hand through his hair. "You're making it really hard for me to leave."

I laughed, enjoying the effect I had on him while having an equally hard time letting him go.

Joshua strode into the room. "I have a meeting in thirty minutes with King Brian. We must go now." His hands twitched like he wanted to drag Andrew away.

Andrew rolled his eyes, annoyance radiating off him. "I'm coming." He lightly brushed his lips against mine. "I'll be back soon, my love."

Malsin seemed to be ready for me to break down at their departure. Once they left my sight, he handed me a vial with pink liquid. "Drink this. You'll feel better."

I downed the contents that tasted like strawberries, and my emotions—veering to depression—settled into a quiet calm. "Thank you, Malsin." I smiled.

"You should be delighted to hear that I am allowing you to return to your room for more rest and recuperation." Malsin grinned, knowing how much I detested his cots.

Surprise flitted across my face. "Really?"

He laughed at the eagerness in my tone. "We may go now if you like."

I stood too quickly; Malsin caught me as I swayed. "Careful now."

"Sorry." I looped my arm though his, and together we ambled out of the healing rooms.

"There's something I don't understand," Malsin said as we walked.

I glanced at him, noticing the furrowed eyebrows and overall confusion showing on his face. "What?"

"As the healers arrived, I worried we had lost you. I was about to tell everyone not to hope. Then suddenly everything turned around." Malsin scratched his head. "It became almost too easy to extract the poison out of you—like it wanted to be vanquished—when before, it acted the complete opposite. Most of the work we did was repairing the damage."

"I don't know what happened," I lied. "I don't remember much."

He nodded, accepting my answer. "Well, I can say one thing. Someone is watching over you."

"A guardian I owe my life to," I agreed as we reached my door.

I didn't like lying—it left a sour taste in my mouth. But I couldn't let Malsin know about Haldren. I noticed a growing trend when I mentioned his name: uneasiness and a quick subject change. *Why?*

Malsin pointed a finger at me. "You are not permitted to leave your room until I have agreed to it. I will instruct the kitchen to bring meals to you."

I nodded. "Fine."

He eyed me for a moment as if searching for a hint of rebellion. He handed me a green vial procured from his pocket. "To help you sleep." Then he walked away.

"Passiflora," I whispered at the door, and entered.

I leaned against the closed door, my hands behind my back. My eyes swept around the room to see if anything had changed. I half expected someone to have rummaged through my things while I stayed in Malsin's healing rooms, but everything appeared exactly how I left it except for a fresh bouquet of pink roses and lilies residing on the desk with a little white card.

I opened the card. Andrew had penned one line.

Your beauty surpasses the glamour of these flowers, but I hope you enjoy them.

I lay on my bed picturing Andrew in my mind while my fingers traced over the bracelet, enjoying the sparkle when the sunlight touched it. I started with the golden-brown hair that fell into his eyes and around his ears, moving down to his heart-stopping blue eyes. Then onto his straight nose, full lips, and the curve of his jaw, dusted with stubble. My eyes unwillingly filled with tears when I realized how close I'd come to losing him. I felt indebted to Haldren for giving me more precious time to be with Andrew.

A knock on the door that evening startled me.

I opened it expecting to see the mute kitchen lady who had brought my meals the last time I was confined. Instead, Henry stood there holding a dinner tray. Immediately my face changed from dreamy smiles to chagrin and panic. I went to close the door.

"No, Isabelle, wait!" Henry pleaded.

I hesitated.

"I ... I brought you dinner," he stammered, trying to say something that would keep me from slamming the door on his face.

"I don't want it," I said coldly, swallowing down my fear. I took a deep breath and exhaled slowly, my hands trembling, hidden behind the door.

Henry pleaded. "Please, I had to beg Tilma to let me take this up to you."

"Tilma?" I didn't recognize the name.

Henry shook his head impatiently. "The head cook."

"You probably poisoned it since your last attempt at killing me failed." I eyed him suspiciously, my fingers curled hard around the door handle to stop them from shaking.

Henry acted like I had slapped him in the face. He opened his mouth, then faltered. "I didn't, I promise. Please just let me talk to you." He fidgeted. Desperation showed in the crinkles of his eyes and the curve of his lips.

I sighed, figuring he wouldn't stop badgering me until I let him in. I opened the door wider and stepped aside, gesturing for him to come in. Henry set the tray on the table next to the flowers.

"These are nice," he commented lightly, touching the petals on the lilies. "Andrew has good taste in flowers."

Henry stared pointedly into my face as if hoping I would reveal something, a blush maybe? If he inspected close enough, he would see the anxiety reflecting in my eyes, the tight shoulders, clammy hands, trembling lip. Blood pounded in my ears. I regretted letting him in.

I cut to the chase, folding my arms. "What do you want, Henry?"

Henry's composure broke. "You survived."

"Barely," I answered softly, wrapping my arms around my chest.

He nodded. "I wanted to know if you would let me repent for my mistakes." He fiddled with the ring he wore on his right hand as he spoke. "If you would give me a chance to be a friend."

"I'm not sure that would be a good idea," I told him honestly. "I can't trust you."

Henry sighed and ran a hand through his disheveled hair. The move, so familiar, reminded me of Andrew. "I'll give you some time to think about it. I won't give up. There's a lot between us that needs to be reconciled."

"I agree," I answered with pursed lips.

"Good. I'll see you later then." Henry rushed out the door, leaving me with the tray, which was rapidly turning cold.

I collapsed in the chair. I clamped a hand over my mouth to stop myself from screaming. Tears trickled down my cheeks. One encounter with Henry and my mind became trapped inside a fiery cell.

CHAPTER TWENTY-FOUR

ALSIN CONFINED ME TO my room for two miserable days. I spent the morning of Gods Day pleading with him, determined to convince him to let me go out.

"Malsin, please! I've been stuck inside forever. Centuries. How am I supposed to get better if I can't feel fresh air on my face?" I begged.

Malsin planted his feet and crossed his arms, undeterred. "I know you don't like it, and by the Gods, you don't look that sick, but you are. I am the healer. I know what's best." He pointed a finger at himself. "Besides, we've had a few light dustings of snow. It's been unseasonably cold this fall, and I can't have you catch your death. Not after I've worked so hard to preserve it. My goodness!" He put a hand on his forehead and shook his head, appearing thoroughly bewildered.

My bottom lip jutted as I pouted like a child denied sweets. "How about a short walk around the school? I won't overdo it! Just walk down a few hallways, get a change of scenery." I wanted to find a window that gave me a view of the castle.

Malsin pursed his lips, and his eyes narrowed as he crossed his arms again. "Well, I can see there's no stopping you. You're going to keep pestering me until I give in or you end up sneaking out of here." He held up his hands in surrender. "All right, you may go, but you must be escorted." He pointed a finger at me. "If you feel tired at all, you must come straight back to your room. You're still confined for the most part. I don't want you to go into the main hall for any meals yet." He shuddered. "Too much excitement there."

I sighed, and my shoulders slumped. That was as good as a no. Other than Malsin, the only person I considered a real friend was Alzmire, but I didn't want to bother him on Gods Day. Malsin sensed my disappointment. He put a hand on my shoulder and patted lightly.

"Look," he said. "It's hard being confined. You're an achiever, a fighter. Staying in bed is like a death curse to you. I get it." He let go of my shoulder and pointed a warning finger at me. "But you're going to do more harm than good if you go out there on your own and end up collapsing somewhere." He gestured to my body as a whole. "Your body needs more time to regulate since we flooded it with healing magic. That torture room was no joke."

I relented. "You're right."

Malsin smiled. "I knew you would understand."

I sat down in the chair and rubbed my temples. "Guess I'm trapped in here forever. There's nobody here I'm willing to bother."

"I know someone," he said.

"Who?"

"Henry."

I shook my head. "No way."

Malsin shrugged. "Then I guess you're stuck."

I bit my lip. My desire for freedom outweighed my animosity to Henry. I couldn't walk around the school terrified of him forever. I needed to face him sooner or later. "All right, but don't tell him I asked."

He grinned. "All right." He slung his bag over his shoulder. "I'll let you be. You've seen enough of me already."

I laughed. "Oh, never."

Not long after Malsin left, someone rapped on the door. Henry leaned against the doorframe, hands in his pockets, a mischievous grin on his face. "I'm busting you out. Malsin says you can walk around the school. He also mentioned something about looking like a cat ready to claw at the walls to get out." He casually inspected his fingernails, then met my eyes and smiled. "Of course, you wouldn't do that."

I raised my eyebrows, folding my arms. Apparently, Henry didn't joke when he said he wouldn't give up. He wasn't my first choice, but I'd take it.

"Don't look too shocked. We've got lots to talk about." He shoved his hands in his pockets again.

"Lead on then." I closed the door behind me.

Henry beamed. "Looks like Malsin was right." He fell in pace with my even stride. "Do you need my arm for any support?" He lifted his elbow out.

"I'm sick, but not that sick." I bit my lip, trying to rein in the caustic attitude brought on by his presence. "But thank you."

He shrugged. "Just thought I'd ask."

We meandered down the end of the hallway. Henry matched my slow pace but stayed far enough away that a person could slide in between us. I appreciated the distance. My emotions ranged from blatant fear to doubt and confusion. My enemy now wanted to be my friend? I didn't think I could accept it.

I stopped by a window and placed my hands on the windowsill to rest and watched the light snowflakes swirl. Malsin was right. What happened to fall? I couldn't see the castle due to the weather. I frowned; my daydreaming plans evaporated. I glanced at Henry and flinched, having momentarily forgotten that he stood beside me.

He caught my reaction, and his face contorted in horror. "You're still afraid of me, aren't you? I scare you now."

The memory of him pushing me into the cell flashed before my eyes. I turned around and leaned my back against the wall. I closed my eyes and clutched at my rolling stomach. Then I heard the gut-wrenching wailing. The fire consumed everything in sight. A child kicked and screamed in her mother's arms as her precious baby doll melted. *No.* I clenched my jaw and pushed back the false memories that had imprinted in my brain as though I lived through them.

I didn't realize I shook until Henry put his hands on my shoulders to steady me. The first thing I saw when I opened my eyes was Henry's startling blue ones. Without hesitation, I blurted out, "Your eyes are identical to Andrew's."

Henry smiled. "Yes."

I gazed into his eyes and pretended they belonged to Andrew. That Andrew held on to me instead of Henry. He made it easy to imagine. Henry had the same straight nose, full lips, strong jaw. I swallowed my fear and within a matter of moments my shallow breathing became strong. "You can let go of me. I'm all right."

Henry released me and stepped back. He fluttered with his hands for a moment before shoving them in his pockets. He hid his regret well, but not well enough.

I forced a smile. "So what did you want to talk about?" I started a conversation, hoping it would lead me to Henry's motives. I moved away from the wall and started down the hallway. I wanted to forget that he had seen my emotional breakdown.

"I don't know." Henry shrugged, matching my pace. "Anything. I hardly know anything about you other than your wicked talent in class and Andrew's obvious deep affection for you. Which is big news by the way. How long did you think you could keep it hidden?"

"Keep what hidden?" I feigned ignorance.

"That my cousin is courting you."

"Forever," I said.

Henry laughed. "Hiding a relationship with the Crown Prince of Aberron is like hiding a dog in your room. Sooner or later, he's going to bark. You know how many girls would kill to be in your position?"

"Many, I'm sure." I'd never forget the girls from the parade shouting "Make me your Princess."

"How did you two meet?" Henry asked.

I tucked my hair behind my ear. "Andrew found me badly wounded in the forest on his Walk and saved my life."

"I feel like you're leaving a lot out," he said perceptively.

"I am," I agreed. "If you're that curious, ask Andrew."

Henry nodded. "I might do that."

"So how are you two related?" No one had gone as far as to explain how they were cousins, only that they were.

"My mother is King Brian's sister," he explained. "My real father died when I was seven, and when I was twelve my mother married Lord Leavesden."

I raised my eyebrows. "Lord Leavesden is not your real father?"

Henry shook his head. "No, but it's not bad. He's really good for my mother, and if she's happy, then everybody's happy. So ... it works out." He pressed his lips together in a tight line, and I wondered if they had unresolved issues between them.

"Sorry about your real father." Firsthand experience had taught me the devastation of losing a parent.

"Thanks ..." Henry said softly, clasping his hands together. He took a breath. "So what do you do for fun?"

I sighed and stared at the stone tiles. "Fun is a foreign word to my ears."

"Surely you must want a break sometime?" he asked, his blue eyes catching mine.

I mulled it over. "Sometimes."

"What did you do for fun back home?" he inquired, sidestepping to the right as Professor Breldian briskly marched by. His cat Ginger followed, close on his heels.

I thought for a minute. "I sewed or baked ... strummed on an old guitar, played at the creek with friends." More often than not, I went to the creek to meet Stefan. I tucked that thought away quickly. It hurt to think about Stefan when I missed him so much.

Henry froze. He held his hands up, his eyebrows raised in surprise. His mouth parted. "Did you just say guitar?"

I paused and shrugged. "Yes, Nathan got one from an old performer in trade when I was ten. I played occasionally. I'm not very well accomplished." I smiled ruefully and stepped out of the way of a maid heavy laden with towels. "What do you know of them?"

"Oh, just about everything." Henry started walking again. "I live for my guitar."

"Really?"

"I think we've found the first thing we have in common." He grinned and raised a finger in the air. "I knew there had to be something; other than a love of swords, of course." He pushed his ruffled hair back. "Hey, let me show you mine. It's in the culture room."

"I would like that."

I'd heard of the culture room in passing but never actually went there. It sounded like a large room for the students to hang out in on Kings and Gods Day or whenever they didn't have class. If Malsin didn't want me in the dining hall, would he approve of the culture room? I bit my lip, worried about breaking Malsin's rules.

As I suspected, it was crowded with chatting students playing games. Tables and chairs took up most of the space along the walls, leaving the middle of the room empty. Immediately I wished I would have said no. I took a step backward, ready to bolt.

Henry carefully observed me. He put a hand on my shoulder. "Relax. I've had a talk with everyone. They're going to have to get used to you or lose me as a friend." He let go of my shoulder.

I eyed him with disbelief. "Are you sure?"

"Yes," Henry said firmly. He took on the persona of a professor when they stressed something of importance. "I said, 'Guys, I'll lay it out straight for you. She stays, and if you don't like it, you can go. Take it or leave it.'" He laughed and shrugged.

I shook my head, still doubtful. "Guess we'll see."

The students watched us like hawks as we strolled deeper into the room. Henry smiled and waved at a few groups huddled together. I envied his relaxed state. He picked up his wooden guitar resting on a stand and strummed his fingers over the steel strings. "This is it. She's my lady." He pulled a rickety chair over and gestured for me to sit, then grabbed one for himself. He played a few chords. A rich sound emanated from the strings, far better than the old guitar Nathan had. "What do you think?"

"It's lovely," I praised, crossing my ankles.

He held it out to me. "Play something."

I plucked a few strings, letting the music enclose me. *Gods forbid it sounds good.* It brought back memories of playing by the fire on cold winter nights with Nathan, Adel, and occasionally Stefan, Mava, and Carl as my audience.

"Do you sing?" Henry asked.

"Only in front of select people," I said.

He grinned. "Oh, we'll have to change that."

We passed the guitar back and forth, discussing different chords and fingerpicking styles. Henry taught me easier ways to hit chords I hadn't been able to reach before, and I showed him some of the melodies I had come up with. The students gave us a wide berth as we played.

Nearly an hour passed without me noticing until I started to feel the effects of my feeble state more strongly. Curse Malsin. He knew I couldn't last long outside, but I didn't want to believe it. I now understood why he wouldn't let me go alone. I worried I wouldn't have the strength to make it to my room without resting every few minutes. Henry seemed to sense my weariness because he set the guitar down and suggested we head back.

A shadow loomed over us. I looked up and gasped. My heart stopped and restarted.

Andrew wore a creamy white, long-sleeve shirt embroidered with silver, and black pants with black boots up to his knees. His golden-brown hair pushed away from his devastatingly handsome face. A smile reached his stunning blue eyes as he rested his hands on the back of my chair.

He caught my eyes and gazed. His smile grew, showing perfectly straight, white teeth. Mischief danced along the planes of Andrew's face as he extended his hand. The constant hum of chatter ceased. Consciously aware that the students watched, I allowed him to pull me up and into his arms.

Without hesitation, he brought his mouth down hard against mine. I closed my eyes and tangled my hands in his hair. He kissed me with intense passion, like he was starved for the taste of my lips. I breathed deeply, taking in the scent of his cinnamon woodsy cologne. Everything faded until only he and I remained: two people desperately in love, scurrying in a run-down world. I fell into the kiss with all the strength I had left, giving Andrew my love and adoration, my breath, and my life.

My cheeks flamed by the time we broke apart, and I looked into Andrew's delighted blue eyes. He wore the biggest, cockiest grin I had ever seen, easily rivaling Henry. Using Andrew as my shield, I peeked at the students. They stared opened-mouthed in shock and jealousy. I sensed more than one girl wanted to battle.

"I've been waiting a long time to do that," Andrew said. As if unable to stop himself, he lightly kissed me once more.

I laughed softly. "It's been three days."

He cupped my cheek and rubbed it with his thumb. "Three grueling, insufferable days."

I couldn't disagree. "I didn't expect you to be here so soon. How did you manage to get away?" I asked, bewildered, and delighted and worried all at the same time.

He gazed above my head at the students, then spoke louder, addressing everyone in the room more so than me. "I need to speak to the students. I must address the reports of their disturbing behavior."

Imaginary ice froze everyone in place as they watched Andrew and me interact.

I grimaced and stared at the floor, not wanting to meet his eyes. "If this is about me, don't. I'm fine." I didn't want to cause any more trouble.

"Isabelle Mirran, don't lie to me." He cupped my face in his calloused hands, forcing me to meet his eyes. I saw anger, determination, and love reflecting back. My lips parted in surprise as I realized Andrew wanted to fight for me. "I will not sit back and let them persecute you any longer. They need to know that if they hurt you in any way, I will be their retribution."

I grabbed his hand, pleading. "You can't save me from everything."

"This isn't about saving you from everything," he repeated. "This is about me protecting the woman I love. If they know I'm behind you, they won't dare touch you again." He squeezed my hand. "Don't worry; I'm just going to have a little friendly chat."

Andrew left my side and strode forward until he stood in the midst of the immobilized students.

I swiveled around and leaned against the wall.

Henry joined me. "This is going to be good. Andrew's temper can be fierce. Best if these students start running now."

I eyed Henry with disbelief. "He said this would be friendly."

"He lied," he said candidly.

"Great." I folded my arms and watched with nervous tension at the pit of my stomach.

"Could I have everyone's attention please?" Andrew called to the crowd. "Come closer if you can't hear me." He waved his hand, indicating for everyone to move in.

The students all shuffled closer, leaving their seats, games, and conversations. Their eyes fixated on Andrew like starving wolves. He planted his feet, his posture stiff. He held his head high. His neck exposed, the tendons jutted out. His sharp eyes observed the group, not leaving anyone out. *A true Prince.* I'd forgotten how easily Andrew acted regal and intimidating, using only his facial expressions and stance.

"I've read some concerning reports detailing your extracurricular activities." His lips curled in displeasure. "You're lucky I didn't bring my sword into the room, or heads would roll."

A few eyes shifted in my direction. I gulped and huddled against the wall.

"See what I mean?" Henry said.

I grimaced. "Right." His friendly chats were more like a court proceeding than anything else.

Nearly all the students hung their head in shame. The room suddenly felt heavy and strained. Even I wanted to escape Andrew's glare.

"Dominic." Andrew suddenly addressed him.

"Yes, Highness?" Dominic attempted to sound formal, but his face blanched, giving away his nervous anxiety.

Andrew folded his arms, his pensive eyes drilling into Dominic. I'd been under that glare many times and knew it couldn't easily be held. I wondered how long it would take before he buckled under the pressure.

"What do you know about Isabelle Mirran?" Andrew asked, gesturing to me.

"Isabelle?" Dominic furrowed his eyebrows in confusion, and his eyes fleetingly met mine.

"Yes. Tell me about her," Andrew commanded.

"Well … there's—there's not much to tell," he stammered, pushing his black hair out of his eyes.

"Oh, come on." Andrew rolled his eyes. "There has to be something." Andrew acted like he conversed with an idiot. He gestured to Dominic. "You're telling me she's been here for a month and you know absolutely nothing about her save her first and last name?"

"Well … uh … she's good at classes." Dominic's voice gradually became small and insignificant as he spoke. He shifted on his feet, giving the distinct impression that he wanted to dash.

"Just good?" Andrew leaned forward, unleashing his full princely power and authority. It wouldn't have surprised me if Dominic soiled his pants.

His hands trembling, Dominic shoved them in his pockets, then swallowed. "She's obviously skilled and hasn't had much of an issue in any of our classes except magic."

Andrew smiled, but it lacked warmth and meaning. "That's right. You kicked her out of magic class because she's dangerous." He stepped forward. The crowd hastily stumbled backward in fear. "She's a—what did you call her?" Andrew furrowed his eyebrows, feigning ignorance. "Oh yes, a soul-sucking monster that will blind you with her rainbow powers. She'll attack when you're unaware and unguarded in your beds. Ironic how the exact opposite happened." He shook his head with disgust written all over his face.

Dominic went pale. Sweat dotted his brow.

"Shouldn't have started that one, Dom," Henry muttered.

"He came up with that?" I asked, my eyebrows raised.

Henry nodded.

Andrew's intense gaze fell upon Falden. "Falden, maybe you can make up for Dominic's ignorance. Tell me, what do you know about Isabelle Mirran?"

Falden turned ashen and shifted his weight uneasily. "She has one brother, Joshua, who commands your armies, and she comes from Saren, a farming community."

Andrew's expression morphed from menacing to completely and utterly bored. He inspected his fingernails as an added effect. Truly, he mastered facial expressions. "Those are mere facts anyone could know. Do you know anything about her habits? What food does she like? What is her favorite color?"

Falden's eyes widened. "I—"

"Speak up," Andrew ordered.

"I don't know, Highness," Falden spoke louder and grimaced.

"Of course you don't." He sighed and rubbed his forehead. "Anybody else?" Andrew glared at everyone standing in the room. When no one spoke, he addressed Henry. "Henry, can you shed some light on the subject?"

"I'm afraid I know about as much as these two idiots." Henry gestured to Dominic and Falden, speaking loudly to be heard from the wall. He folded his arms and met Andrew's formidable gaze head-on, not showing any trepidation. "She's wicked good at class, though. The professors are constantly trying to come up with new material for her to learn." He shrugged. "I don't even know why she's here, because it can't be for the lessons."

Andrew strode forward until he was a breath away from Dominic, Falden, and the students surrounding them. They hurriedly stepped back, stomping over one another in their haste. "If you don't know her, why do you persecute her?" he asked, his voice dark and merciless. He held his arms out wide and turned around in a half circle addressing everyone in the room. "Why do any of you? What has she done to deserve this?"

The tension in the room rose steadily. Andrew's piercing blue eyes sought out everyone, reading the shame and guilt written on their faces.

Many students shuddered as his gaze left them, and I wondered if they felt he saw their weaknesses displayed.

"Nothing!" he shouted, throwing his hands up in frustration. "Nothing but demonstrate her skill in class at the professors' requests. Does that merit the torture she has endured from day one? You nearly killed her!" he roared at them, his chest heaving as he raged.

Several younger students, Ellis particularly, looked on the verge of tears.

Andrew took a step backward and ran a hand through his hair, composing himself to a quiet calm. He turned his head to me and smiled wistfully. My heart ached at the sadness reflected deep in his eyes. I held my breath, wanting to rush over and comfort him.

Andrew fought to keep the emotion out of his voice. "When I found her shackled, burned, and unconscious, I thought she was dead." He balled his fists and raised his eyes upward. "Truly, you do not want to experience the emotions I felt when I looked at her lifeless body."

He faced the students and gestured to me. "By the grace of the Gods or some unseen power, she is miraculously recovering. Soon the injuries that covered her body will be nothing but a memory." He pointed at them, his face in a controlled rage. "A memory that will be a cause of heartache for her and you, because you did this to her!"

Not a single person dared to object.

Andrew folded his arms, shifting his weight from side to side. "You know the King gets reports on the Sorrenian. Now I will get them too. There is nothing you can hide from me."

Everyone in the room, including me, grimaced.

"Don't think for a second that I won't be back here, and next time it won't be just a friendly chat. Next time, I'll bring my sword," Andrew warned with an edge in his voice. He swiftly strode to me with a rather mischievous grin. He reached out for my hand, and I let him take it.

"That is what you call a friendly chat?" My blood pulsed, my heart raced. His harsh words and quick emotions alarmed me. I quivered. "I think you took it a bit far."

"No, he didn't," Henry disagreed. "We deserved it. Every word."

"I'm glad to see you recognize that," Andrew said, appraising Henry with something akin to respect.

Andrew tugged on my hand. "Come on, let's get out of here."

On our way out, he paused at the door, turned around, and addressed the frozen crowd once more. "Remember, I have eyes and ears everywhere. Don't take my threats lightly."

"Where are we going?" I asked as we navigated through the maze of hallways.

"Back to your room. Malsin said you would get tired easily."

I sighed; my shoulders slumped. "Malsin knows everything."

Andrew chuckled. "Healers often do."

"I'm surprised Joshua isn't with you," I commented. "Isn't he supposed to be our chaperone?"

"He's got his head buried in reports." He paused by a window and stared out of it.

A break in the clouds let the sun shine through and touch my face. I tilted my face to the rays, closed my eyes, and enjoyed the warmth.

"I didn't want him to come anyway," Andrew admitted.

"Why?"

"Because then he couldn't scowl at me when I kiss you," he said blatantly.

"Is Joshua against kissing? Or relationships in general?" I asked. I knew next to nothing about his personal life.

Andrew shook his head. "Only when it comes to us."

I frowned. That would need to change. "When will he admit that we are good for each other?"

"When the Goddess Amora appears and tells him so." Andrew shrugged. "It's not likely to happen."

Oh, Joshua ... I sighed. What kind of brother did I end up with?

CHAPTER TWENTY-FIVE

WOKE TO A LOUD pounding at my door. I covered my face in my hands and groaned, positive Malsin waited to reprimand me for going to the culture room. I glanced out the window; it was barely dawn. Malsin wouldn't get up this early for something that trivial. Who could want me up at this hour? I rolled out of bed and pulled a robe over my shoulders.

"I'm coming!" I shouted at the incessant knocking.

I wrenched open the door. Henry leaned against the doorframe, bright-eyed.

"Henry, it's barely dawn. What are you doing awake?" I grumbled, rubbing my eyes.

"I know, but I couldn't sleep, so I thought I'd badger you." He grinned.

I froze, alarmed.

He rubbed his face. "Not literally." He sighed. "I told you I wouldn't—" he started muttering unintelligible words under his breath. I saw the frustration on his face.

I took pity on him and stepped aside. "Come in."

"Does this mean you're giving me a chance?" Henry closed the door behind him. "'Cause I didn't come with a dinner tray this time."

I held my lips together, not exactly sure what I wanted. "I'm not sure." I headed to my bedroom door. "Give me a minute to change." I slipped on a light green dress and sat on the chintz chair adjacent to Henry.

"What can I do to change that?" He leaned back, folding his hands together.

I decided to be blunt. "Help me to not fear for my life every time I look at you. If you can manage that, then I'll give you a chance."

Henry grimaced at first, but gradually his face morphed into determination. "I'll do it."

"Good luck. You're going to need it."

Henry's expression turned grim again. "Thanks." He glanced at the empty fireplace. "Are you cold?"

"No." My answer came out too quick. Since Andrew rescued me from the cell, I hadn't started a fire. Anything bigger than a candle flame scared me.

Henry raised an eyebrow.

I cleared my throat, embarrassed. "I'm fine, thank you."

He rubbed his face and sighed. "You're afraid of me, and fire." He shook his head. "While I waited for Joshua and the healers to come, I heard you screaming. That wasn't pain-related, was it? Something else happened to you with those chains."

I shuddered as the memories rose to the surface. "Yes."

Henry grimaced. "What did they do to you?"

"Do you really want to know?" I met his eyes.

"Yes," he said without a hint of indecision.

I took a deep breath, gripping the armrests for support, and told him about the fiery hallucinations. My voice sounded eerily calm as I spoke, surprising me. I hoped that maybe if he knew the scars went deeper than what he saw on the outside, he would learn from it. That he would think twice before doing something hurtful to someone else. "So as you can see, my love for fire has gone out."

Henry leaned back in his chair, horrified. He opened his mouth and closed it. He swallowed and tried again. "I'm so sorry. If I'd have known, I never would have—"

I cut him off. "I know." I took a deep breath and exhaled. "Can we talk about something else now?"

Henry nodded. "Sure. How did your day go with Andrew yesterday?"

I smiled. "It was great but short-lived. Some dignitary showed up at the castle and the King demanded that Andrew come home for dinner."

A soft knock at the door got me out of my chair. I answered it, and the mute kitchen lady came in carrying a tray laden with food. She set it between Henry and me and left quickly.

"Guess Malsin still doesn't want me in the dining hall." I sighed, picking a grape. I glanced at Henry and gestured to the food. "You hungry?"

"I'm pretty sure it's for your protection." He grabbed a piece of bacon. "There are several girls—and by several, I mean every girl in the entire school—plotting against you."

"Great," I muttered sarcastically. I picked up another grape and threw it in the empty fireplace.

The clock chimed and Henry glanced at it. "Gods forbid, I'm late to meet Dominic." He stood. "Thanks for letting me in this morning."

I stood. "You're welcome."

"See you later." He strode out the door.

Later that day Malsin cleared me for classes again. "Now I better not see you for a health-related matter again. Only for magic lessons. Otherwise, stay out of trouble." He pointed a warning finger at me.

I nodded. "I'm done taking risks."

"Oh, and on another note: I've lost count of how many girls have come into my office begging for some calming remedy. Next time Prince Andrew decides to show up and display his affection in front of the whole school, tell him to bring the anxiety medication. I'm clean out!" Malsin threw his hands up, then let them fall back at his sides, clearly perturbed.

"I'll tell him." I tried to hide the humor I felt at Malsin's predicament but failed. I laughed. "I'm sorry. It's just—I never—I never thought this would happen to me." I gestured to myself. "And yet, here I am." I let my hands fall to my sides, my shoulders slumped.

Malsin chuckled. "You silly girl. You can't expect your life to go exactly how you planned it. Unforeseen circumstances are going to happen."

I sighed, rubbing my temples. "Yes ... I'm learning the hard way."

I spent more time than I usually did getting ready the next morning. Standing in front of the mirror, I brushed my chocolate-colored hair in long strokes. I braided a portion of it and left the rest to cascade down my back. I dumped out my school bag and reorganized it in a methodical fashion.

Underneath my skin, I buzzed with nervousness. Usually when I felt this way, I went to work, organizing everything in sight even if it didn't need to be done. I hoped that if I could keep my hands busy and focus on something else, maybe my feelings would disappear. It never worked, but I never ceased to try.

The clock ticked closer to breakfast, but I couldn't bring myself to open the door. I stood by it as still as a statue, my bag slung over my shoulder, barely focusing on the grains of the wood.

Today would be different. I could feel it. It reminded me of changing weather. Like how some people can step outside, close their eyes, and feel it shifting deep in their bones. Even if there are no obvious signs, somehow they know. It's not magic, but rather a sixth sense ingrained from living in the same place for generations. For towns like Saren, where storms escalate quickly, causing mass destruction, those who sense the weather altering course are important. We treat them with respect because we know that without them, we would never get enough time to prepare.

Andrew had kissed me passionately in front of nearly all the students. His visit had changed the weather.

I could handle the insults when they were directed at me only, but I didn't think I could endure the invectives aimed at my relationship with Andrew. He patched me up and made me whole, physically, and emotionally. I couldn't see the best thing in my life abused. Without him, I wouldn't be here. So, I stood there, knowing I needed to go down to breakfast but unable to take a single step forward.

Henry knocked on the door. I'd started to recognize his knocking pattern. I took the few steps forward and answered it.

"Hey." Henry smiled. "You coming to breakfast? I didn't see you there so I thought I'd come up. Malsin did clear you for classes again, right?"

"Yes, he did." I held my shoulder bag with a vicelike grip.

"So what's the holdup?" He leaned casually against the doorframe and crossed his arms over his chest.

"I can't go out there," I said in a rush. The words spilled out as I gestured to the open door.

"Why not?"

"Because I'm going to be terrorized," I exclaimed, throwing my hands up.

Henry raised an eyebrow, clearly waiting for a better explanation.

"Andrew kissed me in front of everyone," I hissed. "There's bound to be jealous girls out there ready to rip our relationship to shreds." I sighed and put a hand to my forehead. "Look, Andrew is the best thing going for me right now, and I can't handle the sabotage I'm going to get if I walk out that door. Which is why I'm not coming." My voice faltered at the end, though I tried to sound resolute as I folded my arms.

Henry shook his head. "The Isabelle Mirran I know would walk out this door with her head held high and would revel in the fact that out of all those girls out there, Andrew chose her." He pointed to me. "I can't guarantee that you're not going to face some backlash, but I promise that I will stand by your side and support and defend you."

I heard the conviction in his voice and knew he meant it. A smidgeon of my nervousness subsided.

He beckoned. "Come on, you can't start the day on an empty stomach."

I smiled tentatively and took a step forward. I stared at Henry, falling in step with his casual gait. Everything about him from his face to his clothes and stance screamed confidence and self-assurance.

"How do you do it?" I asked.

"Do what?" His blue eyes, bright and curious, met mine.

"Everything about you shouts confidence." I stepped out of the way of Professor Morel pulling a large cart of plants behind her. "I knew from the first moment I laid eyes on you that you were the ruler of this school. How do you do it?"

"First moment. Really?" Henry grinned, shoving his hands in his pockets.

I nodded. "It's pretty obvious."

"In simple terms?" he queried, stopping to let a group of younger students shuffle along. They stared at us wide-eyed. "Some of it is birthright, and the rest is acting the part until you can deliver."

"And once you deliver?" I asked as we reached the steps to the entry hall.

"Then it doesn't have to be an act. I can be as cocky and confident as I want because I know if someone challenges me that I can prove it." He shrugged nonchalantly.

I envied him.

"How do you do it?" Henry shot back at me, mischief shining from his eyes.

"Do what? I don't do anything."

"Act so fierce. Even when you were trying to blend in with the walls—and don't think I didn't notice because I did—you always had this fierce look about you that said don't mess with me. It's partly why I couldn't stop taunting you. I envied your intensity," he confessed.

"My fierceness is based on circumstance. Had you met me in Saren before I was attacked, I would not have been so intense." I shifted on the balls of my feet. "I know it's not exactly the right thing to say, but have a few bad things happen, and you go either of two ways: develop a thick skin, or crumble."

"Good to know," Henry commented softly.

As we neared the dining hall, a girl, fifteen or sixteen I guessed, with flowy blonde hair and a bright pink dress, blocked our path. Her face contorted in an ugly rage, marring her pale complexion in hues of pink.

She pointed a perfectly manicured finger at me. "There's the Prince stealer."

I took a deep breath and exhaled. My body surged with adrenaline and anxiety. The girl blocking my path stepped closer. I hastily stumbled backward as she got right in my face. I half expected her to knock me down.

"You think if I almost die the Prince will save me too? Think he'll fall in love with me too? Huh?" She flicked her long blonde hair away from her face.

Her pushiness unnerved me. She had absolutely no reservations about confronting me.

"Watch it, Iris," Henry warned. He stepped in between us, putting me behind him. Undeterred, she leaned around him to speak to me.

I wished a professor was around to see this, but we stood in an empty hall with no one in sight.

"Prince Andrew was meant for me, not you. My family and I have had plans since birth, and you stole him from me," Iris accused sourly.

"I didn't steal him. He made the first move. Not me," I said, trying to correct the issue.

She eyed me with skepticism. "With your bewitching powers, you tricked him into choosing you."

My weak appetite vanished. My very presence ignited a fury within this girl. My frustration with Andrew bubbled up to the surface. Joshua's words at our first meeting screamed in my head. "You're effectively feeding her to the vultures!" I shuddered; the full impact of his words stared me right in the face.

"This was a mistake," I said to Henry. I started to back away, but he followed by my side.

Iris floated over, a sneer on her pale face. "Prince Andrew may love you now, but that is going to change. Soon you'll only be a memory, dead and long forgotten."

"You act on your threat, and you'll pay for it." Henry folded his arms.

"Who said anything about threats? I'm only voicing my opinion." She held her head high. As she stormed passed, she shoved her bright-colored book bag into my shoulder, knocking me into Henry, who caught me from behind.

I balled my hands into fists as I straightened. "Oh, if you were here right now, Andrew, I'd punch you."

Henry heard and responded, "He could use a good punch."

The bell rang shrill in our ears, and the hallways quickly filled with students and professors leaving the dining hall. With breakfast over, Henry and I changed course and headed to our first class.

I spent the morning fuming. My thoughts kept switching back and forth between my love for Andrew and Joshua's foresight. After this experience, I appreciated Joshua a little more. He'd had good intentions when he tried to spare me from jealous girls brokenhearted over a fantasy. Only, I couldn't see it then. Is this what it meant to be in love with a prince? One moment in the clouds and the next neck deep in the mud. *Is it worth it?* I felt guilty for even thinking the question. Thank the Gods Andrew couldn't read my expression now.

Henry passed me a note during Alzmire's class. I opened it quietly and read.

It was bound to happen to any girl Andrew chose. If it wasn't you, then it would be someone else facing the same treatment.

I sighed, knowing Henry made a valid point. It didn't matter who Andrew chose to show his affection to, there would be at least one jealous girl intent on ruining it. But what mattered more to them, Andrew or the crown? The thought of wearing a crown made me wrinkle my nose in disgust. I wanted nothing to do with glory and power. Deep down I knew the driving wedge between us would be his fate to rule Aberron. I wondered if my love for Andrew was strong enough that I would forego my wishes and take on the duties of being a royal.

Aliyah caught up with me right before lunch. She flipped her long blonde hair out of her face and smiled. "Don't worry; not everyone is in love with Prince Andrew. Some of us have our eyes on somebody else." She glanced at Henry as she spoke.

"That's a relief." I smiled.

"Look, I'm sorry about what happened. Henry's right. We've been real jerks to you, and that's not how I want it to be. Henry's turning over a new leaf, and I'd like to do the same. I mean, I'll be eighteen in a few days. I don't have time for childish games anymore."

Because nearly killing me was childish ... right. I bit my tongue, holding back my sarcastic response because I could see her sincerity.

"So will you come sit with us for lunch?" she asked.

"Oh, I actually have plans. Maybe for dinner?" I bit my lip, hoping she wouldn't see through my lie. I didn't feel brave enough to sit with them just yet.

"What plans?" Henry turned around and asked. I didn't realize he had been listening.

My face felt hot as I scrambled to come up with something. "Oh, well ... it's been a while since—" I cleared my throat. Sudden inspiration struck. "Since I've visited Nisha, my horse."

"But you'll see him this afternoon for riding class," Henry countered. "You can't skip out on breakfast and lunch; you'll be no good as a partner for defensive classes."

"I'm sure I can manage." I stopped walking and stood off to the side. Henry and Aliyah cornered me.

Henry shook his head and folded his arms. His blue eyes blazed. "No. I'm not going to let you do this to yourself. You need to eat. I'll figure out something with the girls."

"I can help," Aliyah offered.

I sighed in defeat. "All right."

Aliyah looped her arm through Henry's, and I followed them to the dining hall, feeling like an outsider. Aliyah obviously centered her affections on Henry, and I wondered if he reciprocated them.

Several girls glowered at me as we entered the dining hall, but they made no move against me. Then I noticed Lord Leavesden sitting at the head of the room, surrounded by professors, and it made sense. They wouldn't try something when he watched. The tension in my stomach lessened.

Henry handed me a tray. I picked up an apple.

"No." He speared a large slice of turkey and placed it on my tray. "You need real food."

"An apple is real food," I protested.

"Yeah, for a horse. Maybe I should plan your meals. You're skin and bones as it is." Henry clicked his tongue in disapproval.

As we continued down the line, he added additional food to my tray, more than I could possibly eat. I decided it would be futile to argue. I hovered at the end of the buffet for a second, letting the worry gnaw a hole through my stomach. Sitting at the table of my enemies was asking for trouble.

"None of that. Come on." Henry gently gripped my shoulder and steered me over to his crowded table. I couldn't help but feel like a deer being led to a table of butchers.

"I just want to know one thing," Dominic addressed me as I sat. "Does Prince Andrew know your favorite color?"

The question caught me off guard. I expected him to say something more on the lines of "Are you really a danger to us or not?"

"He does not," I admitted. "I do know his, though."

"I knew it!" Dominic slapped the table. I jumped. "I'd like to see the tables turned and have him answer all those questions." He eyed me perceptively. "How many do you think he'd get right?"

"Oh, um ... a couple, maybe." I shrugged.

"You mean he gave that whole impassioned reprimand without actually knowing half the questions he threw at us?" Henry's jaw dropped.

I nodded slowly.

Henry started laughing. Immediately Dominic hatched plans to get back at Andrew. It involved surrounding him in the culture room and pelting questions at him. In between bites of lunch, Henry and Falden gave suggestions.

"So what is his favorite color?" Aliyah asked, setting her cup down.

Everyone stopped talking to listen.

"Green," I said.

"And yours?" Aliyah continued.

"Sunset." I picked up a slice of bread.

"Excellent." Dominic grinned. "That's harder to guess."

Toward the end of lunch, Malsin came to me and said he would be gone for the week to a healers' convention.

"If I could get out of this, I would." He shuddered. "I absolutely dread these things, but it's completely unavoidable when I'm the main speaker." He placed a hand on my shoulder. "I'm so sorry, I feel like I've been the worst magic teacher to you."

"But you have been the best healer I could have ever asked for." I smiled, placing my hand on his.

"Yes, which reminds me." He pointed a finger at me. "Since I won't be here for the week, please be safe. In fact, it'd be better if you just went to class and then stayed in your rooms. And tell Prince Andrew not to come either. He's liable to stir up all kinds of trouble." He frowned. "Then maybe I might rest easy."

"I promise to be safe." I grinned and put a hand on his arm. "Don't worry about me. Go, enjoy yourself with all those healers. Make it a party."

Malsin grimaced. "Oh, it will be a party all right."

CHAPTER TWENTY-SIX

 FROZE IN FRONT OF my door after riding class, my stomach coiled in knots. In bright red glittering paint, someone had written *Gretlin*. It felt like I'd been slapped in the face.

A mythical creature, the Gretlin was a female of surpassing beauty who preyed on men on the eve of their wedding. I'd heard many versions of Gretlin's tragic past. Some said she had been jilted at the altar; others said her lover had died the night before their marriage. Regardless of the method, in every story she lost her betrothed. To console herself, she turned to her other great love: precious metals and gems. Unwilling to get her hands dirty, she lured the promised men out of their beds and turned them into her slaves to dig for them. After working them to the brink of death, she set them free. She never kept them for long. Aberronians got married every day, and she had no shortage of men to lure.

It was common to hear Aberronians tell a betrothed man to lock the doors and keep watch for the Gretlin lest she steal him away. Most considered it a joke, and usually stories would emerge on the wedding day of her failed attempts.

However, the Gretlin had two connotations: one a lighthearted warning for the couple in love and the other an insult for women. I could see how they thought it would be a fitting name for me. A prince stealer, with gold, gems, and power at her fingertips. Everything the Gretlin ever wanted.

Numb, I whispered the password and entered my room. I hung up my sword, then went to the bathroom and grabbed a bucket. I filled it with hot, soapy water and grabbed a small rag. I went back outside and started scrubbing at the red paint. It didn't come off easily. The paint soaked through the rag, staining my hands red. I tried not to think as I worked despite being unable to ignore how much the slur hurt.

I heard multiple footsteps coming toward me but didn't turn to see who traipsed down the hall until they spoke.

"This has got to stop." Henry sounded angry.

"Definitely," Aliyah agreed, sounding equally concerned.

I dipped my rag in the red water. "Skipping dinner?" I tried to keep my voice light, but I didn't think I managed it very well.

Henry rolled his eyes. "You know what I mean."

"Of course, she does," Aliyah said.

Henry set the plate of food he brought down. He sat, pulling Aliyah with him. They leaned their backs against the wall. "You don't deserve this. You're not what they called you."

I laughed bitterly. "Aren't I? The Prince is in love with me. No one will believe it happened by accident." I scrubbed harder at the letters.

"You can't seriously believe you are a—" Henry had trouble even saying the word. He grimaced.

I finished his sentence for him. "A Gretlin?"

Henry nodded.

I set the rag down in the bucket with a small splash and stared at the slur, half washed off but still clearly visible. "Five days." I met Henry's eyes with my own. "Five days of inseparability is all it took for Andrew to fall in love with me. Tell me how many people you know that have fallen in love in that amount of time."

"My parents," Henry said immediately. "One dance at a winter ball and they were devoted. Uncle Brian met Aunt Averly at the Healers Guild as she trained to become a healer. One chance meeting, and she took his breath away. He visited her every day while she was an apprentice there. My family is known for falling in love hard and fast."

"Really?" My lips parted in surprise.

Henry smiled. "Yes. It's not out of character for Andrew to follow in his parents' footsteps."

"Don't forget about King Jason, Henry's grandfather," Aliyah added. "He had two weeks to find a wife or else he'd lose his right to the throne. He found the girl he wanted with one week to spare, but she wanted nothing to do with him. He spent that entire week pleading with her to marry him. On the last day, she finally agreed, and they lived happily for quite some time."

Henry and Aliyah's assurances relieved me. "So, you don't think I could have bewitched Andrew?"

Henry and Aliyah both shook their heads.

"No. Many girls have spent a considerable amount of time chasing after him, and he's only ever shown polite interest, if any," Henry said. "At his farewell party for the Walk, I asked him why, and he said 'The girl I want hasn't arrived. I'm waiting for her.'"

"He said that?" I heard the surprise in my voice.

"I swear it's the truth." Henry stood and reached for Aliyah, helping her rise. She looped her arm through his. "So, don't for one second think you are what they call you." He glanced at the half-washed word and grimaced. "We'd stay and help, but we've got to get to magic class. Don't forget to eat." He pointed at the plate of food.

I smiled. "Thanks for bringing me dinner."

"You're welcome," Henry and Aliyah said simultaneously, causing all of us to chuckle. Arm in arm, they turned and strode down the hall seeming very much like a couple in a budding romance.

I scrubbed furiously at the painted words until my fingers hurt, but I managed to get the paint off the door. I brought in the cold plate of food and set it on the table, then I rinsed out the bucket of red, soapy water. I washed my hands five times but still couldn't get rid of all the traces of red paint.

With only one small candle lit, I ate my dinner in the semidarkness with a blanket wrapped around me for warmth. My eyes had grown used to doing everything in the dark, and I found solace in it. I pretended not to feel lonely by remembering Andrew's sweet embrace.

Bright and early the next morning, Henry showed up at my door. I let him inside and went back to the bathroom to finish putting in the last hairpins. He leaned against the doorframe, watching me twist my hair. "So, Aliyah's informed me that Iris has gotten a group of girls together and they are planning something diabolical against you. She tried to find out more, but no one would tell her. They've cut ties with her since she has been seen associating with you."

I stuck the last pin in my hair and faced him. I frowned. "I'm sorry I've caused so much discord among your friends."

"Oh, Aliyah doesn't mind. She says it's a relief not to pretend to like the same things they do now. She's just sorry she couldn't find out what they're planning," Henry said.

"Oh." I picked up my bag, not sure what to say.

"Which is why I've opted to be your bodyguard." He grinned. "Their chances of succeeding will be relatively slim if I'm by your side."

"Oh, Henry, I couldn't ask you to do that. I'm sure I'll be able to handle it." Henry by my side all day reminded me of the King's order for Andrew to not take his eyes off me until I met Joshua.

Henry folded his arms. I saw determination in his countenance. "You're not asking. I'm doing it. Now come on, we're going to be late for breakfast."

His persistence worked in his favor. My fear of him started to diminish, though I couldn't help but keep my guard up. I sighed. "All right."

Nothing happened that day or the next, but Henry, and occasionally Aliyah, faithfully came to my door every morning and dropped me back off at my room after dinner each night.

Henry's group of friends made more of an effort to include me, though I suspected Henry was behind it. Dominic seemed the most standoffish, and sometimes when Henry thought I didn't notice I saw him giving Dominic a look. I knew he couldn't force us to be friends, but it didn't stop him from trying.

After the third day of Henry greeting me in the morning, he said something that caught me off guard. "You know what? I like you. The real you. I don't know why I didn't try to get to know you first; we could have avoided a whole lot of suffering on both our parts."

I chuckled softly. "Yes."

That night after dinner, the jealous girls struck. As we walked out of the dining hall, Iris shouted above us. "Gretlin!" She leaned over the railing with ten or so other excited girls. In her hands she carried a metal pail.

"Isabelle, look out!" Henry pushed me out of the way as Iris dumped the contents of the metal pail over our heads.

Henry didn't have time to move out of the way. I watched in horror as the red glittering paint doused him from head to toe. "Argh!" he cried out, his face grimacing in pain.

For a moment, the red shimmering paint covered Henry and dripped onto the floor. Abruptly, it disappeared, leaving behind tiny painted marks in his skin like a tattoo. "Gods forbid, it burns!" He shook out his arms and legs and danced around.

I stepped forward. "Are you all right?" I stared at the tiny red marks and gasped. Henry brought his hand up to his face and cursed. The red marks were painted words. Insults. I read several of them on his face and hands. Gretlin, Prince stealer, leech, seducer.

I felt sick to my stomach. I tilted my head to glare at the girls, but they had vanished, and not a single professor had been in sight to watch them do it.

"They are going to wish they hadn't done that," Henry muttered. "Come on. I'm not going to let them get away with this."

"What are you going to do?" I asked.

"I'm going to Leavesden." Henry turned and marched down the hall to his office. I trailed behind.

"I'm so sorry, Henry," I apologized, taking two steps to match his one long stride. "Are you still in pain?"

"No. It doesn't burn anymore." He stopped in front of Lord Leavesden's office and knocked.

"Enter," Lord Leavesden called from inside.

Henry opened the door and walked in. "You willing to dole out punishments?"

I shut the door behind us and hovered beside him.

Lord Leavesden raised his eyebrows. He set the paper he'd been reading down. "What's happened now?" He did a double take. "Henry, what's that all over your skin?"

He shoved his hand in front of Lord Leavesden's face. "Read it."

Lord Leavesden's lips curled in displeasure as his eyes darted back and forth, reading the insults on Henry's skin. "They obviously meant it for Isabelle, but I pushed her out of the way."

Lord Leavesden glanced at me, then back at Henry. "Give me a list of names, and I will see to it." He eyed Henry over and grimaced. "Your mother is visiting tomorrow evening. You might want to figure out a way to wash that off before she sees you. I will excuse you from magic class tonight."

As Henry wrote the names of the girls, Lord Leavesden proceeded with general pleasantries, inquiring about my health and classes. I assured him all was well.

"Some of the professors have mentioned that they think you would be better off as a tutor to the other students instead of following the normal course work. Would you be interested in that?"

I nodded. "That would be preferable."

Lord Leavesden smiled. "Perhaps that can be arranged."

Henry handed him the piece of paper and stood. "I didn't get a good look, but I'm positive on these names at least."

"Thank you, Henry. You may go." Lord Leavesden eyed the paper, his lips in a thin line.

"Are you sure you're all right?" I eyed Henry doubtfully, feeling terrible that he had gotten the brunt of the vendetta against me.

"I'll be better when I get his paint off me," he said, wrinkling his nose in disgust.

"Come with me. I might have something that will help."

In my bathroom, I pulled out several different bottles of soaps for Henry to try. "Maybe if you wash your hands and see which one works, you can take the bottle back to your room and get it off the rest of your body?"

"Good idea." He nodded.

Henry lifted his shirt, revealing the toned muscles underneath. I blushed and turned away but not before noticing the words covered his stomach.

"I think every inch of my skin is covered." Henry grimaced as he pulled his shirt down.

"I'm sorry," I apologized while handing him a bottle of soap.

"It's not your fault. Don't be sorry." Henry lathered his hands in soap and attempted to wash the insults away. They didn't budge. I handed him a different bottle, and he tried again with no success. "Gods forbid, what did they put in this paint?"

"I don't think they intended it to wash off." I frowned.

Henry clenched his jaw in frustration. Something about seeing him in this predicament changed how I felt about him. I replayed the scene in my mind. Henry pushed me out of the way as the red paint drenched him, taking the fall for me. He didn't have to, but he did, knowing he didn't have time to save himself. In that moment, I realized that he didn't scare me anymore. Henry had become my friend. Someone I could rely on. I trusted him.

I pulled out Haldren's face cream. "Now, I know for a fact that this will help your face. Unfortunately, it's not intended for anywhere else." I poured a little of the green cream on my hand and rubbed it into his cheek.

Henry laughed. "It tickles."

I smiled. "Sorry, but look, the paint is gone."

He stared in the mirror; his face incredulous as he eyed the side of his cheek. "You're right." He rubbed his cheek. I poured some of the cream into his hands, and he rubbed it into his face, then watched as the paint miraculously disappeared. "Thanks." He inspected his hands. Despite touching the cream, the insults remained there.

"You're welcome. Maybe Aliyah has something better. You could ask her," I suggested.

Henry nodded.

I took a deep breath. "Henry?"

"Yes?"

Our eyes locked. "I forgive you for pushing me into the cell." The words tumbled out of me. "I'm not afraid of you anymore."

Henry's face lit up. "I feel like I've been waiting forever for you to say that." He took a deep breath and exhaled.

"Friends?"

He grinned. "I thought we already were."

"We are, but now it's official." I walked out of the bathroom. With Henry in my room, I had lit more lamps than usual, and the brightness caught me off guard.

"Isabelle."

I turned around. "Yes."

"Your room is freezing." He shivered.

"I've got blankets." I had two blankets folded neatly on the red chintz chairs.

"Is that what you've been doing to stay warm?" His face contorted in anguish.

I bit my lip and nodded slowly.

Henry rubbed his forehead and sighed heavily. "Can I try something?"

"What?" I stepped back warily, the back of my legs hitting the chair.

He stepped forward. "I want to make a fire."

My eyes darted to the empty fireplace, and I shuddered. "No."

Henry closed the gap between us. He put his hands on my shoulders and leaned down until his blue eyes met mine. "You can't spend the rest of your life afraid of fire. You'll freeze to death."

"Fire is death," I shot back.

Henry shook his head. "Not always." He reached behind me and grabbed the blanket. "What are you doing?" I heard the suspicion in my voice.

He grabbed the additional blanket resting on the other chair and held them both in his arms. "I'm taking these away."

"No, don't!" I reached for them, but he jumped out of the way.

"You can have them back when you get over your fear of fire," Henry said calmly.

I eyed him spitefully.

Henry grinned. He took the blankets and set them on my bed, closing the door behind him. I sat while he threw logs into the fireplace. My heart rate started to accelerate; despite it being freezing, my hands felt clammy. I curled up in a ball and turned my face away from the fireplace and Henry.

I heard the crackle and pop and smelled the smoke wafting off the burning wood. After a few minutes, I felt the warmth against my back, but I felt no relief. I clutched at my sides; my head buried into the back of the chair. I waited for the burning hallucinations to start.

I felt Henry touch the back of my shoulder, and I flinched.

"Gods forbid, you're shaking like a leaf." I saw him crouch beside the chair out of the corner of my eye. "Come on, Isabelle, turn around."

"No."

"Nothing is going to happen to you, I promise. Come on, you can't be afraid of this forever." Henry lightly pulled on my arm.

It took more courage than I thought I had to uncurl and face him, but I did it.

He grinned. "See, it's not so bad."

I stared at the orange flames greedily licking the wood. Henry stood and pulled me up. He guided me over to the fire. I trembled, but I fought against it. Henry had a point. I couldn't be afraid of it forever, but I didn't know how not to be.

"Put your hands out and feel the warmth." He held his hands out and sighed, a happy smile on his face.

Tentatively, I copied him. "It's warm."

"Nice, isn't it?"

I shrugged. "I guess."

Henry rolled his eyes. He picked up a piece of kindling and handed it to me. "Now put this in the fire."

I hesitated at first, but I dropped the stick into the fire. A plume of ashes rose. I took a deep breath to steady myself.

"Are you still afraid?" He asked.

"A little," I admitted.

"The only way you're going to get over it is to be around it often." He lifted the small bucket hanging on a large nail on the side of the fireplace. "Add hot coals in this and put the lid on it. In the morning use it to start another fire. If you continuously keep hot coals in this pail, you'll be able to start a fire quickly."

I nodded.

"Think you can do this?" he asked.

"I've got to try," I said.

"That's the spirit." He grinned. "I'll leave you be now."

"Henry?"

He paused by the door. "Yes?"

"Thanks. For everything."

"No problem."

As the night wore on, I found myself more grateful to Henry. I stared at the fire, forcing back the fiery hallucinations that popped into my head, and worked on a better resolve. Before I went to bed, I added hot coals to the pail just like Henry said to do. I fell asleep that night without shivering.

There was a noticeable difference in the air the following morning after news of Henry's debacle spread. The mood shifted in support of Henry over Iris and her group of jealous girls. I saw no doubt in anyone's mind who had orchestrated the assault intended for me, despite Henry and me not being vocal about who did it. By lunch it became a bit of a joke as he rolled up his sleeves and read off the more ridiculous insults.

"This one's my favorite," Henry said, pointing at the crease in his elbow. "Mifflaurd."

More than one person, including myself, furrowed their eyebrows in confusion.

"What does that mean?" Falden asked.

Henry laughed. "I have no idea, but it's funny to say it. Try it."

Everyone erupted in laughter as we all attempted to pronounce it. By the end of lunch, we decided it meant idiot or dolt. Aliyah brought a basket of soaps for Henry to try, some of them specifically made for getting paint off. Henry tried them right before dinner, but none of them worked. I worried he would wear the insults for the rest of his life.

Dinner ended up being a solemn occasion when Henry's mother arrived, her arm draped over Lord Leavesden's. The normal chatter died down to whispers. She wore an elegant lilac silk gown. A small tiara rested in her elaborately styled blonde hair. Around her neck hung a dazzling diamond necklace, and on her ears teardrop earrings. She had a ring on every finger and jeweled bracelets on both wrists. With her stoic expression and glamourous appearance, I found her intimidating.

Her blazing blue eyes swept the room, no doubt searching for Henry. Lord Leavesden leaned down and whispered something in her ear. She smiled and let go of his arm, then waltzed straight over to Henry.

"Hello, Mother." Henry smiled exuberantly, showing off his charm.

"Henry." Her voice sounded warm, and it caught me off guard. I expected it to sound lofty. On second thought, I recognized her voice. A memory flashed of Lord Leavesden speaking into a locket when I received the first note from the employer. I now understood he'd been speaking to her. "Lyle said you were covered in insults, but I had to see for myself."

At my confused expression, Aliyah whispered in my ear, "Lyle is Leavesden's first name. Henry's mother is Princess Liliana Sorren."

"Oh," I said.

Henry's mother grabbed his hand and started reading them; her eyes narrowed, and the corners of her painted lips turned into a frown. "What have you tried?"

"Everything Aliyah, Isabelle, and I had," Henry said. "I managed to get it off my face with a cream Isabelle had, but it's not intended to be used anywhere else."

Her eyes snapped to mine, but I quickly ducked my head, afraid to meet her gaze. I stared at my half-empty plate of food.

"Henry, meet me in Lyle's office after dinner," Princess Liliana ordered. "I will not let you wear those insults any longer."

Henry groaned. "Don't put me through one of your beauty regimes."

"You have no other option." Her tone gave no room for refusal. "Nice seeing you all. Aliyah, you look wonderful as always." She drifted away, clinging onto Lord Leavesden's arm. They strolled out of the room without so much as a backward glance.

Henry grimaced. "This better not take all night. I've got to get some sleep."

With the help of his mother, Henry managed to get every painted insult off. He spent the following week complaining about the torture she'd put him through. No one gave him much sympathy, stating he should be grateful to be back to normal. The girls responsible turned into the laughingstock of the school as they were forced to take on the chores the hired help normally did. Lord Leavesden made them wear the muted brown attire of the maids, and for two days they cleaned the Sorrenian instead of going to class. Incidentally, the maids enjoyed two paid days off—a rarity. I also heard that Princess Liliana put them to shame with a stern speech on proper etiquette and behavior.

Throughout all of this, I tried not to think about magic, but it nagged in the back of my mind incessantly. It had been made perfectly clear to me that I could not get rid of it. I figured I had to do something—tame the wild beast despite my loathing. With Malsin gone to the healers convention, I had no one to teach me. I hated sitting around doing nothing about it.

On Kings Day, I voiced my frustrations to Henry in the library. After spending most of First through Fifth Day watching him leave for a magic class that I couldn't be a part of, I decided I would try it out on my own. Henry studied for an upcoming land and business management test while I perused the stacks of books for something to read.

"Where's the section on magic in here?" I sat next to Henry.

"You tell me which vegetables cross-pollinate, and I'll tell you." He twiddled a pen between his fingers. He had a large square on his worksheet where he had to plot a successful garden by writing down the names of each plant and how much space it needed. The professor docked points if we planted noncompatible plants together.

"Do not put pumpkins next to your zucchini."

"But they're both a squash," he argued. "They should like being around family."

"They may cross-pollinate, and you won't get the desired shape or taste."

He scratched out the word pumpkin and wrote it on the opposite side of his chart.

"Now will you tell me where the magic section is?" I questioned.

Henry put down his pen, clasped his hands together, and crossed his ankles. "Why?"

"I'm going to teach myself, that's why. Malsin's not due back yet," I explained, frustration leaking out of my voice.

"How much did you learn with Malsin? Did you find out what color you are?" He put a hand on his chin, the other leaning against the armrest.

"No. We got interrupted when he tried to teach me." I frowned. "Every time I attempt to find out, it flashes between all of them. It hasn't decided."

"Or you're all of them," Henry perceived.

"I don't know." I bit my lip, feeling unsure.

"You have the Mark of the Gods on your hand. It's entirely possible that they messed with your magic. Gave you more power or something." He gestured to my birthmark.

I quickly hid my left hand from view, an automatic reaction when anyone acknowledged it. "Maybe."

"I think there's something special about you. Something you just don't know yet." He leaned forward as he spoke.

His words reminded me too much of Haldren. I scoffed. "And you're going to tell me what it is?"

Henry shook his head. "No. I haven't a clue."

I got up. "Well, if you're not going to tell me, then I will go searching myself."

Henry shot up from his chair. "Now wait a second. I never said I wouldn't help you."

"So you will?"

"You're not going to find what you're looking for here. The professors don't just hand out magic books freely," he said.

"Why not?" I put my hands on my hips.

"Ever wonder why I don't do magic all the time?" Henry folded his arms.

"No," I answered truthfully.

He raised his eyebrows. "Really?"

"Really."

"Well, there's a catch." He fidgeted on the balls of his feet. "We aren't supposed to do magic outside of class."

"Why not?" I folded my arms.

"Because not all of the students have that ability, and they consider it an unfair advantage." He shrugged. "I could do some serious damage with a wave of my hand," Henry said smugly.

"I see." I bit my lip, frowning. "And no one thought to tell me this because ..."

"It probably slipped Malsin's mind, and you haven't exactly been eager to try it out." Henry crossed his arms over his chest, calling me out.

His perceptiveness reminded me of Andrew. I wondered if the royal line had some extra sense that came with their intense blue eyes.

"But one hour First through Fifth day can't be enough to learn everything there is to know about magic," I argued, fidgeting on the balls of my feet.

He nodded in agreement. "It isn't. Most people who have the ability go on to hire a private tutor or go to a secondary school specifically for mages." His expression turned serious. "Those who have tried to fumble their way through it without help generally get into trouble."

I narrowed my eyes at him. *I never fumble anything.* "So what should I do?"

Henry pursed his lips and scrunched his eyes in thought. "All right. You convinced me."

"Convinced you to do what?" I asked slowly.

"I'll teach you." He smiled, pointing to himself.

My jaw dropped slightly in spontaneous surprise. "You will?"

"It must be kept quiet, though. I can't afford to get into trouble again." He glanced furtively around him, but we were alone.

I nodded. "All right. When do you want to start?"

"How about you help me with my homework, and I'll teach you a little of the basics," he proposed. "Enough that you won't kill yourself at least."

"Deal." I stuck out my hand. "Now hand me your paper, and I'll fill it out."

Henry grinned and reached for his paper. "This is going to be great."

CHAPTER TWENTY-SEVEN

WITHIN FIVE MINUTES I completed Henry's garden plot. "Study this and you won't fail the test." I handed it back to him.

"You're so gracious." He accepted the paper. "All right let's get out of here." Henry shoved the paper into his bag and slung it over his shoulder. "We're going to need a place to practice."

"What about my room?" I suggested.

Henry shook his head. "No, too many people walk down that hallway. Someone would eventually notice."

"What did you have in mind?" I knew he could be inventive when he wanted to be.

"What about an old classroom? There are a few that aren't in use right now. We could go check some of those out," he suggested.

I smiled and gestured to the door. "Lead the way."

As it was one of the last sunny days to be enjoyed, few students and professors roamed the halls. Henry's normal entourage—Dominic, Falden, and Aliyah—along with most of students, had left for Kings and Gods Day to visit their families. Henry and I just happened to be the lucky ones with family too busy for casual company.

I felt apprehensive about practicing magic and tried to push those feelings aside. *I need to learn this,* I thought vehemently. To get over my aversion, I tried thinking about it as a defensive tactic, like fencing. I reasoned with myself that magic had saved my life in the past, and I could use it against an enemy. Maybe if I knew enough, I wouldn't have to go to Joshua for help. I could take care of myself.

Since I'd kept Joshua's counsel and remained in the school, only going out when I had class, I hadn't come across anything suspicious. His plan may have been working but I didn't expect it to last.

Henry led us to an old classroom in a part of the school I hadn't been around much. Dusty chairs and tables squished together along the side of the wall, and a few small windows let in bright sunlight. Henry pulled the drapes over them, shrouding the room in dim light.

"This should work." He surveyed the room, hands on hips. He pulled two chairs out of the tangle and dragged them to the center of the room.

"All right, show me what you got." Henry sat.

I sat in the adjacent chair. "The only thing I've done so far is open it up."

"Show me," he urged.

I took a deep breath and opened my hand, palm facing up. "Spintry."

A flame spontaneously appeared, rapidly changing colors.

Henry surveyed it. He opened his hand, and immediately a blue flame appeared without him saying a word. "This is how it should look. One flame with one color."

"I've tried focusing on one color. Like this." I thought blue, and the flame instantly switched, identical to Henry's. "But the second I think about another color, it switches." I wished for the flame to be red. "See, now it's red. When I don't focus on one color, it flashes through all of them at random."

"Hmm ..." He made a fist, and the blue flame vanished. "What we need to do is look at your mage core. I need to see it."

"I don't know how to access it," I confessed. "I found it once, accidentally, while Malsin healed me."

"Well, you're about to learn." Henry grinned and leaned forward. "Put your hand in a fist and wish for the flame to disappear; then close your eyes and try to clear your mind. Got that?"

I followed Henry's instructions exactly. The flame disappeared, and I worked on clearing my mind by imagining a blank sheet of paper. I took a deep breath and exhaled. "Got it."

"All right, now only think about your magic, and build up a desire to see it. Imagine the swirls of color like the flame in your hand and ask it to show itself," Henry directed.

I imagined the flame in my hand and its rapidly changing colors and built up a desire. *Let me see you.*

In my mind's eye, I transported into my mage core. I stood inside a large glass sphere, brightly glowing swirls of colored smoky ribbon spiraled around me, exactly how I remembered it. I could feel myself sitting in the hard chair next to Henry, but I could also see my entire body inside the magical core. Maybe I was in two places at once? I didn't know what to make of it.

"Can you see it?" Henry asked.

"Yes." I touched the ribbons, and they seeped into my skin like they had done before.

"Now take my hand, and wish for me to see it," he instructed.

Henry clasped his hand in mine, and I immediately thought how soft it felt compared to Andrew's. *Focus,* I reminded myself. *Show Henry.* I thought of nothing else as I wished for him to see what I saw.

Henry materialized in front of me inside the glass sphere. I jumped and gasped.

"Wow, it worked!" He grinned.

I narrowed my eyes at him. "I take it you've never done this before?"

He shook his head. "No. But I've read about it. It's not done very often. Most people find it invasive." He started walking around, gawking at the swirls of red, yellow, green, and blue. "I can't believe this is your mage core. This is crazy!" He ran a lap around the sphere, his hands out touching all the colors. I noticed that only the blue smoky ribbons seeped into his skin and made his hand glow as it recognized the connecting magic.

I laughed, his enthusiasm infectious. "It's pretty, isn't it?" I touched a red ribbon as it swirled past. My hand glowed red for a second.

"Pretty? It's astounding!" Henry exclaimed. He rested his hands on top of his head. He turned around in a circle, his eyes wide in bewilderment.

"My mage core is nothing like this. I only get blue." He dropped his hands to his sides.

"So, what can you do in here?" I asked, walking around, and touching the ribbons.

"Oh, right." He rubbed his forehead. "I forgot I was here for a reason. This is so awesome!" Henry ran over to me. "You enter your mage core to check your levels. See how much magic you have available and when you need to recharge."

"Recharge?" I wanted more of an explanation.

"Yeah. Since I'm blue, and that is associated with the element of water, when my levels are low, I go to a water source and draw the energy out, which fills up my mage core and enables me to practice magic," he explained.

"So how do I check mine?"

"You ask." He shrugged. "Tell your magic you want to check your levels."

"All right. I'm going to try it." I fidgeted on the balls of my feet and shook out my hands. *Magic levels.* I focused my thoughts on a physical representation of the magic. *Show me, please.*

Four glass balls materialized out of thin air and hovered at eye level. A layer of colored sand resided in each, filled to the halfway mark.

"Wow—this is unbelievable!" Henry practically bounced with excitement.

I stepped forward and grabbed a glass ball filled with green sand, feeling the weight of the sand inside. It felt real, tangible, and heavy. The glass, originally cold to the touch, warmed with the heat from my fingers.

Henry stood next to me. "If you were at full power, the ball would be completely filled with sand, not an empty space visible." He scrutinized the rest of them hovering in midair. "It looks like you're about halfway right now."

"Why? I haven't used it except to open and close it a few times with Malsin."

Henry furrowed his eyebrows and rubbed his chin. "When you first activate your magic—like the first time ever—it uses at least a quarter of your power. Plus, you had that magic light show, and while I don't know for sure, it looked like something else was going on too. Am I right?"

I nodded but didn't want to go into details of the images that flashed in my mind when the magic activated. "And what happens when it's empty?" I let go of the ball. It zoomed back in place, suspended at eye level.

"You die. You absolutely cannot empty all your magic." Henry spoke in a clear and firm tone. "You'll start to feel it, though, when your levels are low. You'll feel tired like you haven't slept in ages, and your body will ache. Kind of like the start of the flu."

"So, I get somewhat of a warning then," I commented drily, eyeing the colored balls of sand.

"Yes." He nodded, shoving his hands in his pockets. "Usually, when I start to feel sick, I check my power levels first. If they are low, then I'll recharge. If I feel sick and my levels are high, then I know I've caught a bug, and that's when I go to Malsin."

"I'll keep that in mind." I held on to the glass ball filled with red sand and twirled it between my hands. "So, now what?" I glanced at Henry. He had picked up the one containing the yellow sand and studied it intensely.

"We test it out." He let go of the ball and watched it float back into place. He faced me with a wicked grin as he rubbed his hands together. "I can't wait to see what you can do."

"Oh, come on, you're looking at me like I'm a science experiment." I lightly shoved him, letting go of the ball of red sand.

Henry stumbled backward with a laugh. "So what? This is completely uncharted waters here. I would kill to have this much power." He gestured to the four glass balls filled with colored sand. He sighed heavily. "All right. Time to head back to reality. Focus on the classroom and you'll be there."

In the classroom, I felt Henry let go of my hand. In the mage core, I watched him dematerialize. I focused on the hard chair underneath me, wishing to be there instead of the mage core. I held my hands out in front of my face and observed myself dissolve. *Crazy.* I shivered. When I opened my eyes, Henry wore the most exhilarated expression I had ever seen. It made me laugh.

"That is an experience I will never forget." Henry stood and stretched.

"Gods forbid, I feel stiff." I held my arms out away from me as I stood.

"Yeah, that happens. Sorry, should have warned you." He rubbed the back of his neck. "Time doesn't mean much in the mage core, and you can spend hours in there without even realizing it." He slung his bag over his shoulder. "We better get out of here before someone comes looking for us."

"Good idea," I agreed.

I walked out of the classroom pleased and grateful that Henry had agreed to teach me. I knew it was only the beginning, but I felt like I had accomplished something. From here on out, my knowledge of magic would only expand.

I didn't sleep much that night and woke every couple of hours. My brain wouldn't shut off as I pondered the possibilities of magic. By the time dawn approached, I decided to stop trying and got out of bed.

I roamed the cold halls seeking Henry's room. I shivered, wishing I would have brought a sweater. I found a sign directing me to the boys' sleeping quarters, but I didn't know which one belonged to Henry. I had just decided to chance it and knock on a random door when I saw Ethan, a boy from class, and asked him for directions. He pointed to a door farther down the hall.

I knocked on Henry's door and waited, rubbing my arms to stave off the cold. I hoped he had a fire going in his room. When he didn't answer, I knocked again. A minute later Henry opened the door, bleary-eyed, his hair ruffled. He wore a dark blue robe, hastily tied.

He rubbed his eyes. "Isabelle?"

I grinned. "Payback. I can't sleep, so neither are you."

Henry ran a hand through his hair, his expression sour, and muttered something unintelligible. He opened the door wide for me to come in.

I stepped into Henry's room. The setup was identical to mine but decorated in dark blue instead of crimson red. His stuff was scattered about—piles of papers rested on his desk with boots kicked off by the fireplace. His school bag spilled out on a blue chintz chair. The King's crest, embroidered on a flag hung over the mantelpiece, caught my attention.

"All right, what's so important that you had to wake me before dawn?" Henry appeared more awake by the second but unhappy about it.

"Magic." I crossed my arms. "I need to know more."

He rubbed his temples. "And you couldn't wait just a few more hours?"

I pretended to inspect my fingernails. "Of course not."

Henry sighed. "Fine. Let me get dressed."

I moved his school bag off the chair and sat. The minutes ticked by slowly; I tapped my foot impatiently against the blue rug.

"You take longer than I do, and I'm the girl," I called to Henry through the closed bathroom door.

"It's easier to get ready when you're actually awake," he called back.

He came out of the bathroom, his wet hair pushed back and his eyes bright, smelling like soap and pine. He rummaged around his room, shoving stuff into a bag so fast I didn't catch what he put in there.

"All right, let's go." Henry slung the bag over his shoulder.

We headed off to the abandoned classroom, not passing a single soul. The anticipation I felt heated my skin, and I didn't feel as cold when we entered the room.

Henry's face lit up with excitement as he rubbed his hands together, all drowsiness evaporated. "Time for action."

"Don't get too excited." I laughed. "I might accidently blow something up."

"You?" He shook his head. "Nah ... You'll do fine. Besides, I brought a few things for you to work on." Henry dragged a table to the middle of the room, and then he opened his bag and brought out an assortment of items. A wooden bowl, a small jug of water, a stick, and a knife.

"What's this?" I asked, picking up the stick.

"That's a stick," Henry said pointedly.

I rolled my eyes. "I know. I mean what do you plan to use it for?"

"We're going to use it to test stuff with," he said.

"All right." I set the stick down.

Henry sat on the table, letting his legs dangle, and started explaining. "All right, so you know each color is associated with an element, but they are also particularly good at one other thing." He held up a finger and counted them off. "Blue creates, red destroys, green heals, and yellow is camouflage. We're going to test all of those with these items." He pointed to the array of supplies next to him.

"Show me an example." I leaned against the table, arms folded.

Henry jumped off the table and poured a little water into the bowl. His hand took on a subtle blue glow that I wouldn't have noticed if I hadn't been looking for it. He lifted his hand over the bowl and waved upward. As he did so, the water froze, and an iced horse figurine rose out of the bowl.

I stared intently. "Wow." I touched it, feeling the hard ice, and quickly brought my hand back. "Brr that's cold."

"Cool huh?" Henry grinned. He waved his hand over the ice figurine. It melted into the water with a splash and spilled onto the table.

"I want to do that," I said, eager to create something just as beautiful. I pointed a finger at him. "But first, you've got to teach me how to open up my magic without speaking out loud."

"You just have to focus mentally on it, like really hard. Don't let any kind of errant thought enter your head, and you'll have it open." Henry shoved his hands in his pockets. "So ... basically think *Spintry* in your mind and focus on it, building up a desire to use it. It's the same thing with closing it. Think *Findel* and focus on making it go away. You have to remember that magic is based on desires and focus."

"All right." I nodded, shaking out my hands as I mentally prepared myself.

"It also likes encouragement and will sometimes respond better to small nudges than a flat-out command, which may come off as too harsh," Henry said.

"Now you're making it complicated," I complained, flipping my hair over my shoulder.

"Magic is complicated," he shot back. "There is so much about it that we don't even know and limitless potential. You ready to try it out?"

I took a deep breath and tried my best to clear my mind of any errant thoughts. I kept my lips compressed as I mentally focused on opening the mage core within me. I could tell the second it worked; I felt a buzz of new energy flow freely through my veins. "Got it!" I shook my hands out and bounced on the balls of my feet, a silly smile resting on my face.

"Just for practice's sake, you might want to try it again. This could have been beginner's luck." Henry grabbed a chair and sat, crossing his legs.

"Right," I agreed.

I closed my eyes and centered my thoughts on shutting it down. Suddenly a memory of Haldren popped into my mind, and I recalled him saying magic was like a pet—a dog to be specific. It seemed natural to picture the magic as Boomer, the stray black-and-white dog that nearly scared me to death when I ran from Saren. *Now what?* I thought about what I would do with the real Boomer and led him to a thick, strong, wooden crate. I went to close the door. Boomer yelped softly, and I got the distinct impression that the magic didn't want to be locked up.

I opened one eye and glanced at Henry. "What happens when it doesn't want to stay put?"

Henry rolled his eyes. "You imagined it as a pet, didn't you? What is it? A cat, a dog, bird?"

I opened both eyes, feeling guilty. Was it wrong to picture it as an animal? "A dog. Boomer, the stray in Saren."

Henry uncrossed his legs and leaned back in the chair. "Really? I expected you to be more of a cat person. It'd match your feisty personality."

"It wasn't me who suggested that magic was like a dog," I muttered, crossing my arms.

"Who did?" He eyed me perceptively.

I shifted on the balls of my feet. "It doesn't matter. Just tell me what to do, will you?"

Henry grinned and gestured to me. "You're the master; don't let it run all over you. You wouldn't let a real dog get away with it, so don't let your magic do it either."

I nodded. "Right."

It surprised me how easily I pictured the magic taking on the form of Boomer again. He stayed right where I left him, in the crate with the door swung open. He wagged his tail excitedly, eager to come out and play. Except this time, I knew I had to be firm. I closed the door and latched it, thinking *Findel* as I did so. Boomer and the crate disappeared, and I felt the buzz of magic drain out of my veins. I had shut the magic off.

I took a deep breath and exhaled. I leaned against the table, my hands resting behind me. "I did it. I was firm."

Henry grinned. "Good." He stood and leaned against the table. Crossing his arms, he glanced at me. "Now open it again."

I didn't think I could picture the magic as anything else but Boomer now. I imagined the large, fluffy black-and-white dog in the crate. His chocolate-brown eyes stared at me forlornly, and he yelped. I undid the latch, thinking *Spintry* like it was a password to open the crate. Boomer jumped out of the crate, wagging his tail excitedly, and jumped up and down. I chuckled softly, feeling the buzz return.

"Got it." I grinned.

"You want to know what I picture my magic as?" Henry asked.

"What?"

"A falcon."

I gasped. "Oh! And you made me feel like an idiot for picturing a dog!" I briefly contemplated shoving him but then wondered if my magic would react.

Henry laughed, completely oblivious to my musing. I rolled my eyes and chuckled, deciding I'd ask about that later.

He moved to the other side of the table. "Which one do you want to try out?"

"How about the blue? I want to make an ice sculpture like you did." I pointed to the bowl of water. "Do I still need to focus on keeping it open when I want to try something?"

"No. It's like a water faucet. You turn it on, use what you want, then shut it off. Pretty simple." He shrugged.

I sighed in relief. "Good, because that would be too much to handle."

"Yes," Henry agreed, rubbing his forehead. "It would give you a headache to focus on both at the same time. That's why it's easy to associate an animal as your magic—something you can lock in a cage. Nearly everyone does it. Dominic pictures a red fox, and I think Aliyah's is a butterfly."

"And you the falcon," I said, resting my hands on the table.

Henry nodded. "Yes."

It's no wonder Haldren said magic was like a pet if everyone pictured one to turn on or off their magic.

"All right. Here goes nothing." I placed my hand over the bowl of rippling water and took a deep breath. My hand pulsed, taking on a subtle blue glow as I thought about using the blue magic. I felt a surge of productiveness, an eagerness to create and keep on creating forever. My feelings raced ahead of my mind, yearning to be useful. I enjoyed it.

I pictured Nisha in my mind. His strong, muscular black body, the white swirl in between his eyes, and his flowing black mane. His proud posture and his loyalty. I stared at the still, clear water. Not even a ripple formed. I sent the mental picture of Nisha to the water, desiring it to form into an iced replica.

I watched, amazed, as the water started to ice over. "It's working!"

"Don't lose your focus." Henry leaned forward and gripped the table, his eyes bright with excitement.

I nodded and continued my trail of thoughts, imagining Nisha. I put a little more force behind my desire. *Come on,* I egged the magic on, my brows furrowed in concentration as I lifted my hand up over the water. The ice started to grow.

The water froze over until a replica of Nisha formed. One foot on the ground and the other pawing at the air in a proud stance. I put my hand down and rested it on the table, exhilarated.

"Incredible," I whispered, my eyes fixated on the glistening ice.

"That's some good detail there," Henry complimented. "You even got the swirl right." He pointed to Nisha's head.

"Hey, you ever notice that the swirl matches that part on your birth-mark?" Henry asked.

Of course I had. "We were meant for each other."

"Maybe." Henry came around to my side of the table. "I think it's safe to say that you have blue magic in you. Should we try something else?"

"Sure," I readily agreed.

"Why don't we try red? Reds are great at destroying things. They can form a fireball in their hands." He cupped his hands together.

"A fireball?" Fire left me with mixed feelings as I continued to work hard to not be afraid of it but hadn't quite removed all traces of my fear.

"Yes." Henry nodded, letting his hands fall to his sides. "King Brian prefers to have Reds in his army. They rise quickly through the ranks because of their special destructive abilities."

"Which would partly explain why Joshua is a commander," I said, biting my lip.

"Not just *a* commander. He's *the* Commander," Henry corrected. "Youngest one we've had in about a century."

"Youngest, really?"

He nodded.

"So, what did you have in mind?" I put a hand on my hip. "I can't go destroying tables and chairs in here." I gestured to the stacked chairs. "Unless we want to be discovered."

Henry frowned and tapped the side of his cheek. "Right." He thought for a minute. "Why don't you try conjuring a fireball and throw it at the horse sculpture? It won't destroy anything major."

I pursed my lips and glanced at the sculpture. "I guess I've got nothing to lose; the ice is bound to melt anyway."

"Exactly," he agreed.

"How do I to create a fireball? That sounds a little more difficult than making water freeze over."

Henry shrugged. "Can't help you there, I'm not a Red." He put a hand on his chin. "What about thinking about fire?" he suggested.

I grimaced but couldn't think of another option. If I wanted a fireball, I would have to think about fire. It seemed like the logical solution. I held my hand out, palm facing up, and closed my eyes. *Think hot.* I flinched when the haunting images of a burning village immediately flew into my mind, but I pushed them back. *You're not hurting me today.*

Henry put a hand on my shoulder. "You can do this," he encouraged.

I felt invigorated. I took a deep breath and bounced on my feet, shaking off the bad feelings. I let myself truly feel the magic coursing through my veins. Henry stepped away from me.

One fireball, coming up. This time, when I thought hot, I felt strong and fierce as though I'd been coated in a powerful body armor. I didn't feel domineering but protected. It surprised me to think of fire as a protection instead of a destroyer, but I liked it. I wondered how differently the attack in the forest would have gone if I had felt this way. Would the men have gone near me if I carried a fireball in my hands?

I nudged the buzz of magic, sending it my thoughts and desires. Slowly, I directed it to what I wanted. *Give me fire.*

"I think you got it," Henry said in approval.

"Really?" I opened one eye and peeked. A small flaming ball fit in the center of my right palm. "I'm on fire!" Instinct kicked in as I jumped and shook out my hand. The fireball didn't budge, blazing in hues of red and orange.

Henry held up his hands. "Whoa there. It's not burning you, is it?"

I froze, feeling like an idiot. "No." I brought my hand up to eye level. "I feel no pain."

"You shouldn't. It's magical." Henry laughed, folding his arms. "Make it a little bigger."

I narrowed my eyes at the flame and ordered it to grow. The flame doubled in size until it covered my entire palm.

He grinned. "That's what I'm talking about. Show me some fire!" he said enthusiastically, pumping his fist into the air.

"Keep your voice down; you're going to get us caught," I scolded with a grin.

He mockingly put a hand over his mouth.

I took a few steps back. "All right, Henry, watch out. I'm aiming for the ice sculpture."

Henry hastily stepped out of the firing range and hovered by my left side. I swung my right arm back and threw, centering my thoughts on its destination. The fireball hit the sculpture and exploded. Pieces of ice flew across the room. We dropped to the floor. Henry threw his hands up, creating a shimmering blue shield that blocked us from the shards of ice.

"Whoa," I said breathlessly. "I figured it would melt, not explode."

Henry laughed. "I think you put a little too much power in that one."

"Oops." I shrugged guiltily.

He shrugged. "Don't worry about it. We can cross red off your list. Only got two more to try."

We stood and assessed the damage. Pieces of ice melted on the floor, creating puddles of water. Surprisingly, the bowl was still intact, just slightly singed.

"It might be a little slippery, but I think we're good," I said with an uncertain smile.

"Let's do green next," Henry said. "We need a little healing after all that destruction."

"Green is healing," I repeated, remembering.

Henry picked up the knife and twiddled it between his fingers.

I shook my head and crossed my arms, realizing his intentions. "Don't even think about it."

"Come on," he argued, brandishing the knife. "You'll be able to heal it in a second."

"I can't ask you to cut yourself just to see if I can fix it or not."

"You're not asking. I'm doing," Henry said, determination leaking through his voice.

I opened my mouth to argue, but Henry moved too fast. Using the tip, he sliced into the palm of his hand without so much as a flinch. I raised my eyebrows in surprise. *Wow, he handles pain well,* I thought with admiration. A trickle of blood oozed, dripping down the palm of his hand and onto the floor. He set the knife down, tinged red, and held out his palm.

"Heal it."

I frowned but grabbed his hand. The second my skin touched his, the green magic within me reacted. Sensing the injury, it rose eagerly, flooding me with intense adrenaline and power. I gasped. My heart raced as I drowned in an uncontrollable urge to heal. Everything came into sharp focus as I saw through the eyes of healing magic. I didn't have to look to know all of Henry's issues. I felt them as though they were my own: a ghost of his pain.

Besides the cut he inflicted on himself, I knew he had a bruise on his left thigh. I remembered accidentally smacking him with a staff on Fifth Day. His muscles were stiff and tense, and I became just as rigid. I felt his lack of sleep acutely and the subtle throb of a headache. I heard and felt his heart beating strong, and I knew if I centered my thoughts on it, I could see it just as I could see and feel every part of his body. Every bone, organ, and vein. Nothing could hide from my view.

I discovered all of this within seconds as I let the green magic dominate. Without warning the magic surged, taking me to where it saw the most damage—Henry's sliced palm. I imagined the skin sewing itself together, meshing to become whole and clean. The magic responded enthusiastically, and I watched wide-eyed as the cut disappeared, leaving behind a dried bloodstain.

I couldn't stop it from jumping to the next issue: Henry's bruise. Once it healed that, it raced to ease the throbbing headache. Even if I wanted to, I knew I didn't have the strength to stop it from healing every inch of Henry's body.

I felt an intense wave of disappointment emanating from the green magic when it ran out of things to heal. My breath caught in surprise, and a tear leaked out of my eye as the strong emotions consumed me. I let go of his hand. The feelings vanished as I stumbled backward. I leaned heavily on the table, taking in large gulps of air. I hadn't realized I'd been holding my breath.

Henry held up his hand and inspected it. "Good as new. Thanks."

There was an awkward pause as I thought about what to say.

Comprehension dawned on me as I thought about Andrew's inability to stop healing me when I nearly died due to the burns and poison. How much worse had it been for him? Henry's issues seemed inconsequential to the injuries I had sustained, and yet I couldn't stop the green from taking over. How did Malsin do it?

"If this is how Malsin feels when he has his magic opened, then I am truly amazed at the control he has." I shuddered. "I'd prefer not to have to use that one until Malsin can train me. Otherwise, I might accidently heal more than I can handle."

"Good point." Henry nodded. He poured a little water into the bowl and dipped his hand in it, washing off the dried bloodstains.

"How's your head by the way?" I smiled.

He grinned. "Better, thanks."

"You ready for the last one?" I asked.

Henry shook the water off his wet hands and bounced excitedly. "We saved the best one for last."

"Yellow is camouflage, but what does that mean exactly?" I furrowed my eyebrows in thought, then folded my arms.

Henry sat on the edge of the table, his legs swinging back and forth. "Yellow is tricky. It's rarer than the other colors and easily manipulated by egotism. It's the one color that's always vying for an easy way out. That's why you catch most yellows in trouble with the law. 'Distract and steal' should be its slogan. I'm sure it has other qualities, but I don't know them. We haven't had a yellow here in ages, and since they have such a bad rap for being thieves, those who do possess the ability are loath to admit it."

"I see." I paced back and forth. "I'm sure there's a redeeming quality somewhere. It can't only want to break the law."

Henry picked up the stick. "I thought we'd try something easy. Turn the stick into something, or make it disappear. I'm not sure."

I grabbed the stick from Henry's hand and inspected it. "Take the camouflage thing literally?"

"Right." He nodded.

"All right. Hold out your hand." I passed the stick back to Henry.

He held the stick out in front of him as I turned my attention to it. First, I focused on bringing the yellow magic up to the surface using thoughts and desires of disappearing. It wasn't that long ago that I tried to blend into the walls using the soundest logic I knew. *Can't hurt what you can't see.* The yellow magic within me flared, filling me with a strong feeling of—superiority? Surprised at the word choice, I couldn't think of another word to describe it. Confidence and sly recklessness boosted my self-esteem to the point that I didn't recognize myself in the throng of feelings.

I took a step backward and held my hand out to halt. My eyebrows mashed together. "Wait."

"What's wrong?" Henry stared at me with concern.

I shuddered. "I don't like the emotions the yellow magic is giving me. I can't find myself in them."

"What's it feel like?" Henry twiddled with the stick between his fingers.

"Undiluted power, like nothing can stand in my way." I clutched at my sides. "I don't like it." Fear crept up on me, and I felt the magic surge wildly for control. My breathing wavered as I tried to rein it in, but I felt off-balance. A small part of me wanted to let the yellow magic take over, consume me in the same way the green magic did. I stared at my hands, watching them glow bright yellow, then dim as it fluctuated with my warring emotions.

"Then shut it off," Henry said.

I closed my eyes and focused on shutting it down. The magic—Boomer—ran wildly with no conscience. It took a few tries for me to lock him up in his cage, but I did it. I sighed with relief and stumbled over to the chair, then sat.

"You all right?" Henry asked with worry.

"Yeah. I just need a minute." I took several deep breaths to calm down.

"Want to talk about it?" Henry pulled a chair closer to me and sat.

I rubbed my forehead, shading my eyes from view. "What do you do when the magic makes you feel and want things that go against your nature?" I didn't want to feel superior and cocky.

Henry pursed his lips, deep in thought. He leaned back, and his startling blue eyes caught mine. "Magic cannot make you feel something that you don't or haven't felt on some level. Everyone has a dark side, whether they want to admit it or not. The point is to not let it control you. Take what it gives you, and mold it into something good. Don't ever use magic for something you wouldn't be proud of."

I let that sink in.

Henry picked up the stick. "Now, all we're trying to do is make a stick disappear. I don't consider that too devious." He smirked. "Unless you keep it camouflaged and trip people with it."

That did it. I laughed. "I know a few people I wouldn't mind tripping." Not so long ago, Henry would have been on that list. It amazed me how much had changed in a few short weeks.

"You want to try again?" He held the stick out in front of him.

"Yes." One moment of pure focus, and Boomer jumped out of the cage. With Henry's perspective in my thoughts, I handled the surge of emotions better as I brought the yellow magic up to the surface.

I narrowed my eyes on the stick, noticing the exposed smooth wood grains next to the few patches of rough bark making up the outer layer.

I bit my lip, unsure as I concentrated. *Blend in ... please?*

Half of the stick dissolved in Henry's hand.

"Well, you got half of it." He eyed it. "See if you can get the other half."

I built up a stronger desire, feeling bolder as the seconds ticked by. I didn't let the fear get to me this time; instead, I focused on crafting my emotions into something useful. Fear couldn't be a part of that. *Hide.*

The stick completely dissolved into Henry's hand.

"Is it still there?" I asked, leaning forward.

Henry closed his hand and opened it. "I can still feel it, but I can't see it. Crazy!" He laughed. "See for yourself."

I reached for Henry's open palm and touched the rough bark. My eyes didn't register it, but there could be no mistake that it lay in his hand. "Wow, that's incredible."

"Now let's see it again," Henry instructed.

I let go of the stick and refocused my thoughts on Henry's seemingly empty hand, recalling a desire to be seen and cherished. I inflated the yellow magic's ego, giving in to the strong emotions I rejected earlier and directing them to the invisible stick. Slowly it started to reveal itself, glowing in a yellow hue before returning to normal.

Henry put the stick back on the table. "You created an ice sculpture, then made a fireball and destroyed it. You healed a cut on my hand and made a stick disappear and reappear. I think it's safe to say that you possess all the abilities of the four colors." He paused for a second and grinned. "You are a rainbow. The first of its category."

I sighed. "Well, they got half of it right, then."

"Half?"

I smiled. "Yeah. I'm not a soul-sucking monster, but I do have rainbow powers."

Henry laughed. "Right." He got up and started putting everything back in his bag.

I spent a moment focused on shutting down the magic. I'd used enough of it today. I led Boomer inside his crate, thinking *Findel* as I latched it shut. I breathed an easy sigh of relief when I watched the crate disappear as the magic became dormant.

As we walked out of the old classroom, I turned to Henry and asked a question on my mind. "This magic I have, how much interest to do you think it would garner?"

"Tons," Henry said with certainty. "With a bit of training you could be the most sought-after mage alive."

"I see." Unease coiled in my gut. I thought of the employer.

Henry lightly nudged my arm. "Hey, it's your magic. You choose what you want to do with it."

I nodded.

CHAPTER TWENTY-EIGHT

THINK THERE'S ONLY ONE thing left to teach you, and then you'll have the basics down," Henry said, straightening up.

"What's that?" I asked, moving out of a stretch.

We stretched in Professor Trisgeld's class, First Day afternoon. The weather had been rainy with cold gusts of wind, so all outside classes had either been moved indoors or canceled, like horseback riding. We shared the space with Professor Lildren and his class. One half sparred; the other half stretched.

"How to charge your mage core." Henry grabbed his foot. "Once you learn that, you'll know enough to continue testing out your abilities. I'll come get you tonight."

I copied his move. "Great."

Lord Leavesden handed me a note that evening during dinner informing me of Malsin's delay due to the bad weather. He would not be arriving until it cleared. It would have been frustrating had Henry not opted to teach me.

Henry, Dominic, Aliyah, and Falden came to my room after their magic class. I raised an eyebrow in question, having only expected Henry.

Henry shrugged and said, "They caught me on my way out, and I couldn't shake them off." His expression turned apologetic. "I sort of told them that we had spent the last two days testing out your abilities."

"You told them everything, I take it?" I folded my arms.

"Four colors?" Dominic shook his head in disbelief. "Gods forbid, no wonder you turned into a light show."

Falden and Aliyah nodded in agreement while Henry rolled his eyes. "They know."

I took a breath and eyed the three newcomers. "All right, but you come by your own free will and choice. If something crazy happens, you can't blame me."

"We understand," Falden said.

"We're still coming," Aliyah said.

"I'm not missing this," Dominic said.

"I told them the same thing on our way here." Henry appraised me. "Dress warm, we're going outside."

"In this weather?" I raised an eyebrow.

"It's the perfect kind of weather to recharge with water. Easy access," Henry pointed out.

I grabbed my jacket, which was draped over a chair, and pulled it on. The halls were sparse with people. With Henry leading us, no one even gave us a second glance. I quickly realized being the stepson to Lord Leavesden and second in line to the throne came with a lot of perks.

The wind howled in the dark sky when we stepped outside. Trees swayed back and forth. The last of the golden leaves rustled loudly. The rain showered us with heavy, fat droplets. We sprinted to a gazebo barely distinguishable in the downpour.

"Whew, it's really storming out there!" Henry shouted to be heard over the wind as he pulled his hood back.

"You think?" I said sarcastically. I wrapped my arms over my chest, shivering against the biting wind. I noticed Dominic and Falden doing the same.

"Oh, come on, a little rain won't hurt anybody. Lighten up a little. Live in the moment." Henry stood behind Aliyah and wrapped his arms around her to keep her warm. If possible, I think she shivered more than I did. The happy grin she wore on her face told me she thought coming was worth it.

I pulled down my hood. "All right, all right."

Dominic and Falden sat on the bench and shoved their hands in their pockets. They kept silent but watched with interest.

Henry shifted his weight from side to side as he spoke, using the movement to keep warm. "So, to recharge, all you have to do is touch the element you are associated with and let it soak in. With your magic activated of course."

"Could you explain that a little better?" I mirrored his movements as I fought to stay warm. "That's not much to go on."

"Touch the element and draw it to you. Focus on it filling you up. Like—" He paused, seeming to search for the right analogy. "Drinking a cup of water or something. Your magic will respond to the element like a thirsty man in a desert. Once you think you're completely charged, drop down into your core to check," Henry explained, rubbing his hands over Aliyah's arms.

"That's a better explanation. Thanks," I said.

"Once you do it, you'll understand. You ready to try it out?"

I nodded but then realized he probably couldn't see that very well, so I spoke. "Yes."

I closed my eyes and focused on lighting the magic within me. Once I felt it activated, I opened my eyes and stared at Henry's dark form. "Ready."

"Bet you a Sundal something crazy happens." Dominic nudged Falden.

Falden held out his hand, and Dominic shook it. "Agreed."

"It would work best if you stepped into the rain. Hold your arms out and concentrate on letting the water soak in." Henry pointed to the deluge.

I made a face as I contemplated stepping away from our shelter, then I took a deep breath and stepped out of the gazebo. The rain pelted me with huge droplets. I closed my eyes and titled my face upward, gasping at the cold liquid that splashed across my face. I felt the wind whip at my hair and pull at my clothes. My boots sunk deeper in the squelchy mud, keeping me firmly planted. I lifted my arms and stretched them away from my body, palms facing outward. I became completely still, in tune with the elements. It took a single determined thought, and my world exploded. *Charge.*

I expected to only charge the blue using the rain, but I hadn't factored in the wind. The air element connected with the yellow. I hadn't been very specific when I said charge. I realized my mistake when the wind changed course as the yellow called for it. Instead of blowing in one direction, it centered directly on me, then enveloped me in a funnel and lifted me completely off the ground. It carried me upward about ten or fifteen paces. *Gods forbid, I'm in a tornado!*

I could feel the magic absorbing the wind and water and churning it into a magical energy. Huge surges of adrenaline pumped through my body as the yellow and blue charged simultaneously using the storm. My body glowed faintly, changing back and forth between soft hues of blue and yellow as the magic reacted with the storm. I hovered in the air drinking in the two elements until I felt like I couldn't hold anymore. The magic, now full, set me gently on the ground. The wind reverted to its original course, and the rain continued to pour down as if nothing had happened.

I stumbled in the mud, trying to regain my footing. Henry, Falden, and Dominic ran out of the gazebo. Falden got there first and grabbed onto me. He held me steady.

"Isabelle! Are you all right?" Henry asked.

I patted myself down, shocked and amazed. "I'm fine. Gods forbid what a rush!"

Falden helped me over to the gazebo while I stumbled; my legs felt like jelly after the blast of power. I sat on the bench, shivering and drenched.

"Are you all right?" Aliyah asked with concern as she sat next to me.

I nodded. "I'm fine."

"I can't believe the wind lifted you into the air," Henry exclaimed, running a hand through his wet hair.

Dominic turned to Falden. "Pay up."

Falden cursed and reached in his pocket. He handed Dominic a Sundal.

"I should have given the magic a more direct thought. I didn't think about the wind when I said charge," I said.

"Try to be more careful." Henry shuddered. "You had us all racing to figure out a way to save you when you floated down."

"Maybe you should check your core and see what happened," Aliyah suggested.

"Good idea," I agreed.

I dropped into my mage core and checked the levels of magic in the glass balls. Two spheres, the yellow and blue one, were filled to the brim with grains of sand. The other two, green and red, appeared slightly under the halfway point. I needed to come into closer contact with earth and fire for them to gather energy as well. As I exited my core, I noticed the smoky swirls of blue and yellow ribbons appeared brighter than before.

"What did you see?" Henry asked as I opened my eyes.

"Blue and yellow are completely charged, but green and red are a little under the halfway mark," I said. "So, what do I have to do to charge the other two?"

"Green is easy. Immerse your hand in the earth and it will gather energy. You're going to need fire for the red, so that will have to be done inside," Henry answered.

Aliyah stood. "I'm a Green, so I will do it with you. There's plenty of mud to go around."

I got up and followed Aliyah, hoping nothing crazy happened like a chasm ripping open for me to fall into. At this point, I could easily imagine something going wrong.

Aliyah pushed her sleeve up and crouched on the ground. I copied her. Around us the storm raged on with gales of wind and sleek, icy cold rain.

"Just stick your hand in and focus your thoughts on charging," Aliyah directed. She pushed her hand into the dirt and suddenly started glowing in soft hues of green.

I sunk my hand in the squishy, soft mud and dug my fingers into it. I centered my thoughts on charging the green only. The magic responded enthusiastically as it drew the energy out of the earth.

"Pretty easy, huh?" Aliyah smiled.

I nodded. "Yes."

Thank the Gods, nothing dramatic happened as I filled up on the natural earth element. Smaller surges of adrenaline buzzed through me. I felt more stable rejuvenating one color than I had charging two colors at once. I shuddered to imagine what it would feel like to renew all colors at once. Was that even possible?

Henry walked out of the gazebo and stood by us. He held his hands out, touching the rain. He glowed blue as his magic drank the element.

I pulled my hand out of the mud with a loud squelch around the same time as Aliyah. Henry dropped his hands to his sides.

"I'm soaked and covered in mud." I gestured to myself.

"But you got three of your colors recharged," Henry said. "Come on, let's get out of the cold." He waved at Dominic and Falden, and they walked out of the gazebo.

We sprinted inside, then took a good look at ourselves in the light and laughed. Our clothes and hair were plastered to us. Aliyah and I had mud caked on half our bodies. The boys, less so, but enough to make a trail of dirty footprints.

"We're a sight, aren't we?" I grinned.

"We wear this look so good we'd be fit for a dinner party," Henry joked. He shook his head, and water fell from his hair onto Aliyah, who stood beside him.

"Hey," she complained. "Watch it."

"Sorry." Henry kissed her cheek, causing Aliyah to blush. "We better take our boots off before someone catches the trail of mud." He crouched down to unlace his boots. "We still have one more color to charge. Meet at Isabelle's room in a half hour."

Everyone nodded in agreement. We held on to our shoes and went our separate ways to change.

I spent a moment to shut down the magic then started the bathwater. I peeled off my wet clothes and left them in a pile. I would deal with them after I cleaned up. I sank into the hot water. I scrubbed every speck of dirt I saw off my skin. My hair took longer to wash, as the wind had tangled it into an unrecognizable muddy mess. I changed into dry clothes, then brushed my hair and braided it away from my face.

I picked up my dirty clothes and hung them on a rod to dry. A note fluttered to the floor as I shook out my jacket. My stomach lurched as I retrieved it. With shaking hands, I unfolded it.

I love watching your potential come alive—Employer.

I recognized Henry's knocking pattern on the door. Forcing my feet into action, I answered it. Henry, Dominic, and Falden walked in with a plate of pumpkin spice cookies and a pitcher of apple cider.

Dominic threw a fireball into the fireplace, lighting it. "That should do it."

"Thanks," I said, mind distracted. The employer had been outside with us, close enough to put this note on my person and I hadn't seen him. I had no doubt he could snatch me anytime he wanted.

I jumped and swiveled around at the hand on my shoulder.

"Whoa there." Henry held up his hands. "You're awfully pale. Everything all right?"

I shoved the paper in my pocket. "Fine," I said quickly.

The boys and Aliyah stared at me with disbelief. I hadn't even realized she'd arrived.

I inflected as much interest as I could as I gestured to the fire. I had no intention of telling them my problems. "So, I'm not going to burn my hand, am I?"

Dominic shook his head and picked up a cookie. "No, but this one requires a bit more concentration than the others. You have to make sure your magic knows exactly what you want before you touch the flames, or you will get burned. With the others, you can touch it first and then concentrate on what you want."

I stepped closer to the fire. "I'm not so sure about this," I said uncertainly. "What if I make a mistake and get burned?"

"You hardly batted an eye with the others, and the air literally lifted you into the storm. Don't start questioning now," Henry urged as he poured a drink.

Dominic, perched on the edge of the stone fireplace, spoke. "Just watch Falden and I do it. We're Reds."

I backed away from the fireplace as Falden moved to take my position. I watched their faces appear deep in concentration for one minute, then their bodies start to glow in hues of red. Together they plunged their hands into the fire and chuckled.

"If you noticed, they didn't put their hands in the flames until they started glowing first," Henry said.

"Right." I nodded.

Falden and Dominic removed their hands and moved out of the way.

"Now it's your turn," Falden said with a soft smile.

I took a deep breath and knelt by the fire, feeling the intensity of the heat. I pushed my sleeve past my elbow.

"Don't forget to tell your magic what you're planning. It's very important," Dominic reminded.

"I remember," I said.

Falden turned to Dominic. "Bet you a Sundal she laughs."

Dominic shook his head. "No deal. Odds are too high in your favor."

Why would fire make me laugh? I wondered as I activated the magic and focused on the buzz within my veins, bringing it up to the surface. In my mind's eye, I imagined the red ball of sand with its half-empty status and thought *Charge red.* I stared hard at the fire, ignoring the heat and smoke burning my eyes. Once I had a clear picture of the fire in my mind, I sent the mental picture to the red magic—to Boomer. Trying to show it what I wanted, I repeated the thought. *Charge red.*

I felt a stronger kick of adrenaline as I watched the magical version of Boomer bark excitedly. I glanced down at my hand and saw that it glowed in soft hues of red. Hoping it got the right message, I took a deep breath, held it, then snapped my eyes shut. I turned my scrunched-up face away from the heat and plunged my hand into the burning flames.

My hand and forearm submerged, I gripped a crumbling log, feeling no pain. It felt more like a—tickle. *What is this madness?* I opened my eyes and peeked, then opened them wider. The breath of air I held whooshed out of me. I took another breath without thinking and coughed on smoke.

I glowed bright red; the flames licked my hand as the magic soaked up the energy from the element.

I couldn't help it; I laughed. *It tickled!*

Dominic chuckled. "Told you."

Falden shook his head. "Right."

"What's so funny?" Henry raised an eyebrow, smiling slightly.

"It tickles!" I started laughing uncontrollably.

"Really?" Interest flickered across Henry's face.

Soft laughter went around the room as they watched my reaction.

"I can't stand it any longer." I let go of the log and pulled my hand away from the flames. I shook my hand repeatedly, trying to get the sensation to go away. I felt like a thousand ants had crawled over my hand and wrist. A shiver went up my spine.

I moved away from the fireplace and sat on the floor, then shut down the magic. I eyed Dominic and Falden. "You should have warned me it feels like bugs crawling over your skin."

"And miss out on your reaction?" Dominic chuckled. "All Reds have to learn for themselves."

"Consider it an initiation," Falden said. "If you really want to know what it feels like to have bugs on your skin, ask that spider right there." He pointed to a large brown spider scurrying to me.

I shot up. "What?" I backed into the side of the fireplace and clutched at my stomach.

"Somebody kill it!" Aliyah lifted her feet off the ground and brought her knees up to her chest, mirroring my horrified expression.

The boys clearly struggled to not laugh at our response.

"Are there any bugs girls are not afraid of?" Dominic asked.

Falden scratched his head. "Butterflies."

Henry used a cookie as bait and lured the large brown spider onto it, then threw it into the fire. I shuddered. *Nasty, vile creatures.*

"All safe," Henry declared. He reached for Aliyah and pulled her up to him. He wrapped his arms around her trembling body, and I found myself wishing Andrew were here to do the same to me.

"Kill a spider and get a girl," Dominic mused, rubbing his chin. "Not a bad idea."

"Not that easy, guys," Aliyah said, letting Henry lead her back to her seat.

Henry faced me. "I didn't think you would be afraid of spiders."

"I'm not—I just don't like them is all." I spoke too quickly, not wanting to admit my fear.

It became obvious everyone saw right through my lie. Henry folded his arms and raised an eyebrow. "You looked pretty scared to me."

I sighed and held my hands up in surrender. "All right, all right, so I have a little fear of spiders. You do realize that there are a thousand different kinds, and some are considered lethal to humans."

"A brown jumping spider isn't going to hurt you," Dominic scoffed.

"Spider bites are common in Saren, and I've seen some revolting bites on people. It's a habit to run from a spider regardless of its species," I explained, trying to calm my quivering heart.

"What else do you run away from?" Henry asked, taking a step closer to me.

"Snakes," I said slowly. "Bees." As I spoke, Henry gradually shuffled closer until we stood face to face. "Grabby men." Especially the ones I couldn't see like the employer. I shivered.

The boys chuckled; I shut up.

Henry gestured to the vacant chintz chair. "Come sit. The danger is gone."

I took a deep breath and exhaled, then took the seat next to Aliyah. "Pretty silly, huh? I can wield a sword like it was my right arm, but along comes a spider and I jump."

"They scare me too." Aliyah shuddered. "I'd spend the rest of my life happy if I never saw another one."

"It's natural to have a fear of something." Henry sat on the stone fireplace.

"But you're not afraid of spiders." I felt ashamed to have this ridiculous fear.

Henry shook his head. "No, but put me in a room with a bunch of old, pampered ladies, and we have a contender."

Dominic's face lit up. "Your mother's tea party over the summer."

Henry grimaced and nodded.

Dominic laughed. "Oh, what a disaster!"

Falden nodded vigorously as he started to chuckle.

Henry joined in. "Worst experience of my life!"

We spent another hour dredging up stories to make us laugh. Meanwhile the note seemed to burn a hole in my pocket. My hand rested on the outside of my pants, feeling the thick parchment. The logical thing to do would be take it to Lord Leavesden and then contact Joshua. Something within me resisted. Twice I'd voiced my concerns to my brother over me staying at the Sorrenian and he never listened. I didn't think a third time would make a difference. I might as well keep it quiet and figure my own way out of this mess.

I knocked on Malsin's door the day after he got back, feeling like he needed a reminder. I'd waited a whole day for him to contact me, and he had yet to do so. I knew he had a busy schedule, but he had agreed to teach me magic, and so far he'd done a poor job of it.

"Enter." Malsin looked up from his pile of books and stacks of wrinkled paper. Balls of scrunched paper littered the floor of his tiny office. "Oh, it's you, Isabelle. What's happened now?"

"Nothing," I assured him.

"Oh good." He ran a hand through his disheveled hair. I noticed his hollow eyes and the tired lines on his face.

"You look exhausted," I said bluntly, folding my arms. "What have you been up to?"

"It's this Gods-forbidden report!" Malsin exclaimed, throwing his hands up in frustration. "The Healers Guild threw it at me as I was leaving." His expression turned sour. "And it's so frustratingly technical that I'm losing my mind. I mean really, how many times do I have to explain my healing procedure for a simple sprain? I don't have time for this!"

"What you need is a calming cup of tea and someone to help." I stepped closer. "Perhaps you could dictate, and I could write it down?"

He smiled genuinely; his shoulders slumped in relief. "Oh, Isabelle, would you?"

I gestured to myself. "Put me to work. I've got the time. But first, make some tea. You need it."

Malsin grinned. "Right."

He jumped out of his seat and threw some books and papers into a bin, creating a little more space on his table. He grabbed an extra chair and shoved it to the desk. I sat, pulling his half-finished report to me as he left the room to make tea.

I spent the next hour listening to Malsin dictate as he sipped on his steaming tea. I wrote hastily. The ink still wet as I moved on to the next line, I had to be careful not to create any smudges. Malsin's half of the report appeared barely legible, and he had crossed out many sections. I blew on the page to dry the glistening black ink. "Done." I handed it to Malsin, who eyed it over.

"You are a gift from the Gods," he praised, setting the finished report in a folder.

I wondered if he'd be able to find it later in his messy office. "It's not a problem, really," I said. "Everyone else is either working on homework or in magic class, and since I have no homework and I'm banned from the magic class, I have the free time."

Malsin frowned, guiltily I thought. "Right—magic. I'm supposed to help with that."

"How do you do it?" I asked in turn. "How do you maintain control—resist—the urge to heal everything?"

Malsin put a hand to his mouth, a startled look in his eyes. "You practiced magic while I was gone."

"A little," I admitted, biting my lip.

"By yourself?" Malsin leaned forward in his chair.

"No. Henry taught me the basics," I confessed. "I can open and close it without saying a word, check my energy levels and recharge, but that's about it."

"But you healed someone," Malsin protested, pointing a finger at me.

"Remember when you said we were going to test it out to be sure I was all four colors? Well … Henry and I did." I crossed my ankles and explained, "I created an ice sculpture using blue magic, then I created a fireball and destroyed the sculpture using red magic. I made a stick disappear in Henry's palm using yellow magic," I took a breath and continued, "and I healed a cut on Henry's hand using green magic. The magic never needed to make a choice. I am all of them."

"Four colors! I've never heard of that happening before." Malsin seemed flabbergasted. He put his hands on his head, his eyes alight with disbelief.

"And yet here I am, defying all known logic." I shrugged. "Henry has classified it as a rainbow."

Malsin chuckled softly as he resituated in his chair. "Rainbow? Really?"

I nodded.

"I'd like to see this in action. Would you be willing to demonstrate?" He asked eagerly.

I handed him the pen. "Hold onto this."

I let the magical version of Boomer out of his cage and directed my thoughts to the pen. I started with the most difficult one, yellow. Having done this once, I knew what to expect when the feelings of superiority tried to drown me. I fought for control and focused on the task at hand. Slowly, I made the pen disappear.

"Amazing!" he exclaimed. "I can feel it, but I can't see it." He made a fist and hit the table. I heard the distinct sound of the pen tapping against the desk despite not being able to see it.

I smiled. "Crazy, right?" I pictured the pen in his hand and made it visible again. Malsin set it on the desk with reverence.

I grabbed my half-empty cup of tea and brought it closer to Malsin. I hovered my hand over the top. Switching to blue, I made it ice over and created a frozen maple leaf on top. "Tea isn't any good cold, though."

I put my hand over the cup again and melted the tea into a liquid form. Using the red, I heated it until tendrils of steam rose before I took a sip.

"That's better." I set the cup on the desk. "I don't suppose you have anything you want me to heal, do you?"

"Not on me." He stood. "But I've got a plant that could use a little help." He brought back a wilting orange calendula from the healing room adjacent to his office. "Emilia—Professor Morel—forgot to water this one while I was away." He set the plant in front of me.

"We can heal plants?" I hadn't thought about the broad-spectrum healing magic could have.

Malsin grinned. "There's so much green magic can do, and we've only scratched the surface." He sat. "But to put it simply, Greens can manipulate any living thing." He pointed to the plant. "Plants are alive."

"Right." That made sense. "All right, I'll see what I can do with this." I hovered my hand over the calendula as I brought the green up to the surface, then I touched one of the leaves.

As when I'd healed Henry, I didn't need to see the wilting petals to know what it needed. I felt my own throat parch in response to the dry roots. The magic eagerly entwined itself with the plant and revitalized it. I didn't even try to control it; I knew I couldn't stop if I wanted to. When the calendula stood upright and healthy, again I felt the magic's disappointment, but softer this time. I wondered if the magic reacted differently to what it healed. Did it prefer to heal humans over plants?

I removed my hand. "It's healthy now."

Malsin picked up the pot and inspected the plant. "This is incredible!"

"You act just like Henry when we started testing. He was excited too," I said.

"Excited cannot even begin to explain the depths of what I'm feeling. This is a complete conundrum. This shouldn't be happening, and yet it is!" Malsin threw up his hands. "What is the world coming to?"

"You're not angry, are you?" I asked softly, fearing a reprimand. "Because you were supposed to teach me, but you were gone, and I didn't want to wait."

He put his hand on his chest. "Angry? Gods forbid no. I would have done the same thing in your position. But you do need a teacher before you try anything advanced." His expression turned serious.

I nodded. "I can wait now that I know the basics."

"Good." Malsin grabbed his cup of tea. He took a sip and grimaced. I took the cup from his hand and heated it up for him.

He gave me wry smile as I handed it back.

The clock chimed. We both glanced at it.

"I should get to my room." I sighed, then stood and stretched. I spent a moment to shut the magic down, locking Boomer firmly in his cage.

"Thank you for your help." Malsin stood. "And for showing me what you can do. You've relieved and enlightened me."

"Just remember to ask for help when you're in over your head." I pointed a finger at him.

Malsin grinned sheepishly. "Right."

CHAPTER TWENTY-NINE

OVER THE NEXT TWO weeks, Malsin and I focused on expanding my knowledge of magic. I fought an internal battle over it. I needed to learn and control my powers, but after that last note about my potential, I also believed every day I grew stronger, brought me closer to the employer.

Malsin wanted a full account of what I did with Henry. I explained everything in detail, including picturing Boomer when I opened and closed the magic.

"Did Henry teach you that trick?" Malsin asked.

I shook my head. "No, but Henry made me feel like an idiot until he admitted he does it too."

"I've heard that Professor Slystream actually makes them pick out an animal when they start his class. It's purely a mental trick; there's no meaning behind the animal you choose, but it does make it easier to put a face to the magic," Malsin said.

"What do you picture?" I leaned forward, curious.

"A grizzly bear," Malsin admitted with a smile.

I raised my eyebrows in surprise. "But you're so gentle." I couldn't imagine Malsin as a ferocious bear.

He burst out laughing. "I'm not as gentle as I've led you to believe."

It reminded me that I hardly knew anything about this man despite spending a considerable amount of time together. His personal life was a complete mystery, but I didn't think it right to pry. He'd tell me what he thought I should know.

We delved into the basics again, going over opening and closing and charging. Next we tackled emotions.

"It's mind over emotions," Malsin said. "You've got to keep a firm grip on them or else the magic will run all over you." He crossed his legs, speaking with his hands. "See, the magic fills you with these feelings because it wants to be used, and it knows that people make decisions based off what they feel. For example, the green magic will make you feel disappointed almost to the point of grief when you've stopped using it. It does that because it hopes that you will use it again to get rid of the undesirable feeling. Of course, once you shut it off, it cannot influence you."

Malsin constantly expanded my knowledge and never moved on to the next thing until he felt sure I had completely understood the concepts he taught.

"People generally categorize the four colors of magic into what they are best known for and particularly good at." He held up a finger and listed them off. "Creating, destroying, camouflaging, and healing. A common misconception is that the magic is limited to doing only those four things. That is not the case."

"It's not?" I asked, surprised.

Malsin shook his head. "I'll show you some examples with the green." He put his finger on the stem of the calendula we had worked with. I watched in horror as it withered. When he removed his hand, it was completely dead.

I picked up the pot and stared at the dried remains. "You killed it." I couldn't help but feel a little sad over the plant. I had grown rather fond of it.

"And I could do the same to a person," Malsin said candidly.

I frowned, not happy with this news. It made the green magic, and the people who possessed it, seem much scarier than I wanted them to be. "I want my calendula back."

He chuckled. "I'll get you a new one. Promise."

Unexpectedly, Professor Breldian's cat walked through the slightly ajar door and into the healing room. Malsin smiled. "Ah, perfect." He coaxed

Ginger to come to him and picked her up. "I can show you another example."

"You're not going to kill Ginger, are you?" I asked with alarm.

"Of course not." Malsin looked mildly offended. "I happen to really like Ginger. I wouldn't dream of hurting her." He petted her head leisurely. "But I am going to make her sleep." With his hand on her head, I watched the cat's eyelids droop until she went limp in his arms. Malsin set her on a cot. "She will sleep for a couple of hours and wake up refreshed."

"You used green magic, but you didn't heal anything," I noted.

Malsin nodded. "A better term for the green is manipulation. I can make any living thing experience what I want it to." He gestured to the sleeping cat. "Put it to sleep, wake it up, and as you saw with the plant, even kill." Malsin shifted his weight from side to side. "Which is why we are working with plants until you have complete control over your emotions and errant thoughts."

"And it's the same for the other colors?" I started to feel uneasy with this knowledge.

"Yes, but before I get into what the other colors do, I must confer with Professor Slystream. I want to make sure I explain everything correctly. Best if we stick to what we're doing now."

Every class after that we focused on controlling emotions. Malsin said it was the most difficult thing to master and therefore needed the most time. To do it, I used magic in increments doing the four things I had already tried. Freezing water, creating fireballs, healing plants—because Malsin would not let me near people—and making small items camouflage until it seemed like they had disappeared. Through each exercise, Malsin would make me stop unexpectedly, making me feel the range of emotions and show authority.

I hated discovering that the more I used magic, the more I wanted to give in to it. I often found myself begging to do more, to do something bigger.

"It's worse for you because you have four colors vying for your attention. But you cannot relent." Malsin paced back and forth, his boots slapping against the stone floor. "Letting magic have control is exactly how mages get killed."

I had the hardest time with green and yellow. Green played with my heartstrings the most, its eagerness to heal—manipulate—overruling any deliberate thought I had to discontinue. Frequently, Malsin took the plant away because he knew I couldn't stop on my own. Yellow's ability to make me feel undiluted power and superiority warred with my usually kind nature. Once when I meant to camouflage a teacup, I accidentally made my lower half disappear. I had to focus to keep errant thoughts out when I used the yellow, or it would try to comply before I even finished thinking the random thought.

Out of all the four colors of magic, I enjoyed red the most. I couldn't get enough of that feeling of protection as though I'd been clothed in an impenetrable shield of strength. Red made me feel safe in a sea of worry.

Henry cornered me after riding class on a Third Day afternoon. "All right, what is going on? You've been stewing over something ever since we taught you how to recharge your magic."

I sighed. "Henry, I really don't want to bring you into it."

He crossed his arms. "Too late. Whatever it is, is seriously affecting you and I want to know why."

Reluctantly, I confessed everything about the employer, including my fears that he bided his time until I knew enough about magic to be useful. "I know he's watching—waiting for the right opportunity to strike."

"Gods forbid." Henry's eyes widened then suddenly narrowed. "If the employer knows you're here, why haven't you moved somewhere else? It's not like you're really learning much, except magic."

"Joshua thinks being around others and the extra guards are keeping me safe," I explained. "I don't think it will make a difference when the employer decides he's done waiting."

"Maybe," Henry mused. "Well, I'll keep my eye out in any case. I don't want to see anything happen to you."

I smiled. "Thanks."

Haldren occasionally dropped in on my dreams. He spoke directly to me once to tell me he left a gift for Nisha on my desk. I discovered a basket of exceptionally large golden-yellow apples. Nisha's joy could not be contained, causing quite a commotion in the stables as he whinnied and danced in his stall. When several hostlers came running, I showed them the basket. "He's just excited."

They stalked off, scowling, and muttering under their breaths about running for nothing.

"So, what's the deal?" I picked up an apple and fed it to him.

"Part of our agreement," Nisha explained in between bites. *"He owes me for leaving my herd."*

Apparently Haldren had a beloved apple tree that he never allowed anyone to touch. He promised to give Nisha a basket of his precious fruit when it came time to harvest. When I bit into the apple Nisha offered, I understood the excitement. Had any apple ever tasted this sweet, juicy, and crisp? I didn't think so.

On the morning of Kings Day, ten people stood in front of my door, Henry at the forefront and the rest of his tablemates behind him.

"Grab your coat," Henry said, eyes twinkling. "And some gloves."

"Why?" I asked suspiciously.

Henry grinned. "Snowball fight."

I pulled on my coat, gloves, and boots and followed the group. It had snowed heavily throughout the night. The first real storm of the season. The thick layer sparkled and shimmered against the glinting rays of the sun.

Henry explained the game to me as we stepped outside. "Capture the handkerchief without being hit by a snowball. If you get hit, you have to sit out for two minutes while your teammates go on without you."

Falden stuck a staff into the ice, a red handkerchief tied to the end of it. I learned we couldn't take the staff and run but had to untie the red cloth from it. We separated into two groups in the practice fields. Henry and Dominic were chosen to be the leaders of the two groups.

Immediately Dominic started throwing insults. "You're going to lose! My skilled team is better than yours!"

Henry laughed. "Keep trying, Dominic. I'm waiting for your wit to catch up with your mouth."

Dominic shut up. I could almost see the gears of his mind working behind his eyes.

We distanced ourselves from the staff; each group went the opposite direction. We huddled while Henry dished out orders.

"All right, we've got five minutes to make as many snowballs as we can. We need a quick surrounding wall to protect them as we throw. We're gonna need jobs for everyone. Separate into what you think you'll do best, either making snowballs or being a runner. Who's got the best throwing arm?"

Ethan raised his hand.

"Great. Ethan, you'll need to stand here." Henry started drawing out a map with his gloved finger.

We made as many snowballs as we could in the time limit given and situated ourselves according to Henry's map. Henry and I became designated runners, while Aliyah and Dominic ran for the opposing team. The remaining three people on Dominic's team, Ryan, Cole, and Amarilla, and the four people on ours, Falden, Marie, Roanna, and Ethan, carried snowballs in their hands, wicked gleams on their rosy faces. Falden opted to switch back and forth between teams after every game to keep it even. If Henry and I got hit, the others would run while we waited to get back in the game.

"Ready?" Dominic called.

"Ready!" Henry shouted.

"Go!" Dominic and Henry shouted simultaneously.

I ran, my feet sinking in the deep snow, dodging snowballs. "Oh!" I fell backward when Cole hit me. Dusting off, I laughed and waited to get back in the game. We rotated positions and played several games. We won once due to Ethan's excellent aim, while the other team won twice. Dominic, quick on his feet, scored the win both times for his team.

We played for an hour and a half, then quit. The snow started to fall heavy and thick, making it hard to see. Soaked and freezing but delighted, I ran over to Henry as he pulled the staff out of the ice. The rest of the group practically sprinted back to the school to change and warm up.

I grinned. "Thanks for inviting me. I had a great time."

"You're welcome." Henry gripped onto the pole.

Something dark caught my eye as I started to turn around to head back inside. I paused. Two men lurked by the tree line, clearly watching us. By now I recognized everyone at the Sorrenian, even if I didn't know their names. They seemed unfamiliar. I couldn't make out their profiles as well as I wanted with the pouring flakes, but every nerve in my body screamed danger. My mind raced through several possibilities. I thought of the employer.

I nudged Henry, fighting the feeling to bolt. He would know who they were, and I could stop overreacting. "Since when do two men loiter by the trees in the middle of a storm? I don't recognize them."

Henry glanced behind him and frowned. "You're right. I better inform Leavesden."

One of the men brought something out and pointed it directly at us. I squinted through the flurries attempting to discern what it was.

I gasped. "Henry, look out! He's got a crossbow!" I grabbed Henry and tried to pull him out of the way. I didn't move fast enough. A bolt hit him squarely in the back of his shoulder.

"Argh!" He cried out. He dropped the staff as he fell unconscious from the bolt.

"Henry!"

I toppled into the snow with Henry slumped on top of me. I couldn't push him off me despite using all the strength I had in my arms. How much did he weigh?

"Help! Help!" I screamed, hoping at least one of the other students hadn't made it inside, but my cries were muffled under Henry. Could anyone hear me? "Gods forbid, Henry, you better not die on me! Help!"

Fear clutched at my heart. I shivered as the ice melted through my clothes and touched my skin.

The men who shot the crossbow trudged to us. They wore heavy fur-lined coats and had covered up their faces in scarves till only their brown eyes showed.

"They can't help you now," one of the men spoke, his voice gruff. "They've all gone inside." He crouched beside me.

"What did you do to Henry?" I spat.

"He's not dead. Just unconscious. Just like you're gonna be in a minute." He reached in his pocket and pulled out another bolt. I struggled under the weight of Henry and took a large gulp of air to scream as he jabbed it into my shoulder. The world went black.

CHAPTER THIRTY

U GH ..." I GROANED as I slowly started to wake up. I rubbed my forehead and scrunched my face against a headache. I felt like a sledgehammer pounded me right between the eyes. My shoulder throbbed where the bolt punctured my skin, so I rubbed that too.

"Isabelle?" Henry's voice cut through the fog, piercing my ears.

"Henry?" My eyes flew open to total darkness. I froze.

"You're awake." He sounded relieved.

"I can't see anything," I squeaked like a terrified field mouse.

"Don't worry, you're not blind. There's no light in here. I can't see anything either," Henry assured me.

"Are you all right? Are you hurt?" I gasped as a new thought occurred. "What if we're both blind?"

"Calm down. I'm fine. A little sore where they hit me, but I'm all right." He spoke in soothing tones.

His voice became my anchor. "How long have you been awake?"

"Not long. A half hour maybe. Can you move at all?" Henry questioned.

I patted my body from the top of my shoulders and down my legs, using my sense of touch to figure out my situation. I drew my hand up to my chest as though I'd been stung when my fingers touched something cold attached to my ankle. I took a deep breath, swallowing back my fear, and explored the metal. A cuff and chain.

Panic set in. I started hyperventilating. "No, I've got a chain around my ankle." My hands shook. "Gods forbid, I can't move!" A sob rose in my throat. What if these chains had the ability to torment their prisoner?

"I'm chained too," Henry said, clearly vexed.

"How long do you think your chain is? Maybe we can sit closer." I scooted as far as I could, groping in the pitch black. I felt immensely relieved to not be alone but also guilty that Henry had gotten into this mess. Why had they taken him when I was the intended target?

A warm hand grabbed onto mine. "Henry?"

"It's me." He moved closer.

"We need to get out of these chains." I closed my eyes and imagined Boomer in his crate. I pulled on the latch, thinking *Spintry* like normal, but nothing happened. Boomer whined pitifully, but no matter what I did I couldn't open the crate.

"I can't get my magic to open," I said sullenly. "It's not working."

"I think it's these chains stopping it, and I don't know why. I've never encountered anything that stopped magic before," Henry said. "I tried it when you were still unconscious. I was hoping you would be strong enough to break them."

"I'm so sorry, Henry. I wish I could." Tears leaked from my eyes and fell on my face. Disappointment ran clear through every fiber of my being. What happened to all those years I spent learning how to defend and take care of myself? How come none of it was helpful now?

"Well ... it was worth a try," Henry said in a disheartened tone.

Heavy footsteps echoed, and the door opened, flooding the tiny room with light. Henry and I shielded our eyes against the blinding flame. A man held a lantern high above his head.

"He is here." The man who stabbed me with the bolt spoke. He hadn't removed the thick winter clothes; his face still hid behind a scarf.

Henry and I leaned forward and asked simultaneously. "Who?"

The man pulled down the scarf and grinned, revealing a strong, stubby jawline, a few missing teeth, and a crooked nose. "Your King."

"King?" Henry and I repeated, confusion clear in our voices.

"King Brian wouldn't do this to us?" I glanced at Henry.

"I don't think he's talking about Uncle Brian." Henry clenched his jaw.

"Well then who do you think he's talking about?" I asked in whisper.

Henry shook his head, indicating he didn't know.

The crooked-nosed man set the lantern on the ground, spun on his heels, and exited the room. He left the door open and stood guard outside of it. I saw part of his profile by the doorframe. The light from the lantern gave us a clear view of the room. It appeared big enough to fit a large poster bed and a few dressers were it a bedroom. But except for us, the chains, and the lantern, it was bare.

Multiple sets of footsteps echoed down a set of stairs and into the hallway.

"I think we're about to find out," Henry muttered.

My breathing slowed, then hitched and sped up.

The footsteps stopped just outside of the door, but the people could not be seen. The guard bowed, and half his body appeared in the doorway. "Your Majesty." His voice sounded soft, reverent, and very uncharacteristic.

"I trust they are alive and well?" a man questioned, his voice fluid and smooth; a nobleman, I decided.

"Yes, Your Majesty," the man groveled.

"Good," the man answered in a clear, clipped tone. He stepped into view.

His wavy hair—medium brown streaked with blonde—fell a little past his shoulders. His sun-kissed beard was short but well-groomed on his chiseled face. He had a straight nose and full lips and a scar above his right eye. He wore sturdy clothing: a dark blue, long-sleeve shirt and black pants with boots that rose to his knees. His hazel eyes caught mine and penetrated deep into my very soul.

I leaned back into the cold wall and brought my legs up to my chest. I huddled closer to Henry and wrapped one arm around my stomach. This man put the fear of the Gods in me.

His eyes leveled on mine as he crouched. He scrutinized my appearance; his lips curled into a half smile. "My, your description does not do you justice. You're even more beautiful than I believed." He reached out and touched my face with rough and calloused fingers. I shuddered and pushed his hand away. He chuckled and stood. "Feisty too. We need some of that around here."

"What do you want?" Henry asked in an acidic tone.

The man smiled, directing his attention to Henry for the first time. "Ah, Henry. We've never officially met. You look just like your mother. Same shade of blonde hair."

"What do you know about my mother?" Henry spat. His blue eyes flashed.

The man's hazel eyes turned deadly as he stared directly into Henry's face. Henry clenched his hands, ire radiating off him. I admired his courage and tenacity as he stared coolly back, not once breaking eye contact.

"My dear boy, I know everything." His voice sounded sharp and confident as he folded his arms. "She is, after all—" He grinned, clearly enjoying what knowledge and power he held over us. "My aunt."

Henry's face morphed into shock, then anger and disgust as he recognized the significance of the man's revelation.

"What's he talking about?" I nudged Henry.

The man waved his hands, gesturing to himself. "Allow me to introduce myself. I am Braidus Alexander Sorren, firstborn son of King Brian."

What? I cocked my head to the side and eyed Braidus, trying to understand or see the resemblance. Should his name sound familiar? Instinct screamed yes, but I couldn't place it. I searched fruitlessly in my memory, feeling like I had forgotten something major.

"I don't understand," I said. "Andrew is the only child of the King."

Henry shook his head at the same time Braidus did, both disagreeing with what I'd believed to be truth—with what every child in Aberron had been taught.

I turned to Henry again, pleading for answers from him. "Henry, what don't I know?"

"Yes, Henry, explain it to the poor girl." Braidus stepped back until he leaned against the stone wall. He folded his arms, the corners of his mouth lifting in a small smile.

"King Brian has two sons. He's telling the truth," Henry said tersely.

My mouth dropped open. I shook my head slowly and spluttered. "But … that can't be. Why didn't—Andrew?"

Braidus interrupted my babbled nonsense. "I was the little indiscretion King Brian had at sixteen. When my mother died in childbirth, his dreams of living happily as a family were foiled, and he got stuck with me. A bastard son without the love of his life."

I recoiled from his bluntness. "What do you want from us?" I voiced the question I thought most important. Someone could fill in the backstory later.

His hazel eyes burned into mine. "I want you to work for me."

"Don't even think about it," Henry muttered quickly, not taking his eyes off Braidus.

"Why should I work for you when you're holding me against my will?" I gestured to the shackle and chain.

"Necessary to get your attention." Braidus shrugged.

"And Henry?" I tilted my head in his direction. "If it's me you're after, why have you brought him? What good is he to you?"

"Leverage. He's of no use to me otherwise." He reached inside his boot and pulled out a dagger, then started twiddling it between his fingers. The unspoken message came out loud and clear.

Work for Braidus or Henry dies. *Great.*

I couldn't help but ask despite feeling like I already knew the answer. "You're the Employer. You've been watching me, sending me notes."

Braidus grinned. "Yes."

Under my breath I muttered, "I knew I wasn't safe at the Sorrenian."

Braidus apparently heard me because he said, "switching locations would not have mattered. I would have found you regardless."

My tone was caustic. "What about the men who came after me in Saren? Did you mean for the archer to shoot me?"

Braidus frowned. I saw a hint of regret. "That was—unfortunate."

"Unfortunate?" My voice went up an octave in disbelief. *I nearly died.*

Braidus raised an eyebrow. "I had to make the threat real to get you where I wanted, now didn't I?" He shifted his weight and continued to toy with the dagger in his hands, running his finger along the sharp edge. "I've answered enough of your questions; now you answer mine. I'll give you two minutes to decide."

I sighed and gripped my forehead, fighting off the pounding headache. Henry shook his head at me, eyes wide. He obviously thought I should refuse, and yet I found myself leaning toward saying yes.

Braidus had an answer for everything. He had clearly spent a significant amount of time planning this out. Henry and I faced an unbeatable reality. Braidus had been clever when he captured Henry as well. I could stand up to someone when only my life was at stake, but this was different. Henry's fate rested on me. Saying no to Braidus would be sentencing Henry to death. I would hold myself responsible even if I didn't wield the sword that did the deed. His blood would be on my hands—forever. I stared into Henry's face and saw the despair. The rims of his eyes were red with exhaustion, his hair disheveled and his hands shaking. He had proven to be a true friend, and I would do everything I could to protect him. Even if that meant going against my morals.

"Have you made a decision?" Braidus asked when the two minutes had passed.

Anger clouded my vision. I balled my fists and fought to speak clearly. "I will work for you on one condition." I held up a finger. "You let Henry go."

Braidus's eyes lit up. "Tempting, but no. If I let him go, how can I trust you to do what I want?"

"You have my word," I said sharply.

"Your word is not enough." Braidus pointed the dagger at me.

I met his gaze and held my chin high, refusing to be submissive. "Then I want better accommodations."

Henry and Braidus's eyebrows raised. Henry stared at me open-mouthed. I saw a hint of amusement at my audacity from Braidus. I had no power to make demands, and yet I acted like I did.

"Keep Henry," I spoke harshly, my voice ice as anger fueled my demands. "But give him heat, dry clothes, food. Treat him like a guest, or you can kill us both."

Braidus grinned, then stuck the dagger in his belt and bowed. "Well said, my queen."

His comment caught me off-guard, and I immediately reacted, speaking before I thought. "I am not your queen, nor anybody else's!"

Braidus chuckled softly. "All right. We have an agreement." He pointed at Henry. "But if you do not deliver, he dies."

I nodded. "Fine."

Braidus turned away from us and started making arrangements with the two guards stationed outside the door.

"Isabelle, what are you doing?" Henry spoke through gritted teeth.

I smiled bitterly. "Saving your life."

"But you don't know what he has planned. You can't work for him," Henry argued, a hint of pleading in his tone.

"I'm not letting you die," I said.

A new guard came into the room and unlocked the cuff on my leg. As he hooked his hand under my arm, I activated my magic and sent it my pent-up ferocity. Boomer jumped from his crate, snarling with hackles raised. The man cried out in pain, then fell to the ground in a heap as my green magic set his nerves on fire. I didn't feel a single shred of remorse.

"Yes! Annihilate them!" Henry roared. He brought his knees up to his chest to give me as much space as possible.

I reached for the key lying beside the crumpled man, but it rose from the ground, shimmering under the power of magic, and landed in Braidus's outstretched palm. At the same time, the two guards waiting outside rushed into the room and hovered beside Braidus. They drew their weapons, two short swords.

"Nice try." Braidus smirked.

"I'm just getting started," I snarled, my chest heaving as I fought for breath. My blood boiled inside my veins. I trembled with power and adrenaline, and I had barely tapped into it. I took a deep breath and exhaled, loving every second of my undiluted fury.

Undeterred by the failed attempt, my hands ignited in red flames. Braidus and the guards dived out of the way as fireballs shot out of my hands. They hit the wall behind them and exploded in a shower of sparks and flame yet did little damage. It would take more power to break the stone around me.

One of the guards swung his blade toward me, but I ducked out of the way.

"Don't hurt her!" Braidus yelled as he straightened.

The guard lowered his sword and backed away with an angry expression. *Only natural,* I thought, considering I had just tried to incapacitate him.

I swiveled around to face Braidus. "Release Henry."

"No." Braidus showed no fear despite the growing flames enveloping my hands.

I stepped forward, ready to become more aggressive. Then Braidus completely vanished before my eyes.

"No!" I shouted, dismayed. I couldn't fight what I couldn't see.

"Gods forbid, he's got yellow magic," Henry said, shocked.

My eyes darted around the room as I turned, searching for any indicators of his presence. Abruptly Braidus reappeared, crouched next to Henry with his dagger poised over his throat. Henry turned rigid as stone as he eyed the dagger with alarm.

"Henry!" I cried, distraught. I gritted my teeth, sweat trickled down my forehead. My magic surged wildly for control, and I fought to keep myself together.

"One wrong move and he dies." Braidus pointed the tip of the blade into Henry's neck. He gasped as it pierced his flesh and a bead of blood formed and dripped.

"Stop!" I shrieked. "Don't hurt him." The flames extinguished from my hands as I forced the magic to back down. I all but dragged Boomer back to the crate and swayed unsteadily on my feet as I crashed from the adrenaline high.

Braidus removed the dagger from Henry's throat. "Try that again and I won't be so forgiving." He stood, leaving Henry chained against the wall. Striding to me, he gripped my arm, gentler than I expected, and said, "Come with me."

I mouthed "I'm sorry" to Henry, hoping he could see the apology on my face as the prospect of freedom dissipated.

CHAPTER THIRTY-ONE

RAIDUS HELD ON TO me as we walked into an underground stone hallway. Torches hung on the walls at intervals, lighting the way. We'd taken a few steps and paused when a group of small boys, ranging in ages from five to nine and wearing worn and patched clothes, raced into view. They held short wooden swords in their hands, and peals of laughter rang as they stopped to do battle.

"There are children here," I breathed, surprised. Regret punched me in the gut for throwing the fireballs. Thank the Gods I didn't blast through the stone.

"More than an orphanage should hold," Braidus answered.

"Get the King!" the oldest boy shouted, brandishing his weapon.

"Guards defend me!" The littlest boy skirted behind two bigger boys.

Braidus chuckled as he lightly tugged on my arm to start moving again. As we passed the boys, they stared wide-eyed at me and greeted Braidus with waves and hellos. I noticed they called him Brady instead of Braidus.

He opened a wooden door and entered a fully furnished room with two very drastic sides. On one half, two plush green chairs resided near a roaring fire. A small table with a tea set rested between them. A large desk had been pushed up against one wall, with books and sheaths of paper littering it. It reminded me of an office.

The other side had one long green couch against the wall, a bookshelf with small children's books, and wooden chests with toys spilling out. A large space in the middle gave room to play.

Braidus led me to one of the green chairs and took the adjacent one. "Please have some tea. It will warm you up." He gestured to the tea set.

"No thank you." I had no desire to eat or drink anything.

"I promise there's nothing toxic in it. Here, I'll take a sip as an act of faith." He turned a cup right side up and poured the steaming golden-brown liquid. He brought it to his lips and sipped, then set it back on the saucer.

Braidus poured tea into the remaining cup and handed it to me. I accepted it, sensing the mistake it would be if I didn't. I brought it to my lips and tasted chamomile and peppermint.

Braidus rested his elbows on the chair, touching the tips of his fingers together. I could see resemblances between him and Andrew: straight nose, strong jaw ... I refused to search for any more, hating that Braidus could remind me of Andrew.

Braidus assessed me. I saw intelligence behind his eyes, and it sent shivers down my spine. I set the cup down as politely as I could and folded my hands in my lap so he couldn't see them tremble.

I could faintly hear the commotion of children—boys and girls—outside the room and an older lady bellowing at any misbehaving. It didn't seem to fit. Ruthless killer intent on seizing the throne—for I had little doubt he desired anything else—surrounded by innocent children? What ulterior motive did he have?

I wondered how he could get away with doing dastardly deeds in a place full of children. How could people turn a blind eye to kidnapping? I couldn't stop from asking, "What are you doing in an orphanage?"

Braidus smiled. "Turning the hearts of children against their King."

I raised an eyebrow in question. "Why should they hate King Brian?"

"The laws against illegitimate children are why more than half of them reside here," Braidus explained in a matter-of-fact voice.

I eyed Braidus with suspicion. "I'm not familiar with these laws." I couldn't take his words at face value.

Braidus stood. Going over to the desk, he picked up a book, thumbed through a few pages, and handed to me. "Read."

Using a finger to hold my place, I closed the book to see the cover. *The Complete Set of Aberronian Laws during the Reign of King Jason. Unabridged version.* I'd seen this book sitting on Alzmire's desk. He'd often read parts of it to us in his history lessons. Alzmire said King Brian had changed little of his father's laws and therefore considered this book to be accurate enough for our current times. Braidus apparently thought the same.

I flipped back to the page Braidus wanted me to see. The header read, "The status of illegitimate children." Braidus pointed to a sentence halfway down the page. "This line is the most important one. 'A child born out of wedlock shall not be entitled to any birthrights, nor shall he receive any portion of his parents' estate should they die.'" He pointed to another sentence at the end of the page. "'Should the parents marry at a later time, the status of the illegitimate child remains the same.'" He took the book from my hands and closed it with a snap.

I heard the bitterness in Braidus's voice, and I could suddenly see why no one knew he existed. He had no importance, despite being of royal blood and the firstborn son. With this law in place, he had no chance of ruling Aberron.

Braidus set the book on the desk and returned to his seat. "My grandfather—King Jason—wrote that law in retaliation for King Brian fathering me. King Jason gave little thought to how it would affect the citizens of Aberron." He gestured to the room. "Thus, the orphanages are filled with abandoned children, and my father has done nothing to correct it."

I feared the consequences of believing everything that came out of Braidus's mouth. I wanted someone I trusted to validate that King Brian willingly let this injustice go on. "Forgive me if I don't regard your words as outright truth."

Braidus seemed to take no offense, much to my relief. He waved his hand airily. "By all means, ask someone you know. Let them confirm it."

I narrowed my eyes in disbelief. How could I ask someone about it when he held me captive? In an orphanage, no less. *Who does that?* Someone who didn't want to get caught, I decided.

Braidus lifted his chin slightly while his hazel eyes darted back and forth, searching my face. "If you're wondering if I enjoy holding you captive, think again. There's no glory in kidnapping for the fun of it."

I tried to keep my voice even. "Then why have you done it?"

"There are some things I need that you can provide." He picked up his tea and held it in his hands. "It's not every day you run into someone with your special abilities."

I spoke before I could stop myself, "you sent men to claim me in Saren. How did you know then, when I didn't, that I had 'special abilities?'"

Braidus smiled. "You wear the Mark of the Gods in an interesting location. That does not happen to just anyone. I knew you had to be of value."

And then you decided to wait until I came into that knowledge to stake your claim, I thought. I took a deep breath, terrified of asking but knowing I needed to. "What do you want of me?"

He sipped his tea, then spoke. "First I need you go back to the Sorrenian and make up an alibi. I can't have people looking for my hostages."

"What if they don't believe me?" I asked quietly, staring at my folded hands.

"If you truly cared about Henry, you wouldn't be asking that question." Braidus said it lightly but left no confusion that it was a threat, one I believed he would carry out with no compunction if I didn't comply.

I blanched, causing Braidus to chuckle. He rose from his seat and went back to the desk. He reached inside his pocket, inserted a key into a drawer, and unlocked it with a turn of his wrist. He pulled out a small white box, closed the door, and locked it again.

I had little time to worry about the contents of the box when Braidus stood in front of me. As he lifted the lid, I found myself leaning forward to see. A delicate gold chain followed by a pink tourmaline-and-diamond-encrusted golden blossom. *Jewelry.* I exhaled the breath I'd been holding.

Braidus stood. "Allow me the pleasure of seeing you wear this." He came around the back of my chair and clasped it around my neck.

I shivered as the cold necklace met my bare skin. I touched the flower with no doubt in my mind that I probably wore something worth more than Saren altogether. What purpose did it serve? *No.* I amended my question, knowing it hit closer to the truth. What *magical* properties did it have?

Braidus faced me. He reached underneath his shirt and showed me a similar gold chain with an apple tree charm made of gold and red rubies. It clicked. I wore the blossom to his tree.

"These necklaces are a pair," he said. "They were made from the same gold."

"They're beautiful." I waited for him to tell me the catch. There had to be one somewhere.

He smiled in agreement before he spoke. "They are also spelled. The only way to remove yours is to join the tree and the flower together with the key on the back."

He brought his necklace closer. I saw a raised key in the shape of a star on the back of the trunk. I turned mine over and noticed the same hollowed shape. I couldn't take it off. *Great.* What else could they do?

"It will allow me to hear everything you do." Braidus spoke clearly, making sure I could not mistake his words. "And let me to talk to you when I want." He slipped his necklace underneath his shirt, hiding it from view.

"You've thought of everything, haven't you?" I stated it more as fact than question.

Braidus leaned down, resting both hands on mine. I reared back until my head hit the back of the chair. His face so close, I could smell the tea on his breath. I trembled in fear, wishing I hadn't let my tongue get away from me.

"Every detail counts." Eyes locked, he considered me for a moment longer with an expression of curiosity and then abruptly stepped away. "I will escort you to my guard—Stanly—who will deliver you to the Sorrenian and bring you back."

I rose from the chair, put weight on my shaking legs, and allowed Braidus to steer me out of the room.

"Brady!" A girl wearing a loose, brown, patched dress, no older than six and sickeningly thin, waylaid Braidus by throwing herself onto his legs.

Tears threatened to spill over onto her flushed cheeks. "They're doing it again. They're telling me I can't be a soldier in your army."

Braidus gently pried the girl off him and crouched down to meet her eyes. "If you want to be a soldier, then so be it, but I think you would be better suited for a different profession. One that would take more cunning and skill than a common soldier."

The girl's eyes widened in anticipation. "What?"

He smirked. "Wait for me near the kitchen, and I'll tell you."

The girl's eyes quickly flashed to mine with inquisitiveness etched in her face. Abruptly, she swiveled around and ran in the opposite direction, her dark, riotous curls bouncing against her back.

Braidus straightened and gripped my arm once more. "My apologies; the children often accost me with matters of grave importance."

"You treat them better than I would have expected," I said as we moved down the stone hallway and up a stairwell.

Braidus scowled, clearly taking offense at my comment. "Despite what you must think of me, I'm not inherently evil. These children deserve far better than what they receive."

I kept my mouth shut, knowing I'd be liable to say something I shouldn't. I couldn't disagree with his statement, but I struggled with the idea of Braidus not having an evil bone in his body.

Stationed by the door, a guard bowed low to him.

"Take Isabelle to the Sorrenian and wait for her," Braidus ordered as he let go of my arm.

"Right away, Your Majesty." Stanly bowed once more.

Braidus faced me. "You should know, this building is concealed. So should you try to alert someone of your whereabouts, they will spend the entirety of their days searching for something they will never find." He reached inside his pocket and procured a black strip of cloth. "As an added precaution, you must be blindfolded." He tied it over my head, shielding my eyes.

"Fantastic," I muttered.

Braidus whispered as though his lips rested on my ear. "I am nothing but thorough."

I flinched, causing Braidus and Stanly to chuckle. A new hand gripped my arm a little harder than necessary—Stanly, no doubt—and led me inside a carriage reeking of cats, dust, and mold.

He sat next to me and called to the driver, "Drive on!"

I gripped onto the side of the carriage for support. The seats had very little cushion, and the bumpy road jostled me. More than once I bumped into Stanly, but he didn't seem to mind. I would have preferred a horse.

Since I couldn't see and had nothing better to do, I voiced a question that suddenly popped into my mind. I knew Braidus would hear me.

"Can anyone else hear you or just me?" I whispered as quietly as I could. I didn't want Stanly to think I addressed him.

"Anything you say to me will be heard by those around you, but only you can hear my voice," Braidus responded.

Despite the distance between us, I heard him clearly. I took a deep breath and exhaled. *I am doomed.*

As the minutes ticked by, I contemplated Braidus. The few children I had seen in the hallway reacted warmly to him. The little girl went as far as to seek refuge from her tormenters. Their unspoken devotion to him left me little uncertainty that he *was* turning the hearts of children against King Brian. But to what end? What could children do in a fight created by—and most likely for—adults?

"We're here." Stanly pulled the blindfold off. "Don't take too long. I'll be waiting."

I shielded my eyes from the afternoon sun coming in through the carriage window. He opened the door and I stepped out, eager to get away from the stench. I all but ran to the school, marching through the snow and ice. Once I entered the Sorrenian, I headed straight for my room. I needed dry clothes.

In record speed I changed into something dry and warm, not caring if my clothes matched. I tucked the necklace under my shirt. I couldn't have people asking questions about it. I washed my face and patted it dry, hoping to hide that I'd been going through a range of emotions.

I paused by the door and spoke to Braidus through the locket. "If you don't mind, I would like to ask Alzmire about the laws regarding illegitimate children before I make up an alibi." I wanted him to validate Braidus's claims concerning the children in the orphanage and perhaps get a better understanding of my captor. If every detail counted, I wanted many in my arsenal to use against Braidus.

"Go ahead." Braidus spoke casually. "You'll soon learn that I do not lie."

Right. Grateful that he couldn't see the skepticism on my face, I headed out the door in search of Alzmire. I found him in his classroom, sitting behind his desk using the afternoon light to read the paper in his hand.

"Hello, Isabelle." Alzmire greeted me in Nistieran like always. "What brings you here on a Kings Day afternoon?"

My hopes of talking candidly with Alzmire were dashed when Braidus said in perfect Nistieran, "Don't think about it."

I forced a smile and centered my attention on Alzmire. "I have a question for you concerning the laws about illegitimate children."

Alzmire raised an eyebrow. "Should I be concerned? You haven't gotten carried away with Andrew, have you?"

Braidus's enveloping laugh made me flinch. I clamped a hand over my mouth. Crimson heat flushed my cheeks. "No! Gods forbid." I hurried to tell a lie to set the record straight. "I picked up a book in the library—this book actually—" I pointed to the one on Alzmire's desk, *The Complete Set of Aberronian Laws during the Reign of King Jason. Unabridged version.* "I thought I should study up on some laws if I am to continue courting Andrew."

Alzmire pursed his lips and eyed me with suspicion. "Isabelle, you know you can tell me anything in the strictest of confidence, and I will do my best to protect you. If Andrew has—"

I cut him off, sorely regretting asking in the first place. Curse Braidus. No wonder he was so willing to let me ask. "I swear it's not like that. I have not been compromised in that way." Kidnapped, on the other hand ...

Alzmire had the decency to appear a little sheepish at his remarks. "All right. What is your question?"

"I just wanted to know if these laws are still in effect." I grabbed the book on his desk, thumbed through the pages until I found the correct one, and held it out to Alzmire. I pointed to the sentences Braidus had shown me.

Alzmire read through them quickly, then looked up at me and nodded. "Yes. These laws still apply to our current times. King Jason wrote them six years before his reign ended and meant them as a deterrent for courting couples."

I groaned inwardly.

Braidus spoke in a smooth, velvety voice. "The year of my birth, to be exact."

I pasted on a smile to keep myself from reacting to Braidus. "All right. That's all I wanted to know. Thank you." I turned to leave, but Alzmire held up a hand.

"Isabelle, a word of caution. A brief moment of passion, however desirable it may seem, can have lasting consequences. Children born out of wedlock suffer greatly for something they had no control of. Just think about that the next time you see Andrew."

I nodded slowly, flooded with embarrassment from Alzmire's pertinent questions and ire for Braidus who laughed softly in my ear. "I will. Thank you." I hurried out of there as fast as I could.

"Do you believe me now?" Braidus asked, a hint of amusement lacing his tone.

"Yes." I trusted Alzmire to tell me the truth, though I cringed at the conjectures he made.

"Good." Braidus sounded like he genuinely meant it. "Now make up an alibi and come back to me."

My stomach coiled in knots. Despite not having a concrete plan, I knew exactly who I needed to go to. *Dominic.* I headed for the first place I thought I could find him on a Kings Day afternoon. The culture room.

I sighed in relief when I found Henry's usual group lounging, cards and dice in hand. I rushed over, maneuvering between tables, chairs, and students milling around. *Game on.*

Dominic set his cards down. "Isabelle, where have you been? Where's Henry? We looked for you for like half an hour."

I forced my face to appear apologetic. "I'm so sorry. We were right behind you when Henry tripped on some ice. He landed hard, so I took him to Malsin."

Dominic sat up straighter, concerned. "Is he all right?"

"Oh yes, he's fine." I waved nonchalantly. "Just a bruise. Turns out he—" I wrung my hands and fidgeted on the balls of my feet. My mind raced ahead to come up with a believable excuse. *Hold it together, Isabelle!* I mentally screamed.

My chest tightened under the pressure. It hurt to make up lies about Henry, knowing it was my fault Braidus chained him to a wall. "He has the start of the flu. All that running around in the snow this morning made it worse. Malsin said he has to stay in his room for a couple of days and rest. No visitors or you'll get it too. Henry asked me to inform you all." I stared at the faces of Henry's friends, hoping they only saw impassiveness.

Dominic folded his arms and eyed me suspiciously. "But he didn't seem sick this morning."

"It's fast acting. One minute you think you're fine, and the next your limbs go weak and you're throwing up," I said quickly. With a stroke of genius, I added. "Henry said it could have been the roast duck last night. Perhaps it's food poisoning. Did any of you have that?"

Sudden gasps went around the table. Roanna, Marie, and Amarilla clutched their stomachs and clamped a hand over their mouths.

I fed into their fear. "He could be wrong." I shrugged. "Malsin wouldn't pinpoint it on anything specific, but he said Henry is very contagious." I wrinkled my nose. "I don't suppose any of you want to spend the next several days vomiting."

Everyone but Dominic nodded vigorously. He tilted his head slightly and eyed me. Mistrust came off him in waves. I hoped he didn't notice the nervous sweat on my brow. Gods forbid, I wished I could lie better.

"What about you? You were right next to him." Falden pointed at me.

"I'm actually going against Malsin's orders to tell you about Henry. I'm supposed to be in my room. Malsin said I have to be quarantined since Henry threw up on me on our way to the healing rooms." Their faces transformed to disgust. I held up my hands. "Don't worry, I changed before I came down here." I dropped my hands. "Malsin is afraid it will spread through the school like wildfire, so I better not expose you any longer. If anybody asks where we are, tell them what I told you." I sighed and rolled my eyes. "I'm going to be so bored."

Braidus chuckled in my ear. "You wish." I flinched.

I heard murmurs of agreement among the group as I turned to leave. Dominic shot up from his chair and followed me. "Isabelle, wait!"

I made him follow me out to the hallway before I paused.

"Henry's not really sick, is he?" He folded his arms.

"Yes he is." I tried to sound like I meant it.

Dominic shook his head. "Cut the lies. People only fidget like you just did when they're lying. What's really going on?"

"Choose your words carefully," Braidus interrupted.

"I am," I muttered tersely.

I took a step closer to Dominic, my eyes pleading. "Please, for Henry's sake, don't question me."

Dominic's eyes widened. "What have you done?"

"I haven't done anything. I swear it." I balled my fists, trying to keep my emotions in check. "But I am trying to keep him safe. I can't do it without your help."

"Whatever mess you're into, Henry shouldn't be involved. He doesn't deserve it." Dominic took a step back, his face contorting to a mix of hatred, concern, and apprehension.

Without Henry, I knew Dominic and I would never willingly be friends. We were opposite sides of a coin, never meant to meet except molded together with one single purpose. Save Henry.

My voice broke. "Don't you think I know that?" My hands pressed together in front of me, I begged. "Please—help me."

He sighed and rubbed his temples. "I'll do it for Henry, not you. Get him out of whatever problem you're in. Now."

I nodded, fighting back the tears of remorse. "I'm doing everything I can. I promise."

"So, what do you need?" Dominic glanced around the hallway as he leaned against the wall once more.

"Just stick to the story I gave, sick with food poisoning," I said quickly. He nodded.

"Thanks," I whispered.

"Don't thank me," Dominic snarled. "I knew you were going to be trouble; I'm just sorry Henry had to get mixed up in it."

I flinched.

"Thanks all the same," I said quietly, wringing my hands. I stared at the ground and took a deep breath. "I've got to go." I looked up, and my breath caught in my throat. My eyes widened as I backed up against the wall.

Andrew.

Dominic raised an eyebrow, seeming confused at my expression, until he heard the footsteps and turned around. Andrew strode down the hallway, a soft smile on his face. Dominic stepped away so Andrew could join us. But he couldn't. I wouldn't let him get mixed up in all of this.

I reacted out of fear as I put my hand out and shouted. "Don't come any closer!" As soon as the words came out, I clamped a hand over my mouth, realizing my stupidity. Braidus would surely want to know who I shouted at. Could I lie? I made a mental note to keep my mouth shut whenever possible.

Andrew stopped, his eyebrows raised in surprise. I put a finger to my lips signaling silence. He narrowed his eyes at me but heeded my command. I walked slowly to him, my heart beating out of my chest.

My shout brought people peeking out of the doorway from the culture room. They stared openmouthed but, thank the Gods, silent.

"I'll say this once, so listen carefully." Braidus spoke in clear, clipped tones. "If you truly want to undermine me, you have to lose the fear. Your attempts so far have been admirable but weak. Think over your situation carefully, then ask yourself if hiding this person from me is worth more than Henry's life."

I groaned and thought up every single insult and curse the jealous girls had painted on Henry and directed them at myself. I hadn't expected Braidus to school me on how to undermine a master villain. Which, once again, left me questioning his motives.

I spent less than a second to think over my situation. In this case, Henry mattered more.

I stood far enough away that Andrew couldn't touch me and thought fast. "I'm so sorry, Andrew, but Henry caught the stomach flu. He threw up on me, and Malsin said I need to be quarantined. I don't want to get you sick as well."

"Andrew ..." Braidus mused. "Did he come alone or with Joshua?"

"Alone," I muttered.

"Allow me to escort you to your room," Andrew said cordially.

I gave a short nod. "Thank you."

"Well then, let's make this interesting," Braidus said.

My stomach lurched at his words. I clenched my jaw. I imagined Braidus sitting in a green plush chair, a drink in hand, listening to my interactions for entertainment. Perhaps the children played around him on their side of the room.

Andrew turned around and we strolled amiably out of the hallway. I wanted to grasp his hand and tell him everything, but I fought the urge. I needed to hold it together for Henry's sake.

As we reached the entry hall, I pointed to the double doors. "Could we get some fresh air? I'd like a moment to breathe before I'm shut in my room."

Andrew nodded. We strolled out the front doors and into the snow. I led him over to the gazebo where Henry, Dominic, Falden, and Aliyah had shown me how to recharge my core during the storm.

"You seem upset. Are you all right?" Andrew asked as we sat. He reached for my hand, and I took his. I closed my eyes and breathed deeply. I didn't know how much time I would get with Andrew or if I'd ever see him again. I'd take what I could get.

"I'm all right." I forced the words out, surprised that they sounded genuine. Andrew's presence worked wonders. "It's just been a rough day with Henry and all." I sighed and admitted a different truth. "I miss Saren."

Andrew frowned. "I see." He rubbed my hand with his thumb.

"That was good." Braidus sounded surprised but pleased. "Now let's see how far you're willing to sacrifice your own happiness for someone else. End your courtship with my brother."

"No!" My whisper came out strangulated. My heart clenched as tears threatened to spill from my eyes.

"Isabelle?" Andrew eyed me with concern. "If it's bothering you so much, I'll make Joshua take you back. You probably didn't get much of a goodbye since you had to run away."

I blinked my tears away and focused on Andrew. "No. Winter has started, it would be foolish to go now. I just need time to think, and to do that, I'm going to need some space." I took a deep breath and spoke the words that would crush my spirit. "Andrew, I don't think I can court you any longer."

He let go of me as though he'd been shocked. He leaned away from me. "I don't understand." A range of emotions from confusion to hurt flitted across his face. "Tell me you do not love me."

"I ..." I couldn't do it. I put a finger to my lips, signaling silence as I sank onto the wooden planks of the gazebo. My knees sunk into the snow that had blown over. I did two things simultaneously, knowing any pause in speech would make Braidus suspicious.

"I'm just a little confused right now about me—about us," I said as I wrote **Braidus control** in the snow.

Andrew stiffened; his face masked into something I couldn't read as he stared at the two words I'd written.

I reached underneath my shirt, careful to not let the chain give me away, and showed Andrew the necklace. I pointed to my ear, so he'd get the message. He narrowed his eyes in anger, and his whole body tensed.

Underneath my first message, I wrote **No help or Henry dies.** I spoke. "I just need some time to reevaluate my life—my priorities. I don't think you can be a part of that."

"How is he taking it?" Braidus asked.

"Not good," I whispered.

Andrew eyed me like a predator watches prey. When I responded to Braidus, he pointed to the necklace and then to his ear, with comprehension. I nodded.

Andrew cleared his throat. "If that's what you think you need." He spoke softly with some emotion I couldn't pinpoint. Hurt, worry, or anger? He took a breath and exhaled slowly. "Will you do something for me?"

I stared at him expectantly.

Andrew held on to my hands. "When you decide what's best for you, let me know. Until then, I will wait for you." Reaching down, he wrote in the snow, **I'll save you.**

"All right." I stood with Andrew's assistance and used my boot to wipe out the messages. "Goodbye, Andrew." I brushed my lips against his cheek and left him standing there.

I trudged through the ice to the school. I waited on the front steps until Andrew had ridden out of the Sorrenian, then I headed to the carriage.

"Well done, my little soldier," Braidus praised. "You take orders very well."

"You are cruel," I said, fighting through emotion.

Stanly put the blindfold back on when I got to the carriage, and off we went to the orphanage.

My emotions twisted around like a corkscrew wedging its way through my heart. Why didn't Andrew tell me he had a brother? An evil one at that.

Betrayal and hurt ran deep in my veins. My heart said to forgive Andrew, that he probably had a legitimate reason for keeping Braidus a secret. And yet, I couldn't dislodge the thought that Braidus was only the beginning to a series of secrets Andrew didn't want revealed.

I knew without a shadow of a doubt that I loved Andrew, but as I reflected on the words I said to him, I found myself truly believing it. I needed space to deliberate. If we couldn't be open and honest with each other, what kind of relationship did we have?

The carriage jarred to a halt. Stanly gripped my arm, led me inside the building, then removed the blindfold. Braidus casually walked to us, a hint of a smile resting on his lips.

"They are just serving dinner. Would you care to join me?" He held out a hand and I let him take mine.

"Is Henry all right?" I asked as we moved in the direction of the chatter echoing down a torchlit hallway. The building reminded me of a nobleman's home. Fleeting memories of my parents' house in Korrun came to mind, and I remembered running down hallways very much like this one as a child.

"Henry is perfectly fine. With the exception of new clothes, he has everything we agreed upon," Braidus assured.

We rounded a corner and walked through an open archway into a dining hall. Several rectangular tables had been pushed together to create two long tables for the forty or so children. They ranged in ages from infant to fourteen. One small table for the adults rested in the corner of the room. There seemed to be no sense of order for the seating arrangements, but as I stared, I noticed a pattern. One older child or teen assigned to a younger one. Three middle-aged women hustled and bustled, placing bowls of soup and pieces of bread on the tables. Pitchers of cider had already been poured into tiny cups.

"Brady's brought a girl!" a boy who looked about seven shouted.

He didn't need to shout; all eyes were already on me; the children's faces full of curiosity. Braidus seated me at the empty table. Before he had a chance to step away, one of the ladies serving soup approached him.

Hands on hips, she stared up at Braidus, reminding me of a mother hen. "Brady, you know I don't like you mixing your business with the children." She glanced at me furtively with eyes the shade of amber. "I've agreed to let you stay here, and for the most part there's been no trouble. But Gods forbid, fireballs? Are you trying to bring this house to the ground?" An exasperated look crossed her roundish face. "I've got Nestor holed up in bed and in a healing sleep. That woman set his nerves on fire. *Fire*, Brady."

"I assure you, Greta, she will be quite cordial now," Braidus said smoothly.

"If you're gonna keep prisoners with mage abilities, then at least make them wear the chains. I'd feel safer that way," Greta said with a huff.

"Oh, I don't think that will be necessary." He looked at me. "Will it?"

"No," I said quietly with a shake of my head.

Braidus smiled and faced Greta. "See, she's quite docile now."

Greta frowned and muttered something unintelligible under her breath, though I thought I picked out the word *dog*. "I'll bring you your soup and bread." She stalked off.

Braidus sat across from me. Around us the children conversed happily, and several conversations centered around Braidus and me as they speculated about the relationship between us. I kept my eyes firmly on Braidus but listened to the chatter.

"Think Brady's courtin' her?" a boy said.

"She's awful pretty; if he ain't, he better ask her quick," another boy said.

"Sure got fancy clothes—where you think she came from?" a girl asked with a wistful tone in her voice.

"The factory," another girl said in a matter-of-fact tone. "I heard they make 'em real smart with manners and everything for the noblemen."

"Brady's a nobleman," a boy pointed out. "He probably picked her out. Gods forbid, he's gonna get married."

Braidus chuckled softly, and I could tell he listened to the children as well. My cheeks flushed, and I stared at my clasped hands, unable to look at him any longer. Greta arrived with soup and bread and two cups of cider.

I focused on the food in front of me, surprised by how delicious the hearty soup tasted.

After a few mouthfuls, I got enough courage to talk to Braidus. "May I ask you something?"

He nodded as he picked apart his piece of bread with his fingers.

"The chains, how are they able to stop the magic?" I chose a question I figured had the best chance of him answering.

"There is a rare plant, commonly known as the Enchantress. It produces a white flower with golden edges that is intoxicating to mages. Most are unable to resist its hypnotic beauty and aroma. Once they touch it, the Enchantress feeds off their magic. The plant is harmless to people without the ability but lethal to those with and can live for hundreds of years off a single mage." Braidus set his bread down and picked up his spoon. "It has many uses, one of them being the ability to stop mages from using their powers. I simply coated the chains in a solution." Braidus shrugged.

"I see." I picked up my bread. "It won't hurt Henry, will it?"

Braidus shook his head. "No. It only prevents him from using his magic."

I breathed a sigh of relief. "Good."

When dinner ended, Braidus led me to a bathroom so I could freshen up, then took me to Henry. "We shall reconvene tomorrow." He opened the door and gestured for me to enter. I walked through and he closed the door behind me.

"Isabelle!" Henry threw his arms out as though he wanted to rush to me, but he didn't move his legs. The cuff shackled to his ankle prevented him from going far. "Are you all right? What happened?"

Henry had a thick wool blanket over him, a basket of apples and bread, a canteen, an empty bucket, and a large lantern for light and heat. I raised my eyebrows in surprise. Braidus did hold up his end of the bargain. I sat next to Henry and leaned my back against the wall.

"I'm fine." I pulled out the necklace and pointed to it then at my ear. Henry's eyes flashed, but he nodded.

"What happened?" He repeated. "You've been gone for hours. I swear I've been hearing children in the hall. Where are we?"

"In an orphanage." I shrugged, making it clear I didn't know why Braidus chose this place as his lair. "Braidus wanted an alibi so we wouldn't be looked for. I went back to the Sorrenian and told everyone you got food poisoning from the roast duck we had last night," I explained.

"Roast duck, huh?" He propped one leg up and glanced at me ruefully. "You know that's my favorite, so many people eat it. If no one else gets sick it's hardly likely anyone is going to believe that."

"It is?"

Henry nodded.

I grimaced. "Well, it better work because that's all I could think of." I rubbed my eyes and sighed.

He searched my face. "You've been crying. What else did he make you do?"

"I saw Andrew." My voice wavered.

"You did?"

"He came to visit." My lower lip trembled as I spilled it all. "Braidus told me to end my courtship with him, so I did. I told him I needed some space to think things out."

Henry rubbed my shoulder. "Don't worry, Isabelle, Andrew will understand."

My face crumpled in pain. "I don't know. I meant every word I said." It hurt that Andrew had neglected to tell me about Braidus, and I needed time to get over that.

Henry opened his mouth and closed it, appearing at a loss for words. "Oh." He removed his hand and folded his arms, not seeming to know what to do.

I pulled a portion of his blanket over my legs. Knowing Braidus was privy to all my conversations, I wouldn't tell Henry that I told Andrew about our predicament. I held on to a sliver of hope that he would find us. And even if he didn't or couldn't, at least he knew what had become of us.

"I know why the chains are stopping the magic. Braidus told me," I said.

"Why?"

I launched into the explanation about the plant, Enchantress.

"Must be super rare if I've never heard of it," Henry finally said with a frown.

I nodded and closed my eyes, exhausted emotionally and physically. I fell asleep leaning against the wall.

CHAPTER THIRTY-TWO

I DIDN'T DREAM, BUT AS I drifted in and out of consciousness, I felt watched. Even asleep I couldn't forget who controlled me.

Braidus hovered over me, a breath away from my face when I opened my eyes. I yelped and slammed my head against the stone wall. Braidus chuckled while I rubbed the back of my head and cursed. Henry, his head leaning against the wall already, opened his eyes blearily, searching for the source of the commotion. His face hardened when he discovered Braidus.

"Come with me," Braidus said softly, reaching for my hand.

I had no choice but to obey. I accepted his hand and he pulled me up. I looked over my shoulder once and gave Henry an apologetic smile as we left. Braidus led me to a bathroom. "Freshen up, then Stanly will escort you to me."

I nodded.

A frivolous dark blue dress and undergarments hung on a hook. A drawn bath made the room steamy, and I relaxed a smidge. I turned on the water faucet to relieve myself as I had done last night so Braidus wouldn't hear me. Silly, but I couldn't help it. I sunk into the bath and vigorously washed, wiping away the grime and the dried tears. I couldn't hide the internal tension despite appearing fresh.

I patted myself dry with a towel and dressed. I slipped on the dark blue dress he expected me to wear. I brushed my hair back and pinned it with a large silver butterfly hairpin. I left the necklace out in the open.

I sat in a green plush chair. Braidus had tea and a plate of small cakes set in between us.

He gestured to the food. "Please eat."

"Thank you." I picked up the cake and bit into it.

Braidus didn't touch the food but sipped on tea. He watched me with interest, and I wondered what crossed his mind but couldn't bring myself to ask. Thankfully I didn't have to wait long. He spoke. "Have you ever considered your worth?"

"If you're talking monetary value, I have no idea how much money I have. Joshua hasn't told me," I said. "If you mean me personally, the only thing I'm good for is attracting trouble."

"Your powers alone are worth more than every coin in the Royal Treasury." Braidus set his teacup down and draped one leg over the other. "I have traveled extensively, and I can say with absolute certainty that I have never met your match."

"What are you getting at?" I narrowed my eyes. "You're not going to try and sell me off, are you?"

He half smiled and shook his head. "Absolutely not. I wouldn't have spent the last several months trying to secure you, only to give you away. I'd guard you with my life if I had to."

"And yet I'm your prisoner." I scowled. "That doesn't make much sense. Shouldn't prisoners be expendable? Henry is to you."

Braidus scoffed. "Henry isn't you. He isn't worth even a quarter of what you are despite his status as second in line."

"What makes you say that?" I leaned slightly forward. "What do you know about me?"

He chuckled at the eagerness in my voice, but I couldn't help it. I'd spent so much time trying to unravel the mysteries in my life and hardly got anywhere.

"You do a few more things for me, and I promise I'll tell you something," Braidus said.

I sighed. "What would you have me do?"

"I was thinking about the children this morning." He rubbed his chin. "Their clothes are starting to show their wear, and they could use some new ones. It's about time I sent a message to my father, so I thought I could do both." He took a breath and met my eyes. "I want you to steal two bags of gold Sundals from the Royal Treasury and deliver them to me."

My jaw dropped a little. "Steal?"

"Yes. Stanly will drop you off in front of the castle." Braidus stood. "The Treasury is located at the base of the castle, and it is guarded by ten highly skilled men every hour of the day. You have three hours."

"And If I'm not back in time?" I asked, worry gnawing a hole through my stomach. I feared he asked too much of me. I'd only just discovered my powers, after all.

"Henry's here for your sake. Not mine," Braidus reminded. "Make sure to camouflage yourself to avoid Joshua and my family. It would not bode well for Henry should they discover you."

"Right," I muttered.

Stanly blindfolded and shoved me into the stinky carriage. While we rode, I focused on opening the magic. Boomer danced, excited to be free of his cage. Then the magic brought back to remembrance the cuff and chains that prevented him from coming out. Boomer growled, and I got the distinct impression he wanted to tell me how much he hated it. I dropped down to my knees and petted him. I spoke to him in soothing tones. "I know, I hated it too, but I'm going to need you to work for me now, all right?" I let him feel my strong need for him. Boomer barked and wagged his tail. I felt the magic buzz more intensely in my veins. I smiled. The magic and me united. Together, we could work to accomplish a seemingly impossible goal.

I dropped into my core for a minute to check my levels: three-quarters full. I hoped that would be enough.

"We're here."

I blinked back in reality. Stanly took the blindfold off. "I will wait for you here with the driver."

I nodded and stepped out into the snow. I shivered as the wind bit through my clothes. Many carriages drove up to the castle gates, letting people in and out. Multiple guards warmly dressed milled about, keeping tabs on the richly clothed people arriving and departing. My dark wool coat and blue dress blended in perfectly with the other patrons.

Stanly had parked a little way down from the front entrance. I didn't think the guards would be watching me as I headed straight for a large bush and hid behind it. I needed time to formulate a plan.

Once hidden, I let all my emotions play out. I buried my face in my wind-chilled hands. *What am I going to do?* I paced back and forth trying to come up with something sustainable.

I had never stolen anything in my entire life, let alone two bags of gold from the Royal Treasury right under the King's nose. Alzmire's recent history lesson on the treasury popped into my head. I replayed it in my mind, skipping over the mundane parts to the vital information.

Alzmire had paced back and forth, his hands resting behind his back. "The judgment is the same whether you take a single copper Starlet or every last coin in the vicinity." He paused and whipped around to face us. His eyes flashed to steel. "Death."

I remembered how uncomfortable the air got then, and the nervous chuckles that followed. Alzmire started pacing again, a soft smile on his lips, and I suspected nervous fear was exactly what he wanted to instill in us. "Now who can tell me why?" And with one question, spoken in the mild manner of a professor, the room thawed.

It was Henry who answered the question, as perhaps one day he might be the one giving out the judgments. "It acts as a deterrent. With a sentence so severe, it might persuade many to desist. Though, action and judgment are swift with hardly a trial if they don't."

I kicked at the evergreen bush in anger and watched the snow dust the ground. There would be repercussions somewhere down the line, I knew it. Was Braidus insane to think that I could just waltz right in and take two bags of money without them noticing? I wanted to scream and pound my fists into something. I wanted to sink into the snow and forget I even existed. What had I—or Henry—done to deserve this? What kind of sick infatuation did Braidus play out through me?

Did it matter?

No.

I closed my eyes and mentally stripped away everything about me. My heart, my dreams, my wishes, even my name. I entered one thought—the single command Braidus had given me—and I felt the magic within me surge to a new level. Had I not peeled away my persona, I would have been terrified at the level of power coursing through my veins. Instead, I felt mildly happy. *Strange.*

I called on the yellow magic and focused on blending myself into my surroundings until I couldn't see my body. *Fantastic.* I grinned, drunk with power.

I walked through the gates completely undetected. Not even my footprints showed up. Then I realized my feet weren't touching the ice. I walked on an air current, hovering a little above ground level. *Amazing.* I followed two elaborately dressed old men and slipped in through the front door as it closed. The air current disappeared, and my feet touched the hard stone with hardly a sound. I barely gave the grand entrance hall a second glance. My eyes darted to the two sets of marble stairs. I chose the descending set, remembering Braidus had said the treasury was located at the base of the castle.

I padded nearly silent through the halls, scarcely looking at the extravagant palace décor. Two guards rounded a corner, and I sneaked up behind them. I listened to their conversation, hoping it would lead me to where I needed to go.

"Did you watch the sword practice today?"

"No, what did I miss?"

"Dadel got clobbered by the Commander."

The other guard snorted. "That's nothing new. No one has beaten the Commander in months. Mirran is brutal."

My ears perked up at the sound of my last name.

"Yeah, but you should have seen it. Dadel was all jelly by the time Mirran was done with him. They had to drag him off the floor," the man persisted.

I smirked, feeling proud to call Joshua my brother. Too bad he couldn't help me now; Braidus made sure to convince me not to go to him. Another guard ran down an intersecting hallway and nearly crashed into the two men I followed. I froze.

"Watch it!"

"Sorry!" he called, hightailing it down the hallway.

"Hey, where are you going in such a hurry?" the story-telling guard asked.

The man didn't answer but continued running.

I trotted out from behind the two guards and chased after the sprinting man. Anybody that ran that fast had to be going somewhere important. I trailed behind him as close as I could so that his footsteps would muffle mine. I followed him through the labyrinth of hallways and descending stairs.

He breathed in labored puffs and sweat dripped off his brow as he ran at a fast but steady pace. It occurred to me that I should be breathing just as heavily, and yet I felt like I barely exerted energy despite matching his speed. And in a dress no less. Should that bother me? *Yes.* Did it? *No.* In this state of mind, nothing the magic did worried me; instead, it left me intrigued, giddy even. I welcomed the magic as though it were a food source. It raced through my veins, feeding me with its power but never quite satisfying my needs. I wanted more.

At the last minute, the guard ran into an office. Not the treasury. *Great.* I slowed my pace and continued down several hallways with no success. The castle was worse than the Sorrenian.

Just when I started to lose hope, I stumbled upon the treasury. At the same time, a guard made it to his post—a big bare room with a wooden door, in front of which nine men stood stock-still and silent. The guard was immediately reprimanded by another sentry. I backed into a corner and watched.

"Gods forbid, Jason, where have you been? I was ready to start a search party for you."

The man—Jason—gripped his knees as he caught his breath. Apparently, he'd been running too. "Commander Mirran wanted me." He straightened up.

"You're not in trouble, are you?" The guard narrowed his eyes.

He shook his head and fell into position, breathing heavily.

I took a good long look at what I was up against. I eyed the men first, noticing an array of weapons—short knives, batons and the like—tied securely to their belts. They were armed to the teeth.

I cast my eyes to the wooden mahogany door, so plain and simple it could have led to a broom closet. Had the men not guarded it, I would have thought nothing special lurked behind it.

I looked for hidden triggers in the ceilings and corners of the room, but I didn't see anything. I lost my concentration once as I wondered what the men did for entertainment. Standing in an empty room for hours had to be boring.

Focus, Isabelle, I reminded myself. Ten men couldn't be enough to protect the Royal Treasury. I closed my eyes and willed for the magic to show me what my physical eyes couldn't see. When I opened them again, I saw through the yellow magic.

Bolts lined the doorframe, something I didn't see before because they had been painted to match the mahogany. I focused on the bolts and watched as they transformed into little points. They would impale anyone that tried to enter unlawfully. I smiled. *Clever.* Now where was the switch?

I suspected there to be a button of some sort to shut it off. How else did the King get in and out without spearing himself? Nevertheless, I couldn't find anything remotely helpful in sight.

I presumed one of the guards carried something on their person, but my fear of discovery made finding out for sure impossible. Perhaps they said a certain word, a password that disabled it. I shifted uneasily on my feet. I didn't have all day to guess. I needed a better option and fast. I called upon the green magic while maintaining the yellow, deciding to test out the only option I could think of.

But first, I needed a distraction—something to get the guards' attention. I searched for something on the men that I could use, but I didn't see anything I could reach without someone noticing. I pulled the large silver butterfly hairpin out and let my hair fall freely down my back. I held it tightly in my hand and tiptoed around the men until I stood in the middle of them all. I kept a watchful eye on my escape as I willed the hairpin to become visible and dropped it onto the ground. I dodged out of the way.

It clattered onto the marble floors. The guards jumped into action and turned to find the source of the ringing. They huddled together staring at the butterfly hairpin.

"Somebody fess up," the reprimanding guard said. "Rule number five says that no guards shall have anything on their persons that is not related to guarding the treasury. Which one of you was holding on to this for your lady friend?"

Instant commotion. The guards talked over one another to defend themselves.

"Wasn't me—"

"How dare you accuse—"

"Ben has a date tonight with—"

I bit my lip to keep from laughing as I ran to them at an almost inhuman speed. Using the green magic, I touched parts of their bodies—their arms, backs, or whatever I could reach—and put them to sleep. I managed to get four down before the others noticed something was going on.

"We're under attack!" a guard shouted as he drew his sword. The others still standing quickly followed suit. Their eyes darted for something they couldn't see.

Me.

"Reveal yourself, yellow mage." A guard swung his blade around, cutting through the air.

No thank you, I thought. I sneaked up behind two guards back-to-back with their weapons held out in front of them. I touched their shoulders. They dropped to the floor, asleep. Four more to go.

One of the guards kicked at his comrade, who groaned and then started to snore. "Gods forbid, there's more than one guy in here. They're putting us to sleep."

"Group together. Hold your swords out, and we'll move in a circle. Aim your swords high and low." A guard motioned for the other two to come to him.

A good thought, but they couldn't outmatch me. As the three guards raced to their companion, I beat them to it. I slid behind the guard calling the others and in one fell swoop got them all as they moved into position. It took me less than twenty seconds to knock them all to the ground.

I pumped my fist. *Success!*

Then it hit me. I stumbled backward and clutched my heart under the crushing disappointment emanating from the green magic. In my mind's eye, I saw Boomer whine, and the sleeping men flashed before my eyes. I knew he wanted me to go back and heal the ones with injuries underneath their uniforms. But I couldn't. I sent a very firm mental *no* to Boomer. He dropped to the ground; his tail tucked between his legs. I sighed in relief as the overwhelming depression lifted.

I swiveled around and stared at the door until an idea flew into my head half a minute later. I grabbed a dagger from one of the men and threw it at the door. The bolts transformed into sharp points and shot from their holes, lodging into the opposite sides of the doorframe.

I frowned and rested my hand on my chin when I realized my assessment had been a little off. The sharp points connected to long rods, creating a metal gate that appeared impenetrable.

I thought of a number of different things to combat this and started off with the simplest one: a fireball. It created a shower of sparks as it connected with the metal but did not explode.

I stepped forward and inspected the gate for the least bit of damage. I rolled my eyes. Great, a few singe marks. *Super helpful.* I tried out the next idea. I called upon the blue magic and touched the metal. Cool mist wafted off the bars as I froze them.

I stepped back and created a larger fireball. I fueled my anger for Braidus into it, and I imagined him as the gate. I lobbed it.

I ducked as metal pieces flew everywhere, hitting the unconscious men behind me. They hardly stirred. The noise, louder than the guard's shouts, had me praying that no one came running to investigate. I rushed to the door and yanked on the handle. When it didn't open, I iced the handle and threw a smaller fireball at it, breaking the lock. The door creaked opened.

The room easily rivaled the size of the dining hall at the Sorrenian. I sprinted to the first pile of tan bags, not bothering to study the numerous treasures before me. Once it was untied, I ran a hand through the bag to check. I grabbed a second bag and did the same, confirming they contained only gold Sundals. I heaved them over my shoulder, groaning slightly under the weight, and made them invisible.

Two hours had already passed. I trudged past the unconscious men, not bothering to shut the door behind me. Anyone could get through it now; I'd broken every lock. I felt my physical and magical energy start to drain as I tiptoed through the maze of hallways, searching for an exit. Sweat beaded on my brow as I labored, lugging the two bags of gold and fueling my desire to stay invisible. My shoulders became stiff and sore, my hands sweaty. My heart beat out of my chest and pounded in my ears. The only thing that kept me going was Henry. I couldn't let him down.

I skirted around the people loitering about in the hallways, guards and servants and nobles alike, careful to make as little noise as possible. More than once someone nearly bumped into me unbeknownst. I didn't know what I would do if I saw Andrew or Joshua, but I didn't have to worry because I didn't see a single person I recognized.

As I got down the front steps of the castle, a wind current masked my steps in the snow again. I successfully made it through the entrance gate before a loud gong from a tower bell rent the air.

"Close the gates!" a guard shouted. "The Royal Treasury has been robbed!"

The sentry men rushed to slam the gates shut, bewildering the people arriving.

"Everyone must be searched!" a guard screamed.

Ha, not me, I thought slyly.

Stanly waited a considerable distance away from the front gates. I hid behind a large tree and unveiled my body. I kept the money bags disguised. I balled my hands into fists and held them at my sides so it seemed like I staved off the cold. Stanly sat next to the driver; his face impassive as his muddy brown eyes roamed.

He caught sight of me and jumped off the seat. His feet dug into the snow as he opened the door for me. I climbed inside the carriage and set the bags down. The coins jangled. I led the tired Boomer back inside his crate, shutting off the magic, and revealed the two tan bags.

With a twitch of his mouth, Stanly blindfolded me again. I suspected he enjoyed doing it.

"How much time have I got left?" I asked no one in particular.

Braidus answered. "Twenty minutes."

I sighed and leaned my head back, hoping we could make it back in time. I closed my eyes underneath the blindfold and brought my persona back to life. Every thought that I had discarded to do this job came roaring back. My hopes, dreams, and morals.

I clutched at my sides, crushed under the guilty weight of my actions. I stole from the King. The very essence of my moral fiber had been violated. My long-standing belief in upholding the law and protecting and defending others and myself against criminals had been turned against me. I was the criminal now. I had to live with the consequences of my actions, but Gods forbid it hurt.

Braidus sat in a green plush chair when we arrived, watching the children play leisurely with hand-carved wooden toys.

"Brady's girl is back," a boy noted, pushing his curly red hair away from his eyes.

Stanley set the two bags on the desk. Braidus stood, moved over to the desk, and untied the strings, letting the Sundals spill out.

There were audible gasps from the children and Greta, who was sitting on the green couch watching the children. Braidus scooped a handful and presented each child in the room with one Sundal. "This is but a small portion of what your King owes you for the injustices you've been served."

They held their coins in their clasped hands, with wonder in their eyes.

"Greta, can we go to market?" a girl asked, clutching on to her Sundal with reverence.

Greta stood. "Not today, but we'll go soon. Children, run up to your rooms and get your books. It's time for lessons."

The children reluctantly filed out of the room.

Greta faced Braidus. "Stolen money, Brady? Is that really how you want to get back at your father?"

"You think he would let me waltz into his study and speak to him?" Braidus scowled. "He would rather execute me than look at me."

Greta shook her head impatiently. "You're not going to win him over if you're stealing from his treasury."

"It doesn't have to be his treasury." Braidus flexed his fingers, anger showing on his face. "It can be mine."

Greta put her hands on her hips. "And how are you going to do that, Brady? Try to kill him again? Because that worked out so well for you last time."

"No. My plan was flawed. I was foolish when I acted out of resentment." Braidus spoke bitterly. "I won't make that mistake again."

Greta pursed her lips but nodded.

Braidus reached in his pocket and handed her a medium-size velvet drawstring bag. "Order new clothes for the children. They need it."

My eyes widened when I realized he gave her his own money, not what I had stolen for him. Greta took the bag and swiftly left the room without a word.

Braidus swiveled around and faced me. He held out his hand. "Come, I'll take you to Henry."

I placed my hand in his and let him lead me out of the room. Curiosity got the best of me, and I blurted my question before I could stop myself. "Greta treats you like a son. Why is that?"

Braidus chuckled. "In many ways, she is my mother. The same night my mother birthed me; Greta also had a baby. The Gods were exceptionally cruel that day, for she lost her child as I lost my mother. Greta became my nursemaid and the only one who ever saw true potential in me."

I had little doubt pity showed on my face. I couldn't even begin to imagine the pain Greta must have felt.

We paused outside of Henry's door. Braidus faced me, his hazel eyes meeting mine, and for a moment I wondered how evil he really was. How much was a front? I couldn't condone what he had done to Henry and me. I never would. And yet, I found myself wanting to peel back the layers of Braidus and see the real man underneath. What he truly hoped to gain out of all of this. A kingdom?

I couldn't be sure.

"I'm sure Henry is anxious to hear about your escapades today." Braidus opened the door. "Enlighten him."

I walked into the room in a daze. I collapsed next to Henry and leaned my head against the wall, staring blindly at the ceiling. Confusion riddled throughout me, from the top of my head to the tips of my toes. Nothing made sense anymore.

Henry stared at me, concern and pity showing on his face.

"I'm a villain," I said softly.

"What happened, Isabelle?" He placed a hand on my shoulder.

I turned my head sideways to meet his eyes and spoke listlessly. "I stole two bags of gold from the Royal Treasury."

"You what?" Henry exclaimed, visibly taken aback at the news. "How did you do it?"

My voice sounded bland as I told him my master plan to steal the money.

"Gods forbid, Isabelle. I can't believe you did that." His eyes widened in astonishment. He ran a hand through his hair and shook his head. I wondered if he wanted to believe it was a lie, a dream. I certainly wished it so.

I tried to defend my actions. "Braidus gave me three hours, or you would be dead. I had to do it." I buried my face in my hands and shuddered.

Henry rubbed my upper back, but even his face seemed grim. We all knew what the outcome of this would be. I would continue to be Braidus's puppet as long as he held on to Henry. I was his to command.

CHAPTER THIRTY-THREE

 FELL ON MY KNEES into the hard, icy snow, gasping for breath. Tears streamed down my face. "What is happening to me?" I cried out.

My hands shook uncontrollably. Cold shivers ran down my spine. I was clammy, sweaty, and covered in garbage. I saw blood on my dress. Was that my blood or someone else's? I reflected in horror. *What have I done?*

The sky started to darken; I guessed it to be six or seven in the evening. I'd fallen in an alley soiled with a smell that would rapidly make milk curdle. It reeked of rotten fish and animal remains. I had no memory whatsoever of getting here. The last thing I remembered was Braidus pulling me away from Henry. *Why am I here?*

My thoughts turned to one action. *Find Henry.* I started to stand before realizing my mistake. I cried out in pain. Blood bloomed before my eyes onto the lower half of my ragged light pink dress. My fingers trailed down my side. My hand became sticky with the congealing blood. *There.* My fingers wrapped around cold metal lodged in my upper thigh. A knife.

I groaned. *Gods forbid, why?* Again, I desired to know what had led me to this circumstance, but my memory blanked out. My breathing came in short gasps as the pain caught up with me. How much blood had I lost? Was I close to death?

My magic already opened, I called on the green and put a hand on the wound. I hoped to heal it myself, but the second my hand touched the wound, the magic sputtered. I didn't have enough power to heal it. I quickly shut the magic off before it latched on the wound and killed me while, ironically, it tried to heal.

I launched into a slow crawl. My fingers clawed the icy snow and burned from the cold. I searched for a section of earth to plunge my hand into but found only cobblestones underneath me. I dragged myself to the side of a building, wheezing at the effort. I wept from the pain and gripped my leg.

I turned my head and saw it. A broken flower pot a few paces away. I moved to it, stretching out my arms as far as they would go to pull my body along. I gripped the pot's jagged edge and tugged it to me. I sunk the tip of my finger in the remaining dirt and charged.

Taking a deep breath, I squared my shoulders and gripped the knife. I couldn't stop the scream ripping out of my chest as I yanked it out. I threw it away from me as though it were on fire and swiftly put my hand over the wound, healing it.

I stumbled over to the edge of a building, sat, and leaned against it, shivering against the penetrating cold.

"Oh, Henry," I whispered. "I've failed you now."

"Isabelle?" Braidus's voice infiltrated my ear.

"Braidus?" His cool voice sent a jolt through my system, shocking me into reality.

"Where are you?" he asked.

"I don't know. In some alley. I just pulled a knife out of my leg." I sniffed, attempting to stanch the steady flow of tears.

"I'm coming to you," Braidus said, a slight edge of concern in his voice.

"Fine," I agreed, wrapping my arms around my chest.

I lost track of time, quivering in the snow. My mind raced as tried to remember what I had been doing. I didn't know how much time had passed since I had lost my memory. Weeks, days, hours? How long had I worked for Braidus? I gasped and thought in horror, *What if I killed someone?*

My breath came in faltered gasps as I hyperventilated, persuaded that I had killed or seriously injured someone. Why else would I have had a knife in my leg? This had all gone too far.

I broke down and sobbed, terrified of the criminal that I had become and convinced that whatever I did was so horrendous that maybe I couldn't remember it because I didn't want to. Perhaps I erased my memory so it wouldn't haunt my conscience. *Is that possible?* I didn't know.

I buried my face in my hands. *Andrew.* Why hadn't he found me yet? I told him Braidus held me captive. *Please, someone help me out of this nightmare ... please.*

I fell into a daze, falling in and out of consciousness as I waited for Braidus to come.

A rough hand shook me awake. I opened my eyes blearily. Braidus crouched in front of me. He didn't say a word but gently lifted me into his arms and carried me into the back of the smelly carriage. He held on to me, and my head rested on his shoulder while we rode through the city to the orphanage. It was the first time that I remembered not being blindfolded.

Braidus carried me inside and down a flight of stairs. We didn't pass a single soul as he moved to his room. I hated that the one time I could see, I was too delirious to pay attention to the surroundings. I had nothing to go on.

He laid me on a couch and sank to his knees. "Do you need a healer?"

I shook my head. "I took care of it myself."

"Are you sure you're all right?" Braidus's tone still conveyed concern.

I scowled. "I came to my senses in an alley filled with rubbish with a knife in my leg. Do you think I'm all right?"

"Came to—" Braidus furrowed his eyebrows as he rested his hands on the edge of the couch. "You have no idea what you were doing, do you?"

"Not a clue." I bit my lip as anxiety rocked through me, terrified of what I didn't know.

Braidus muttered something unintelligible, though it sounded like curses. I closed my eyes and ignored him. Suddenly he spoke as if the thought had just occurred to him. "Does your dress have pockets?"

I had never worn this dress before. "Check."

Braidus fished around my dress. To my great surprise, he pulled out a small scroll tied neatly with a red ribbon.

"What is that?" I asked, alarmed. I sat up quickly. Is that what caused my injury? Did I steal a scroll—and murder someone in the process? I shuddered.

"I won't know until I read it," Braidus said. "But I suspect it is an important piece to the puzzle I'm trying to solve about you. Possibly the most important of all."

I scoffed and let my mouth run away from me. "You're just as bad as the rest of them."

Confusion flashed across his face. "As whom?"

"Andrew, Joshua—I bet even King Brian—allude that they know more about me than they're willing to tell," I snapped. "It's not fair to be left in the dark when the information pertains to me." I took a breath and continued, my pent-up frustration reaching its breaking point. "It's like having a huge spider on your back. Everybody can see it, but they'd rather let you die from the bite than tell you."

Braidus listened to me rant with fascination, a small smile resting on his lips. "I've held you captive against your will and made you break several Aberronian laws. You wouldn't believe me even if I did tell you everything I know."

I frowned but didn't correct him.

Braidus stood, clutching the scroll in his hand. "I need some time to study this."

"Wait," I called after him as he moved to leave. He paused and stared down at me. "I need to know. What day is it, and is Henry safe?"

With patience in his eyes, Braidus smiled wryly. "You robbed the treasury yesterday. Henry is safe." He gestured to the couch I sat on. "Rest here for the night."

I sighed in relief and placed a hand on my forehead. "Thank the Gods."

I closed my eyes and slipped into the dream memory of my parents' deaths. I found myself on the ground instead of inside the tree where I hid at the time of their murder. I walked around the scene, able to pause and play specific parts. I'd never been able to do that before, and it intrigued me.

Redwood trees fenced us on all sides, and little light fell through the top. Fifteen grungy men, each holding a weapon, surrounded my captured parents. Their clothes were ripped, filthy, and bloodstained. Sweat dripped off their dirty brows. The air felt stale with mistrust and fear.

"Your plan failed. The King still lives," my father said. His dark brown hair was untidy, and a cut above his right eye leaked blood down his bruised cheek. His forehead was lined with stress, and a few days' stubble grew on his chin. His hands were bound behind him with thick rope, and his knees sank into the soft dirt.

My mother knelt next to him. Her black hair cascaded down her back, covering the rope that tied her hands. Her red lips curled in disgust, and her emerald-green eyes reflected anger. No bruises or cuts showed on her face. She wiggled closer until her shoulders touched my father, attempting but failing to reach his hands.

Rooted on the spot, I couldn't take my eyes off my parents. My chest tightened; my breath came in short gasps. I felt as though a jagged knife had been plunged through my heart. I wanted to run away, to turn back on the scene in front of me, but I couldn't. This was the last memory I had of my parents. I couldn't leave them no matter how much I wanted to.

I moved to my parents and dropped to the ground beside them. I reached out a hand to touch them but hesitated at the last moment. Instead, I spoke. "I'm here. I love you."

An insurgent stepped forward. "That may be so." He played with a knife, twiddling it between his dirty hands. "But this is not the end of us. We will rise again and in greater numbers and power." He spoke with authority despite his lackluster appearance.

My mother laughed mockingly; contempt written on her face. "Rise again, and the good people of Aberron will send you running with your tails tucked between your legs."

Bold and passionate, I thought.

I walked around the band of ruffians, fixating on their angry, sweaty, dirty faces. Their tattered clothing had streaks of blood and grime from open shallow scratches. They appeared to have just run from a fight, perhaps through a blackberry patch?

I stood by my parents again, unable to stay away from them for long. Despite this being a memory, I wanted to believe that they felt my silent love and support.

"No!" the insurgent screamed at my parents, flinging the knife in their direction. It whizzed past and lodged into a tree. "Braidus will obtain what is rightfully his, only this time, you won't be in his way." He raised his hand and signaled to his men. "Goodbye."

Wait. I paused and replayed the scene over again, listening closely to the insurgent speak. I gasped in shock. This was what I had forgotten. Why Braidus's name seemed familiar but I couldn't place it. Braidus had caused my parents' deaths. I ran around the men again, searching for anything that indicated his presence. I had to believe he was here, watching this unfold like I had in the tree. *There.*

He stood a few yards away, nearly out of view. I almost didn't recognize him with short hair and a clean-shaven face with hardly a blemish. The scar above his right eye would appear later. He leaned against a tree, acting like a casual bystander, but he couldn't hide the smoldering arrogance on his face. I stood an arm's length away from him. He seemed young, sixteen or seventeen at most. *My age.*

Braidus grinned as he listened to the insurgent promise his return and rise to power. My hands balled into fists as I fought the urge to slap him across his face. He obviously loved the worship he received from his followers. I watched in horror as he caught the insurgent's eye and nodded subtly. That's when the insurgent signaled his men.

I turned around. "No! Please!" I sprinted to my parents and fell to the ground before them. I reached out to touch, but my hand moved through them as though I grasped smoke. I couldn't change a memory of the past. I couldn't stop this from happening.

Horrified, with tears streaming down my face, I screamed, "Gods forbid. No! Please!" The grungy men rushed forward, walking through me with no awareness of my presence. They ran their swords through my parents in one swift motion.

"Curse you, Braidus!" I screamed through broken sobs as I crumpled to the ground.

I pounded my fists into the dirt and tree roots, seeing my parents' death in a new light. It all made sense now. They had stopped Braidus in his first attempt to take over. He failed because of them. So Braidus killed my parents so they would never be able to stop him again. Only now he had me to contend with.

I woke up with a jolt, my face wet with the tears I had cried in my sleep. Henry's face loomed in front of me. I gasped, quickly sitting up. I swiveled around to search for Braidus, but he wasn't in the room. He never left my side for long.

Henry held out a hand and pulled me up.

I glanced at the clock as we tiptoed our way to the door. Eleven. Only a few hours had passed, and yet so much had happened. Powered with knowledge of Braidus's actions, my emotions had escalated to the point that I could barely see straight.

Henry opened the door a sliver and peeked out. He beckoned me to follow.

We moved slowly down the hall, fearing any loud noise would cause someone to investigate. The hour late, I assumed all the children, Greta, and her helpers were in bed. I could never be sure of Braidus and his guards, though. Something told me they didn't keep the same hours.

We reached the door, and I pulled on the handle, coming face-to-face with Braidus and two of his guards. I gazed into his face, noticing the tired lines, scar above his right eye, hazel eyes, light brown beard, and long, blonde-streaked, wavy hair. Seconds felt like minutes as we stared at each other.

Whatever he saw in me was enough for him to take a few steps backward. His guards flanked him, fear in their eyes. Henry glanced at me and did a double take.

"Isabelle?" Henry moved his hand as if he wanted to touch my shoulder but hesitated.

My pulse elevated; adrenaline rushed through my body. The cold air hit my face, but it did nothing to relieve my flushed skin. Muscles tense, I saw through narrow slits of rage.

"Henry, put up a shield. I don't want to hurt you." I lunged at Braidus and snatched his wrist. He couldn't disappear if I held on because I'd still be able to feel him. Braidus stiffened and eyed me with alarm but didn't struggle against my grasp. No doubt he saw the murderous look in my eyes and thought better.

I spoke, my voice cold, dead, and merciless. "You better pray to the Gods that I don't kill you right now."

I let loose the fury, hurt, vengeance—every emotion that set me on fire—along with my magic. Boomer broke down the crate I had locked him in. His hackles raised, he snarled. My balled fist ignited with red flames.

Henry backed into the wall; a softly glowing blue shield wrapped around him like a second skin. I hoped it would be enough.

Braidus leaned away from my flaming hand as he put his hand up and spoke warningly. "Isabelle."

"Did you think I wouldn't figure it out?" I tightened my grip.

Confusion flashed across Braidus's face for the briefest of moments.

I spoke harshly and quickly. A minute section of my mind kept tabs on my magic. I couldn't kill him yet. Not until he knew this. "I knew your name sounded familiar, but I couldn't place it." I cocked my head to the side and gauged his reaction to what I said next. "Did you know I was there when you murdered my parents?"

Shock showed on Braidus's face.

I smiled without warmth. He hadn't known, then. "I saw it all, hidden inside a redwood tree my father converted to a playhouse. I should kill you now to avenge them."

"Killing me won't bring them back," Braidus said, lowering his hand.

"You're right, it won't," I agreed. "But why should your life matter more than theirs? Gods forbid, they were good people, and you took them from me."

"What do you want me to say? That I regret it? That I would take it back? That I'm sorry?" Braidus spoke heatedly. "There is nothing I can say that will change the past." His expression turned pained. "Don't turn into me, Isabelle. You're not a killer."

I spoke through gritted teeth. "Don't tell me what I am." A surge of magic escaped my tight hold. A fireball shot out of my hand, narrowly missing Braidus and headed to his guards.

They barely had time to dive out of the way. The fireball hit the ground and exploded. Pieces of ice and dirt flew into the air as the ground shook beneath me.

Braidus placed his hand on mine. "If you kill me, you'll never know what you are destined for or why Haldren has taken an interest in you."

I felt a brief flash of surprise. As far as my memory served me, I had never mentioned Haldren to Braidus. How did he know? The flames momentarily vanished as I considered his words. I could call them back in a second if I needed to.

Braidus took that as an opportunity to speak. "I can tell you everything you want to know about Haldren and why he visits you."

I narrowed my eyes and pursed my lips. "I can ask Haldren that myself."

Braidus shook his head. "He won't tell you, and neither will Joshua, Andrew, or my father. They don't think you're ready."

"Ready for what?" I asked slowly. A small part of my mind screamed at me to kill him anyway, regardless of what he said to stall as he searched for an escape.

Braidus reached in his pocket and pulled out the scroll I had stolen. "Promise not to kill me, and I'll give you this. Consider it a starting point."

"A scroll over the head of my parents' murderer?" I scoffed. "I don't think so." My hand ignited once again.

Henry came up beside me, still glowing softly with his shield wrapped tightly around him. "Isabelle, take the deal and let's go. Death is permanent. You can't come back from that."

Braidus's guards flanked him and eyed me warily. Their hands hovered by their sides, ready to draw weapons if need be.

Tears welled up in my eyes. "But he doesn't deserve to live."

"You're right," Henry agreed. "But if you kill Braidus, no matter how justified you think his death may be, you're still a murderer. Do you want to be that, Isabelle?"

No.

Slowly the flames rescinded. I sighed and let go. Braidus grimaced as he rubbed his wrist. I tugged at the necklace wrapped around my throat. "Take this off. I refuse to be your puppet any longer. I make my own choices now."

Braidus stuck the scroll in his pocket and reached behind his neck, then unclasped his apple tree necklace. He held it out to me. I snatched it and unlocked the apple blossom necklace I wore. I ripped it off and threw both necklaces back at him. Braidus caught them both.

I held out my hand. "Give me the scroll."

Braidus handed it to me. "Take it."

I put the scroll in my pocket and pointed a finger at Braidus. "If you ever try to use my friends or family against me again, I will kill you without hesitation."

Braidus nodded. "I'll take that into consideration."

I turned swiftly on my heels and marched to the gate. Henry wasted no time following. I glanced at the orphanage to see many little faces pressed against the upper windows. Greta stood at the open door; arms folded with ire.

The bitter cold air whipped at our faces. Henry created a ball of blue light and let it hover above us, giving us the light we needed as we walked the icy, snow-covered street lined with old manors. Henry didn't try to speak, and I found myself grateful for the silence.

I'd been faced with my parents' killer, and I hadn't avenged them. I let him go. Had I made the right choice? The dream still fresh in my mind, I pictured my parents as I last saw them: bound with thick ropes, my father bruised and bloody, my mother putting on a brave face. My father had died almost instantly when the swords sliced through his body. But not my mother; she lasted a few moments longer.

I remembered her turning her head to me, staring straight up at the oval window as though she could see me through the illusion. Perhaps she could. I recalled not being able to understand her expression as I looked at her. I'd never seen true regret, remorse, and love paired together before.

Adrenaline continued to throb strongly through my body. I clutched at my rolling stomach, my breath coming in gasps as my chest tightened with sharp stabs of pain. Some strange noise came out of my throat, and it took me a while to realize I was sobbing since I couldn't feel my face.

As we got to the end of the street, Henry stopped. "Isabelle, turn off the magic. It's making you feel more intensely."

I nodded and imagined a new, stronger crate for Boomer. It took me several tries, but I managed to lock my magic inside. Henry caught me as I stumbled and started to topple over. With the magic sealed, the pain dulled but remained constant.

"I know I'm not Andrew, but maybe a hug will help?" Henry asked as he wrapped his arms around me. "Girls like hugs, right?"

I chuckled and some of my pain lifted. "Depends on who's giving them."

"Oh." Henry didn't seem to know what to say to that.

I stepped away. "Thank you, Henry."

He grinned. "Sure. No problem."

I needed to get my mind off what happened, or I knew I'd turn around and go back to confront Braidus again. As we started walking, I asked Henry how he escaped.

"I noticed the guard that came in to give me food and check on me had a key hung on his belt that looked like the one Braidus took when you first tried to escape. I knocked over my water and complained loudly that I was thirsty. As the guard crouched to grab the canteen, I smashed his head into the stone wall. Then I kicked him with my boot and knocked him out. I took the key from his belt and unlocked the chain. Then I went looking for you."

"Impressive," I said with raised eyebrows. We crossed an intersecting street and continued forward.

Henry shrugged but held on to a smug grin. "Not really. But it worked." He sighed and shoved his hands in his pockets. "I totally get it if you don't want to talk, but I've been trying to put together what happened back there, and I have a question, if you're willing to answer it."

"Ask away," I agreed, jumping over a half-frozen puddle.

"Who is Haldren?" He asked with some trepidation. "You were completely set on killing Braidus until he mentioned that name."

"Haldren is a mystery, but I'll tell you what I know." I stopped and leaned against a large fir tree, wrapping my arms around my chest to fight off the cold. "He is a God who has taken a special interest in me."

Henry eyed me skeptically, shifting his weight side to side. "A God? But there are only four." He listed them off quickly. "Zadek, Amora, Tomas, and Nachura."

I shook my head. "That's what I thought too until he started visiting me in my dreams; or maybe he transports me to another plane of existence?" I wondered.

Henry raised his eyebrows.

"The point is I know absolutely nothing about him." Frustration leaked into my voice. "Joshua, Andrew, and Braidus as it turns out, do." I made a face. "They won't tell me anything more than what he is. A God that I should be wary of. Every time I've mentioned Haldren, Joshua gets this horrified look on his face and Andrew turns stiff like petrified wood. I've tried doing my own research, but I've come up empty."

"What do you and Haldren talk about?" Henry moved to lean against the tree with me. The blue ball of light followed him, hovering above his head as though tied to him with string.

"A number of things." I shrugged. "He seems to think I'm important, but he won't tell me why. Randomly he pops in and helps me." I gave

Henry two examples. "That face cream I used on you to get the insults off came from Haldren, and he pulled me away from death after the poisonous chains incident. The healers hadn't actually gotten to me in time."

"Oh." Henry grimaced, and I wondered if I should have left that a secret.

Oh well. I was past the point of caring.

Henry ran a hand through his hair as we started moving again. "Gods forbid, the second I think I've got you somewhat figured out you throw something new at me. Your life is never dull, is it?"

I shook my head. "Not anymore."

I hate it.

CHAPTER THIRTY-FOUR

ENRY EYED ME UP and down as we walked; his blue orb of light let us see each other clearly.

I stopped. "What?"

"You're a sight. There's blood on your dress." He pointed at the lower half of my light pink dress.

I glanced down and assessed myself. Mud and who knows what else covered a great deal of my tattered dress. Dried blood covered a large portion of my hip reaching up to my stomach and down the side of my leg. A slit near my upper thigh exposed my skin, but the blood hadn't been washed off so it blended in.

"Did Braidus do that?" Henry asked tentatively. "Are you injured?"

I addressed his second question first. "I'm all right. I took care of it. Braidus never physically harmed me." I grinned, wanting to lighten the mood and not think about Braidus. I poked Henry in his side. "You don't look or smell any better, for that matter." Henry never got the new clothes I'd requested, and he still wore the ones he'd been captured in: a long light blue shirt and brown pants, minus the fur-lined jacket.

"Well, you smell like you've been in a garbage heap," he retorted, jumping out of the way as I came after him again. "Where were you?"

"An alley," I said.

Henry raised his eyebrows in surprise. "Hmm ..." He stretched his arms out. I stepped out of the way. "I'm never going to complain about exercise again after being chained to a wall for three days." He grimaced and dropped his hands. "They gave me a bucket to go in. It wasn't pretty."

"But you're alive. That's what matters." I patted him lightly on the shoulder.

He nodded. "Hey, you got any money?"

"No. Why?" I furrowed my eyebrows.

His shoulders slumped in disappointment. "I thought we could get a ride to the Sorrenian. We could change into clean clothes first and then move on to the next course of action."

I held back a laugh. "After all that talk of enjoying exercise, you're so keen on riding now? Besides, it's the middle of the night. You're not going to find a driver at this hour."

"Come on, it's Carasmille. We're bound to find someone. It's going to take us ages to get back to the Sorrenian. I'm freezing out here." He shivered.

I couldn't disagree. I felt the cold seep through my tattered dress, but I worked hard to ignore it since I couldn't change our circumstances. "Where's your jacket?" I asked.

"One of the guards liked it, so he took it." Henry shrugged.

"You're in luck." I skirted in front of him. I bent down and picked up a silver Moonel peeking out of the snow, glinting off Henry's blue light orb. "Is this enough to get us there?"

He grinned and snatched the coin. "Close enough. Now all we need is a driver."

We picked up our pace and hurried to the busier street in sight. The middle of town, I thought, as I recognized the statue of Aberron from a distance. With lanterns lit and coming into view, Henry shut off his magic, extinguishing the light he had created for us.

"See, what'd I tell you?" He pointed at a carriage with a sign offering rides. The driver seemed to be waiting for someone, bartering with a man over salted pork.

Henry called to the driver. "Hey, can you give us a lift?"

The driver wrinkled his nose at the sight of us. "You're too dirty to ride in my carriage."

"Aw, come on!" Henry begged. "I've only got a Moonel on me, but I promise I'll make it worth your while if you take us."

"Where are you headed?" the driver asked.

"The Sorrenian," Henry answered.

The driver seemed to rethink his earlier refusal. He rubbed his chin with a black gloved hand. "The Sorrenian, you say?"

Henry nodded. "That's right."

He peered down at us. "What kind of worth your while are we talking about?"

"Ten Sundals." Henry folded his arms. "That's more than you'll make tonight."

The man licked his lips, an eager expression on his face. "Done. Get in."

The man bartering turned around. "Hey, that's my ride."

"Not anymore," the driver said. "Unless you're willing to pay the ten Sundals he's offering." He jabbed his thumb in Henry's direction.

The man scowled and cursed under his breath. "No. Go on then. I'll find another ride."

Henry flipped the silver coin up to the man, who caught it and stuck it into his pocket.

"Good negotiating skills," I said as we hopped in the carriage and the driver took off.

"For the right amount of money, most people are willing to overlook something they don't like." Henry spoke it as fact.

We huddled together for warmth. Our shoulders knocked into each other as the wheels spun through the ice and snow. Henry leaned his head against the side of the carriage and rested. The city became a blur before my eyes as I formulated a plan.

I had to leave the Sorrenian for good. I couldn't let Braidus get to me again. Once I got cleaned up and my stuff packed, I'd go to Andrew. I'd tell him everything and hope he could convince his father to pardon me. I couldn't see another course of action. I didn't want to stay the criminal I'd become.

My gut twisted at the potential drawbacks—including death.

As the carriage rolled to a stop, so did my thoughts. I gently prodded Henry awake. "We're here."

Henry asked the driver to wait, promising to return in a few minutes while he went inside to get his money. His blue orb of light appeared once more as we trudged to the Sorrenian.

As Henry went to grab the door handle, I put a hand on his arm, stopping him. "I forgot to tell you: Dominic knows that you weren't sick, and I'm pretty sure he hates me because I couldn't tell him where you were."

"Now you tell me?" Henry sighed and ran a hand through his hair.

I hoped my face appeared apologetic. "Sorry."

"I'll meet you at your room in an hour. Don't go to sleep on me," Henry said.

I nodded. "Wouldn't dream of it."

I chose the shortest route to my room and whispered the password. I entered, shut the door, and leaned against it with a resounding sigh. I pulled the scroll out of my pocket and set it on the mantel above the fireplace. I would open it when I felt ready.

I spent the next half hour in the bath taking off the layers of dirt and blood on my skin. I scrubbed vigorously, wishing I could erase my sins as easily as the grime. I went from feeling intense, murderous anger at Braidus to being almost numb. A small part of my mind replayed everything I did while trapped under his control. The worst part? I would never know who I hurt—or killed—to retrieve the scroll. With every ounce of mental effort, I tried to remember but came up with nothing. When I started to feel again, I knew it would eat me alive.

I should have killed him, I thought. If I had already murdered once, would it matter if I did it to someone deserving of it?

I slipped into clean undergarments and a crimson dress that felt like an outward representation of the blood on my hands. I didn't have the heart to look at myself in the mirror. I'd only see the villain I'd become.

I started a fire and waited. When Henry arrived, he carried a plate of cookies.

"I snuck some cookies out of the kitchen on my way over here." He set them on the table and held out his arms. "Come here."

I stepped closer, and Henry wrapped me in a bear hug. I breathed in the smell of pine soap.

"I never properly thanked you. Without you, I'd probably be dead."

"Without me, you wouldn't have been in this mess in the first place," I said sourly.

I stepped back, but Henry held on to my shoulders. "You did what you could. I hold no animosity toward you." His blue eyes locked with mine. "Don't beat yourself up over this." He let go.

"Henry, I think you should know something." The serious tone in my voice made him stiffen. In a rush of words, I explained to Henry how I circumvented Braidus by writing a message in the snow, telling Andrew of our demise. "I need to find him, tell him we are free, and then I'm confessing everything." I took a deep breath and exhaled as I wrung my hands. "If I am pardoned—"

"You will be," Henry interrupted.

"Then I'm going away," I said. "I can't live at the Sorrenian knowing Braidus could be privy to my every move."

"I don't want you to go." He frowned while his eyes pleaded.

I suspected mine mirrored the same sadness in his. "But you and I both know I need to."

Henry gripped his forehead, his expression showing frustration and weariness. "Well you're not doing this alone. I'm coming with you."

I smiled. "I'd hoped you say that."

Henry seemed mockingly offended that I would even question his involvement. "Of course. I spent the whole time in the bath thinking about how to convince you to go with me to Uncle Brian. Thank the Gods I didn't have to."

Henry followed me around my room, a cookie in his hand as I packed things into my cream-colored bag. "Isabelle, when you get pardoned, where are you going to go?"

I paused, holding a hairbrush. "If I get pardoned." I sighed. "Perhaps Joshua or Andrew can help me find a new place, someplace Braidus won't suspect." *Surely they wouldn't deny a move now,* I thought. "I just need some time to figure things out, atone for robbing and Gods know what else."

"What do you mean what else?" Henry grabbed the hairbrush out of my hand and put it in my bag. "What else happened?"

"I don't know!" I threw my hands up and dropped them to my sides. "I came to my senses in an alley with a knife in my leg. Henry, I don't know what I did to get that scroll, and I'm afraid to find out."

He eyed me with disbelief. "You have no memory at all?"

"None," I said firmly. "I might've killed someone and never known I did it." I put my face in my hands and shuddered. "I should have killed Braidus when I had the chance. I'm already a murderer anyway."

Henry placed a hand on my shoulder. "Oh, Isabelle," he sighed. "I don't think you killed anybody."

My voice came out muffled through my hands. "How would you know? I robbed the treasury. The next step up is murder."

"Come on, Isabelle; you can't start thinking that way," Henry said adamantly.

"Right," I muttered, stepping out of his reach, and tied the strings on my bag.

He picked up the scroll. "Have you read it?"

I shook my head.

"Don't you want to know what it says?"

"Honestly?" I pushed my hair away from my eyes. "I'm not sure. You go ahead."

"How about we do it together?" Henry suggested.

"Fine."

Henry untied the ribbon and carefully unfolded the scroll. We bumped arms as we read it together.

Find a girl beautiful and fair,
Preordained to a fate not chosen.
At birth, a mark shall be imprinted.
A spiraled red sun,
a gift from the Gods as one.
Given powers beyond measure,
two will seek to make her heir.
Her allegiance to one will be the deciding destiny
in the struggle of power for the Kingdom of Aberron.
Heed the warning now given:
without her presence in the fight,
both will lose to a mightier foe.

Underneath the writing, the Mark of the Gods had been stamped like a seal in red wax.

"This is a prophecy," I whispered.

Henry read it over again. "At birth, a mark shall be imprinted. A spiraled red sun." He reached for my left hand and brought it up to the paper, comparing the two marks. "These are identical." Henry folded the scroll, tied the ribbon over it, and handed it to me. "This prophecy is about you."

I untied my bag and placed it on top, then closed it again. "I don't believe it. Braidus could have written that."

"No way." Henry folded his arms. "That scroll is ancient. Didn't you feel how brittle the paper was? Someone way before his time had to have written it. Besides, the handwriting was off. No one writes like that anymore."

He took a breath and continued. "Isabelle, I think the reason why Braidus is so focused on you is because of this prophecy. He believes in it."

"That doesn't mean I have to." I faced him. "I'm not going to let some piece of paper decide my destiny. I should have a choice in the matter."

"It doesn't work that way," Henry said patiently. "The prophecy isn't deciding your fate at all; it's just foretelling what will happen. Your decisions will fall in line with what is prophesied."

"Are you sure about that?" I eyed him.

He nodded. "Positive."

"Well great." I set my bag on the floor and sat in the chair it previously occupied. I rubbed my temples, feeling the stress consume me.

Henry sat in the opposite chair; his face grim. "You have to take this seriously. Especially since anyone who knows you and has read the prophecy believes you are the one to fulfill it."

"So, who cares what I think, right? I have no choice in the matter because Braidus and whoever else has read it thinks it's about me." I stood, upset over every injustice life served me.

"Right," He agreed.

I scowled. "I hate my life."

Henry chuckled. "I have to admit I don't envy you so much anymore. I think you have it worse than anyone I've ever met, but you have friends to help you. You have Andrew."

"Right." I picked up my bag and set it on the chair again. I took a deep breath and exhaled the nervous tension. "I've got everything ready. Why don't we sleep, and I'll meet you in the dining hall for breakfast? We can go after we eat. Dominic will want to know you're all right."

Henry nodded. "Agreed. See you in a few hours." He strolled to the door, rubbing his eyes, and exited.

I lay on my bed and closed my eyes, but I couldn't fall asleep. I felt silly for trying to sleep in day clothes, but I couldn't bring myself to change. I'd packed mostly everything already. Fifteen minutes went by before I finally decided to go to the stables and see Nisha.

I ran into Malsin, who looked worn out on the front steps of the school.

"Isabelle?" Malsin grabbed my shoulders.

I smiled sheepishly. "You caught me."

"Where in the Gods have you and Henry been?" He let go. "Why did you pretend to be sick?"

I opened my mouth to answer but was momentarily caught off guard by the horde of soldiers in full Aberronian armor riding to us. The man leading the party held up a black gloved hand and halted the group. Seeing Malsin and me, he jumped off his horse and marched to us.

"Can I help you?" Malsin addressed the soldier.

The soldier completely ignored Malsin and stared at me. "Isabelle Mirran, you are under arrest for the robbery of the Royal Treasury."

CHAPTER THIRTY-FIVE

Y BLOOD WENT COLD. Time moved at a snail's pace as I stood there, trying to comprehend my fate. I took a deep breath and smoothed out the lines of my dress. I'd known it was only a matter of time before someone linked the robbery to me. I had just hoped to do it my way. Talk to Andrew first with Henry by my side.

Which is why I couldn't let them take me. "You can't arrest me."

"We have orders from the King," the soldier said, his voice deadpan.

"Let me see it." Malsin held out his hand.

The soldier produced a piece of paper and handed it over. Malsin read it in the flickering torchlight, then eyed me with suspicion and alarm. "This is signed by the King. There's nothing we can do."

I shook my head, eyes wide. "No." I backed up until I hit the closed door. "This isn't how it's supposed to go." I needed Henry.

The soldier motioned for additional soldiers to flank him. They jumped off their horses and stood behind their leader, eyeing me with cold calculation.

Malsin ran a hand through his hair, appearing bewildered. "I can't believe I'm asking this. Isabelle, did you rob the Royal Treasury?"

My eyes trained on the soldiers, I glanced at Malsin for the briefest of moments. "Yes."

The soldier smiled. "See, she admits it already. Now come with us."

"Take me directly to the King and I'll go," I demanded.

The soldier shook his head. "That's not how it works. The accused don't get to make requests."

"Then be prepared for a fight because I am not going with you." I used the only weapon I had on me. Magic. My hands ignited with red flames. I held them up, ready to defend myself if necessary.

The soldiers drew their swords and pointed them at me. Malsin looked between me and the soldiers, blatant dismay on his face. He put himself between us.

"I don't know what has gotten into you, Isabelle, but this isn't the girl I know. Shut off your magic now." Malsin pointed a warning finger at me. "Those soldiers are only doing their job. They don't deserve your wrath. Just do what they say, and I promise I'll get it sorted out."

I cared for and trusted Malsin. I knew he had my best interests at heart. Reluctantly, I closed my magic. "All right." I prayed I hadn't made a mistake in listening to him.

I held my hands out in front of me as several soldiers surrounded me, weapons still poised. I opened my mouth to tell Malsin to find Henry, but one of the soldiers touched my hand, and everything darkened.

I awoke to find myself in a jail cell. I lay on a thin and dirt-stained mat pushed against the back wall with a faded gray wool blanket over me. A bucket stood in the corner on the opposite side. A small window about the size of a short plank of wood let in sunlight.

The door opened and the soldier entered, holding handcuffs. "It's time."

"Time for what?" I asked warily.

"Your court proceeding with Court Magistrate Philsby," the soldier said.

I scrambled to sit up and pressed myself against the wall. My heart pounded in my ears. "Court proceeding? Philsby?" I shook my head. "No no no. I need to see the King."

"You're seeing the court magistrate, and that's final." The soldier fiddled with the handcuffs. "Now if you try to put up a fight, I swear on the Gods that I will—"

I cut him off, fearing the malevolent look in his eyes. "No need." I held out my hands.

The soldier huffed. "Well all right."

As he put the cuffs on my wrists, I asked him his name.

"Max," he said.

I tried my hand at small talk, anything to keep the terror at bay as Max helped me stand. "You seem like a good soldier. Bet you're sorry you got stuck with me, huh?"

"Not really." Max shrugged. "I get paid more when I deal with high profile criminals."

My breath caught in my throat. I cleared it and spoke. "I'm high profile?"

He nodded.

Oh dear. I frowned.

The two guards posted outside my door followed behind us. We marched down a drab hall devoid of paintings and decor. Another two guards stationed outside a set of double doors opened them upon my arrival.

I stepped into the large room and swallowed as anxiety washed over me like a wave. Every bench angled toward the focal point of the room: a high-backed wooden chair bolted to the ground. A tremor ran through me as we headed to it. I counted the benches as I walked down the aisle. Ten rows on either side and each long enough to fit fifteen people comfortably. I sat in the accused's chair and shivered against the coldness of it. My insides quivered, and I found myself grateful for an empty stomach.

I rested my trembling hands on the armrests, noticing a hole about the size of a Sundal on both sides. The soldier crouched and unlocked the handcuffs. I rubbed my wrists while he fiddled with the cuffs, undoing the chain, and slipping it through the hole, then putting it back together.

When he finished, I rested my arms on the armrest again while he put the shackles back on, effectively tying me to the chair. My breathing became accelerated as panic started in. *Gods forbid, I don't think I can do this.* Max pulled on the chain to make sure it was secure. I gasped as the cuffs dug into my skin.

"Sorry." He had the decency to appear apologetic, and I wondered what he saw when he looked at me. A cold, heartless criminal, or a girl in the wrong place at the wrong time?

He stepped away and sat on the front row bench, nearest to me. I stared ahead, starting with the three steps to the stand, the ornately carved podium, and the six plush, dark blue chairs behind it. Above the stand, the largest flag I'd ever seen had been pinned to the wall, bearing the King's crest. It took up a considerable amount of wall space.

A door to the right opened, and three guards filed in, followed by a rather portly man with white hair, red, flushed cheeks, a thick mustache, and tailored clothes. The court magistrate, I assumed. He chose one of the dark blue chairs while the guards sat on the benches.

I heard the doors behind me open, but I didn't turn around to look. Chained to the chair, I wasn't even sure if I could. Multiple sets of footsteps pounded against the stone floor, turning silent as each person took a seat. The magistrate's eyes darted about the room. He nodded subtly to himself, seeming satisfied that everyone had arrived, and rose. He sauntered over to the podium, gripped the edges of it with his beefy hands, and leered at me.

My stomach lurched at his attempt to be intimidating.

He cleared his throat, and the room became still. "I am Court Magistrate Philsby. Please state your full name for the record."

"Isabelle Elaine Mirran," I said, hearing but not seeing someone scratch pen to paper.

He nodded. "We are here to discuss your involvement in the robbery of the Royal Treasury, where two bags of gold Sundals were taken." He leaned forward, resting nearly all his weight on the podium. "Do you deny your involvement in this incident?"

"No," I said.

Philsby's mouth twitched, seeming to fight a smile. I shuddered. He made me feel like a bug he couldn't wait to squash.

"We will now hear the eyewitness accounts of the robbery." Philsby waved his hand. A guard rose, standing between me and Philsby. "In your own words, please explain what you saw."

The guard took a deep breath and said rather uncertainly, "Well ... I didn't exactly see anything." He fidgeted with the cuff on his sleeve and then spoke in a rush. "I was guarding the gate like always, when suddenly I felt a small gust of wind, and a butterfly hairpin appeared on the ground. I thought Ben, the guard next to me, had dropped it. Then our commanding officer Luke started reprimanding us, and the next thing I remember is a healer shaking me awake. That's when I found out the Royal Treasury had been robbed."

"Anything else you'd like to add?" Philsby asked.

The guard shook his head.

The magistrate nodded and waved him away, calling another guard over named Luke. I recognized Luke as the one who tried to take charge once they realized they were under attack.

"When my men started dropping like flies, I realized we were under attack. I drew my weapon and tried to fight, but one of the robbers had yellow magic, rendering it impossible for us to see them." He continued to explain in detail the events of his fight with his invisible foe, or foes, as he believed.

Next, a young mage no older than twenty-five stepped forward.

"State your name and color of magic," Philsby said.

"Darren Grevledge, and I possess yellow magic."

I stared at him with surprise. I had never met anyone but Braidus possessing yellow magic.

"Yellow magic allows you to see a vision of the last person who touched an object. Am I correct?" Philsby asked.

Darren nodded. "Yes."

"Using your mage abilities, did you see this girl holding onto the butterfly hairpin?" Philsby gestured to me.

Darren nodded again. "Yes."

"Where did you see her?" Philsby propped his elbows up and clasped his hands together.

"In front of the guards near the Royal Treasury," Darren said, glancing at me.

"Do you believe she robbed it?" Philsby appraised the mage with caustic inquisitiveness.

Darren shook his head. "I cannot say for sure."

Philsby nodded. "That is all." He waved him away.

Darren walked past me, eyeing me with what seemed like confusion. I supposed all the people in this room wondered why I did it.

"We have heard all of the witness accounts on the matter," Court Magistrate Philsby said. "We will now question the suspect." He shifted his weight as he stared down at me and spoke harshly. "Isabelle Mirran, were you a part of the group that stole from the treasury?"

I clarified. "I did it alone."

He frowned and gripped the edges of the podium. "It took at least four people, each with a different color of magic, to break into it." He held up his fingers as he spoke. "Yellow to camouflage, green to put the guards to sleep, blue to ice the door, and red to blow it up."

I nodded. "That would normally be the case, except I possess all four colors of magic." I heard gasps and muttering behind me. "I did it alone."

"Blasphemy!" Philsby shouted.

I flinched and opened my mouth to explain, but Philsby cut me off.

"I have no use for liars in my court. Isabelle Mirran, did you aid in the robbery of the Royal Treasury of your own free will and choice, knowing full well what the consequences would be if you were caught?"

I took a deep breath and spoke as clear as a bell. "I did. But you have to understand—"

"I don't need to understand," Philsby snarled. "By the laws of the court and the order of the King, anyone who willingly robs from the Royal Treasury shall be sentenced to death. You shall be made an example to deter others from this course of action. Your execution will be at noon." He slammed his fist on the podium.

"Wait!" I shouted at Philsby, but he was already striding out of the room through the side door without so much as a backward glance in my direction. Three guards rushed to follow behind him.

A tremor ran through me. I glanced at the clock—9:45. How could I get out of this in that short amount of time? Philsby wouldn't even hear my reasoning. I took a few deep breaths, trying to calm the surges of adrenaline. I fell into a daze as Max unlocked the handcuffs, removed them from the chair, and put them back on again. He led me back to my cell and freed my hands once more.

I didn't realize I repeatedly said, "He didn't give me a chance," until Max responded.

"Philsby doesn't give liars a chance. Never has."

"I'm not a liar," I snapped.

"Sure." He shook his head, clearly not believing me.

I paced back and forth in the cell, too angry to sit down. I would die because I told the truth. If only he would have asked me to demonstrate my abilities. I could have shown him I had all four colors of magic. The soldier came back five minutes later with food, but I pushed it away.

"I just don't understand why a pretty girl like you would want to rob the treasury. Was it a game?" he asked, holding on to a bowl of slop fit for pigs.

"Gods forbid, no!" I stopped pacing. "Please, I need to speak with my brother Joshua. He's the Commander." I knew everything could be sorted out if I spoke to him.

"Sorry. We cannot respond to requests made to see higher dignitaries capable of lifting the sentence. The judgment made by Court Magistrate Philsby is final." Max shrugged.

"But he's my brother," I pleaded.

He shifted his weight and spoke in a dull voice. "The last time we let family members visit, the man slated for execution escaped with their help. We discontinued the practice for fear of it happening again."

"So, nobody will know I'm going to die?" I asked softly.

"Oh, they will know." He assured me. "We send the family a condolence letter explaining the crime and the judgment."

Fantastic. I sighed, sat on the mat, and put my face in my hands as Max left the room. What had I been thinking? That I could march up there and explain that I had Henry's life hanging above my head when I broke the law? Who would believe that without Henry by my side? I wanted to shout that Braidus was back and staging a war to take over, but who would believe that either? He'd been banished from Aberron, his very existence erased out of everything, record books and all. No one probably gave him a second thought.

Max came back a few minutes later with a clipboard, piece of paper, and pen. "We are required to ask what method of execution you would like. We have three options. Hanging, beheading, or an arrow through the heart."

"Seriously?" I gripped the top of my head, my fingers digging in my hair. "Like that would matter. It's all going to end in death anyway."

"It matters a great deal to some people," Max said dully. "Just choose one, so I don't have to choose for you."

"I'll take the arrow through the heart," I snapped.

He marked it down. "I am also required to offer a temple priest or priestess to help you come to terms with your sins before you are executed. Are you interested?"

"No." I had nothing to come to terms with. I willingly committed a crime to save Henry's life. I wasn't plagued with regret.

A new soldier arrived. He stood inside the room and lifted his softly glowing blue hands. A bright blue liquid substance a little thicker than water formed on the ceiling and covered it. Then it started trickling down the walls. *Oh no.* I shot up from the mat, ran to Max, and hid behind him, terrified. The mage and Max chuckled at me, but I didn't care. What if that stuff touched me? I shuddered.

When the mage dropped his hands, every wall had been covered. He turned and faced me, a smirk on his face. He gestured to the shimmering blue walls. "Touch it all you want; it won't hurt you."

"What is it?" I asked warily.

"It's called Zadek's shield, for only a God can break through this. It will stop any person with a magical ability from escaping. We've tested it with every color. So even if you do possess all the colors like you claim—" he scoffed, "—you're not getting through this."

I let my mouth run away with me and glared at the two men. "Seriously, do I look like a liar to all of you?"

They shrugged like it wasn't out of the question.

"Then perhaps a demonstration will help?" I gestured to the wall. "If your shield is truly impenetrable, then everything I do will be harmless." I had nothing to lose—I'd already been slated for execution. A small part of me hoped that once the guards saw that I hadn't lied, they could tell Philsby, and we could redo my trial.

A cocky grin formed on the soldier mage. "By all means, go ahead."

I let Boomer out, activating the magic. Adrenaline buzzed in my veins. I touched the shield that felt like cold syrup and watched the green magic shoot from my hands and explore. I felt a wave of disappointment crash over me.

"It's not living," I muttered. "Green is useless."

I switched to yellow. Wind had the power to destroy if it was strong enough. I created a mini, bright yellow, tornado in the palm of my hand with the air in the room. The shield absorbed the wind as though it were nothing. I couldn't knock it down.

"That's three colors," Max breathed behind me in surprise.

"No, it isn't," the soldier mage said. "I've only seen two."

"I watched her use red magic last night," Max argued. "I think she's telling the truth."

"I am," I said tersely as I lobbed a fireball at the shield. Nothing. It didn't even explode but melted, then extinguished.

I switched to blue and turned around to face the two awestruck soldiers. Cool mist wafted off my blue glowing fingers. "Freezing it won't do anything, will it?"

The mage's jaw dropped. He shook his head.

I created a ball of ice anyway and threw it at the blue wall. "I've only just discovered my powers; I don't know how to make shields yet."

"You really did rob the treasury all by yourself." Max eyed me with wonder.

"Yes. Because if I hadn't, then Henry James Sorren, second in line for the throne, would be dead. I had no choice. Now if you find Philsby, perhaps I can explain why I shouldn't be executed," I said in a huff.

Max and the mage stared at each other and nodded.

"Can't make promises, but we'll see what we can do," Max said.

"Thank you." I sat on the mat and waited.

I could see a clock resting on the wall through the bars on my door reading 10:20. Time slipped away faster than I thought possible. I'd done everything I thought I could do. I had to leave it up to Malsin and the two soldiers.

When the clock neared eleven, Max came back and spoke through the bars on the door. "We told Philsby what we saw, but he said it didn't matter if you had four colors. You still robbed the treasury, so that makes you guilty." He shifted his weight uneasily and grimaced. "He threatened to execute us too if we didn't leave him alone."

My face fell as my stomach squirmed, and my heart jumped into my throat. "Thanks for trying anyway." I asked for paper and a pen to write my last words down. With pity shining strong in his eyes, Max agreed. He had to get the mage to lift a small section of the shield for him to slip me the materials: a piece of paper no bigger than my hand and his pen.

I penned a note to Andrew.

Dear Andrew,

I did everything to save Henry. I couldn't let Braidus kill him. I'm not proud of stealing from the Royal Treasury or anything else I did, but I don't regret it. I hope you can understand. Andrew, please always remember that I love you. I pray that you will move forward and find someone who will be a better fit for you. A girl not plagued with bad luck and a penchant for trouble. Stay true to yourself and you'll be a great King.

Love,

Isabelle

I ran out of paper to say everything I wanted. I folded it up and pounded on the door until the mage and Max came back. Max promised he would put the note in the outgoing mail. I believed him.

I moved the blanket off the mat and lay on it. I stared up at the stone ceiling in a daze. *The prophecy is wrong,* I thought shrewdly. I won't be the one to fulfill it, not with this sentence. The more I thought about death, the less scared of it I became. I had come near death so many times already that it wasn't this big fear. I held absolutely no regret for my actions despite feeling guilty. I did what I could to save Henry, and I would do it again in a heartbeat.

I reflected on every person I ever cared about, starting with the people in Saren—Nathan, Adel, Stefan, Mava, and so on. The values Nathan and Adel had instilled got me here in the first place. Life was precious, and we had to do our part to protect it. I didn't think anyone believed that as fiercely as I did.

The sun loomed high in the sky when Max opened the door for the last time, holding on to the handcuffs. He wore a grim expression on his face as he clasped them around my wrists and led me out of the cell. Every guard we passed mirrored the same bleak expression. No one liked to look death in the eyes.

We headed outside into an open area—a training field perhaps? The snow fell lightly; large flakes dropped on my eyelashes, nose, and cheeks as I stared into the sky. It felt right to have the weather match the event: cold and unfeeling.

They'd fashioned a wooden stage in the middle of the field. A wood pole, the girth of a tree trunk shaved of its outer layer, stuck through the middle of it.

I felt a sense of peace as Max led me to the stage. I stood ramrod straight against the post and held my hands out. He unlocked the cuffs, then pulled my arms back until I hugged the trunk. Clasping the shackles around my wrists once more, he yanked on the chain, making sure it secured me.

"May the Gods find favor with you in the afterlife." Max tried to smile, but it came out as a grimace.

"Thank you," I whispered.

He nodded and jumped off the stage. His boots crunched in the icy snow.

My breath came out in visible puffs as I watched the twenty or so soldiers take position. Court Magistrate Philsby arrived and stood near them. He wore a large fur overcoat with a matching fur hat jammed on his head. His steely gray eyes watched with interest and little sorrow. I wondered what made him so callous, so quick to judge without hearing all the facts?

A wagon pulled by two horses came into view and halted behind the soldiers. A painted red sign on the side of it read *Carasmille Coroner*. The coroner hopped down and stood by the edge of the stairs, away from the firing range but close enough to take my body away quickly. He glanced at me with an unreadable expression, then bowed his head and clasped his hands together. At least he had the decency to look solemn for my execution.

The court magistrate took a step forward and spoke in a loud, harsh voice. "Isabelle Mirran, you are sentenced to death after being declared guilty for the robbery of the Royal Treasury. May your death be an example to others that they may be spared from the same fate."

He raised his hand and signaled the archer to step forward. I closed my eyes, unsure if I wanted to watch the arrow fly from the bow. I took a deep breath, savoring the gift of life one last time. I didn't want to think but only feel as the cold, wet snowflakes touched my face and melted. I opened my eyes, wanting one last look at the sky.

Philsby lifted his hand and shouted, "Fire!"

I smiled, grateful that it would be quick. Soon, I would be reunited with my parents. I followed in their footsteps after all. We died to save someone else. The archer notched the arrow and pulled back the string. He squinted through the storm, took a second to aim, then let loose. The arrow zoomed straight toward my heart.

CHAPTER THIRTY-SIX

"S TOP!" A NDREW ROARED, HOLDING his hand out.

Gods forbid. Don't let him see me die. The arrow soared, pierced my red dress, pricked my breast beneath, and—exploded in a magnificent ball of fire. Joshua stood in his saddle on the far side of the field, his glowing red hand outstretched. I pictured his eyes smoldering with rage even from this distance. The breath I held whooshed out as I sagged against the pole. *Thank the Gods.*

Andrew swung off his horse and sprinted, slipping and sliding on the ice to me. He didn't even take the stairs but rather jumped right onto the stage and skidded to a halt a breath away from my face.

He cupped my face with his cold, lightly calloused hands. Concern showed deep in his blazing blue eyes. "Are you all right?"

I opened my mouth, astonished, but nothing came out. I cleared my throat and tried again. "Yes—yes, I'm fine." *I'm not dead!*

Court Magistrate Philsby stepped forward; his cheeks flushed red. "I demand to know what is going on!" He pointed at me with his pudgy finger. "This lady is a thief, and it is the law that she be executed!" He stomped his foot in anger.

"Give me a minute, and I'll free you." Andrew lightly brushed his lips against mine. He jumped off the stage to meet Philsby head-on and thundered, "Is it not also court policy to inform the King and Crown Prince when you plan to execute someone? Why was I not informed?"

Philsby sneered. "I don't have to answer to you. You're not the King yet."

"Maybe not, but I have the power to put you up there instead." Andrew gestured to the execution stage. "Do you want that?"

Philsby blanched and stepped backward into a soldier.

"I thought so," Andrew said harshly. "We are taking Isabelle to the King. I suggest you follow along."

Philsby nodded vigorously.

Andrew addressed the crowd. "Whichever one of you has the key to Isabelle's handcuffs, unlock them. *Now.*" He turned on his heels and raced back to me. Max chased after him, pulling keys out of his pocket. Once I was free, Andrew pulled me into a bone-crushing hug and held me. He kissed the top of my head, then entwined our hands and led me down the stairs.

Passing by the coroner, he said, "We shall not need your services. No one is going to die today. Philsby tomorrow, perhaps. First he'll need a night locked up to reflect on his demise."

The coroner bowed deeply. "Yes, Highness."

Andrew reached in his pocket and handed him a small bag of coins. "For your time coming out here."

The coroner's eyes widened in surprise as he accepted the money. He spluttered. "Thank you, Highness."

Andrew nodded. "You're welcome."

Andrew helped me onto his horse and swung up behind me. He wrapped his arms around my waist, as if afraid to let go of me, and held on to the reins. My brother trotted forward.

"Gods forbid, Isabelle, I've never been more terrified." Joshua was visibly shaken; his glistening eyes met mine. "There should be a warning label attached to you."

I attempted to smile. "Thank you, Joshua, for saving me."

"Always," he spoke firmly.

I smiled truly back.

With a moment to breathe, I stared at the greeting party waiting patiently on their horses. Flanked by guards I didn't recognize were Joshua,

Henry, Malsin, Dominic, Falden, Aliyah, Alzmire, Trisgeld, Lildren, and Lord Leavesden.

I tilted my head to stare at Andrew. "Did all these people come to save me?"

Andrew smiled. "Yes. If it weren't for Henry and Malsin clamoring up a storm, we wouldn't have gotten here in time."

Overcome with gratitude, I sought Henry and Malsin out. "Thank you. I owe you my life."

Henry grinned. "Hey, you saved mine first. I'm only repaying the debt."

"What are the odds of Isabelle robbing the Royal Treasury for profit?" Malsin shook his head, a grin on his face. "One out of infinity. I had to do what I could." He pointed at my breast. "Do you need me to look at your chest? You're bleeding."

I glanced down. "Oh." I covered my breast, my cheeks flushed with embarrassment. The arrow had cut through enough of my clothing to leave a section exposed.

"I've got a pin." Aliyah passed it to through the line of men until it got to me.

I activated the green magic, healed the cut, then shut it off. I pinned my dress together to cover myself.

Somehow, Philsby managed to get on a horse, though I felt sorry for the poor beast that had to support his weight. With Andrew and I in the lead, we rode to the front of the castle and dismounted. We passed our horses off to a group of hostlers waiting by the front steps. By the looks on their faces, I guessed they'd been expecting us. Andrew and I locked hands as we trotted up the steps and entered.

It took me two steps to match one of Andrew's. He strode through the ornate halls with purpose and direction, navigating his way easily. I didn't even try to absorb the elaborate furnishings. Instead I focused on the marble floors beneath my feet. I didn't know how much bejeweled gold and silver my eyes could take. Any person we passed, whether noble, guard, or maid, melted into the wall and bowed or curtsied. Andrew ignored them completely.

Two guards rushed to open a set of double doors. We stepped onto a wide, blue carpet, and Andrew slowed. We'd reached our destination. The throne room. Longer than wider, huge windows spanned the left side showing the snow flurries and bright sun. I barely noticed the marble pillars on the right, the tapestries, or the other various jeweled objects as my eyes centered on the focal point of the room. Three chairs on a dais with the King and Queen occupying two of them.

Pure, unhindered fear gripped me. *Why now?* After everything else I'd faced today, I couldn't explain it. It became harder to walk the closer we got. Every step forward turned into a conscious effort. Had Andrew not been gripping my hand, I would have bolted in the opposite direction. My heart pounded in my chest as we ran out of carpet.

Andrew stopped at the bottom stair and spoke to the King in a strong, sure voice. "Father, we seek an audience with you to pardon Isabelle Mirran of any transgressions against Aberron."

The King nodded subtly. He caught my eyes and held them with his blazing blue, the same shade as Andrew's and Henry's. Intimidated, I shrank into Andrew like a shy little girl hid behind her mother's skirts, but I didn't avert my gaze. King Brian wore a thin gold-and-silver crown encrusted with diamonds and sapphires on his gray-flecked, short brown hair.

His clean-shaven face seemed wrinkled with stress more so than age. He appeared no older than fifty. I saw the resemblance of both his sons: Andrew and Braidus. They had the same straight nose, strong jaw, and full lips, for starters. I knew I could find more similarities if I searched, but now wasn't the time. His expression left me clueless as to the inner workings of his mind.

"You have caused quite a stir in Aberron. Especially among my two sons." His mild voice surprised me. I expected it to be harsher. Perhaps it was a ploy? Make me feel comfortable, then strike? I shivered.

"Oh, the poor dear, she is absolutely frightened," Queen Averly said, pity lacing her tone.

Other than noting her presence when I first walked into the room, I'd hardly given her a glance. I appraised her now, noting the sympathy on her lightly painted face and in her chocolate brown eyes. She wore a small silver tiara with diamonds placed expertly in her elaborately styled, straw-colored hair. I didn't see a single streak of gray. She seemed younger than King Brian, with fewer wrinkles. Maybe five or so years younger? I couldn't be sure.

King Brian smiled. "Do not be afraid. I will not harm you. The Gods know you've been through enough already. Step closer, I want a good look at you."

Probably the wrong thing to do, but I glanced at Andrew first for approval. He nodded encouragingly and let me go. I trembled, feeling as nervous as a bunny rabbit expecting to be eaten as I climbed the three stairs and stood before the King. He held out his hands. Obligingly, I let him take mine. His hands were slightly rough—like a soldier's. Perhaps he trained often?

He eyed me up and down and rubbed his thumb over my birthmark as he gazed at it. Then he met my eyes and grinned. "My, you are pretty. I can see why my boys would fall on their heads for you."

"Thank you," I said in a small voice.

He let go of my hands. "You and I have much to discuss, but this isn't the room for it. Come, we'll go to my study."

I nodded and swiftly stepped down until I stood beside Andrew. King Brian stood. Reaching for Queen Averly's hand, he helped her rise, then addressed the small crowd. "Follow me to my study, please."

He took the lead, hand in hand with the Queen, and exited through a side door held open by a guard. We fell in line behind them. A long table and chairs able to seat twenty people occupied most of the study. Bookshelves crammed with books lined most of the walls. Old maps of Aberron in silver frames utilized any available space. The King took the chair at the head of the table with the Queen on his right. Andrew chose the seat to his left, and I sat next to him. The rest of the group chose chairs at their discretion. Henry sat on the other side of me; Joshua took the seat next to the Queen facing me, and so forth. Philsby sat at the very end of the table with a sour expression that made me believe he did not want to be here.

The King addressed us. "Now before we get into the heavy details, we need to discuss Isabelle's involvement with my Royal Treasury. I assume all of you are here to plead her case?" His eyes flicked from one person to the next. Everyone except the Queen, Philsby, and I nodded. "Then let us begin."

He rested his sharp gaze on me. "You robbed me of two bags of gold."

I opened my mouth, but nothing came out. I cleared my voice and tried again. "I'm sorry. Can I pay you back?"

His mouth twitched, seeming to fight a smile when he meant to be stern. "That's a start." He clasped his hands together. "You were arrested and put on trial, then sentenced to death as my law dictates, except the court magistrate was not given all of the facts when he ordered your death. Correct?" He glanced at Court Magistrate Philsby, whose eyes had widened in surprise.

I nodded. "Yes."

"Why not?" The King asked, eyeing me.

"I was not given time to explain," I said softly. "I tried, but he wouldn't listen. He called me a liar."

"Philsby, is this true?" The King directed his attention at the court magistrate. He gestured to me. "Did you give her a chance to speak?"

Philsby acted flustered. His eyes darted to the door. "Well, she said she was guilty, what more did she have to say?"

"Maybe the fact that while she is guilty of the crime, she acted out of defense. Narrowly saving Henry—the second in line to the throne—from Braidus." King Brian's eyes narrowed.

Philsby gasped. "He's back?"

"You would have known that if you had taken the time to listen to Isabelle." King Brian leaned forward. "Had Henry's life not been at stake, she would not have committed the crime. Don't you think that warrants some attention?" He reclined in his high-backed chair.

Philsby nodded, seeming thoroughly ashamed.

"Before you judge someone of their crimes, whether they are guilty or not, you need to make extra sure that the accused is given enough time to plead their case. Especially when the sentence is as severe as death. You are also supposed to inform me"—he held up a finger—"and Prince Andrew when someone has committed a crime that warrants the death penalty. I do not remember seeing such a note today," the King reprimanded Philsby.

"Nor did I receive one," Andrew said.

"But I sent it. I'm sure I did," Philsby argued, his beefy hands balled into fists.

"Check your errand boy because I did not receive it," the King said sternly.

"Of course, of course." Philsby nodded quickly. I half expected him to grovel at the King's feet. He cleared his throat and said in a small voice. "What about the issue of her having four colors of magic? She convinced two soldiers she had the ability when I know it to be impossible."

The King turned to me. "Isabelle, do you know how to project your mage core?"

I shook my head.

The King smiled. "That's all right. I can help. Open your magic and take my hand."

"All right." I let Boomer out and placed my hand in the King's.

King Brian's strong blue magic connected with mine, and I couldn't help but feel a sliver of terror at the power radiating off him. His mouth twitched. "Isabelle, magic doesn't react well to fear. It's a wonder you robbed my treasury at all with the way you're feeling toward magic."

I swallowed and tried to lose the fear. "Right." I took a deep breath and exhaled, then cleared my mind.

"That's better," he said.

I felt the thrum of magic heighten as King Brian directed it. A shimmering ball materialized and hovered over the table, easily the size of someone's head or larger. It reminded me of the water droplet Haldren had created for me to see the healers working over my body when I had nearly died.

A picture of my mage core formed inside the sphere. Swirls of red, blue, yellow, and green roamed in and out of view. King Brian guided the picture to focus on the four glass spheres with colored sand. Yellow and red were a quarter of the way full; blue and green were at half.

Gasps of wonder went around the table, despite everyone but Philsby already knowing I possessed all four colors.

"You need to recharge, Isabelle. You're starting to look dangerously low on red and yellow," Malsin said.

I heard muttered agreements from everyone but Philsby, who appeared utterly dumfounded.

"Seemingly impossible but not." The King narrowed his eyes at Philsby with an unreadable expression.

"It appears I've been wrong on all accounts. Forgive me," Philsby said ruefully.

King Brian nodded and let go of my hand. The ball vanished. I spent a moment to shut off the magic.

"Given the fact that Henry's life was in the balance between right and wrong and that the real perpetrator is my banished son, who has wittingly arrived in Aberron—not to mention that he retained all of the money—" King Brian grimaced, then met my eyes. "Isabelle Mirran, by order of the King, you are officially pardoned and cleared of all charges."

I let out a breath of relief. Everyone except King Brian and Queen Averly, who smiled warmly, and Philsby, clapped and cheered.

The King clapped his hands. "Now that is settled, we can move on to the important details. I would ask that only my dear wife, Andrew, Joshua, Henry, Lyle, Malsin, and Isabelle stay. Thank you for coming and showing your support for Isabelle."

I saw the disappointment on Dominic, Falden, and Aliyah's faces that they weren't included. Alzmire, Trisgeld, and Lildren had enough sense to keep their disappointment masked if they felt any. Philsby practically raced to the door. I mouthed a thank you to all of them except Philsby as they left. Lord Leavesden gave directions to the three professors to escort Dominic, Falden, and Aliyah back to the Sorrenian.

"I'm glad that's over." King Brian rubbed his temples. "I hate dealing with Philsby. He's always so eager to sentence somebody, and he never listens. I might have to give him another job." His face lit up. "I know; I'll make him the errand boy."

Murmurs of agreement and soft chuckles went around the room.

King Brian turned to Joshua. "Get Philsby back in here, please."

Joshua hurried to obey and returned with Philsby, who trembled.

King Brian spoke. "I have decided that I no longer want you as a court magistrate. Your actions today proved that you are incapable of the job. Henceforth you shall now be the errand boy in charge of bringing messages regarding the accused to me and Prince Andrew." He tilted his head in Andrew's direction. "Should we receive messages after the sentence is carried out, you will suffer the same sentence. Please remove your things from your office and report to the post. They will get you settled into your new duties."

Philsby struggled to speak as he wrung his hands. He cleared his throat and finally said, "Yes, Highness."

King Brian nodded. "You are excused."

Philsby hurried out, radiating dejection. I held back a smile. *Justice.*

King Brian leaned back in his chair and folded his hands in his lap. He angled his face to me. "I want a full account of what happened between you and my son Braidus. Henry was only able to get out the hostage and Royal Treasury part. I know there is more to this story than he had time to explain."

I took a deep breath and opened my mouth.

The Queen held up her hand. "Wait. Isabelle, when was the last time you ate something?"

I racked my brain. Henry had brought cookies last night, but I hadn't had a chance to eat one as I packed. "I don't remember."

"We cannot continue until I have seen Isabelle eat something. She looks dreadfully famished." The Queen stood and gracefully glided to the door. "I will be back with refreshments."

Andrew grabbed my hand and entwined it with his. "Thank the Gods you're all right. I've been in a state of complete panic for days. I hid and watched you get into that carriage at the Sorrenian. I tried to follow. One moment you were there, and the next you weren't. I had no idea where you had gone. Joshua and I spent the last four days searching the entire city for you and Henry." Andrew ran a hand through his hair. "And then to find you on the execution block. Gods forbid, I thought—"

"It's all right." I spoke to Andrew in soothing tones and caressed his pain-stricken face. "I'm safe now." I reached over the table and placed my hand on my brother's. "Thanks to Joshua."

He seemed slightly startled at my show of affection and gratitude. Joshua smiled warmly. "Anything for you, little sister."

The door opened and Queen Averly waltzed in. Three maids trailed behind her laden with dessert, bread, cheese, slabs of meat, fruit, and an assortment of drinks. They set them on the table, curtsied, and swiftly left the room. My mouth watered.

"All right, everyone, eat first, and then we can begin," Queen Averly said.

We busied ourselves with the food in front of us and spoke little. Paired with the King's pardon, everything tasted divine. Once we moved on to the tray of pastries, the Queen declared that we could start. Pumpkin roll in hand, I didn't realize all eyes rested on me until I'd taken the third bite. *Oops.* I chewed quickly and swallowed, having momentarily forgotten that I was supposed to talk.

I addressed King Brian. "Where would you like me to begin?"

"Start from the moment you were captured," he directed. "I am aware of everything else."

"All right then." I paused. "May I enlist Henry's help in telling the story?"

The King nodded. "Of course."

I turned to Henry. "If I forget something, feel free to chime in whenever."

His mouth full of a berry hand pie, he nodded.

I started divulging everything beginning with Henry getting shot and continuing until I reached the point where I tried to break free the first time.

"You set his nerves on fire?" Malsin shook his head, his mouth open slightly with surprise. "My goodness, Isabelle."

I shrugged. I still didn't feel sorry for it.

"It was a gallant effort," Henry said. "Until Braidus used his yellow magic and held a knife to my throat."

I nodded. "Right." I turned to Joshua. "The notes, the men who came after me in Saren, Braidus orchestrated the whole thing to get to me."

Joshua scowled, then nodded. "I came to that conclusion when I heard you'd been taken."

I then spoke about agreeing to do Braidus's bidding and how I discovered we were in an orphanage run by a lady named Greta. I expressed my regret at using the fireballs, having not known beforehand there were children in the building.

King Brian scowled. "Of course. Greta would do anything for Braidus. She believes he is as much her child as he is mine."

I glanced at Queen Averly, wondering how she felt about this. Her lips were taut, and her eyes crinkled, giving me the impression that she was unhappy. Because of King Brian's indiscretion, or that Greta had more claim on Braidus than Queen Averly did? I couldn't be sure.

I took a breath and pleaded. "Please don't go after Greta. She may have been aiding Braidus, but it wasn't in the way you would think. She was trying to help him make better choices. She didn't condone his actions toward Henry and me or the robbing of your treasury."

King Brian shook his head. "She may not have agreed with Braidus's actions, but she allowed them, and that is still a crime."

I bit my lip and nodded, deciding it would be folly to argue with the King.

"Now, Andrew said you wore a locket around your neck that prevented you from coming to anyone for aid," King Brian said, picking up an apple fritter.

"Yes," I said, wishing I could delve into my half-eaten pumpkin roll. "Braidus carries a pair of necklaces. He wore one and I the other. It allowed him to hear anything within my earshot. If I had spoken about our plight, Henry would have been killed." I took a breath and continued. "I tried my best to tell Andrew, but I was blindfolded every time I left, so I wasn't able to give any information on our whereabouts. I do not believe Braidus will have stayed at the orphanage since Henry and I left."

"Agreed." The King poured himself a drink from the tray. I used it as an opportunity to shove the rest of the pumpkin roll into my mouth.

Andrew chuckled at my chipmunk cheeks and handed me a drink to wash it down. Once I cleared my mouth, I talked about robbing the treasury.

"Had you picked up the hairpin on your way out, we'd have never known who did it," King Brian said.

"I didn't know objects could show visions with yellow magic, otherwise I would have," I said, fiddling with the empty cup in my hands. "I don't know if Henry told you this, but we were planning on coming to you to confess. I could never live with that on my conscience."

"I would have preferred that," King Brian said.

I continued with my next prominent recollection: waking up in the alley with a knife in my leg and the prophecy in my pocket. I expressed my confusion for having no memory of how I ended up there and my fear that I had hurt someone in the process. "I'm afraid—" My voice broke and I shuddered. Andrew squeezed my hand in comfort. "I'm afraid I killed someone."

Multiple people interjected simultaneously.

"I told you to stop thinking that way." Henry shook his head.

"You have way too much compassion," Andrew said.

Joshua nodded listening to Andrew. "She incapacitated the guards at the treasury humanely by putting them to sleep."

"Absolutely not," Malsin said. "You're not a killer."

"While possible, I doubt it." Lord Leavesden shrugged.

King Brian held up a hand and the chatter stopped. "I believe I can shed some light on this subject."

My jaw dropped. "You can?"

"You took the prophecy from a temple near the heart of Carasmille. In case you didn't know, temple priests are the handlers of the prophecies. They informed me of the incident after it happened." He set his drink down and cleared his throat. "The scrolls are spelled so that when someone takes one unlawfully, it enacts an immediate memory loss, erasing the last day, or in some cases an entire week, of their life. Most often the priests are able to recover the scroll. If not, if the memory loss is delayed at all, then we hope the thief becomes so distressed with his predicament that he wanders into a Healers Guild seeking help. The scroll is then recovered and the thief properly convicted.

"In your case, the priest could not see who had taken the scroll and threw the knife hoping the person would reveal himself." He waved a hand airily at me. "You obviously had a slow response to it because you managed to get away before losing your memory."

"So, I didn't kill anyone?" I asked breathlessly, gripping the edge of the table. I dared to hope.

The King smiled and folded his hands. "No. You did not."

"Oh, thank the Gods," I cried. Tears welled up in my eyes as I tried to control the overwhelming amount of emotions I felt at once. I covered my mouth with my hand to stifle my cries. My fear, anxiety, and uncertainty over the incident were replaced with relief and liberation. *I'm not a killer.*

Andrew pulled me into his chest as I took deep, calming breaths. His muscled arms wrapped tight around me. Feeling his warm body and listening to his beating heart made my emotional breakdown even worse. A fresh wave of tears hit me. The man I loved held me, and suddenly that's all that mattered. Not the issues we faced as a couple or the issues centered on me with Braidus, Haldren, the prophecy, or anything else. Andrew's hand rubbed up and down my back, and I sensed an overwhelming amount of love emanating off him. That's when I recognized that I was safe, whole, and loved.

The air in the room felt thick, uncomfortable, awkward. Nobody liked to see a girl crying her eyes out, but I couldn't help it. I couldn't stop the floodgates once they'd opened. Andrew's shirt became increasingly wet, but he didn't seem to mind.

Malsin passed me a cloth napkin. He pulled a pink vial out of his pocket and handed it to me. "Drink this; it will help."

"Thank you," I said shakily, understanding why the King had Malsin stay. Had he expected this? *Probably.* I downed the contents of the vial, and a feeling of calm overtook me. I took a deep breath and wiped my eyes.

"Are you ready to continue?" King Brian asked in a patient voice.

I nodded and cleared my throat. My cheeks felt hot. "Yes. Sorry." I wiggled out of Andrew's grasp and resituated in my chair. But he didn't seem to want to let me go. With an expression of mock offense, he wove his fingers through mine and held them with a firm grip. He grinned.

Henry sighed. "Lovers."

"Just wait till it's you," Andrew said.

Henry opened his mouth to respond, but King Brian eyed him, and he quickly shut it and slouched in his seat.

"What happened after you woke up in the alley?" King Brian asked.

"I found some dirt in a broken flowerpot and recharged, then healed my leg. Braidus found me and brought me back to the orphanage. He took the prophecy from me," I answered. "He gave it back, though."

King Brian leaned forward. "You have it?"

I nodded. "It's in my room at the Sorrenian. I can give it back."

"Yes. It must be returned to the temple priests." King Brian poured cider into his cup and took a sip. "How did you escape?"

I smiled and turned to Henry. "Tell them about your amazing escape. You should be proud."

Henry grinned and launched into his tale of knocking the guard out and stealing the key.

"I'm impressed, Henry," King Brian praised. "You showed great wit and ability."

I had the feeling those words rarely came out of King Brian's mouth, for Henry's expression turned incredulous, then radiated happiness.

Henry took a breath and continued explaining our escape. "Once I got free, I started searching for Isabelle. I found her—she was uh ..." Henry seemed unsure if he should tell everyone about the state he found me in—asleep and sobbing.

"She was what?" King Brian raised his eyebrow.

Henry shifted uneasily in his seat. "Crying. It took me a minute to realize she was asleep. She mumbled Braidus's name repeatedly."

Flashes of concern from everyone in the room hit me at once.

King Brian's eyes rested on me. "Is this something we need to discuss or not?"

"Yes." Andrew sounded adamant as he stared at me with blatant worry. "What happened, Isabelle? What did Braidus do? You only talk in your sleep when something has seriously upset you."

"It's nothing I haven't dreamed before, but this time when I dreamed about the murder of my parents it was like I was watching it for the first time." I shuddered as the memories tried to resurface. Andrew pulled me into him and held me while I spoke. "I couldn't figure out why Braidus's name sounded so familiar until that memory resurfaced. He ordered his men to kill my—" I glanced at Joshua. "Our parents."

Wearing a grim expression, King Brian's eyes darted between my brother and me. "Without your parents I would not be alive today."

"How—how did they save your life?" I asked. "I've never been told."

"It is a long story and difficult for me to share," King Brian admitted. "When I feel up to it, I'll tell you." I saw a sliver of pain in King Brian's eyes, and my gut tightened. "Just know that I am eternally grateful for them and the sacrifices they made for Aberron."

"As am I." Queen Averly reached for King Brian's hand and squeezed it. He met her eyes, and they shared a deep look of love, and affection.

The room thickened with solemnity. A moment of silence passed as we waited for the King, seemingly deep in reflection, to tell us to continue.

Queen Averly rested a hand on King Brian's shoulder. "Dear, Henry and Isabelle have yet to finish their story."

King Brian nodded. He took a breath and exhaled. "Please continue."

Henry cleared his throat. He furrowed his eyebrows. "Let's see, I shook Isabelle awake, and we headed for the exit but met Braidus at the door." He glanced at me furtively. He took a breath and spoke in a rush. "Then Braidus gave Isabelle the prophecy, and we ran." He slouched low in his seat with flushed cheeks.

I smiled half-heartedly at Henry, appreciating his attempt at skirting around the truth. I felt lucky to have become such good friends that he wanted to protect me. He and I both knew that telling the King I had tried to kill Braidus probably wouldn't go over well. And yet, it quickly became obvious on everyone's faces that they believed Henry had left out some major details.

"Henry, you know better than to lie to the King. What would your mother think?" Lord Leavesden reprimanded.

"I didn't lie," Henry protested. "It's the truth."

I wiggled out of Andrew's grasp and sat up straight. "It's all right, Henry, it wouldn't be right to keep this a secret. It's better to just say it all and accept the consequences as they come."

Henry ran a hand through his hair, his expression one of unease. "Isabelle ..."

I swallowed my anxiety, then squared my shoulders, took a breath, and stared at King Brian. "I tried to kill Braidus."

I watched everyone visibly stiffen, but no one appeared as shocked as I thought they would. *Huh,* I wondered. Maybe they expected it?

"Explain," the King commanded, his voice sharp. His expression hardened into something I couldn't read.

I flinched at his tone of voice. "I was a little—emotional." I grimaced. "I ran into Braidus, and I lost it." I told him everything, from telling Henry to shield himself, to gripping on to Braidus, the fireball in my hand, and confronting him about the murder of my parents. "He tried handing me the prophecy in exchange for his life, but I wouldn't accept it. I wanted to avenge my parents."

Joshua spoke with a grim expression. "I cannot say I would have acted differently in Isabelle's position."

King Brian nodded. "It is understandable." His eyes darted between Joshua and me. "However, leave the judgment of Braidus up to me." He eyed me. "Because you did not actually kill Braidus, I will let this go. I won't be as forgiving if there is ever a next time."

I nodded meekly. "I understand. Thank you."

"Isabelle was seconds from killing Braidus until he mentioned a name—Haldren. Then she stopped," Henry added. "I convinced Isabelle to take the prophecy and go. So we did."

Surprise flitted across Joshua, Andrew, and King Brian's faces. I assumed it had to do with Haldren and not Henry's persuasive abilities.

"Haldren?" Malsin leaned forward. "You mean the God over Gods?"

I swiveled my head to stare at Malsin, nearly jumping out of my seat as I latched on to this bit of information. "You know who Haldren is?"

Malsin nodded. "Of course. He is the—"

Three sharp looks from Andrew, Joshua, and the King had Malsin retreating before he said another word. He wore a sheepish expression. "Never mind. I know nothing."

I slouched in my seat and cursed under my breath, but Andrew and Henry heard me. Henry glanced at me, mirroring my disappointment, and seeming of a mind to mutter a few curses himself. Andrew frowned, and I could see that it bothered him that I was upset, but it wasn't enough for him to tell me what I wanted to know about Haldren.

Andrew reached for my hand, but I folded my arms and glared, causing Joshua to chuckle and Andrew to scowl as he pulled his hand back.

King Brian's bright blue eyes rested on me. "What exactly did Braidus say about Haldren? I want word for word."

"Braidus said he could tell me why Haldren visits me. That you, Andrew, Joshua, and Haldren won't because none of you think I'm ready." I tried hard to keep my face impassive, but I couldn't hide all traces of the scowl forming on my face. "I do not recollect telling Braidus about Haldren, so I am unsure how he knew about our meetings in the dream world. Unless," I added slowly, "Haldren told *him* about it."

I saw the unease grow on Andrew, Joshua, and the King. Even Queen Averly seemed concerned. Lord Leavesden and Malsin appeared perplexed, and I could tell they wanted more information but didn't think it appropriate to ask. Henry and I wore matching looks of disappointment.

I attempted to ease some of the tension in the room. "Braidus only *said* he could tell me about Haldren. He never actually did. He handed me the prophecy and said to consider it a starting point. But it's not. The prophecy is a bunch of rubbish."

Henry shook his head. "Braidus believes in the prophecy."

"I'm sorry, I don't understand. What exactly does this prophecy say?" Malsin interrupted.

"I have a copy." King Brian stood and rummaged through his bookshelves. He pulled a book out and flipped through the pages until he found what he needed. He handed it to Malsin.

Malsin read through it quickly, then looked at me with wonder in his eyes. He slid the book over to Lord Leavesden. It didn't take long for the book to pass through everybody. Only Henry and I declined, having read it yesterday together.

"Don't tell me you all believe it," I scoffed, getting increasingly uncomfortable with the open curiosity I saw on their faces.

"How can we not?" Malsin said. "You match the description perfectly."

Everyone nodded, including Andrew. I frowned.

Lord Leavesden set his cup down. "So, this is the new threat we are under? Your son wants to come back and overtake the throne?"

"Braidus believes with all his heart that he should be King," I said, my tone serious as I addressed everyone in the room. I wanted to say that I even agreed with some of the policies he desired to change, but I wasn't sure my precarious relationship with the King could handle it yet. I didn't want to appear as if Braidus had persuaded me to fight for him. "I have no doubt that he is planning something. The few loyal followers I saw him in contact with treated him like the King already." I glanced at King Brian and added meekly, "I mean no disrespect to you, Highness."

"None taken." King Brian sighed and rubbed his temples. "Joshua, I want you to dispatch several patrol guards to search for Braidus. Start with Greta. She's our best hope of finding him." His lips formed a thin line. "I think it's about time I met with my son. Also, considering Braidus's deep interest in Isabelle, paired with the prophecy and her unusual abilities, I think it would be best if *we* kept a closer eye on her." He faced my brother. "Joshua, I am recommending that Isabelle reside here until further notice *and* that one of us has her in our sights at all times."

Most of me agreed with the King's recommendation. Living in the castle with Andrew sounded like a dream; however, I couldn't help but wonder if I needed constant supervision. Did I look like a two-year-old?

Joshua nodded. "That is agreeable."

"Good. If that is all, I'm going to rest. This day has given me a headache." King Brian leaned back in his chair. "Is that everything?" His eyes flicked to me. "Isabelle?"

"Yes, I think so." I'd told him everything relevant concerning my time with Braidus.

I listened to the tired sighs around me. It had taken several hours to discuss everything. The afternoon had flown by and evening arrived. A great amount of information had been thought over, absorbed. Enough to make any person tired. Lord Leavesden rubbed his eyes. Henry leaned back, rested his hands on his stomach, and closed his eyes. Even Joshua appeared ready for at least a nap.

Queen Averly smiled. "Perhaps we should all rest. It's been a trying day after all."

King Brian nodded. "Agreed." He gave Malsin, Henry, and me quarters for the night. Lord Leavesden already had a room with his wife, Princess Liliana, who apparently stayed at the castle so often that everyone considered it her permanent residence. We made plans to sort out more the next day. Henry, Andrew, and I walked together through the halls to our rooms. Whether luck or convenience, Henry and I got rooms adjacent to each other.

"That took forever." Henry stretched. He rubbed his stomach. "I am stuffed with pastries."

I felt a little envious. Since I did most of the talking, I'd only gotten the one pumpkin roll. "How many did you eat?"

"Five or six." He shrugged.

"Oh!" I lightly shoved him.

Andrew chuckled.

Henry stumbled. "Hey, cut me some slack. I've had a hard day."

I raised my eyebrows. "Oh, really? Were you slated for execution?"

"No, but not even Tilma, the head Sorrenian chef, can outcook the chefs here."

I shoved him again.

He pushed me back. "But I successfully organized a rescue party, raced to find Andrew and Joshua, then interrupted Uncle Brian's important meeting with the Nistieran ambassador to plead your case."

We stopped in front of Henry's door. I let go of Andrew's hand and wrapped Henry in a bone-crushing hug. "Thank you. I don't know what I would have done without you."

He hugged me back. "It's what best friends do for each other."

Best friends? I smiled.

Andrew shifted his weight from side to side and cleared his throat. I saw the jealousy flash in his eyes despite him clearly trying to hide it. I let go of Henry and snuggled up to Andrew. I kissed him quickly on his cheek. "Don't worry; you still have my heart."

Andrew's whole countenance lit. "Good."

Henry rolled his eyes. "Good night." He went into his room, closing the door behind him.

"I've been waiting forever for a moment with you alone." Andrew's eyes twinkled as he cupped my face.

I laughed as he rested his forehead on mine and breathed deeply. His soft lips touched mine, gently at first and then harder as passion took over. I leaned against my door and pulled him into me, matching his need and desire.

"Will you stay with me until I fall asleep?" Alone, my mind would race through the events of the past week, giving me no solace or rest.

"Until you fall asleep," Andrew agreed. "Then I must be in my room." His expression rested somewhere between a pout and dread. I suspected he'd prefer to stay with me all night if permissible. "I really don't want to take my eyes off you."

I laughed. "Then don't. The King did say he wanted someone to keep their eyes on me at all times."

He grinned. "That's right. Allow me to take the first watch."

I beamed. My heart soared into the clouds as I opened the door, pulling Andrew inside.

CHAPTER THIRTY-SEVEN

That was quite a show." Haldren clapped his hands softly—almost mockingly, but not quite. "I especially enjoyed the part where the arrow zoomed toward you and Joshua stopped it just in time." He shivered, presumably with delight. "Doesn't get much more exciting than that."

I sat on a boulder he'd conjured up, the tall wheat swaying around us. Haldren paced back and forth just on the edge of the dark green forest.

He waved his hand. The wheat field disappeared, replaced with a reenactment of my almost execution. I hugged my chest and frowned, not happy with his tricks. We stood next to Philsby and the soldier with the bow. One look at Philsby's heartless face made me cringe, but Haldren didn't pay attention to them or my reaction.

"Do you see that?" He waved his hand, and in a blink of an eye we moved to the stage. Haldren hovered over the version of me tied to the post. "There's not even a hint of fear on your face. It's remarkable."

Haldren let the scene play out and chuckled when Joshua thrust out his glowing red hand, exploding the arrow. I scowled, not finding it the least bit amusing. With a flick of Haldren's fingers, we arrived back to the wheat field.

I folded my arms. "Where have you been? I haven't seen you since this whole fiasco with Braidus started. It hasn't been like you to abandon me during a time of need."

"I was busy." He plucked a strand of wheat and twiddled it.

I wouldn't let him get away with evading my question. "Doing what?" I narrowed my eyes.

"Someone else needed my attention. Contrary to what you may believe, I have other interests that sometimes take precedence over you." He dropped the piece of wheat and gestured to me. "Besides, you're still alive. You didn't need my help."

I sighed, sensing a losing battle. It didn't matter what I did—Haldren would always have the upper hand. I couldn't demand answers of a God. How ridiculous of me to think that I could. "Right, and if they had been a second too late, I would have been dead. Not even you could have saved me from that."

"Hmm ... maybe," he mused. He conjured up another boulder and leaned against it. "So, what are you going to do? You have two very eligible brothers after your heart."

I raised my eyebrows. "You mean Andrew and Braidus?"

He nodded.

I scoffed. "Braidus is not even remotely eligible." I kicked at the wheat, letting my hands fall to my sides. "He is a tyrant."

"Oh, I beg to differ," he said with a coy smile.

I fought to keep my jaw in place. *Haldren a matchmaker?* Did he expect me to consider Braidus? Haldren of all people should know that my heart lay with Andrew.

Haldren's cold blue eyes penetrated mine. "You are wondering how Braidus knew I visit you."

I reared my head back in surprise. I'd barely finished thinking the question. "How'd you know?"

He smiled. "And now you're wondering if he was right about me refusing to tell you about your importance."

I folded my arms, not liking that he could read my mind. "Well, is he?"

Haldren nodded. "Yes. You are not ready to learn. Soon, though." He rubbed his chin, musing once more.

I groaned. "Why do you have to be so mysterious?"

Haldren chuckled. "I rather enjoy it. Perhaps I should send King Brian a gift." He waved his hand and a box appeared, hovering beside him in midair, wrapped in blue paper with a white bow. "Seeing him thwart your attempts to learn about me has been amusing." He flicked his fingers and the box disappeared. No doubt sent to King Brian.

I rolled my eyes, sensing my sentiments would fall on deaf ears. I changed the subject.

"The prophecy. Is it about me?"

"Yes," Haldren spoke in a serious tone as he clasped his long, nimble fingers together.

I tried not to let it sink in, knowing it would send me into emotional turmoil if I did. I leaned against my boulder. "Did you write it?"

He shook his head subtly. "I did not."

"Then who did?"

"The first King of Aberron, of course." He acted as if I should have known that already. "He had a gift of sight and wrote many prophecies in his time. Though I believe yours is particularly significant." He ran his hands through the tall stalks of wheat, and I briefly wondered why it held his fascination.

"Has he ever been wrong?" I felt almost hesitant to find out the answer, but I wanted to believe that my life wasn't tied to a prophecy written three hundred years ago.

"Never."

My heart sank with what I didn't want to hear. I didn't want this—my mind struggled to come up with an accurate description—this fate I didn't choose. "What does it mean?"

"That is something you must discover on your own," Haldren said dismissively.

I frowned. "You're no help."

He chuckled. "I've given you plenty of information already tonight. Just think it over." He put his hand up in farewell. "Sleep, and bask in the knowledge that, for now, you're safe."

With a wave of his hand, the field disappeared, and I woke up in bed, lying on my right side. A candle burned low beside me, though the rest of the room was dark. Andrew's arm wrapped loosely around my stomach. His breathing sounded deep and even in my ear. For a moment, I enjoyed the comfort Andrew gave and snuggled up close.

My movement woke him. He groaned. "Gods forbid, I fell asleep." He sat up.

I rolled onto my back and eyed him. He rubbed the sleep out of his eyes and sighed. Then he smiled at me and pushed my hair away from my face. "Get some sleep, Isabelle. I'll be here when you wake up." He lightly touched his lips to mine and quietly sneaked out of the room.

I fell asleep faster than I expected, feeling tired right down to my bones.

The next morning, I found Haldren's gift for King Brian beside my bed with a note asking me to deliver it. I briefly contemplated chucking it until the note on my bed glowed. I picked it up and read.

I'll take Nisha back if you do.
—Haldren

"All right, I'll deliver it," I said rather quickly. "Don't take Nisha." It would break my heart to see him go. Despite knowing we would have to part ways at some point, I couldn't bear it right now.

When Andrew and Henry greeted me at the door, I spoke before they could ask about the present in my hand. "It's for King Brian from Haldren." I shut the door behind me, and we headed to breakfast.

"You talked with him last night?" Andrew asked, trying to sound casual as he wrapped his arm around my waist and pulled me close.

"Oh, we talked." My tone gave way to my displeasure. "I'll tell you what he said when I give this to King Brian." I gestured to the box in my hands with a tilt of my head.

The dining room appeared to be a nice size but not overlarge. Tall windows letting in the morning sun spanned most of the room and gave an incredible view of Carasmille. Several paintings of fruit in gilded frames caught my attention.

King Brian sat at the head of a table filled with trays of breakfast food. Queen Averly, Lord Leavesden, Princess Liliana, Joshua, and Malsin had already been seated. Henry sat near his mother, while Andrew and I strode straight to King Brian.

I presented the box to him. "This is for you from Haldren. He said, and I quote, 'Seeing him thwart your attempts to learn about me has been amusing.'" I fought to keep my expression civil. "I believe he wants to thank you for keeping his identity a secret."

King Brian eyed me with surprise. He accepted the box and lifted the lid. He reached inside and pulled out a scroll larger than what I thought the box could hold.

"Hold this." King Brian handed it to Andrew and grabbed what appeared to be a plane of glass, about the size of a book, in a gold frame. He set the box on the breakfast table and took the scroll from Andrew. He moved to a table pushed against the wall and slid a vase of flowers out of the way.

Everyone moved out of their seats and gathered around King Brian as he unfurled the scroll. It revealed a large map of Aberron. He placed the gold frame over Carasmille. We all gasped as the map came to life, showing us a complete three-dimensional layout of the city in the glass.

"It's like you're flying above the city," Andrew breathed. "There are so many red tiled rooftops."

"I've never seen anything like it." King Brian seemed amazed. He touched a tall building in the city, a temple I thought. The map refocused until it appeared like we stood on the empty street around the building.

"The only thing it's missing is people and livestock," Joshua said.

"Indeed." King Brian touched a glowing blue dot that had showed up on the corner of the plane of glass, and the map returned to the full layout of the city. "I look forward to studying this when I have the time." King Brian lifted the frame—dissolving the picture—then rolled the scroll.

We returned to our seats, where the King demanded I tell him everything about my talk with Haldren.

I summarized with a few sentences. "The prophecy is real and about me. I'm not ready to learn about my importance." I waived my hand airily. "Hence the present to you for not telling. And ..." I grimaced, took a breath, and spoke in a rush. "He thinks I should consider Braidus as a possible suitor."

Andrew shot out of his chair, shouting something about Braidus never getting his hands on me again. He hovered next to me, tensed like he would fight anyone who came close. Joshua, having just taken a sip of his hot drink, dropped his cup and started choking. Malsin rushed to help while Lord Leavesden and Princess Liliana threw napkins to sop up the liquid.

Henry gripped his toast until it crumbled. He eyed me with disbelief. "You've got to be joking."

"I wish I were," I said glumly. "I want nothing to do with Braidus."

"Perhaps it would be best if we addressed something else," Queen Averly suggested with alarm on her face.

"Agreed. Andrew, sit down," King Brian ordered. "No one is marrying anyone today."

Andrew reluctantly sat. He held on to my hand, and I could feel his body thrumming with adrenaline. He shot me a look filled with anxious love, and I suspected if given the choice, he would have married me right that minute.

Toward the end of breakfast, the King decreed, with the approval of Princess Liliana and Lord Leavesden, that Henry should live at the castle also. "Lest Braidus tries to use you against us again." His lips curled in displeasure.

I could hardly contain my joy. I'd dreaded leaving Henry at the Sorrenian.

Malsin addressed King Brian. "If I may, I would ask to stay as well." He pointed at me with his thumb. "This girl gets into so much trouble, she's going to need me."

Soft chuckles went around the room. Joshua, Lord Leavesden, Henry, and Andrew nodded. My cheeks flamed with embarrassment, knowing Malsin was right.

The King nodded. "Granted." He looked at me. "I've been told that in the past few months, you've been bruised, sliced, shot, burned, poisoned, stabbed ..." He paused and rubbed his chin. "Oh yes, and a broken arm. It's a wonder you're still alive."

"Exactly," Malsin exclaimed. "She needs me."

I stood and walked around the table. I leaned down and hugged Malsin. "Thank you."

He broke out into a delighted smile as he hugged me back. "You're welcome."

King Brian and Malsin worked out a plan. Malsin would become a tutor for Henry and me in addition to being given his own room to continue his healing experiments.

"But what about defensive classes?" I couldn't imagine not being able to practice every day.

"Joshua can do that, right?" King Brian eyed my brother.

"We start every morning at seven. Including Kings and Gods Day," Joshua said.

"Sounds perfect." I grinned.

Henry's expression turned glum. "Seven, really?"

Joshua nodded. "Before breakfast."

Henry groaned.

Queen Averly had us pick out rooms near the royal chambers. She pointed to the double doors that ended the hallway. "That is our room. Andrew's is on the right, and Joshua is on the left. Next to Joshua is where Liliana and Lyle stay." She gestured to five other double doors. "These are available for you to choose."

Naturally, I chose the room right next to Andrew, across from Princess Liliana and Lord Leavesden. I worried the Queen would disapprove of my choice, since it was awfully close to Andrew, but she smiled and said it had a wonderful view. Henry chose the room adjacent to mine, and Malsin took the room across from him.

Joshua and a small group of soldiers accompanied Lord Leavesden, Henry, Malsin, and me back to the Sorrenian. Andrew and King Brian had meetings with the Nistieran ambassador.

It took me less time than Henry to pack up my room, considering I had already gotten a head start before I was arrested. Once the soldiers hauled everything I wanted into the wagon, I helped Henry.

"This is going to be great." Henry faced me with a grin, his arms full of clothes. "We'll be right next door to each other, so that means I won't have to climb a bunch of stairs to get to your room anymore."

I laughed lightly. "Aw, come on, you love exercise, remember?"

At lunch Lord Leavesden made an announcement. "This may come as a shock for some of you, so please prepare yourselves. At the request of the King, Malsin, Isabelle, and Henry's time at the Sorrenian is over."

The air became thick with silence as the students let that sink in. Iris stood and pointed at me. "Why isn't she dead if she robbed from the Royal Treasury?" From the disgust on her face, she obviously wished that had been the case.

I raised an eyebrow at Henry. He shrugged. "Word might have gotten around while I acquired my search party."

"The King has cleared Isabelle of all charges," Lord Leavesden said in a firm, matter-of-fact tone.

Iris gasped. "Then she's also bewitched the King!" She cast her eyes on the other students in the dining hall with a beseeching expression. Not one person gave her the support she sought with Lord Leavesden in the room.

"That will be enough from you, Iris," Lord Leavesden spoke harshly.

"She is not fit to be with royalty," Iris said loudly as she sat and eyed me with revulsion.

"And you're only fit for a pig farmer!" Henry shouted. Our table erupted in praises for his quick comeback. Even Lord Leavesden fought against a smile.

I stayed silent, knowing it would be futile to defend myself against someone who would never see reason. I believed Iris acted more out of jealousy and a desire to see a crown on her head than out of a pure love for Andrew. I pitied her and wished that one day she would find the kind of love that set her heart on fire like I had with Andrew. Perhaps then she wouldn't act so foolishly.

I stood in the shadows with Dominic, Falden, and a visibly distressed Aliyah while Henry got bombarded with well wishes. I couldn't help but laugh as multiple girls cried on his shoulder. More than once, he had to tell them that he was not dying and that I didn't do it. Despite not being willing to stand with Iris, some girls clearly agreed with her.

"It's Isabelle's fault, isn't it?" a fifteen-year-old girl accused. "She's—she's poisoned you!"

"Why else would Malsin be going with them?" another girl agreed.

Henry's pained expression silently begged one of us to save him.

"I'm not gonna do it." Dominic chuckled as another heartbroken girl latched on to Henry's arm and begged him to stay.

"Me either." Aliyah wrinkled her nose at the sight, but she wrung her hands and shifted uneasily on her feet.

Falden shook his head, his lips in a grim line.

I rolled my eyes. "I'll do it."

I waded through the crowd and pulled Henry out. "Move it, or I'll poison you too."

I stood in the entry hall and said goodbye to Dominic, Falden, and Aliyah. Unlike everyone else at the Sorrenian, they knew why we had to leave. Once Dominic understood that I did everything in my power to save Henry from Braidus, his dislike for me lessened.

"I'm sorry I gave you so much trouble," Dominic apologized. "I won't doubt you again." He held out his hand. "Friends?"

I shook it. "Friends."

While Dominic, Falden, and Henry conversed, Aliyah swooped in with a quick hug. "Keep an eye on Henry for me, will you?" She tried to smile, but her composure broke. Her eyes glassed over, and her lower lip trembled.

I had no doubt in my mind that she was in love with him. "I'll keep him safe," I promised.

"Good." Aliyah nodded and took a breath to steady herself.

I walked over to Henry and pulled him aside. "You ready to go?"

He nodded. "I've just got to say goodbye to Aliyah." He sighed, seeming unhappy at the idea.

Henry held out his arms and wrapped Aliyah in a hug. She rested her head on his shoulder. They stayed in a sweet embrace for a several long minutes, not saying anything. Dominic and Falden moved to stand by me.

"This is hard to watch." Falden grimaced.

"It's obvious they love each other," I said, noting the way Henry had his eyes closed like he wanted to remember this moment forever.

"Yes, but they won't commit." Dominic shook his head. "I've had enough." He marched forward and stood behind Aliyah, facing Henry. "Either kiss her now and mean it or sever ties. You're only hurting each other with your hesitation."

Aliyah stiffened in Henry's arms. She started to step out of Henry's grasp, but he held her tighter. Henry's eyes flashed from Dominic to Falden and me. We all nodded our heads in agreement. Loving each other but not doing anything about it sounded like slow torture on the road to death.

Henry stepped away from Aliyah but held on to her shoulders. He bent his head closer to hers. He took a breath and said in a rather uncertain voice, "Do you want to court?"

Aliyah's cheeks tinged rosy pink. She nodded her head, her voice barely a whisper as she answered. "Yes."

Henry's face softened. "Really?"

"She's been waiting for you to ask her for ages, you dolt," Dominic sounded exasperated as he rolled his eyes.

"You could have said something." Henry glared at Dominic.

"You could have paid attention," Dominic retorted.

"Guys, shut it, will you?" Aliyah said hotly.

"Right," Henry agreed. "Enough talk." He tilted her face to meet his with a finger under her chin and brought his lips to hers. He kissed her soft and sweet, like a promise to grow their relationship until it bloomed.

I felt happy for Henry but seeing him kiss Aliyah made me miss Andrew. I wanted to get back to the castle and into his arms. "I'll be in the stables." I swiftly exited the entry hall.

Henry caught up with me as I entered the stables, his chest heaving from the run.

"You all right?" I asked.

He wore a silly grin. "I'm great." He sauntered past me to get to his horse a few stalls down from mine. I noticed a new bounce in his step.

"Hey, Nisha, you ready to be with some real warhorses?" I leaned against the stall. "I'm sorry it's been so long since I visited." I leaned against the stall. "I got kidnapped."

Nisha turned his head away from me and backed farther into the stall. I got the distinct impression that he was angry with me. *"I know."*

"Haldren told you?" I held my lips in a grim line.

Nisha rocked his head in affirmation. *"You cannot be trusted on your own. You left me here to worry."* He turned around in the stall and flicked his tail at me.

"Oh, come on, I told you I was sorry, didn't I?" I knew better than to come down empty-handed and offered him the apple I'd saved. "Please, Nisha, don't be mad. I'm trying, and it isn't easy." He turned around and accepted the apple. I rubbed his nose. "You know I didn't mean for you to worry." I fished a broken carrot out of my pocket and held it out to him.

Nisha ate the carrot from my hand. *"Don't make me worry again."*

I opened the stall and hugged him. "I'll try not to, I swear."

Henry led his horse over, saddled, and ready to go. "All right, what is the deal with your horse?"

"Why don't I let Nisha do the honors?" I patted his neck. "Nisha, please say hello to Henry."

Nisha bowed his head. *"Hello, Henry."*

Henry visibly jumped. "Gods forbid, he talks!"

I smiled. "Yes, he does."

Henry narrowed his eyes as realization set in. "That day when Nisha tried to kick me, after I called you crazy—I'm sorry for that by the way—he really was yelling at me, wasn't he?"

Nisha spoke. *"Insult Isabelle again, and I will yell at you more."*

Henry slowly backed away, pulling his horse with him. His face showed alarm and a smidgeon of terror, making me laugh.

The whole ride to the castle, flanked with guards, several wagons, Joshua, and Malsin, Henry eyed Nisha like he might eat him. In a low voice, so the guards wouldn't overhear, I explained to Henry how Nisha came to be my horse.

"His true master is Haldren?" Henry asked as we handed our horses off.

"Yes," I said, handing Nisha two sugar cubes, then waved farewell. "He's only mine until Haldren wants him back, but I hope he stays with me for a long time."

The following day, Queen Averly personally helped decorate my new quarters. Although her idea of decorating involved ten palace servants lifting the heavy furniture and art while she directed from a chair, sipping tea. The sitting room alone appeared about the size of a classroom at the Sorrenian, with two slightly smaller rooms serving as bedroom and bathroom. What did people do with so much space? I briefly considered designating a section of the room to be used purely for exercising, then worried I might get in trouble for it. What if I broke one of the beautiful crystal and gold-trimmed vases?

Queen Averly also ordered an entire new wardrobe for me. After she decorated the room to her liking, she sent a seamstress in to take my measurements.

I stood in a breast band and underwear and held my arms out away from me. The seamstress had insisted that this would ensure proper-fitting clothes. Growing up with Adel as Saren's best dressmaker, I believed her.

"She's a bit too thin," Queen Averly remarked to the seamstress. "Make everything one size bigger. I'd like to see her fill out a little."

"Yes, Highness." The seamstress ducked her head in acknowledgment.

I grimaced, imagining the Queen shoving trays of pastries at me.

She caught my expression and said, "You've got to assure people that Andrew has made a wise choice in giving you his love and affection. They will want to see a strong, healthy woman, and I hate to say it, but you look like you have missed too many meals."

I struggled to hold still and wished the seamstress would hurry up. "Why should how I look matter to others if Andrew is satisfied with it?" It bothered me to think of people scrutinizing my appearance like the Queen did now.

"You know Andrew's next step to become King is to find a wife and he has a limited amount of time to do so," Queen Averly said. "The people of Aberron must be assured that he has chosen a woman who appears ready for childbearing. You do not. . . but that can be changed."

I nodded. "I understand." Of course Aberron would want to make sure the line of the King continued.

She set her teacup down and spoke with conviction. "I see the way Andrew looks at you. He is utterly in love with you." She clasped her hands and took a breath. "I'm surprised he hasn't asked you to marry him yet."

The seamstress stepped away and handed me a robe. I pulled it over my shoulders, tied it, and then sat in the chair adjacent to the Queen. I sought her approval, wishing Adel were here to guide me through asking. A mother should be here for this sort of thing, and she was the closest I had to one.

The Queen's acceptance of me would mean everything. It would guarantee that a marriage to Andrew would begin well and establish good relations. "Would you accept me as his choice?"

Queen Averly smiled. "From the moment Andrew started growing into a man, he's had a constant stream of women vying after him." She frowned. "But they look at him like a prize to be won, with greed and lust in their eyes. I haven't once seen that in you. I wish you could see yourself when you look at Andrew." She chuckled softly. "Your eyes sparkle, and your whole countenance glows. You look at Andrew and see him; not his crown or status, but the man he's become. The love you two radiate warms my heart. It's all I've ever wanted for him, and now he has it with you." She met my eyes. "I accept you as his choice and am looking forward to getting to know you better."

I struggled to speak as surprise flooded through me and showed on my face. Queen Averly laughed, light and carefree like the sound of bells tinkling.

The evening snow softly fell three days after my near execution. King Brian, Henry, and I played a game of Pilfer in a sitting room. I enjoyed the time getting to know King Brian and found him to be quite agreeable. Mild mannered but stern and decisive when he needed to be. Malsin and Queen Averly, engaged in amiable conversation, sat in soft chairs near the roaring fire. A tray of drinks and small cakes lay between them.

Suddenly the door opened. Andrew charged in, a piece of paper in his hand. He strode directly over to me and held up the paper. "You wrote me a goodbye letter." He read slowly out loud. "Andrew, please always remember that I love you. I pray that you will move forward and find someone who will be a better fit for you. A girl not plagued with bad luck and a penchant for trouble. Stay true to yourself and you'll be a great King." He let the paper fall over our game and folded his arms.

"He sent it. The soldier actually sent it." I brought a hand to my mouth in surprise. I picked up the letter. "I wrote this after I was sentenced to die. I wanted you to know how I felt about you."

Andrew opened his mouth to respond, but at that exact moment Joshua marched in and headed straight to us. He also held a letter. "I just received this." He peered at the paper and read it off. "We regret to inform you that your sister, Isabelle Elaine Mirran, was convicted of robbing the Royal Treasury and sentenced to death. We send our condolences to you and any family or friends associated."

King Brian set his cards down. "Joshua, set up a meeting with Philsby. I may have to sentence him sooner than I expected. It's been three days and I still haven't received a note informing me of Isabelle's sentence—and now you have one saying it's been carried out already."

Joshua nodded. "I will see to it."

With a beseeching expression, Andrew turned to my brother. "Joshua, please."

Andrew didn't need to say any more for Joshua to seem to understand. Joshua's eyes flicked to me and then back to Andrew, giving me no doubt that they were rehashing an old conversation or argument about my courtship with Andrew.

"And if it doesn't go your way? Are you willing to accept that?" Joshua asked.

Andrew straightened his posture until he stood regal with the power of his kingly blood. His blazing blue eyes met Joshua's emerald green. Andrew spoke with firmness and conviction as though nothing in the world could ever persuade him to say or feel something different. "If I were only given a day with Isabelle as my wife, I would take it and consider myself gratified. At least I would know that she was mine."

My eyes darted between Andrew and Joshua. A nervous and wary tension bloomed inside me as I wondered if they were referring to Braidus or the prophecy. I decided on the prophecy because thinking about Braidus made my blood boil. My mind skipped to the end of the prophecy, where it talked about the warning. I mentally recited the last two lines from memory.

Without her presence in the fight, both will lose to a mightier foe.

I could think of nothing else that would fit. No one talked that way when they asked for someone's hand unless they anticipated something dreadful happening. Joshua must be worried about whatever the last part of the prophecy meant—if he did know, or even if he didn't. I vowed to delve deeper into it so I could prevent that last line from happening.

Joshua appeared to consider Andrew's words. He shifted his weight from side to side as he reflected. Then he nodded. "You have my blessing."

Andrew broke out into a delighted grin. He placed a hand on Joshua's shoulder and spoke with emotion. "Thank you, brother."

Joshua smiled, bordering on the edge of a grin. "You're welcome." He shook his head, appearing bewildered but pleased as Andrew stepped back.

Andrew swiveled around to face me, positively beaming.

I raised an eyebrow. "Forgive me if I don't believe what I just watched. For truly it must have been the imaginings of a tired mind." I glanced at Henry and King Brian. "Unless you both saw it too?"

Henry nodded. "Sure did."

"Us too," Queen Averly remarked, with Malsin nodding by the fireplace.

Andrew chuckled as he got down on one knee. "You didn't imagine it, love." He grabbed my hand, and his expression changed to one of soberness. "The moment my world collided with yours, I knew I'd never be the same. At first glance you plunged my heart into a sea of emotion. Little did I know then that you would become my safe harbor and heart's desire."

His eyes glistened with emotion. "I am in love with you, Isabelle, and every day I fall more in love with you—your smile, the sparkle in your eyes, your tenacity and passion. I cannot bear another second wondering if I will ever have you by my side." Andrew took a deep breath, appearing slightly nervous as he asked, "Isabelle Elaine Mirran, would you please accept a proposal of marriage and do me the honor of becoming my wife?"

I blinked several times to hold back the tears threatening to overflow and spill down my cheeks. No words ever compiled had sounded so beautiful or rung so deep in my soul. I felt my heart might burst with love, affection, but most of all devotion.

As I opened my mouth to give my answer, the door opened for a third time. A soldier stood panting, his hands on his knees as he fought for breath.

"Dregaitia—" he choked out, still gasping heavily from his apparent flat-out run to notify King Brian. "The Dregans are attacking."

THE END

NOTE TO THE READER

I really appreciate the time you took to read Fate not Chosen; I am thrilled you chose to add it to your home library. If you enjoyed reading this book, it would mean the world to me if you would do two things for me.

1. Share on social media or tell your friends about my books.

2. Leave an honest review by simply visiting my website:

www.ScribbledReads.com
click on the series,
click on the book you read, and
click the "Write a review" button,
or email me your review Tara@ScribbledReads.com

Thank you. Your reviews, and support help me to write more new worlds scribbled in ink!

ABOUT THE AUTHOR

Tara Lytle is the talented author behind the captivating Fate Series, and enthralling Matching Series. She draws inspiration from her love of clean young adult fantasy and paranormal romance. With a steaming cup of hot chocolate, her Spotify playlist, and an open word document, she embarks on crafting worlds where love, adventure, and epic fantasy intertwine. Tara Lytle's passion for the genre fuels her creativity, resulting in two completed series in the last three years and more novels on the horizon. If you're seeking enchanting tales that transport you to new realms, her books are a delightful choice! Visit: www.ScribbledReads.com

OTHER NOVELS BY AUTHOR TARA LYTLE

THE FATE SERIES

FATE NOT CHOSEN
FATE CHALLENGED
FATE CONQUERED

THE MATCHING SERIES

MATCHING FEATHERS
MATCHING FOXES
MATCHING FIRE